Caught

Caught by the Bad Boys
Book One

BY RAATHI CHOTA

Caught

Limitless Publishing, LLC
Kailua, HI 96734
www.limitlesspublishing.com

Formatting: Limitless Publishing

ISBN-13: 978-1-64034-508-9
ISBN-10: 1-64034-508-6

Dedication

To the strongest woman I know. I love you, Mom.

Chapter One

Lana

I held my books against my chest as I walked up the stairs to another day in hell. Senior year only started a few weeks ago, but I couldn't believe it was my last year. As I walked into the building, teenagers lurked in every corner. A group of boys stared at me, but I kept my head up high. A stupid idea, though, because the next thing I knew, I was on the ground.

"Geeky Lana," they said and laughed as they walked away.

"Douchebag Benny," I muttered as I stood up and fixed my glasses. Of all the days I wore a skirt, it had to be today when I got tripped, and my skirt rose. I had dressed in a black skirt, striped shirt, a denim jacket, and boots. I pulled up my maroon knee socks and picked up my books. As I walked to my locker, people greeted me with the term of "Geeky Lana" or "Good girl," which I got used to by junior year. I turned the corner, and my sad face lit up when I saw my best friend. "Hey, Miranda."

"Hey girl...how was your weekend?" She smiled. Miranda Stevens had been my best friend since she arrived in sophomore year. Seniors teased me, and she came out of nowhere and rescued me. From that day, we became friends.

"It was boring...I finished my English assignment and went with my parents to that boring dinner," I groaned as I took my books out. Before Miranda spoke, someone turned the corner.

"They're coming!" the girl squealed. She set her top so it'd be more "revealing" and adjusted her skirt so it'd be shorter. I rolled my eyes as I got my Calculus book out, then shut my locker. I turned around and leaned on my locker as I watched them turn the corner. Them. They did it ever since the new guy arrived, well not just them, but the whole school. Everyone gave them space to walk like they were knights who saved an entire village, and everyone congratulated them, but no, they were just a bunch of narcissists. The biggest ego heads the school ever had and it made me sick to watch them every day as they walked past and got acknowledged by everyone.

Ethan Baxter. Jefferson High's jock. He had dark brown hair with blond highlights that he got when senior year started. He was team captain, and his dad owned the biggest, most popular sports store in Illinois. I had to do a project with him last year, and we got an A for all my work, even though he came to my house. He had broad shoulders and a significant tattoo on his chest that was only exposed to the public during practices or after a game. I hadn't seen it up close, but I'm sure the girls he slept with had.

Aidan Rowley. The school's prankster. He always had a mischievous grin on his face and was up to no good. He's the shortest out all of them, and he had brunette hair and a six-pack that made the girls swoon. At the start of senior year, I walked to my Calculus class and saw Mr. Bronx with the rest of the class. The door was locked. Mr. Bronx opened it, and I kept in a laugh. Aidan and his friends had turned everything upside down. The desks and chairs were on the ceiling, and the posters were upside down. Aidan got away with it because it was the first day and Mr. Bronx was a cool teacher.

Carter Halls. He was the nicest—well, the smartest one of all. He was a player with his platinum blond hair and indigo blue eyes; he got any girl he wanted with his looks. Also, he was sarcastic, so I barely spoke to him. As soon as he talked to a girl, they'd be the most hated girl in school.

Blake Gunner. The new guy became friends with them on the very first day; I wish it were that easy. Blake and Ethan were the tallest. Every day he had headphones on, music at its loudest setting as he looked straight ahead. It's rumored that he sold a kidney and used the cash for an upgrade on his motorcycle. Cliché and scary at the same time.

As they walked past me, I saw Aidan's and Blake's gazes on me. My jaw tightened as I eyed them. Once they turned the corner, I bit the inside of my cheek because they never looked at me. The bell interrupted everyone, and I headed for my first class of the day.

***

"Good morning, Mr. Bronx."

"Morning, Lana, how was your weekend?" he asked, propping his legs on the table, then putting his hands behind his neck. Griffin Bronx and my dad were friends in college, and he always used to play with me when I was small. It turned out that he was my godfather, so to have him as a teacher was a bonus.

"It was good, and yours?" I smiled as I opened my book.

"Boring." He laughed. I watched everyone come into class, and Mr. Bronx took the attendance. I sat right in the back because I didn't want to catch any attention. "Where is Mr. Rowley?" Mr. Bronx asked as he looked around the classroom. He opened the door, and of course, there was goofy Aidan. "Aidan…you're late, sit down!" Mr. Bronx warned as Aidan sat down next to me. "Right, class, please take out the homework that I gave you last Thursday."

"Homework? I don't recall," Aidan shouted. Mr. Bronx walked to the back of the class where Aidan and I sat and looked at him.

"Exponential Functions, Aidan. It was mainly practice, which you requested!" Mr. Bronx exclaimed, then turned to me. "Lana, show him."

"Well, I didn't do it," Aidan said. Mr. Bronx turned around and sighed.

"You should be more like Lana Willson, Aidan. Otherwise, you'll fail."

"GG," Aidan coughed out. There were a few snickers as Aidan looked at me. I rolled my eyes and raised my middle finger at him.

"Detention," Mr. Bronx coughed loudly for the whole class to hear. Everyone laughed, and I smirked at Aidan, who rolled his eyes.

***

Next, I had Phys Ed, and the only good thing about Phys Ed was I had Miranda in the class, but there's always a bad when there's a good. *They* were in my class. I changed into my uniform and walked out of the girl's locker room to stand with Miranda. I glanced over and found all four of them there, which was rare, since they ditched a lot.

"Okay listen up…since my throat is a bit sore, we're going to do some stretches, then have a good game of dodgeball, all right? Good? Okay. Stretch!" Coach Harris, who was also the coach of the varsity football team, said in a raspy voice. After doing a few stretches, we were in two groups. None of them were on my side.

"Shit," I muttered to myself as we got into position. Aidan glared at me, and he must've told the rest to get me for revenge since I got him detention. At least I had an active girl in front of me who did all the work, but I still had to be careful.

It was halfway into the period, and on my team was another guy, Miranda, and me. On the opposite end were Blake and Ethan. We. Were. Screwed.

Ethan grinned as he rested his palms on his knees while Blake stared. Ethan came out of nowhere and knocked down the poor boy. I looked back at Miranda, who got the ball. She was good at sports, but Ethan was better. She ran up and threw it yet missed both of them. I backed up as Blake took the ball. He threw it immediately, and I dodged it, then sighed in relief until I heard a scream. I turned around to see Miranda on the floor. I ran up to her, completely forgetting about the ball.

"Miranda, are you okay?"

"Willson, back in the game!" the coach said, his voice loud and clear. What happened to his sore throat? I made my way to the ball, picked it up, and looked at the guy. I stared at Ethan, taking careful aim. I threw it, but it didn't hit him. It hit Blake. I smiled to myself as his face changed as he realized he was out. Blake scoffed and sat down by Carter. Ethan turned to look at me with determination in his eyes. He picked up the ball and threw it without any aim. It hit Miranda on the head again as she tried to walk to the nurse. "That's it! Game over, everyone. Go change!"

"Are you okay? I'm going to kill him!" I grumbled as I ran over to Miranda.

"I'm okay, and no, you're not. See you later." She sighed as she walked to the nurse's office.

Miranda went home, and I heard Ethan and Aidan were looking for me, so I hid in the girls' bathroom and ate my lunch there. The final bell rang for the end of the day, and I walked to my locker and got my bag. I was about to go to Miranda's locker but remembered she went home…which meant I had to walk home because Miranda usually drove me. I groaned as I began to walk. I lived ten minutes away, but that was by car. So for the next half an hour, I strolled until I heard something. Music, not any music, it was "American Slang" by *The Gaslight Anthem.* I turned around to see a black BMW. It stopped right next to me, but I continued to walk and look straight ahead. I could see from the corner of my eye that it continued to follow me. So I stopped, and the car did too.

"Get in, Lana," the deep voice said, and I furrowed my eyebrows. I stepped over to the car and looked down to see them.

"Excuse me?" I asked. Ethan drove while Aidan sat in the passenger seat and glared at him.

"Get in. I'll drop you off." Ethan shrugged. The music was off by now, and from the corner of my eye, I saw Blake and Carter in the backseat.

"That's okay, I just live around the corner…"

"No, you don't. Now get in," Ethan demanded. I scrunched my nose up at his attitude, then backed away from the car. As I reached the sidewalk, my heel slipped, and I landed on the ground with a thud. I cursed as I looked at my foot, stuck on the edge of the sidewalk. Out of the corner of my eye, I saw someone get out of the car. I glanced up to see Carter's blond locks fan my face as he helped me. I tried to walk, but my foot ached as I gripped onto his arm. He dusted the dirt off from my back, then rested his hand on my shoulder.

"Are you okay?" His voice was deep as I looked up at him. His blue eyes stared down at me with concern. I slowly nodded as my mouth fell open, yet nothing came out. "Come on, we'll take you home." The corners of his mouth pulled up into a smile. Carter held the door open for me as I got in.

"Thanks," I mumbled and sat next to Blake Gunner, who had a cigarette rested in the corner of his mouth. He didn't seem fazed as he stared out the window. "Hi." I forced a smile to see what he'd do.

"'Sup," he said. I rolled my eyes and looked straight ahead as Ethan drove.

"Err…sorry about your friend," Ethan broke the silence.

"It's okay…but it's not me you should be saying sorry to." I muttered the last part. I think Blake heard me when he scoffed. I watched as he threw his cigarette out the window, then looked at Aidan.

"Hey, Aidan…put on *Happy Song*," Blake said. Aidan had that grin on his face as he took his phone and searched for the music. My eyes widened as I knew what would come. I took off my glasses as if to clean them, but I wanted to surprise them. The song started as they watched me. I lip-synced as the song went on because I liked Bring Me the Horizon. I sang with a smile plastered on my face and banged my head to the beat while everyone fell silent in the car. I lip-synced the entire song like it was nothing, yet they took it as a big deal. Once the song was done, they gaped at me.

"What did I do?"

"What was that?" Carter asked as a look of confusion crossed his face.

"That was "Bring Me the Horizon". Keep up, Carter."

"No, I mean…how do you know the song?"

"I like their music."

"You like rock?" Aidan asked as he turned in his seat.

"Yeah, what's wrong with that?"

"Well, it isn't normal for a goodie like you to like music like that," Blake scoffed.

"Well, I don't care. You don't know me, and I don't know you. Aren't we all full of surprises?" I laughed as I put on my glasses.

"Whatever, put on "American Slang"," Ethan told Aidan, and he did. We sang along and bobbed our heads to the beat even though they found it weird. We came to a red light, and I turned to look at the car next to us.

"Shit," I mumbled and ducked down.

"What? What?" Carter asked as he looked around.

"It's Kelly."

"So?"

"She hates me, I hate her, she sees me, and then she'll embarrass me," I said as tried to keep level.

"Ah, the good girl doesn't want to get caught, does she?" Aidan asked, and I pictured that grin. I kicked his seat and told him to shut up. We moved again, and I lifted my head up. All of them had smirks on their faces, which I didn't like.

"What?"

"You're the ultimate good girl, Lana." Aidan laughed.

"But we all know good girls are masterminds at being bad girls," Blake whispered in my ear, which sent a shiver down my body.

"Whatever...I just don't like getting into

trouble." I rolled my eyes even though Blake was right.

"We're here," Ethan said as the car came to a stop. Carter got out of the car to make way for me, and I got out. Once he was in, I turned back around.

"Thanks for the ride, Ethan." I smiled at him. By now, my foot was settled to walk. "Listen...nobody has to know that this ever happened, right? I mean, for the sake of you guys and mine...like, I almost got caught back there with—"

"No problem. We wouldn't want you getting into trouble, now would we?"

"Thanks, and bye." I smiled then spun around. I heard their conversation behind me, yet I continued to walk.

"Why is she so scared?" Blake asked.

"Her dad's the sheriff," Aidan replied as I laughed. My joking manner immediately changed as I frowned. I let out a sigh as I thought of the recent event. Who am I kidding? They didn't want to get involved in my sad life. In the end, they'd scream their way out.

Chapter Two

Lana

I groaned as I stretched my arms to the alarm clock; I hit it continuously, but it wouldn't budge. I opened my eyes and turned the alarm off. The time read 6:31 a.m. I took a while to get ready in the morning, and I had a bus to take, therefore I had to wake up an hour and a half earlier. I took a quick shower and brushed my hair. I slipped on some blue jeans, a cream sweater, and my white Converse. I looked in the mirror and almost vomited; my hair was a mess, so I slipped on a cream beanie to match my outfit. I went over the persuasive speech I had to do today, which I was nervous about since Carter and Benny were in my class. Once I was done, it was 7:15. I went downstairs to the kitchen, where I found Mom and Dad.

"Morning, hun. How'd you sleep?" Mom asked as she placed a cup of coffee in front of me. She did the same for my dad, who sat opposite me.

"Good, I guess, and you two?"

"Fine," Dad mumbled.

"Everyone okay at work, Dad?"

"These stupid punks who are doing drugs and all that…we can't seem to get them, and it's a real pain in the neck."

"Well, you should be glad I'm not like that, Dad."

"I know my girl wouldn't do anything like that."

After breakfast, I walked to the bus stop. In the morning, I'd take the bus, and in the afternoon, Miranda dropped me off. Hope she came today, I wouldn't survive another lunch in the bathrooms. I got off the bus and adjusted my beanie. It was going to be a long day. As I headed toward the main building, something caught my eye. I turned my head and saw them. They sat on Carter's classic GMC truck. Carter was making out with a girl, and Ethan and Aidan were talking; then there's the one who was staring at me. I looked at him, and he immediately looked away to his friends. Blake had his headphones on and acted as if he was in the conversation. I rolled my eyes and walked into the building. I got my things from my locker as the bell rang. I jogged to English class because I didn't want to make way for them, especially after what happened yesterday. I entered the classroom and frowned when I saw Benny Nielson, not the teacher.

"Hey GG, ready for the speech?" Benny asked. The teacher moved us around, so Benny sat in front while Carter sat beside me.

"Yes, unlike you, who didn't even start."

"Let's see," Benny said, grabbing my cards.

"Benny, give it back!" I demanded as I tried to

reach for it.

"Come on, put more effort into it!"

"Blah…blah…big words…blah…blah," Benny said as he went through my cards. I was annoyed. I leaned back to sit in my chair, but I fell, and my butt hit the ground. As I got up, everyone laughed, and when I straightened up, Carter Halls towered over me with a grin. "Here you go, loser," Benny said, then threw the cards over his shoulder. I bent down and picked them up.

"All right, class, settle down," Miss Rosa exclaimed as she walked into class. I sat in my seat and stared at the cards. "Ready for those speeches?"

Miss Rosa was one of the friendly teachers, she was caring and helpful, but if anyone misbehaved, they'd be sure to see her bad side, and nobody wanted to see a nice person's bad side. She wore a formal black skirt and jacket, black heels, and had a tight bun. She was young, in her mid-twenties, which annoyed me and was the reason why there were so many guys in her classes. I gave my speech, which was about bullying; I hoped I'd given a clear message to everyone who did. I walked back to my seat with a satisfied look. The rest of the speeches were good, yet Benny came up, winging it. Carter, on the other hand, was classic Carter Halls. He talked about animal abuse and how he saved a stray dog and took it to the pound, which made all the girls clap and wipe away their tears. The bell rang, and I got up for Physics. I looked over my shoulder and noticed Carter was still in his seat. I squinted my eyes at him as I pushed up my glasses. As I walked out of the classroom, I was hooked by two arms. I looked at Ethan and Aidan, who were on either side of me.

"What do you want?" I asked as their arms flexed against me. They didn't say anything as they walked past everyone. I was pushed as people came toward me, but Ethan quickly shoved them away. I saw my Calculus class, but I didn't think we'd stop. "Mr. Bronx! Uncle Griff! Sir…help me!" I shouted as we walked past the class. Aidan quickly put his hand over my mouth, and Ethan shook me. They opened the doors at the back building and quickly walked out. I finally realized where we were going—the empty part of Jefferson High. It was still used for the local ditches, smokers, make-out sessions, and not to mention…beating. "No! Please, I'll do anything. I'll do your homework for the rest of the year. I…I'll do anything!"

"Would you shut up?" Ethan growled as his grip tightened on my arm.

"Well, I'm sorry, it isn't every day you get kidnapped by…Them." I muttered the last part in Ethan's ear. Nobody said anything after that until Aidan took out his phone and I saw his reflection in it, which made my eyes widen. "Please tell me you're not going to take a picture?"

"No…I'm taking a video for Snapchat."

I rolled my eyes and looked forward. A tall figure leaned against a wall as we got closer. The person sat on the broken bench, which usually fit at least eight people, but now it fit three.

"Here she is," Ethan mumbled, then put me down. I had to focus my eyes to see who the figure was. Blake Gunner.

"What am I doing here? I'm gonna be late for class, and I don't want to—"

"We get it, Lana. Now sit down," Carter said, and I turned around to see him walk toward us. I glanced down to see my beanie in his hands. "This fell off when they were carrying you." He threw it at me. I caught it with ease and put it back on, then sat down. The bench felt as if it was going to collapse under Blake's butt and mine. It shook, and I grabbed the first thing I got my hands on. Blake's thigh. My eyes widened as I realized what I did. I slowly looked at him and gave a fake smile. He, on the other hand, looked as if he'd kill me.

"Ugh, please, it's not the first time a girl touched you," I said, then let go of his thigh dramatically, like he had a disease. The rest of the guys laughed, but Blake glared, which quieted them. "So what am I doing here?"

"What's your deal, huh? We always play loud music, and chicks always look at us like we're crazy, so they tell us to turn it off or put on the radio for mainstream music…but you?"

"You're a nerd, for crying out loud," Aidan said as he took a seat next to me. The bench shook again, but I managed to keep my balance.

"So…why is it such a big deal to you guys that I like rock music? Is it such a crime?"

"It just doesn't make any sense. Is this all an act? Do you hack into the school system to change your grades?" Blake asked as he raised a brow at me.

"Are those glasses even real?" Aidan asked. I looked at him as he took off my glasses. He put them on but immediately removed them.

15

"Okay…they're real."

"Or do you do it because you're scared?" Ethan asked, then folded his arms. He grinned at me. I raised a brow.

"Scared of what?"

"Not what, who."

"Your dad," they said in unison. I scoffed.

"You guys really think I'm doing this because I'm scared of my dad? I'm doing this because I want a healthy future. I don't want to waste it, unlike some people," I said, then got up. I walked toward the building with clenched fists because I was already late for class.

"Yeah, you guys were right. She's too much of a good girl," Carter said. I quickly turned around, but none of them looked at me.

"Yeah, bet you she was boiling inside at how much she was missing since she never ditched before."

"What do you mean?"

"You're such a good girl. We thought good girls are bad, but you're just an ugly old GG," Blake said, then stood up. He walked toward me as I folded my arms.

"Ha, you don't even know me," I said, then pushed up my glasses. "You don't know what I'm capable of, Blake Gunner."

"Okay…then let's have a bet." He smirked and looked down at me; I couldn't take it anymore, so I stood on my tippy toes. "You have to be the bad girl of the school for two weeks. If you break and go back to being a nerd, then you have to be our little puppet for the rest of senior year."

"And if I win?" I asked as I kept a grin, because I knew if I did it, then it'd result in old habits that were bound to come back.

"If you win…we'll make sure you won't get picked on anymore," Carter said. I looked over Blake's shoulder at the blond. "I'm sure you don't want to end your senior year with the nickname Geeky Lana."

"What do you think, GG?" Ethan asked as he rested his arm on Blake's shoulder.

"That's ridiculous. You expect me to be a bad girl for two weeks, and if I lose, I have to be your puppet for a year? That's so unfair!"

"So what you're saying is you're gonna lose?" Aidan tilted his head.

"What? No! This is ridiculous. I'm going back to class!" I said, then spun around.

"You have three days to think about it, Lana!" Carter shouted.

"See you, GG!" they said, and I walked faster, yet I heard their laughter behind me. I could be bad. It shouldn't be hard, thanks to him.

***

It's been two days. Two long days, and in those two days, the guys called me GG whenever we had classes together. It annoyed me. At lunch, I'd stare at them as they were noticed by everyone.

"Yeah, so my mom had to go to the store and look for pads, then go to the pharmacy and get my medication…"

"Uh-huh."

17

"Lana, are you even listening?" Miranda scowled as she banged her hands on the table, which got us a few looks.

"Yes! You were sick from the ball, because when the ball hit you, your tummy was sore, and then you had to go home."

"Yeah, and—" Miranda said as I looked at her, but she immediately stopped and moved her gaze to something else.

"What? Is something on my face? Are my glasses dirty?"

"Lana Willson," someone said. I didn't have to turn around to see who it was. By the voice, I immediately knew it was Blake Gunner. He came and stood on our table. Miranda's eyes widened as he towered over us. "Can I have your attention, Jefferson High students?" he asked as loudly as he could. He caught everyone's attention easily since he was scary and tough.

"Blake, get down!" I yelled. Apparently, he didn't listen.

"Does everyone know this girl here?" Blake asked as he pointed at me. I froze and looked for help, but there were no teachers, and the lunch ladies couldn't care less. "Do you guys know her name?"

"Yeah, her name is Geeky Lana."

"I like Loser Lana."

"But we all know her as...drum roll, please," Blake said as he pointed to Aidan, who drummed in the air, then pointed at Blake.

"GG!" everyone exclaimed. I was irritated...no, I was angry. How dare he embarrass me? I've been humiliated enough in my life, and out of nowhere, he wanted to ruin my life even more. I quickly stood on the table and cut off Blake.

"Hi, you must know me. I'm Lana Willson," I said, then glared up at Blake. "You must know Blake Gunner here, typical bad boy, if you ask me." I rolled my eyes. Everyone went silent and waited for Blake's response, but I beat him to it. "Think he's all tough with that look…what's his name?" I dramatically put my finger to my chin. "Man-whore…narcissistic…son of a—"

"Enough! You two! Get down!" Mr. Bronx appeared out of nowhere and yelled at us. Blake and I got down and followed him. "I'm gone for two minutes and come back to this."

"Mr. Bronx, he started it. He came out of nowhere."

"She called me—"

"I don't have time to take you two to the principal because he's all the way on the other campus, so I'll let you two go, since it's also your first time getting into trouble." Mr. Bronx sighed, then ran a hand through his hair. He disappeared down the hallways. I sighed in relief and walked back to the cafeteria. It wasn't normal for me to get shouted by Mr. Bronx, but when I did, I wanted to cry. Considering he's my godfather, it'd be a disappointment if Dad ever brought me up in their conversation and said I'd been disruptive.

"Typical…" a familiar voice said behind me.

"What, Blake?" I groaned, then spun around to see him leaning against a locker. He looked at the ceiling. Blake was dressed in a black crew neck

19

with pushed-up sleeves that showed the tattoos on his arms, black jeans, and Converse. I looked back at his face, and he smirked at me. I immediately looked away and felt my cheeks warm up. The only reason they warmed up was because of how similar he looked to someone else I once knew, also with the tattoos and a nose ring. Footsteps neared me, but I made sure not to look at him. I felt heavy breathing on my neck and looked down to see his Converse right next to me.

"Teacher's pet," he whispered in my ear, and I instantly pushed him away.

"Fine!"

"Fine, what?"

"Fine, I'll do the bet," I mumbled. He clapped his hands, and out came Ethan, Aidan, and Carter. "What is this?"

"I told you that she would!" Aidan said, then swung his arm around me. "Ready, GG?" He pinched my cheeks. I removed his arm from my shoulder, and he immediately backed away.

"So, for the next two weeks, starting on Monday, you'll be a bad girl. You'll ditch, disrespect teachers, do drugs, sex—" Ethan said.

"What?" I cut him off.

"He's joking...but surprise me, Willson. Let's see who can be more of a badass here," Blake said as he looked down at me with that cruel smirk.

***

"Lana!"

"What, Mom?" I groaned, my eyes still shut as I

covered my face with the duvet. My bed shook, and I groaned again. "If it's you, Miranda…please stop." I groaned as I threw a pillow over my shoulder. She sometimes slept over, especially Friday nights.

"Ouch." I heard a deep voice, and I knew it wasn't my dad, because he'd gone to the station. My eyes shot open as I turned around.

"What are you guys doing here?" I asked as I got out of bed. I looked like a dinosaur in the morning, and the four hottest guys in school were in my room.

"Your mom let us in," Aidan said as he rubbed his head and nudged his head to the side, where my mother leaned against the doorframe and cautiously took in Blake Gunner's appearance.

"Do you know what time it is?" Carter asked as he motioned to my clock. I looked at it, and my eyes widened because it was noon.

"I thought I'm only going to be a bad girl on Monday," I whispered as I felt my mother's eyes on me. The bet was stupid. I didn't have to prove myself to anyone. I put on my glasses and glanced around the room. Aidan sat on my desk chair, Ethan looked at my bookshelf, and Blake leaned against my bathroom door.

"We're going shopping," Blake mumbled, then turned to my mother, who nodded with a small smile.

"I'll be just down the hall, and I expect you boys are staying for breakfast?" They nodded eagerly, and she clasped her heads together. "Breakfast will be ready soon then. Don't be up here *too* long."

"What's wrong with my clothes?" I frowned once my mother left the room, then glanced at my wardrobe. I wore basically anything if it looked good on me.

"N-Nothing's just..." Blake stuttered then looked away.

"Okay, let's see what you got," Ethan said, then walked to my wardrobe. I bit the inside of my cheek as he looked at my clothing. "Nice band shirts. Why don't you wear them at school?" he asked, referring to the Green Day and Led Zeppelin shirts, along with a few others, which caught Blake's attention as he walked toward Ethan.

"Well, considering I'm known as the good girl in school, people would think I'm looking for attention if I came to school dressed all rock chic and stuff," I mumbled, then looked down at my pajamas.

"We'll just tell people you're one of us, and if they want to start shit, they have to go through me," Blake said as he took out clothes and shoved them into my arms. "Go shower. We're going to turn you into a badass chick." He ruffled my hair. I rolled my eyes and walked to the bathroom. I showered, brushed my teeth and hair, and headed back to my room. I looked down to what I wore because I didn't have time to look at what Blake threw at me. I liked it. It was some black jeans and a maroon jersey. I slipped on my ankle boots and walked downstairs to the kitchen, where the guys were eating pancakes.

"These are divine, Mrs. Willson!" Aidan moaned as he stuffed his face with pancakes.

"Why, thank you, Aidan."

"Coffee...hun?" Mom asked as she held the coffeepot. I nodded, and she poured some into my cup while I sat next to Ethan. "So what are your guys' plans for the day? Just shopping?" she asked as she cleaned up. Mom was okay with me having a boy over; I never really had more than two over, so I guess she was excited there were four in her house.

"We're just going to the mall...I guess," I said, then glanced at the guys. They were too engrossed in the food, but Carter's eyes met mine as he shrugged.

"Well, you guys have fun. I have to be at the hospital soon, so I'll just go and get ready."

***

After breakfast, we cleaned up and walked to Ethan's car. We sat in silence, Blake and Aidan on either side of me.

"Turn on the radio, Ethan," Blake said. Ethan turned it on, and we got a fright as the loud music began to play.

"Softer!" Aidan yelled. Carter seemed too engaged in his phone, so I leaned forward to turn down the music. I heard snickers behind me as I leaned forward. I forgot that my butt was up in the air, so I immediately sat back down with two smirking idiots.

"What?" I snapped my head toward them. They shook their heads but didn't stop smirking. I elbowed them in the stomach, they groaned, and this time they looked out their windows. We passed the mall, and my eyebrows knitted in confusion. "Aren't we going to the mall?"

"No…unless you want to get those cliché Ramone and AC/DC shirts that everyone gets at Target." Carter rolled his eyes as we passed the mall.

"So where are we going?" I asked as I took out my phone.

"Rodney," Blake answered.

"Rodney?"

"Rodney…if you want the best and rare band tees, go to Rodney. If you want any records, go to Rodney," Aidan said as if he memorized it.

"Cool…I've been looking for vinyl for a while," I said.

"Really? Who?" Ethan asked as he looked at me in the mirror.

"Alt-j." I smiled up at him. His eyes flickered to the road, then at me with a smile. I looked at my phone and noticed I got a message from Miranda, then I remembered she stayed over, but I didn't remember when she left.

Miranda: Hey, woke up before you as always. lol You have some guests waiting for you…well by the time you read this, you'll already know, so don't worry about me and just enjoy the day.

Chapter Three

Lana

Ten minutes later, we arrived. I got out and saw a small shopping center, a few small shops here and there, but the biggest one was:

RODNEY'S ROCK & ROLL

"Wow." I looked at the big store in front of me; it consisted of two floors with band posters and guitars that surrounded the windows.

"I know, right!" Carter grinned at me. He held his hand out, and I stared at it. "Come on then. I won't bite."

I slowly took his hand as we walked into the store. Holding his hand was weird. Carter Halls was attractive, and I'd never pictured myself in the position I am right now, with him. The first floor was huge. It had records, CDs, guitars, comics, and books. I made out most of the bands as we walked past them. There was even a separate section for

25

The Beatles. We went up the escalator for the second floor, where all the clothing was.

"I'm in heaven," I sighed as the corners of my mouth curved.

"You got that right, babe," Blake said, then swung his arm around my shoulder. I furrowed my eyebrows at him as my grip tightened on Carter's hand.

"I'm not your babe!" I scowled as I dropped Carter's hand and shifted out of Blake's hold.

"Rodney!" Ethan said as a guy came out with a box in his hands. He looked to be in his late thirties, he had a few tattoos and dirty blond hair, and he also wore a band tee, jeans, and Converse.

"What's up, dude?" Rodney said as he greeted each of the boys. His gaze shifted toward me as I smiled. "Who's the chick?"

"This is Lana," Aidan said. "We've been going out for a while."

"In your dreams, pretty boy." I smiled sarcastically, then stepped aside.

"Feisty, nice…I'm Rodney."

"Lana. Pleased to meet you. This is a cool store you got."

"Thanks…so what can I do for you guys?"

"We want to turn our little geeky friend here into a badass chick," Blake said as he draped his arm around my waist. I stiffened at his touch yet didn't say anything because they'd continue to do it.

"Cool, okay. Now what are some of your favorite bands?" Rodney asked as we walked to the women's section.

"Err…The 1975, Arctic Monkeys, Bring Me the

Horizon, Green Day, My Chemical Romance, The Gaslight Anthem…I can go on for days." I laughed at myself, then pushed up my glasses. I awkwardly coughed the laugh away and looked back at Rodney.

"Girl has good music taste," he said, then winked at Blake. "Okay…hmm…err…" Rodney said as he observed me; he walked around and took in every inch of my body. "Blake…come on," he said, and Blake followed, probably going to get clothes for me to try on. Carter and Aidan disappeared to do their own shopping, which left Ethan and me.

We stood near the dressing rooms for five minutes and looked anywhere and everywhere but at each other. Then I finally took the chance and asked him, "Why did you stop?" He looked at me in confusion, but after a moment, he finally understood.

"I felt sorry for throwing the ball at your friend, and I knew you lived quite far so…" Ethan shrugged his shoulders.

"Oh…thank you."

"No problem." He smiled, but it looked forced.

"Are you okay?"

"What do you mean?"

"I don't know. You don't really talk compared to the other guys."

"I don't know, it's weird. I used to tease you, and now I'm spending my Saturday with you. I don't know how Carter and Aidan can be so calm when they used to tease you too, but now…" he said, then looked away. "Now when Blake shows up, he's all…I don't know, interested in you. It's weird because I've known you since kindergarten, and I teased you for no reason. Now thanks to Blake, I see the real you. Shows don't judge a book by its cover."

"Ethan, I don't want you to feel so bad. It's okay," I said, then approached him.

"I'm sorry."

"It's okay," I said, then raised my arms. His arms wrapped around me as he buried his head in my neck.

"Get a room," someone said. We let go, and I bit the inside of my cheek as Ethan rubbed the back of his neck.

"Come on, nerd. Here, get changed," Blake said as he shoved the clothes into my arms again and glared at Ethan. I walked into the dressing room and put on the first outfit. It was a maroon crop top, black tights with a few holes in them, and denim shorts. Rodney gave me some black Doc Martens, which looked like school shoes, but they were cute. I walked out of the dressing room; the guys were too engrossed in a story Rodney was telling to even notice I was there. I did an awkward cough, which caught their attention. Ethan and Aidan had smiles on their faces, and Rodney looked satisfied, but Carter and Blake didn't.

"I don't like it," Carter said as he shook his head.

"Yeah, too revealing," Blake said as I gaped at him, because I liked the outfit. "Try on the other outfits," he said as he took out a cigarette. My eyes widened, but I walked into the dressing room and closed it to change.

After seven outfits—Blake disagreed with most

of them—I came out with the last outfit.

"Is this satisfying for you, Blakey?" I asked with a fake pout. He raised his head from his phone, and I watched as his eyebrows rose. I wore The Killers tank top, black ripped jeans, and a leather jacket with Doc Martens.

"You look...good," he said, then stood up. I frowned because I noticed he didn't really like it. He walked over to me and took my glasses off, then looked down at me. "Now you look hot," he whispered as the corner of his mouth rose. I bit the inside of my cheek as I nodded. I got changed into my own clothes, then Rodney gave me a few other outfits like that one and said it'd look, and I quote, "hot" on me. Blake, Carter, and Aidan walked out of the store, which left Ethan and me at the cashier. I took out my wallet to pay, but Ethan stopped me.

"I got it," he said then took out his card.

"T-Thanks."

"You look beautiful, Lana...with or without your glasses," Ethan said with a smile. My cheeks reddened as he turned to the cashier to pay.

Afterward, we drove and had a late lunch at a restaurant. We sat in a booth, and Blake casually sat next to me, Carter to my left, Ethan in front of him, and Aidan in front of me.

"Err...four burgers and some salad?" Aidan told the waiter as he looked at me.

"Excuse me?" I tilted my head at him. "Make that four burgers and a double," I said. The waiter wrote down our order then walked away. "You think you guys can have delicious burgers while I eat some plants?" I scoffed. Blake smirked at me, but I ignored him and looked around at the customers. I did like salads, but I was famished, and I heard the place served good burgers.

"You're some girl, huh, Willson." Carter laughed as I bit the inside of my cheek. It was a habit.

"Do I really have to do all that bad girl stuff? I mean I have the clothing…"

"And the attitude," Blake chimed in.

"What do you mean?" I raised a brow.

"Just the way you act—it's strange—like you're not afraid, but you are afraid of something," he said as his lips drew into a straight line. Before I argued, he continued. "You'll be okay on Monday. Don't worry. Be yourself and stop trying to hide behind that good girl image," Blake said, then reached up and stroked my cheek. I realized everyone else had their own conversations while Blake looked directly at me.

"But I've been doing it for years," I said, then looked down.

"Yeah…but I've finally caught you, and you're no good girl," he whispered with a smirk plastered on his face.

***

I slipped on my black hoodie and Doc Martens, then tied my hair into a bun. Today's the day. For the next two weeks, I had to become the school's bad girl. Anything could happen in two weeks, and it's scary. I walked downstairs with my bag and entered the kitchen. Mom was busy with the dishes as Dad looked up at me. Yikes. "Morning,

30

everyone."

"Phases." Father sighed and looked at his iPad again. I laughed and took it as a joke, but he raised a brow at me.

"You okay there? You look different." Mom tilted her head.

"The weather looks weird today, so I put this on."

"Nice shoes…I don't remember buying them for you," Dad said as he glanced down at my long boots.

"Yeah, she went—" Mom said, but something cut her off. A car honk. My eyes widened. I knew that car anywhere; it used to honk at me when I crossed the street to school and almost drove me over once.

"Love you guys. Bye," I said, then kissed Dad on the cheek. I raced out of the house to see Ethan and Aidan in the car.

"Come on, we're gonna be late, Willson!" Aidan yelled from the backseat. I turned around to see my parents by the door. Mom said something to Dad, and he nodded then walked back inside.

"I was going to take the bus, you know," I said as I climbed in the passenger seat.

"Yeah, well, Blake said we should get you from now on," Aidan said from the backseat. Before I questioned them any further, Ethan turned on the radio. We got to school and saw Blake and Carter by the doors. Blake looked at me and frowned. After our brief encounter at the restaurant, I kept my distance with him, because he knew me as nothing but bad. Which I found weird, Blake of all people.

I'd never spoken to him since he came to the school, and suddenly, he's interested in me. Blake noticed something in me that some of the Jefferson High students didn't, and I'd been going to school with some of them since I was seven.

"What?" I asked as we approached them.

"Where's your leather jacket? The makeup?" Blake asked, then eyed me up and down.

"It was cold today, and I don't like wearing so much makeup on a Monday!"

"Blake, leave her. She looks gorgeous." Carter winked at me. "Come on, let's go in."

"Wait…do you mean all together? Like that 'cool' walk you guys do?" I raised a brow. I hated that walk. It's lame and squirmy, and from the look on Blake's face, I noticed he hated it too.

"Yeah…now you will also look cool," Aidan said, then swung his arm around me.

"Err…no thanks. That walk you guys do is super lame."

"Come on, please. It will be so cool to have a girl in the middle," Aidan whined as he tugged on my arm.

"It's like you're our princess and we're your knights protecting you." Blake winked at me. A shiver kicked up my spine at the mention of princess.

"I don't need protecting."

"Watch this," Aidan said. He gave a knock, and it magically opened. Everyone gave way as we walked. A look of irritation appeared on my face as people stared. I used to make fun of them and roll my eyes as they walked, and now I walked with them. We passed jocks, and they whistled at me, which was weird since they stole my gym clothes a few weeks ago so I had to wear the school's old, smelly uniform. Out of the corner of my eye, I saw Benny stare. I turned away, which made it worse since I saw Parker Collins, one of Aidan's friends, smirk at me. I bit the inside of my cheek, then walked off. I approached my locker and quickly put in my combination. I took my glasses out of my bag, then put them on. All the attention was too much; I hated it.

"Hey, badass," a familiar voice said. I smiled as I closed my locker and saw Miranda.

"Please don't leave me again with those idiots!"

"Was it that bad?"

"Yeah…I mean, I love the clothes, but it was weird."

"Well, you'll just have to get used to it, Lana…two weeks!"

"Come on, Lana," Aidan said as he leaned against the locker next to me.

"Where?"

"Class…where else?" he rhetorically asked. I closed my locker and said goodbye to Miranda. I looked down at my Calculus book as I followed Aidan. I didn't see where we went because the bell rang. I panicked.

"Aidan…where are we going?" I asked as I looked up. We walked to another side of the school as he grabbed my arm. The hallways got emptier until it was us.

"We're ditching, duh," he stated. My eyes widened as I let go of his arm.

"We can't. We have a pop quiz today!"

"How do you know that?"

"Well, perks of having Mr. Bronx as your uncle, and I heard this quiz is necessary."

"That's exactly why we're ditching," he said as he caught up to me.

"Well, I'm not!" I said as I picked up my pace.

"You can't even survive the first period!"

"So then what's the use of coming to school if we're going to the ditch the first period?"

"Touché," he said as we walked to Mr. Bronx's Calculus class.

"We're already late, you idiot!" I growled as he stopped to get some water from the fountain. I grabbed his back collar and dragged him to the classroom.

"Well, damn, if you want me so bad, Lana, all you gotta do is ask. I'm sure Carter won't mind," Aidan said behind me. I rolled my eyes and took a sharp turn. I made sure he knocked against the lockers. He groaned, but I continued to walk. I couldn't be late for Mr. Bronx; I had upset him already last week. I opened the door to the classroom and dropped Aidan before I got in. Everyone's eyes shot up from their work as they looked at me.

"Lana, Aidan—you're late," Mr. Bronx said flatly, then I looked at him. He had rings under his eyes, which meant he was grumpy.

"Sorry, Mr. Bronx…we…we…"

"Just…sit down, you two," Mr. Bronx said as he rubbed his temples. I quickly sat down; since the only two seats available were in front, we had no choice. "Right, class, take out your homework," Mr. Bronx said as he wrote on the board. I went through my binder and got the sheet out, then I remembered I didn't do it. I was going to do it this weekend, but the guys took my Saturday up, and on Sunday we had a family day. I quickly threw my sheet in my binder, then remained calm, but inside I boiled. I was already late, and now I didn't do my homework. "Switch with the person next to you," Griffin Bronx said as he ran his hand through his hair. The guy next to me was Nick, one of Benny's friends and a jock. He gave me his paper with a smirk.

"Where's your sheet?"

"I didn't do the homework," I mumbled, but he heard me loud and clear. Nick had a shocked look on his face, but it immediately turned into a devilish grin.

"You didn't do the homework, Lana!" Nick shouted. I glared at him, and he smirked at me. I looked down in shame; GG or Geeky Lana didn't do her homework. I saw a pair of shiny shoes appear in front of me; I looked up and saw the disappointed look on Mr. Bronx's face.

"Lana…you've been very disruptive this lesson."

"Yes, sir," I muttered. I had to be a bad girl. It shouldn't influence me; I should get used to it.

"And you do realize I must give you a detention, right?" he asked, and everyone gasped. I turned around and rolled my eyes at them. I looked back at Mr. Bronx and bit my lip as I slowly nodded. The rest of the lesson I made sure I did all my work, but Nick made it hard since he teased me about my detention. Aidan gave me thumbs up and said I did great.

The rest of my day was absolute crap. I was in a bad mood, so Phys Ed was horrible. The guys smirked at me because they enjoyed every moment of it. We did laps around the field when I saw Ethan next to me.

"How's your day?"

"Screw you, Ethan."

"Hey…want to race? First one to Coach Harris wins?" Ethan asked with a grin. He's tall as hell, not to mention muscular. Yet I was stressed about everything that happened today, so doing something fun excited me.

"You're on!" I exclaimed with a big grin. We stopped and took a quick breath.

"One…two…three."

"Go!" I yelled after the countdown. He bolted through everyone, but I jogged. Halfway through, he got tired, and I took it as my chance to run. I ran through the students, which included Blake and Kelly. Ethan's eyes widened as I passed him, but I eventually heard his footsteps. I ran with all my strength and closed my eyes as I crossed the imaginary finish line.

"Lana!" Ethan yelled. My eyes shot open as I tripped and fell into someone, and that someone was an angry someone. Next minute we're on the ground, but it didn't stop there. Ethan came in so fast that he landed on top of us.

"WILLSON, GET OFF ME!" Coach Harris yelled.

"I can't, sir," I mumbled as Ethan crushed me.

He immediately got up and held a hand out for me. I grabbed it as Ethan pulled me up. I turned around to help Coach Harris, but he was furious.

"Willson! Baxter!" Mr. Harris yelled. I groaned at the mention of my surname; it was the fourth time I'd heard it today.

The bell rang, which signaled the end of the day. I groaned as I shut my locker and walked to the detention room. I took my time, though; I'd say I got lost because I'd never gotten a detention before. I texted my mom and told her I'd be late because I'd be in the library doing homework. Like I'd say to her I got a detention. She'd give me a lecture on how she didn't raise me like that, then go on and say how she wasn't like that at my age. I got to the room and looked at it. I gulped and quietly opened the door. An old teacher sat there with his legs propped up on the table.

"Miss Willson, surprised to see you here. Sit down," Mr. George said, and I gave a slight nod. I looked around the room and saw a few people. Until my eyes met theirs, Ethan, Carter, and Aidan sat and stared with proud looks. Yet someone caught my eye, and I tightened my fists as I watched Blake Gunner listen to whatever Kelly West blabbed on about. However, I don't think he paid attention because he kept licking his lips seductively as he stared at her cleavage.

Chapter Four

Lana

Kelly West. Jennifer Brighton. Melissa Singe. The three bitches in senior year. On the day the guys took me home, I saw Kelly in the other car, and I ducked. Blake couldn't get enough of Jennifer, since he said, and I quote, "spoiled-ass bitch." Now to see him, just wanting to get in her pants, showed exactly what kind of guy he was. I tried to play it off and strolled to an open seat, which was in the middle of the class. The tables were joined, so I sat alone. I looked at the clock. Two more hours to go. I took my homework out that I was supposed to do for Mr. Bronx and the homework we got for today. I sat quietly and did my work. Aidan threw notes at me, but I ignored him as I tried to do my homework. As I thought of an answer, I drifted off. I couldn't believe I got my first detention from my favorite teacher. Mr. Bronx must've been disappointed in me. If only I could explain my situation to him. Wonder what he'd tell my dad when he came over for dinner again. My thoughts were interrupted when I felt someone sit next to me. I saw blond locks out of the corner of my eye and sighed.

"What do you want, Carter?"

"Will you be my date to Homecoming?" he whispered in my ear. The sound of Homecoming sent shivers down my back. I completely forgot about Homecoming—it's next week. I didn't bother with school dances; usually, when guys asked me, I'd be so gullible as to say yes, then on the night, they either didn't show up or they did and found ways to humiliate me. I stared at Carter for any humorous gesture but found nothing.

"What? Why? Me?" I muttered the last part. There must've been a catch to it. Never in my life had I ever thought Carter Halls would ask me, Lana Willson, to Homecoming.

"Just…I would like to take you to Homecoming because you're cool."

"Ugh…yeah, right."

"Look, I'm sorry, okay? I truly am. Ethan told me he said sorry to you, and it made me realize that I should be doing the same because you're different, and if we weren't such assholes back then, we would have all been friends or something," he said. The bullying started in middle school when we had dance class. I paired up with Benny Nielson. He couldn't dance, and he'd get annoyed and told me I couldn't dance, so he went and told the whole school I sucked. That led people to make fun and tease me. It wasn't only about the dance, but to have a sheriff as a father made people want to embarrass me even more.

"I'm sorry, Lana. I was so stupid, and I can't believe I did those things to you." He sighed. To think…a week ago he pulled my chair and laughed at me. Now, he apologized. I considered his beautiful blue eyes and noticed how they sunk in sadness. "Do you forgive me?" Carter asked. I took a deep breath and sighed. I leaned my head against his shoulder, which made him tense up, but he eventually relaxed.

"It's okay, Carter. I forgive you," I barely whispered, but he heard it. He rested his head on mine, and I listened to the happiness in his voice.

"Thank you…thank you so much, Lana," he said as he put his hand on my thigh and stroked it. It was my turn to twitch at the sudden contact, but I closed my eyes and tried not to ruin the moment. Everyone deserved a second chance; it was the only way to forgive, forget, and eventually move on with life.

The rest of detention, Carter helped me with the math work since he was also smart but never showed it off. Even though I knew the answers, he helped me so I'd get it done quicker. Once the clock hit four, Mr. George dismissed us. I grabbed my things and made my way to the exit.

"Hey, want a ride?" Carter asked as he came up beside me.

"If it's no problem," I said. Carter nodded, and we walked to his truck. He moved faster, and I playfully rolled my eyes. Carter opened the passenger door for me, and I thanked him as I got in. He shut it, and I never saw him come to the driver seat. I looked up and saw him in front of

Blake. By the look of it, they'd had an argument. I tried so hard not to look, but it was hard not to since they were right in front of me. Carter threw his hands up and walked to the driver's side. My eyes locked on Blake as he turned to me. My eyes widened at first, but it was replaced with a small smile. Luckily, he returned the gesture and walked across the parking lot to his motorcycle.

"Sorry to keep you waiting," Carter said as he got into the car.

"It's okay," I said as I watched Blake get onto his motorcycle and drive off. I tried so hard not to ask what that was about, but Carter grinned.

"It was nothing…just a disagreement," he said and started the car. The rest of the drive home was silent but comfortable. Sometimes I caught Carter staring at me, and I'd yell at him to keep his eyes on the road. We pulled up to my house. I glanced at it and saw my mom's car in the driveway. Dad wasn't here yet; he'd have a ton of questions as to why guys fetched and dropped me off. I looked over at Carter, who already seemed to have his gaze locked on me.

"Err…thanks," I said as I opened the door.

"No problem, and sorry again." He avoided eye contact as he spoke.

"It's okay." I forced a smile, then got out, shutting the door. I leaned on the open window. "Yes," I said, then bit the inside of my cheek. He raised his eyebrow and gave me a questioning look.

"Yes…?"

"Yes…I'll be your date to Homecoming," I said as I felt my cheeks warm. I looked at him, and he had a smile on his face. "See you tomorrow, Carter."

"See you in the morning, Willson," he called. I watched him drive off as I opened the door.

"I'm home!" I shouted as I walked into the comfort of my home. I walked to the kitchen and saw Mom with a phone in one hand while she sipped tea with the other. She smiled and mouthed a hello. I walked up to her, kissed her cheek, then walked to the fridge. I took out a fruit cup and sat opposite my mom at the island.

"That's great, Jade!" Mom said to the person on the phone. My eyes immediately widened at the name. Maybe Mom knew another Jade. "Oh, I can't wait. It will be like old times again." Mom laughed. "Okay, tell Richard and Levi we say hi, okay? Love you…bye."

"Can't wait for what?" I asked as she set down her phone. She looked at me with bright eyes.

"Did you forget, dear? The Radcliffs coming this year?"

"Oh," was all I said. "When are they coming?"

"December, dear," Mom said. The Radcliffs were our neighbors ever since I was six years old. Richard and Jade Radcliff got along with my mom quite well. They had a son a year older than me by the name of Levi. We were best friends and did almost everything together, until a few years ago, when Mr. Radcliff expanded his business to California. They couldn't turn down the opportunity, so they moved, but it didn't keep us apart. Every year, they'd visit. It was fun, but as we grew older, Levi was distant, so I was distant too.

Our parents thought nothing of it, and we spent hours in a room and watched movies, not a word to be spoken. I wasn't very excited because of what happened last year, though. Seeing him again would make things awkward. Hopefully, they'd stay at a hotel. "How was the library, sweetie?" Mom snapped me out of my thoughts.

"Oh, yeah…it was okay, I guess. Got my work done," I said as I made my way up the stairs. *In detention.*

***

I woke up bright and early, ready for day two of being a badass bitch. Over the past few days, as I got to know Blake Gunner, I'd learned a few things from the bad boy himself, and it's to just not give a shit. Today, I decided on a pair of black jean shorts with tights, tank top, leather jacket, and boots. If my looks didn't convince them, then I'd have to take it to the next level. I entered the kitchen, where I found my mother busy. Thankfully, Dad wasn't here, so it'd be more comfortable if Ethan came. "Morning, Mom."

"Morning, hun. Here's your…" She turned around and stared at me. I grinned as she placed the coffee on the table and sat next to me. "Baby, are you okay?"

"Peachy!"

"Why are you dressed like that?"

"Just experimenting, Mom," I said, then stood up from my seat.

"Just…be careful, okay?" she pleaded, and I

knew she'd warned me because of my dad.

"I will…and Mom? What did you tell Dad yesterday when Ethan came?"

"I just said Miranda couldn't give you a ride, so a friend gave you one…the one who came over to do that project," she said, and I couldn't believe she still remembered my project with Ethan Baxter, which must've explained when she said yes the previous Saturday for letting all of them be in my room.

"Thanks, Mom. Where's Dad, by the way?"

"He had a night shift, and now he's tired." She chuckled as she took a sip of her tea. I smiled and thought how lucky I was. My thoughts were interrupted when I heard a loud roar from outside. My eyes widened, and so did my mother's. I walked to the front door and stiffened when I saw him. "Ooh…I like him, Lana. He's handsome. Is he your ride for today?" Mom asked as she looked out the window. She was childish sometimes. I rarely had boys over anymore, and she was tired of me at home every weekend. Well, I had Miranda, but she said I needed to have more male friends that are my age.

"Err…I got to go, Mom," I mumbled as I kissed her on the cheek then grabbed my bag and went out the door. He took off his helmet then eyed me. "What the hell are you doing here? Where's Ethan? Or Carter?"

"Keep the attitude for school, princess," Blake said, then tossed the helmet toward me.

"Please, don't call me princess, and I am not getting on there," I said, then shoved the helmet at him.

"You're going to be late."

"What's your problem? The whole of yesterday, you ignored me and said I could do better, then I get to detention and see you sucking Kelly's face off, and now you offer me a ride?"

"Why? You jealous?" The corner of his mouth rose as he got off his motorcycle and approached me.

"No, I thought you'd have West on the back of your bike," I said. I saw his boots opposite mine; he placed his finger on my chin, then tilted my head. My embarrassed blue eyes met his brown ones. We stared at each other once he'd look at my lips, then back at me, while I did the same.

"Get on the motorcycle." He snapped me out of my gaze.

"No."

"Lana, get on the bike!"

"Make me," I whispered and noticed how he licked his bottom lip.

"As you wish," he said. Next thing I knew, his hands wrapped around my waist as he pulled me over his shoulder. He held me with one arm as his other gripped the helmet.

"Put me down, you son of a bitch!" I yelled as I balled my fists and hit his back. Blake put me on his motorcycle, then got on himself. He looked over his shoulder and handed me the helmet. "Don't you need this more than me?"

"Nope." He grinned. Blake started the motorcycle, then kicked the side stand in. "Hold on tight, babe," he said, and off we went. Well, at least he didn't call me princess.

***

"Err…we're here, Lana," Blake said as the motorcycle came to a stop. Even though I'd been in a fast car before, it was an entirely different experience on a bike. So many times, I thought we'd fall over at the speed Blake went.

"I don't want to let go," I said as my grip tightened around his waist. He took my helmet off, and I blinked.

"You don't have to, babe," he whispered. Instantly, I let go and got off the motorcycle. As we walked toward Ethan's car, I noticed their gaze on us.

"Hey, guys."

"Are you guys together or something?" Aidan asked as he looked at Blake, then me.

"No. Blake's just an ass."

"You look good today," Carter said. I smiled.

"So what's the deal with you and Kelly West?" Ethan asked Blake, who lit a cigarette.

"Just a hookup, man. She's so fucking annoying, trying to get in my pants…all of them."

"But you gotta admit they're good in bed." Carter said, and they all laughed in agreement while I scoffed.

"What's wrong, Lana?" Aidan asked.

"Just so pathetic that you guys sleep around using girls as toys."

"Aww…Sheriff's daughter jealous 'cause she's a virgin," Blake said, and they laughed. I rolled my eyes, then slightly shook my head. "You're not?"

"Who was the lucky guy?" Blake asked, and I noticed how they waited for an answer. From the corner of my eye, I saw Aidan look down as he tried to avoid eye contact.

"None of your business," I said as the bell rang.

***

"You guys are so cute together!"

"Whatever, Miranda."

"Yeah, you guys even have matching outfits! It's so cute!"

"Matching outfits? Carter's wearing navy blue. I'm wearing black."

"Girl, I was talking about you and Blake. Everyone is talking about it!" she said as we stood in line for lunch. My eyes widened. I was never the center of attention. I wanted to crawl into a hole. The only time people talked about me was when they pranked me. "You two were made for each other!"

"Yeah, if I only dress and act like this," I mumbled as I paid for my stuff. We walked to the center of the cafeteria and sat down at a table.

"So which one of them is your date to Homecoming?"

"Me," a familiar voice said. I looked up to see Carter and the rest of the guys. They sat down yet didn't even bother to ask.

"Sure, you can sit," I sarcastically said. Miranda blushed as Ethan and Aidan sat next to her. I rolled my eyes as Carter and Blake sat next to me.

47

"So what's the gossip today, girls?" Aidan asked in a high-pitched voice. We laughed, but apparently, he really wanted to know.

"Actually, everyone is talking about our grand entrance." I pointed to Blake with my pizza. He grinned, then took it from me. "Hey! I paid for that!" I shouted as I tried to get it, but he shoved the whole thing in his mouth.

"What do we have next period?" Miranda asked after she calmed down from the two hot guys on either side of her. She'd always had a crush on Ethan, so I guess it was heaven for her.

"Phys Ed." I mumbled at the thought of being with all four of them again.

"Speaking of classes…thanks for that," Carter mumbled.

"What?" Blake asked.

"Dude, this girl comes and tell the sexy Ms. Rosa we were late for class because she had to get some forms for her dad."

"Nice excuse," Ethan said, then high-fived me.

"Yeah, you saved me from another detention," Carter said as he put his arm around my shoulder.

"Oh," Blake mumbled.

"What?" I asked.

"I just thought of you doing something…with him in class." He avoided eye contact as I gaped. Never ever would I do something like that in a classroom with Carter Halls.

"Hi, Blakey poo," Kelly said as Jennifer and Melissa trailed behind.

"Hey, babe." He rose to his feet. Blake wrapped his arms around her, smashed his lips on hers, and they made out on the table. My eyes widened in shock. Everyone else in the cafeteria either cheered or fell silent like I did. Carter's grip on my shoulder tightened as I stared at them. I would've slapped him with my pizza, but he ate it!

Chapter Five

Lana

I looked at everyone at the table to see Miranda's glare and Ethan's smirk, while Aidan laughed. As Blake sucked her face off, his one eye opened, and he looked directly at me. I squinted my eyes, then turned away.

"Mr. Gunner! Miss West!" The teacher pulled them off each other, then Kelly and her friends walked away. The bell rang, and people got up. I stood up and ran out of the cafeteria. I didn't know why, but I didn't want to be there. I didn't want him to see my reaction. I walked down the hallway until it was quiet. I walked past a door and saw a familiar face. I slowly opened the door and stood there.

"If you have any questions, ask me during or after class but not right now, be—"

"Hi, Uncle Griff."

"Lana, I didn't recognize you there with all that…happening." He pointed at my outfit.

"Listen…I wanted to apologize for my behavior

yesterday," I said as I walked closer to his desk. He stood up and leaned against the desk, folded his arms, and looked at me.

"It's okay, just…why? You've always been an A student, Lana. When I saw you in the cafeteria with that Gunner kid, I already knew something was up, but now seeing you with Aidan when all he is, is trouble…" Mr. Bronx said in disbelief. I looked down at my feet, too embarrassed to meet his eye. "What happened?" I couldn't tell him. It wouldn't be fair. He'd let things be easy for me, which will make the guys wonder.

"If I could tell you, I would, sir, but…I can't."

"Well then, Lana…all I can tell you is be safe and don't let those boys get to you," he said, then approached me. He kissed my forehead and had that smile on his face that could end world hunger.

"Thank you, Uncle Griff," I said as I turned around to walk out.

"I miss those glasses of yours!" he said while I walked out. I laughed and took them out of my pocket, then put them on. He gave me the thumbs up and smiled while I closed the door.

"What just happened in there?" a high-pitched voice asked. I turned around to be met by Melissa Singe.

"None of your business," I stated and walked off.

"Are you having a—"

"No!" I yelled, then spun around. She had a mischievous grin on her face. I rolled my eyes.

"Then what?"

"I just asked him something…which is really none of your business," I said as I walked off.

Benny and his friends teased me and said that I wasn't good enough for Blake, or any hot guy for that matter, and to think, it's all Blake's fault. He made out with Kelly…right in front of me! Miranda gave me a ride home, and I was glad; I didn't want to see the guys again, especially Blake. I couldn't believe this morning he talked about Kelly like she was another bang, then at the cafeteria he's back with her?

"I'm sorry," Miranda said as we drove in silence. I snapped my head at her and furrowed my eyebrows. "About Blake and Kelly." I scoffed and looked out the window.

"Like I care."

"Oh, but you do, girl. Everyone felt sorry for you." She frowned at me. I remembered people stared at me with pity in their eyes—that or they laughed.

"I don't care," I said and sighed deeply. The rest of the ride home was quiet, yet Miranda tried to cheer me up.

***

"What in the world are you wearing?" Dad asked as soon as I got home. I forgot he was on the night shift; he'd probably leave in the next few hours.

"I don't know, Dad." I sighed as I walked up the stairs.

"Young lady, you stop right there and tell me what the hell is going on!" he said behind me. I flinched as I slowly turned around.

"Nothing," I mumbled as my thoughts drifted off

to what happened with Levi and me last year. Right at this moment, I got the same feeling.

"Nothing, my ass! I didn't raise you like this! Why do you look like you've just come from doing...drugs?" he yelled as I closed my eyes. "Lana! Talk to me! Are you doing drugs?" he shouted, then approached me. I looked down and saw his gun in its holster. I got scared at the sight of a gun. He was going to leave soon since he had his uniform on. He was the sheriff of one of the small towns in Illinois, the closest one to the city.

"No, Dad, I'd never do such a thing!" I exclaimed as tears formed in my eyes. How could he think I did drugs? I knew I looked like a mess. My hair was all over the place. My makeup was messed up, and there were holes in my tights.

"Your mother will come home late. If I hear anything about you while you're here at home, I'm coming straight back and arresting those two boys! I don't want them near you!" he scowled. "Go to your room!"

I ran up the stairs, slammed the door, and leaned against it, then sunk down. I closed my eyes and breathed as I tried to remain calm. It felt like I've been doing this for weeks, but it's only day two. I wanted to give in, but I didn't want Blake to win.

A little while later, I heard the front door close, and a car drove off...then I cried my heart out. I barely cried, but when I did, it wouldn't be over one thing—being called the "good girl." Bullied by everyone in the school for the past few years. The feeling that everything that happened last year was my fault. Being treated as a joke in the cafeteria earlier. People said I looked for the bad boy's attention when I wore these clothes. Everything was falling apart.

***

I wasn't going to let my dad ruin everything, so I made myself look at least presentable for the day. I'd cried for two hours last night, then had a bath. Mom came home and saw the state I was in, so we had take-out. No questions were asked, and I always knew Mom would be there for me. I slipped on a big gray shirt, black jeans, and maroon Doc Martens. Like Blake, I just didn't care. I put on my glasses and put my hair up in a bun. I had my usual breakfast with Mom, then Dad entered the room.

"I'm taking you to school today," he said as he grabbed his keys. My eyes widened as I spat out my coffee.

"Oh, sweetie, that won't be necessary. You just got back an hour ago. Go rest," Mom assured Dad as she rested her palm against his chest.

"I want to," he said as he let go of her hand and walked outside. I stared at Mom for help, but she sighed.

"If any cute boy comes, I'll tell them you got another ride." She smiled. I sighed as I sipped my coffee. Then I heard Dad's car, which startled me. I got up and scurried outside.

The car ride felt like an eternity while Dad lectured me and I nodded. We were a block away from the school.

"Err, Dad, you can stop here...I can walk," I

said, then gave him my best smile. He shook his head and drove on. I wish the bell rang, and I'd run in. Everyone seemed to be outside today, even the guys. They sat in Carter's truck.

"Just, please…Lana, don't do anything stupid," Dad said as I got out of the car. I nodded, then shut the door. I looked down at my shoes as I walked. People stared at me—not the stare of why did she come out of the Sheriff's car, but a look of shame and pity. I kept a straight face as I walked up to the building and tried to block out the things I heard.

***

I sat in the back, but I still felt eyes on me. Aidan sat next to me, and Blake was on the other side. Carter and Ethan sat in front of me. I was surrounded.

"Lana."

"Lana."

"What?" I snapped. I realized Aidan spoke to me, so I turned to him.

"Are we still on for the fourth period?" he asked. I almost forgot that Aidan told me to help him with a prank he wanted to do. I breathed in as they watched me. I had to do it. I wasn't scared, and I could do it if I'm careful. I slowly nodded. A small smile appeared on his lips, but I looked away…rather at Blake. He smirked, and I rolled my eyes. I wish I slapped that smirk off his face.

I was in the fourth period, Home Economics. Aidan was in Chemistry, and his prank was up and ready to go. I put oil into the pan to make stir-fry, but I accidentally put too much in but shrugged. I checked the time. 11:18. Two more minutes. Mrs. Hartwell came to look at my food, and her eyes almost fell out of her sockets as she saw the oil.

"Child! Dispose of that now! Too much!" she said. I turned off the stove and picked up the pan and threw it into the recycle bin. Suddenly, I heard sounds of paper burning. Mrs. Hartwell's eyes widened, and I looked at the time again. 11:20. I ran to the emergency lever and pulled on it; simultaneously I heard another one, and I visualized Aidan pulling his. "Everyone, evacuate!" Mrs. Hartwell shouted as everyone ran out. We've practiced it a million of times, but when something happened, everyone went bonkers. I saw Aidan in the sea of students. He ran up to me and grabbed my arm, and we went the other way. The abandoned side of the school was where his car was, and he opened the door for me while I got in. When the emergency lever went off, we could go home; after five minutes, the teachers would go back and check what caused it.

"That was incredible!" I said as we drove off.

"I know, right? The teacher was right next to me, and he told me not to put that chemical in, so I said 'this one,' then added it in and…boom!" he said as we laughed.

"I swear my teacher almost had a heart attack!" I laughed as we drove past all the houses. The area didn't look familiar to me. "Where we going?"

"You'll see." He grinned. I shivered and glanced out my window. A few houses passed, followed by a bunch of trees and then…nothing. My eyes widened as I saw dirt outside. "Relax, we're just going to hang out...somewhere," he mumbled. We pulled up to what looked to be an old cottage. I saw two cars and a familiar motorcycle. I thought it'd only be Aidan and me. "So what was the deal with your dad dropping you off? You do something naughty?" He wiggled his brows, and I playfully punched him.

"No...he was upset with my appearance and the fact that guys are picking me up and dropping me off now," I mumbled. Dad was honestly pathetic; he didn't trust me.

We walked into the cottage to see the rest of the guys. Inside looked much better. It seemed cozy, a big L-shaped sofa with a TV, bar, bathroom, and two other rooms. It had a small kitchen, and band posters were plastered everywhere.

"Speak of the devil," Ethan said as he saw me. I grinned and sat next to him and Blake. Carter and Blake smoked, which bothered me. At first, when we met, they barely smoked, but now all they did was smoke. I turned around to see Ethan light two cigarettes. I didn't like it. Surrounded by four tall, muscular dudes in the middle of nowhere.

"What now?" I looked at them; they were too engrossed with the thing between their lips to even acknowledge my existence.

"Let's get to know each other." Ethan smiled as he blew out the tobacco smoke through his nose.

"Dude...we're not fourteen. I think we know each other too well," Carter said.

"I don't," I piped up.

"All right, let's play," Blake said. "We all have

to answer truthfully, okay?" he asked. "This one is for you, Lana. Are you scared?"

"Of what?" I laughed.

"Getting caught."

"I already did."

"That still doesn't answer the question. Are you scared, yes or no?" he demanded. I looked at the guys for help, but they were too mesmerized with their cigarettes.

"No," I said as I bit the inside of my cheek.

"Then smoke." He smirked at me. My eyes widened at what he said. He held out the cigarette and waited. The guys stopped for my response. I had to do it; he was testing me. I knew if I took it, he wouldn't bother me; if I didn't, he'd say I was scared and win. I stared at the familiar thing between his fingers then took in the scent. I slowly took it as I watched the smirk play onto his face. I closed my eyes and put the familiar scent between my lips and inhaled. The smoke flowed through my lungs, and I slowly removed the cigarette from my mouth and exhaled. I opened my eyes to see their stares. It was common to cough at a first attempt, but thankfully, I'd done it before with Levi. "How did you—?"

"When did you learn—"

"Are you okay?"

"I'm all right," I replied. They looked at me in awe as I inhaled the stupid thing again.

"You're full of surprises, Lana," Ethan said as he wrapped his arm around my shoulder.

"My baby is growing up!" Aidan cheered. Blake stared in shock, but it changed into a smirk. He stretched out his hand and pointed to my cigarette.

"Nu-huh…get your own, pretty boy," I said as I blew out smoke in his face. He grinned and took another cigarette. It was weird at first. Then I thought about my family, mostly my dad. He was right. I was raised correctly and with good manners; things like that should never slip my mind once. I sighed as I crushed the cigarette in the ashtray. I got up and walked to the other side of the sofa, so I was opposite them. "What does this make us?" I asked. They stayed quiet for a bit, then looked at Blake, even me. It made sense since he started the bet.

"I don't know…friends?" he asked, then shook his head. "Look, Lana, if you want to back out of this and return to the normal, boring, bullied, loser, geek—"

"I get it…and no, I don't. It's actually fun with you guys." I smiled. They gave a warm smile in return. It was the first time I'd seen them smile since all they did was smirk at me; their smiles individually were beautiful.

"I'd love to be your friend, Lana," Ethan said while the rest nodded in agreement. It was only temporary, though, so I'd smoke even if it's okay. A few days wouldn't hurt anyone. Even if it meant to bring out the old Lana that only revealed itself when Levi Radcliff came.

"I need to use the bathroom," I said after I smoked another cigarette. Two weren't as bad as Blake, who did eight in a day.

"Sure…down the hall, second door on your left," Ethan said. I thanked him and got up then walked to the bathroom. I didn't need the bathroom. I heard the guys talk as I shut the door. I looked at myself in the mirror. I had bags under my eyes, and my hair was messy. I cupped my hand over my mouth and smelled my breath. Yikes. I opened the top cabinet and searched for mouthwash or something but didn't find any…only cologne and condoms. In the back were weird parcels, but I totally ignored them. I checked the bottom cabinet under the basin and saw more of the strange packages. I sighed, got up, and fixed my hair, then washed my face. I flushed the toilet and still washed my hands, then walked out of the bathroom.

After an hour, Carter, Aidan, and Ethan decided to go. Blake said he'd take me home, and I argued because I was scared to ride his motorcycle, but he insisted.

"Why me?" I asked once silence took over. I laid on the sofa while Blake sat opposite me, for once not smoking. He looked at me in confusion but finally understood.

"I don't know…you're different," he said. I rolled my eyes at his cliché statement. I knew I was different, considering everyone at school thought I was a whore who looked for attention from the four hierarchy guys. "I'm sorry," he mumbled as he played with his fingers. "Sorry you had to get dropped off by your father, and sorry I acted like a dick the past few days."

"Don't worry. That's my punishment."

"That's kind of sad."

"You get used to it," I said. Whenever I did something stupid or behaved weird, my dad insisted on driving me to school.

"I watched you…" he said, and I raised a brow.

"Were you stalking me, Gunner?" I turned to him. His eyes widened but turned into that stupid smirk.

"When I got to school, all the girls were hooked on me, but you seemed annoyed and pissed," he said as I raised a brow. "It amused me to see you roll your eyes at me or look at me in disgust. I asked the guys about you, and they said you're 'Geeky Lana' or just a loser.

"I watched you get bullied by Benny…I thought you'd never speak to me, but when Ethan stopped to pick you up that day, and when you surprised us by rocking out to "Happy Song" instead of blocking your ears or something…I knew something was up. I was intrigued and wanted to know more about you, and this was the only way."

"But why?"

"We're teenagers, Lana. You should act like one. You're too serious. Your dad has you so focused on school and scaring you—"

"I'm not scared—"

"That you're not enjoying your youth. We're teenagers. We're supposed to do stupid, ridiculous things and take chances." He cut me off. I turned to my side and buried my face into the sofa. "I'm doing this to show you how to enjoy your high school experience, take risks, and to bring out the side nobody has ever seen," he said as I heard footsteps. "I went to your place last night. It looked dead. I knocked on the door, and there was no answer, then I went to your window and heard crying."

"I don't want to talk about it," I mumbled into the sofa after a while. I felt the couch sink in, then another body get onto it. His arm dug around my body and wrapped around my waist, and his other hand came up to my face. He took a lock of hair and put it behind my ear.

"You don't have to tell me, but are you okay?" he whispered in my ear as my brows rose. Right then and there I wanted to cry, but I had to keep it in. I slowly nodded, then relaxed into his hold.

***

Blake

I honestly felt sorry for her; she showed up to school in the sheriff's car. I felt like a douche. I didn't know why I did it—though Carter got on my nerves, I wanted to ask her to Homecoming, but I knew she'd say no. She hated me, plus Kelly West was a damn good kisser, so how could I say no one more time?

I went to her house yesterday. The lights were out, no cars were in the driveway, and I wasn't sure if anyone was home. I knocked on the door, but there was no answer, so I went to her bedroom window. It was dark, too. I climbed the tree to get to her window, and I heard a strange sound. As I got closer, the noise got louder. I sat on the branch and listened. She cried. I made her cry. I debated on whether I should knock on her window and go in and comfort her, but a car pulled up the driveway. She turned on the light, and that's the first time I saw her like that, lifeless. Her eyes were bloodshot, makeup ran down her face, and her hair looked tangled. She went to the bathroom. I took it as a sign to leave. Then when I saw her today with a pissed look, it made me laugh. She looked so cute, yet I wanted to annoy the shit out of her. I'm glad Aidan had that ridiculously stupid prank, otherwise we wouldn't be here. She wouldn't be here. I didn't know why I did it; I thought she'd push me off the sofa, but she gave in. I wrapped my arms around her and drifted off to sleep.

"Blake…it's dark."

"Good to know," I said. Of course, it's dark, because my eyes were closed.

"Blake…it's dark outside!" she exclaimed. My eyes shot open as I sat up.

"Shit! My dad's going to kill me!" she yelled as she got up, then grabbed her shoes.

"You? He's going to kill me!" I panicked. Lana stared at me as she put her glasses on; to be honest, she looked cute with those glasses. A smirk grew on her face as she walked closer to me; the smell of tobacco went through my nose as she opened her mouth.

"Is someone scared?" She pursed her lips. I rolled my eyes, then grabbed her hand. We walked to my motorcycle, and she got on with no argument. "Can we stop at the gas station quickly?"

We pulled up at the gas station, and she sprinted into the store as I followed. We went our separate ways to get a few things. Two minutes to be exact, and we were at the cashier. I had a lighter and box of gum while Lana freaked out. She took a pack of mints and three boxes of gum. I chuckled as she took out her wallet. I offered to pay, but she shook her head and quickly paid.

"I am fucking screwed," she said as we walked to my motorcycle. She stuffed her mouth with mints, and all I heard were her grinds. I laughed as we got on my bike; I found it cute when she panicked. Her glasses fell to her nose, and she cussed.

We pulled up to her house minutes later, and I saw her mother's car, which meant no sad Lana Willson.

"He'll be here soon, though," she said as she got off my bike. She looked at me, then at her feet. "Thanks," she mumbled. I raised my eyebrow and looked at her. "I don't really know why, but thank you for…I don't…crap, I don't know, Blake, just thanks." She walked to her house. I smiled as I thought of what other surprises Lana was capable of. I drove to my house, which was a single story that consisted of four bedrooms. I walked into the house where I saw my older brother.

"I'm home."

"Dinner's in the microwave," Axel said as he flicked through the channels on the television.

"Where's Momma?" I asked as I went to the kitchen.

"She's working late, I guess."

"This is the third time this week," I said as I took out the mac and cheese from the microwave.

"Well, at least she has a job, Blake," he said from the living room. I rolled my eyes.

"Yeah…unlike some people," I muttered to

myself.

Axel Gunner, my twenty-two-year-old brother, was jobless and too lazy to go study. Momma was an assistant at a vibrant company that owned a bunch of hotels and stuff, so the money was good. There was enough money to keep a roof over our heads until one day it was all gone, and my mom had to go look for a new job. I sat on the sofa and ate my food in silence. I turned to my brother, who laughed at something the woman said on the television. In no way did I want to end up like him.

Chapter Six

Lana

"Is this a thing now?" Miranda asked as she looked at the cigarette between my lips.

"Just a show, girl," I said as we walked to the side of the school.

"Temporary, right?" she asked for the third time today.

"Yes, Miranda!" I exclaimed. "It's not like I'm going to get addicted."

"Sorry…just asking, because you said that the last time."

"Well, this is only my second one today," I said, then decided to change the subject. "Who you taking to Homecoming?"

"Some guy." She blushed, and I knew it was the right topic to talk about.

"Some guy, huh?"

"Shut it, nerd. It's Marcus Sanders."

"Marcus…the guy that came at the beginning of the year? He's cute," I said, then dropped the cigarette. I crushed it under my foot as she spoke.

"I know, right? We've been talking for a while now."

"Do you like him?"

"Yeah…I like Marcus Sanders," she said, then bit her lip. "And he's my date to Homecoming!" She pulled me in for a hug. I laughed and hugged her back; I was glad my best friend was going to Homecoming with someone she liked. "We're going shopping on Saturday. Don't forget. We need dresses."

"Ugh…I'm sure my mom has something."

"Yeah, if you want to come dressed as a surgeon, then sure," she said sarcastically. I rolled my eyes and gave in. "I can't wait! Plus, your date is Carter freaking Halls. You guys will be the couple to beat."

"Beat in what?"

"Homecoming king and queen!"

"I don't know—"

"Don't worry, I nominated you, and plus, Them are nominated too!"

"All of them?"

"Yep."

"I don't think Blake will come. He probably thinks Homecoming is crap. Aidan will likely be his goofy self…"

"Remember last year when we took a picture then he dumped a bucket of fish oil on you?" Miranda laughed.

"Yeah…I hugged Jennifer and Kelly so tight they almost fainted from the smell!" I chuckled as the memory entered my mind.

"Hopefully this year will be different," she said after we recovered from our laughter.

The last bell went off, signaling the end of the day. After I finished at my locker, I decided to take a slow walk to Ethan's car. I walked down the quiet hallways until I heard footsteps behind me. I walked faster, and so did the people behind me. I looked up and saw a figure close to me. Benny Nielson. My eyes widened, and I turned around to face two other people. Nick and Liam. I turned around again to see Benny's smirk; he nodded, then Nick and Liam stood on either side and lifted me by each arm. They turned around and walked down the empty hallways. A feeling of déjà vu swept inside of me.

"Wh-what are…you…" I stammered as I looked at them. They walked out of the building to the exact place where Aidan and Ethan dragged me last week. Instead, they shoved me against the wall, making my glasses fall off.

"Hold her," Benny said. They roughly pulled and pinned me against the wall. I exhaled deeply as Benny stepped toward me. Liam and Nick slowly released their grip from me and backed off as their leader inched closer. "Don't you get it, Lana? They're using you!" he exclaimed, then grabbed my jaw. "They'll end up hurting you…"

"Look who's talking, you fucking hypocrite," I hissed. Benny snapped as he hit the wall next to me with the palm of his hand, then gripped my jaw again.

"I'm doing you a favor, Lana." He laughed. "They're gonna break your heart just like he did." I tilted my head at Benny as a smile broke onto my face. Benny raised a brow then took a step back. "What are you looking at?"

"An asshole who couldn't take a punch from Levi Radcliff," I said and watched as the vein popped in his neck. Benny raised his fist, then looked at me.

"Do it. You've done it so many fucking times it won't make a difference!" I shouted as he looked at me.

"Will you shut up!" he yelled, then punched the wall. This time he pressed his forehead against mine. He exhaled deeply as I looked at him.

"I will not be silenced!" I giggled. Suddenly, my giggles turned into laughter as I pushed him off me. Benny, Nick, and Liam backed away as I sank down the wall and laughed.

"Are you fucking crazy?" Nick asked as I calmed down.

"Do you really wanna know?" I asked with a smirk. Benny became annoyed, and the next thing I knew, he's right in my face as he held my arms up with one hand and cupped my face with the other.

"Are you on drugs, Willson?"

"Nope!" I said as the corners of my mouth turned up. I was nervous, but I didn't want them to know that, so I joked around. Benny let out a growl as he looked at me. I heard voices, and it looked like he did too as he looked over his shoulder.

"Hey, what the fuck?" Ethan yelled. Benny turned to me, and I smiled.

"I can't hate you, Lana Willson. I'd rather hate myself," Benny said, then shook his head. He got up, and I squinted my eyes through the sunlight.

Ethan approached us, but Nick and Benny blocked him. I sighed deeply as I felt my eyes droop. My head ached as I watched Ethan fight Nick and Benny. I heard laughter in the distance and turned to see Liam. I leaned my head back and groaned as I shut my eyes.

***

My eyes shot open as I looked up. I laid in a bed in an unfamiliar room. I sat up and looked around, yet something told me I'd been there before. I looked at the bedside table and saw my glasses were shattered. The broken pieces brought my memory back, but all I remembered was Benny, who tried to take a punch, but something stopped him. I raised my legs to my chest and cried. I buried my head into my knees as I thought back to what happened earlier. I felt the edge of the bed go down with someone's weight. I saw Ethan with a saddened look on his face. He took his shoes off, then laid next to me. I didn't care if it wasn't normal, so I relaxed next to him. He put his arm around me as I cried into his chest.

"Shh...Lana, don't worry, you're safe now," Ethan mumbled as he rubbed my back. I sniffed, then looked up at him. His eyes were dark, and I noticed that he had a cut on his lip.

"I hate him so much!" I cried into his chest, then remembered when Benny said, that he couldn't hate me. Ethan rubbed my back and assured me that it was all right.

"I'll get him," he growled as he kissed my

forehead. He wiped my tears away with his thumb, then hugged me.

"Ho-how did you know?"

"I was getting worried since you took so long, so I went to look for you, then I heard shouting and saw…"

"Oh, thank you."

"It's okay, Lana," he said, then sat up. "I'll go get you some water." I slowly stood up and stretched after he left the room.

"Ouch," I mumbled as I hit my foot on something. It was the same parcel that I saw yesterday in the bathroom. I glanced at the door. Ethan could be back any second. I quickly crouched down and looked under the bed: more parcels that looked the same. I shoved the package under the bed as the door opened. I sat down as Ethan brought a cup of water with some medication.

"For your head," he mumbled as he set the pills down. I thanked him, then took the pills.

"What happened to your lip?"

"Err…nothing, just practice," he said, then shrugged his shoulders. I knew there wasn't any extracurricular activity that Ethan was involved in today because he offered to take me home.

"I've arrived! Your lives just got better!" an annoying voice said, and Aidan entered the room. I playfully rolled my eyes as he sat down on the bed. I noticed he had a bruise on his chin and his arm, but I ignored it. Aidan was the one who transformed awkward situations into funny ones, so I didn't want our only hope to be uncomfortable, too.

"Where are we?"

"The cottage…duh," Aidan said as he took out some cigarettes. Ethan took out a lighter, then held it in the center as we lit our cigarettes. I didn't protest as I blew out the smoke; it calmed me. I watched Aidan as he stared at the ceiling, attempting to blow smoke rings. I glanced at Ethan, who was already staring at me. He immediately looked away as his cheeks turned red. "You going to the football game tomorrow night?"

"Err…I don't know."

"Please come, Lana. I need you," Ethan said as he stared at me.

"But…what if they start again?" I mumbled.

"Sit with us. They're not going to hurt you ever again." Aidan stood up. "We should probably get you home. I'll be waiting in the car. Don't get too touchy, you children," he joked as he walked out of the room. I blushed as I thought how he'd save us from an awkward situation but made one up when he left. I turned to Ethan, who already had his eyes set on me. I rose to my feet and crushed the cigarette in the ashtray nearby.

"Can I ask you something?" he asked as he got up from the bed.

"You just did."

"Promise me you'll come to the game tomorrow night?" he asked as he walked closer to me.

"Y-yes," I mumbled as I stepped back, then hit my legs against the bed. Ethan firmly placed his hands on my waist and looked at me.

"And will you wear my jacket for, you know…good luck?" He smirked. I must have been as red as a tomato; I nodded, then took another step back but fell on the bed. Ethan landed right on top, our faces inches apart as he stared at my lips. He leaned in slowly as I closed my eyes.

"Hurry up, you two!" Aidan yelled from outside. My eyes shot open as I cautiously slipped from beneath Ethan, who also got off the bed. I looked at my glasses on the table.

"Err…I'll get you new ones." He walked to the table and took a plastic bag from under it; he put the remaining pieces in, then put it in a drawer. "My dad knows a guy," he mumbled, then walked out of the room. I slowly followed as we walked out of the cottage. Ethan held the door open for me as I got in the car. Aidan spoke to someone on the phone, and it looked like a serious conversation, since his eyes slanted and he whispered. He saw us, then told the person he'd call back. He put his phone away and got in the driver's seat. The ride home was awkward, so Ethan switched on the radio.

"How did you guys find that cottage?" I asked from the backseat.

"Ethan's dad was going to use it for extra storage, but it was too small, so he told us we could have it," Aidan said.

"So that's like your…man cave?"

"Yeah, plus it's far away from everything," Ethan said.

"And everyone," I said to myself. We pulled up to my house to see Dad getting out of his car. He turned around and smiled. Dad was okay with Ethan, since he'd come to my house before, and his dad always gave my dad discounts at his stores. I got out of the car and thanked the guys.

"Hey, Dad," I said as we got into the house.

"Hey, sweetie. Your mom will be coming home late. Someone just went into labor," he said as he walked to the kitchen. "So…Mexican or Chinese?" he asked as he held his phone.

"Err…Mexican." I smiled as I sat down at the island. Dad joined me after he placed the order, then gave me a once over.

"You okay, kiddo? You have a bruise on your cheek," Dad said, touching the injury gently. "Was it those boys? I swear I will make sure—"

"No, Dad. I just fell today," I said as I placed my hand on his arm. His jaw tightened as he looked at my cheek again.

"Y'know…your mom approves you seeing all these boys since you haven't mixed much with the opposite sex, and…I do too. You should enjoy your last year of high school." He sighed. "But if any of those boys break you…I will break Ethan and use him as a stick to beat the rest of them."

"Yes, Daddy."

"Food will be here soon."

"Great…I'm just going to clean up," I said as I walked upstairs. I opened the door and immediately shut it. I heard movement in my room, and my eyes shot open. My eyes widened as I saw what it was…or in this case who. "What are you doing here?"

I looked at the blond beauty on my bed, with a smirk might I add. I locked my door to make sure my dad wouldn't interrupt us while I kicked him out.

"Carter Raymond Halls, what the hell are you

74

doing here?"

I pictured him perfectly, well, not really, since his jaw was jacked up.

"What? I can't talk to my Homecoming date?" Carter asked as he shifted on the bed, then patted the space next to him. I slowly sat down as I eyed him suspiciously.

"What happened to your jaw?" I asked. He opened his mouth to reply but got cut off.

"Lana…you okay in there?" My eyes snapped to the door handle, which rattled. I got up and ran across the room to the door. I glanced at Carter, who grinned. I glared and mouthed him to get out, but he opened my sheets and got comfortable in my bed.

"Err…yeah, Dad, I'm good," I mumbled.

"Food's here. Open the door." My dad raised his voice. I slowly opened the door and got out quickly.

"Yum, food, I'm starving!" I said as I looked my dad in the eye. He turned to my bedroom, but I took his hand and dragged him downstairs and into the kitchen. We sat at the island and ate the Mexican food. Dad eyed me suspiciously, but I smiled. I ate my food so fast I swear my mouth was on fire. After five minutes, we heard a thump from upstairs. My father's eyes turned to the stairs as mine widened.

"What the hell was that?" Dad asked, rising from his seat. I stood up and blocked his way.

"It was just my books. I was studying…yeah. That's why I locked the door. So I put my books on the bed, and they must've have fallen off."

A phone call cut off my dad's response. I sighed in relief as he reached into his pocket to retrieve his phone.

"Hello?" He returned to eat his food. I did too, occasionally looking at the stairs. Carter better get the hell out of my house. "Uh huh…got it," Dad said, then ended the call. He sighed heavily and got up.

"Everything okay?"

"Yeah…some idiot robbed Mrs. Evergreen's boutique. Now I have to go in." Dad sighed as he grabbed his jacket and keys. "I don't know how long your mom or I will be, so…stay safe," he said as I walked to him. "And no boys over while I'm gone." He kissed my forehead. I awkwardly chuckled as he walked out the door. I heard the car start and listened as it got quieter. I grabbed the rest of the Mexican food, then ran upstairs to my bedroom. I opened the door to see a shirtless Carter Halls on my bed.

"It's not nice to stare," he pointed out. I scoffed, then strolled to the bed. I sat next to him and opened the food. We ate in comfortable silence. "Are you okay?" he asked as he tilted his head. I sighed and nodded, but Carter didn't buy it. "Lana, has Benny ever done that to you before?"

"Y-Yes, Carter, of course…I mean, you saw it once last year." I laughed drily; he'd asked as if he hadn't seen me like that before.

"I didn't realize it was so…"

"Brutal? Damaging? Painful?" I cut him off. I was mad; now he cared?

"Lana, I'm sorry. I won't let that happen ever again. None of us will," Carter said. He slowly put his arms around me, but I tried to push him away.

76

After two attempts, I gave up and cried in his arms.

"I'm sorry," I mumbled into his bare chest.

"It's okay. They're going to get it someday," he said as he played with a lock of my hair.

"I'm all fucked up and depressed. Why would you want to go to Homecoming with me?"

"Because you're you, Lana Willson. You don't give two shits what people think of you. You're funny, a risk taker, and…you gave us another chance. We were assholes to you, but you gave us another chance, and I can't thank you enough for that," Carter said as he cupped my face. He gently wiped my tears away, then kissed my forehead. "I promise…you will never get hurt again."

After that, we talked about anything and everything. It was funny to lay on my bed, laughing and talking as if Carter hadn't done anything to me. He used to tease me a lot.

"I need to change," I said as I got up from the bed. I walked to my closet and grabbed my pajamas, then walked to the bathroom. "You staying the night?"

"If you want me to," Carter said from my room.

"Well, it's already late so…" I said, then shrugged my shoulders. I sat by my desk and put my arm on the bureau.

"What you thinking about, Willson?"

"How I'm going to get Benny Nielson back."

"Need help?" Carter asked as the corner of his mouth turned up. I walked to my bookshelf and opened a book that I'd hadn't opened in years.

"Middle school yearbook?" Carter raised a brow. I had a devilish grin on my face as I opened the book. Two papers fell out, and I held them in my hand.

"I know you only came here at the beginning of freshman year, but there was an incident that happened in middle school with Benny. If anyone ever brought it up, he made sure they were dead."

"Wait, Aidan told me Benny came to school dressed in his pajamas, thinking it was pajama day?" he asked as I nodded.

"Then the seventh graders dunked his head in red paint and hung him on the flagpole!" I scrunched my nose up and laughed.

"Yeah…but now if anyone speaks of it, he wants them dead," he mumbled. Benny Nielson was known to have a short temper; that's why he always took out his anger on me. Every time he did, I saw something in his eye, something like regret or guilt.

"Well, then, Carter Halls, get out your best black attire, because you'll be seeing me in a coffin soon." I laughed as I held up the two papers, which were photographs of Benny in his Batman pajamas and red paint all over his face while up on the flagpole.

"No way, Lana. He's going to kill you," Carter said as he took the pictures.

"It's a risk I'm willing to take."

"All right. What's the plan?"

***

It turned out Dad had a lot of work to do, so he stayed at the station and Mom didn't come home until three a.m. She was exhausted and went to bed

78

immediately. We stayed up and talked about the plan and messaged the rest of the guys, so they'd be in too. Funny that they were up late. Aidan demanded that we join a group chat, so we finally put the chat to use:

Ethan: Gotta hand it to you, Lana, that's a foolproof plan.

Blake: Yeah, how'd you think of it so quick?

Aidan: Ugh, please. Where do you think she gets her mischief skills from? ;)

Lana: Carter :)

Blake: How the heck did you get help from him?

Lana: I showed him the picture.

Ethan: How?

Lana: His right here…

Aidan: *He's

Lana: Whatever -.-

Aidan: You're not so smart after all.

Blake: What the hell is blondie doing in your house?!

Carter: Snuck in. ;)

Aidan: And to think we dropped you off! You could have invited us too!

Lana: I didn't know! He climbed through my window while my dad was here...

Ethan: I'm coming.

Blake: Me too.

Aidan: Yay! Party!

Lana: No! Hell no! No party! Nobody is coming!

Blake: But you let him in...

Lana: I didn't!

Ethan: Then kick him out!

Carter: I'm right here, y'know, and it's almost 4 a.m.

Lana: Yeah, see you guys at school. Byee...

Aidan: Use protection!

Ethan: WTF Dude, don't give them ideas!

Carter: Lana's phone died, see you in the

morning, guys. Someone is getting it tonight!

Blake: Screw you, dude...touch her, and I'll smack that smirk right off your face.

Aidan: You better sleep with one eye open tonight.

Carter: Oh, I will as I watch Lana's beautiful body right next to me.

Ethan: I will rip your ball sack off and beat you with it!

Aidan: BrUh too far.

Blake: Yeah, dude, just got a freaking visual of that.

Chapter Seven

Lana

I woke up early since Carter stayed the night. It was risky to sleep together. Other than that, it was comforting since he played with my hair as I fell asleep in his arms. I groaned and checked the time. Seven a.m. and Mom was still asleep. I got up to get my clothes, then walked to the bathroom, still half asleep. Out of the corner of my eye, I saw movement. The shower was on. I wasn't in the shower, and I forgot about Carter. My eyes widened as I saw the tall blond in my shower.

"Carter!" I squealed, then turned away. I looked back and sighed in relief. The towel rack on the shower door covered him from his waist down, so I only saw his bare chest. He smirked at me, so I scoffed and looked back at the mirror. I brushed my teeth while I waited. The water stopped, and out of the corner of my eye, I saw him get out. Thank goodness, my parents' room was on the other side of the house while mine was on its own with my

CAUGHT

own bathroom. Carter walked out with a towel draped around his waist as he strolled to my room. I closed the door and got undressed, then jumped in the shower. I let the hot water fall onto my body as I ran shampoo in my hair. I saw movement once again. I turned around and squealed once again. "Carter freaking Halls, what the hell are you doing?" I demanded as I bent down to the towel's length as it covered my chest.

"Nothing I haven't seen before, babe," he said. I rolled my eyes as I stared at him. He went to the mirror and took the comb, brushing his hair. "It takes time to get my hair to look this good." I rolled my eyes as I watched him put the gel in, which belonged to Levi. The hair gel was from last summer, so it was more solid and made the tips of Carter's hair hard. He didn't seem to care, though, and tried his best to smooth it out.

"You're going to be late…and you are wasting water." I scoffed and slowly turned around; my back faced him as I washed my hair. I looked over my shoulder and saw he was gone. I sighed in relief as I turned off the shower and walked out. I put my clothes on, then brushed my wet hair. I walked back to my room to see Carter put his clothes on.

"Do you always carry extra clothing in your bag?" I asked as I leaned against the door.

"Yep…gotta have a spare shirt," he said as he put on a plain black shirt with the same jeans and shoes from yesterday. He walked to the window, and my eyes widened.

"What are you doing?"

"Don't wanna get caught now, do we?" He

winked at me, and before I replied, Carter jumped on the tree outside the window and made his way down. I watched him as he walked to his truck across the road and waited. I strolled downstairs to the kitchen, where my mom turned on the kettle.

"Morning, Mom."

"Morning, hun."

"How'd you sleep?"

"Came home at three in the morning. The woman was in labor for eleven hours. I need more sleep," she said, then stirred her tea. "Dad will be home soon. How was your night with Mr. Blondie?" she asked, then wiggled her brows. My eyes widened as Mom stared at me, grinning.

"What?"

"You're both heavy sleepers, Lana," she said, then sipped her tea.

"Mom, please...don't tell Dad," I begged as I clasped my hands together.

"I won't. Why was he here, though?" She raised a brow.

"We were...busy with a project and lost track of time, so I said he should stay over."

"And he couldn't stay in the guest room?"

"I thought we were getting it ready for the Radcliffs?"

"Oh, Lana...did anything happen?"

"No, Mom, no! Carter's a friend," I said as I got up. She mumbled something, but I ignored it as I walked to the door. I heard voices outside as I opened the door.

"Lana!"

"Lana, come on, we're gonna be late!"

"Willson, hop on!"

"Lana, don't go with him!"

My eyes widened as I saw Carter's truck in my driveway, Ethan's car in the street, Aidan's car opposite him, and Blake's motorcycle on my lawn. It was ridiculous.

"What the hell is going on?" I asked as I looked at them.

"I was here first!" Carter yelled.

"Shut up, Halls." Blake rolled his eyes, and I noticed his swollen eye.

"Come on, Lana…who's it gonna be?" Aidan asked from his car. I looked at all of them as they stared at me. I rolled my eyes and crossed my arms. They got out of their vehicles and stood in front of me while they glared at each other.

"What happened to you guys? Are you serious? Last week, you were all walking down the hall, best friend shit…now you're fighting for who gets the girl?" I asked, then bit my lip to prevent a sudden laugh. "That's just sad."

"Well, of course, we would consider what happened last night with you and—"

"Nothing happened. Yeah, he stayed over, but nothing happened. He's just idiotic." I cut Blake off as I glared at Carter.

"Oh…" Blake, Aidan, and Ethan said in unison.

"So, are we cool now? I don't want things to be awkward while I'm hanging out with you guys," I said, then bit the inside of my cheek. They nodded simultaneously, yet a car honk behind them disturbed us.

"What the hell is this?" a familiar voice asked. I

looked up to the person I did not want to see. The guys turned around and stiffened as Dad got out of his car, slamming the door.

"Morning, Daddy, how was work?" I asked as I stepped forward. I heard the guys snicker behind me, and I knew they'd tease me afterward, but I didn't care. I was frustrated.

"Was all right. Why are they here? And whose cars and—" He cut himself off when he looked at the motorcycle. "And what the hell is it doing on my lawn?"

"Sorry, Sheriff. There was nowhere else to park it," Blake said as he shrugged his shoulders. Well, it was true since the rest of the guys took up the rest of the space with their vehicles.

"I'll ask Lana again. What are they doing here?" Dad asked, then rubbed his temples. I glanced over my shoulder to see their awkward stares.

"Err…they wanted to give me a ride to school," I mumbled and watched as my dad turned to the motorcycle.

"Well, you're no way in hell getting on that thing," he said. I tried so hard not to laugh as I looked at Blake, who glared at my father. "Why are you all here? I thought Ethan took my daughter to school."

I looked at Ethan, who smirked; I rolled my eyes as I glanced back at Dad. Of course he'd choose Ethan; he got discounts on all his sportswear, and Ethan's family was well known in Illinois.

"Well, Dad, I've been on each and every one of these vehicles, and I can assure you, they are lovely drivers and keep me safe."

"Well, go ahead…and have a nice day." Dad sighed, then ran a hand through his hair. My smile grew as I looked at the boys; they were like dogs, waiting for me to throw the stick—in this case, to tell them who I'd go with.

"I'll see you guys in school," I said, then walked past the motorcycle, around the truck, and through Aidan's and Ethan's cars. I stepped on the side of the road and turned around to see their stares. Dad, on the other hand, had a satisfied look as he walked into the house. They stared at each other, then raced to their vehicles. My eyes widened, as I knew what they'd do. I ran when I heard their vehicles, reason being that I didn't choose any of them because I didn't want any favoritism. They'd fight, and it would make things awkward. I ran with all my might as to not to get them to pull up next to me. I looked back and saw Blake on his motorcycle. I ran faster as I heard a car's motor idle. I looked back once more to see Ethan's car right next to Blake, and it's as if Blake's motorcycle came to life at the sound it made. I panted as I ran to the next road; I couldn't hear their vehicles as I took the corner, but something did stop me: Aidan's Subaru right in front of me as he blocked the way.

"Come on, Lana, we're gonna be late!"

I turned around, but a big truck stopped in front of me. I looked to my left and saw Ethan's car. A step closer and I'd be on top of the vehicle. I looked to the right and saw Blake's motorcycle; his back faced me as he scooted to the front and made space for me to sit. I glanced over Carter's truck and saw the way out. Their vehicles cornered me, and in that time, I hatched up a plan. I jumped on Blake's motorcycle with my right foot and pushed my left foot onto Carter's bonnet. I stood on his truck as I heard Aidan's honk. I smiled at Carter, then winked at him as I climbed on the roof of his vehicle then jumped in the back. I quickly jumped off before he drove off and made my way to school.

***

"How's life?" Miranda asked as she leaned on the locker next to me.

"Like every day…shit."

"So far, you're doing pretty good, Willson. Isn't it weird that you rock up to class with the guys and every time you have an excellent excuse?" She tilted her head.

"Nah…just another week, then I will be Benny Nielson free." I smiled as I thought of their protection when I win, yet I'd have to stand up for myself sooner or later.

"What if you lose?"

"Oh, hush, Miranda. That's a big if." I waved her off. If I did lose, I'm supposed to be their little puppet for the rest of the school year. Not how I wanted to spend the rest of my senior year.

"Have you heard the latest gossip?" She changed the subject. I raised an eyebrow at her and shook my head. "Rumor has it that Them roughed up half of the team yesterday," she whispered. I narrowed my eyes as to why Blake, Ethan, Aidan, and Carter would beat up half of the team. Then it hit me.

"W-Why?" I let out a shaky voice. She shrugged

as we walked down the hall. Ethan's lip, Aidan's bruises on his arms, Carter's jaw, and Blake's eye…they beat up those guys from yesterday. For me.

"Lana? Hello?" Miranda snapped me out of my gaze. I glanced up to see a muscular guy who smiled at me.

"Hmm?" I asked as I took in his messy brown hair and sweet smile.

"This is Marcus, the guy I was talking about the other day."

"Hi."

"Hey, Lana. I know we haven't talked much, but since I'll be seeing you a lot, why not start, right?" He chuckled. I laughed too, but my focus was on something else. They beat up Benny Nielson for me. I didn't know how to feel about it. Well, once I saw Benny, then I'd understand. I walked into Physics, and I could've sworn I didn't recognize Liam, Nick, and Benny as they sat right in the front. Their faces weren't pleasant. Benny looked the worst with his blue eye and vivid bruises all over his face. He glared at me as I walked past him, then suddenly, I was on the floor.

"Ouch!" I yelled, as I'd seen him trip me. He muttered something under his breath, but I blocked it out as I pushed myself up. The teacher entered the class, and I quickly walked to the back of the room. Benny looked over his shoulder with a blank look, to which I scowled. He didn't know what would come to him.

***

"Is your revenge on Nielson still in place, ma'am?" Aidan asked as we walked down the hall.

"Of course. Little son of a bitch should get what he deserves!" I said as we walked to the gym. It was lunch, and the football team practiced for tonight. Like always, Coach Harris pushed them for yet another big game. Revenge on Nielson was in place. Everyone knew what they had to do, and nothing should get in our way. The team was out on the field as we walked past the gym and into the boys' locker rooms. The smell of cologne mixed with sweat hit me as we entered. I scrunched my nose as we walked to Benny's locker. With Aidan's lockpicking skills, we quickly got it open and grabbed his clothes, then replaced them with a similar shirt that Benny wore. Aidan walked into the shower rooms and did what he had to do while I kept guard. We heard footsteps from the field and hid in Coach Harris's office as the team came in. Ethan took off his shirt, which revealed his toned abs, and of course the rest of the team did the same. We saw Benny open his locker, and I tensed if he'd notice. I sighed in relief as he opened it to dump his sweaty tank top; he closed it and strolled to the showers. Ethan was already by the showers; it was only him and Benny in there. After five minutes, Ethan came out with a towel around his waist and Benny's gym shorts. Which meant Benny showered and Ethan did his part, which was distract Benny as he took his clothes. Ethan dumped the shorts in the trash, then walked to Benny's locker. The lock was open, so Ethan took out the shirt and threw that in the garbage too. Five minutes later, Benny came out with a towel around his waist as he dried his hair with another. Laughter erupted around the room as he took the towel off his head. Aidan and I chuckled behind Coach's desk as we looked at Benny.

"What?" he asked as they pointed and laughed at him. He opened his locker and looked in the mirror. I swear his face was as red as his hair. When Aidan went into the showers, he put red hair dye in Benny's conditioner and a little bit of bleach in his shampoo. Benny's dark hair was replaced with a red blob. I laughed as Aidan and I walked out of the office and stood in front of Benny. The rest of the team's eyes widened, as some of them were half naked, and covered their crotches. I rolled my eyes and looked at Benny again. I glanced over at the rest of the six-pack beauties in the room and noticed they took out their phones to take pictures of Benny's hair.

"Where the hell are my clothes?" Benny yelled as he turned to Aidan and me.

"Looking for this?" Aidan asked as he raised his clothes. Benny reached forward, but we ran out of the room. I was in front of Aidan as we moved, and I looked back and saw Benny right behind us while he held up his towel.

"Lana!" Aidan yelled as he threw the clothes. I caught them with ease and ran down the hall. Out of the corner of my eye, I saw Aidan attempt to pull Benny's towel off as he ran after me, but Benny pushed him, then fixed his attention on me.

"You're going to be screwed, Willson!" he yelled. I ran faster this time. As I ran, I saw people's eyes widen as we ran past them. I looked up and saw the place where I needed to go and opened the doors, which caught everyone's attention. I stood in the middle of the cafeteria as Benny ran in. I searched the room for natural blond locks and saw him in the corner with a projector. Carter sat with Miranda and Marcus; he gave me a nod, then looked at the wall. The cafeteria went silent as everyone looked at me. Benny walked closer but stopped when everyone laughed, yet some gasped. He looked at the wall and saw the picture of him from fourth grade in Batman pajamas, hanging from a flagpole with a red face. I looked at him as he glared at me. "Lana…give me my clothes, then I'll decide whether I'll kill you now or later."

"You want it? Come and get it!" I said as I ran to the doors on the opposite side of the room, which led to the parking lot. Thank goodness Blake opened it; I didn't know how he opened it since it had been chained up for years, but he had his ways. I heard Benny behind me as I ran out the door into the chilly weather. I saw him, Blake Gunner, on his motorcycle as he smoked a cigarette. His eyes met mine, and he dropped the cigarette, then started the engine. I ran up to him, hopped on, and drove off. We drove in small circles around the parking lot as Benny neared. I threw his clothes up in the air as Blake and I laughed. His clothes landed in a small puddle as Blake stopped the motorcycle. We saw Benny with a murderous look on his face; he grabbed his clothes and walked back to the building. We sat on the motorcycle for a while in silence. I looked down and noticed my arms were wrapped around Blake's waist. I was about to lean my head on his shoulder when I heard a teacher yell out our names.

***

I let out a groan as I opened the doors to the empty room. It was Friday afternoon, and nobody managed to get detention but me and, of course, Blake. It turned out Blake didn't see the teacher when he drove, so Mrs. Singleton caught us immediately. She's strict. She's in her mid-forties and always wore a tight bun. Mr. George was quietly seated at the teacher's desk. He looked at me with a cold stare, yet he had no choice since he signed up for the week's detention. It was my second and hopefully last detention.

"Afternoon, sir," I said as I walked past him. He gave a slow nod as I sat in the middle of the classroom. I looked around at the empty desks. The door flew open, which startled Mr. George and me, and Blake walked in with a straight face.

"Mr. Gunner, you are—"

"Does it look like I care? At least I'm here," Blake snapped. Mr. George didn't want to argue, so he read his newspaper. I prayed as I heard the chair next to me screech across the floor. I opened one eye to see Blake right next to me. I looked around at the empty seats, then back at him. Of all places, he chose the seat next to me.

"What crawled up your ass and died?" I asked as he stared out the window. He propped his legs up on the table and glanced at me.

"I was late because Mr. Basil was talking about

my grades." He huffed as he crossed his arms over his chest. Mr. Basil taught Biology.

"What's wrong with your grades?" I didn't want to ask because Blake was only in my Photography class, which he ditched, and Phys Ed, so I couldn't really tell what kind of grades he had.

"My grades are fine. I just have to explain shit more and use scientific terms."

"What kind of grades do you get?"

"Not straight As like you, nerd."

"Come on…maybe I can help?"

"I get the average…Cs and Bs. It's okay. Don't worry, I'll make it." I slowly nodded, then looked at Mr. George, who was about to fall asleep. "You going to the game tonight?" Blake asked after a while. My eyes widened as he asked me that question. I slowly looked at him and nodded. He raised a brow.

"Yeah, I, err…Ethan asked me to come," I said, then avoided eye contact.

"Why?" Blake demanded. Out of the corner of my eye, I saw his stare.

"To…support him and wear his jacket," I said. A small smile appeared on my lips as I said those words, but I immediately frowned as the thought of yesterday popped into my head. I heard something snap, and again out of the corner of my eye, I saw Blake. I glanced down at his hands as he clenched his fist, but his knuckles looked red and bruised. "Thank you," I mumbled as I looked at his swollen knuckles. I glanced up, and our eyes met; his eyes were a dark shade of brown. I saw the bruise around his eye, faded but still visible. The memories of yesterday ran through my head as I heard the frantic calls of my name. All I knew was Ethan took me home, and the guys beat up Benny.

"No problem, Willson. I don't ever want to see you like that again," he said. I bit the inside of my cheek and nodded at the thought of Benny and Blake in a fight. My thoughts were interrupted when the door opened once again; I glanced at Mr. George, who was asleep. Aidan and Carter strolled in. I narrowed my eyes. Both sat down in front of Blake and spoke.

"Where's Ethan?" I asked.

"He's getting ready for the game tonight," Aidan said as he took out his phone. I noticed Blake's jaw clench as I nodded. I took out my phone and earphones; I plugged it into my phone with the earphones into my ears. I felt the guys' eyes on me, every move I made. It's as if they waited for something. My head bobbed at the song I thought of as I scrolled through my songs to look for it.

"Do you think she can hear us?" Carter whispered. I kept my gaze fixed on my phone as I eavesdropped.

"Don't think so. Let me try," Aidan said then looked at me. "Lana!" I smiled at him as I bobbed my head to absolutely nothing. Aidan looked at Blake and Carter as he nodded. I glanced back to my phone and pretended to keep myself busy as they spoke. "The guy said Tuesday is the day. He's sending a few guys to collect the stuff, and then they'll give us the cash," Aidan said. I inched near them; I put my head on the desk to make it look like I'd dozed off. As I closed my eyes, I tried my best to hear their hushed voices.

"Does Ethan know?" Blake asked.

"Of course. It's his cottage," Carter said.

"Do they want all of it?" Blake asked.

"Yep, all by Tuesday four p.m. sharp. They'll collect everything," Aidan mumbled. It tempted me to ask as the guys spoke more about it. I took one earphone out, and they immediately stopped. They looked at me with nervous yet cautious looks.

"What?" I asked. All three shook their heads as they forced a smile. They stared at me, waiting for me to either put the earphone back in or ask them another question, which I gladly did. "Any of you got a cigarette? I've been craving one since lunch," I moaned as I looked at them. They hesitated at first, then at once, they searched their pockets. Aidan was the first to hand me one; he looked at the teacher as he handed it to me. Then he looked at me like I'd grown a second head. Probably thought I'd get caught, but I didn't care; I craved one. They watched me as I twirled it between my fingers. I tilted my head and smiled. "Well? This cigarette isn't going to light itself."

Carter quickly jumped up and lit it for me. I thanked him as I inhaled the thing between my lips. Out of the corner of my eye, I saw their stares. I blew out, a feeling of satisfaction whirling inside of me as I stared at Mr. George.

"Do you think Mr. George is a heavy sleeper?" I asked as the teacher drooled on the newspaper.

"I don't know. Why?" Carter asked.

"Well, let's find out," I said with a grin. I inhaled the cigarette once again then handed it to Blake, who took it with surprise but put it between his lips. I walked to the front of the classroom where Mr. George was asleep. I grabbed a marker from the whiteboard behind him and looked at the boys. Aidan smirked at me as he caught on to what I was going to do. Carter stared in shock but eventually took out his phone, and Blake came to the front of the classroom as he sat on the teacher's desk. "Detention is now in session," I dramatically said, then took a bow. "First off, never ever leave markers loose when a bunch of disruptive teenagers are around, otherwise…" I trailed off, then did the one thing I'd never thought I'd do. I walked up to Mr. George, bent down, then drew on his face. Once I was done and satisfied with the work, I put the marker back. Snickers came from Carter and Aidan, who took selfies with Mr. George.

"Wait! Before you wake the old man up, let's take a picture…for memories!" Aidan said, then gestured for Blake to join us. We stood together and pulled weird faces with Mr. George, who was still asleep, then laughed at the photo. I walked back to stand behind Mr. George.

"Secondly, never fall asleep as a teacher because…" I continued, then grabbed the cigarette from Blake. Before he protested, I walked up to the sleeping man again and quickly swiped the cigarette across his nose. The guys looked at me with murderous looks. Mr. George immediately sat up as he awkwardly coughed. I promptly hid the cigarette behind me and crushed it, which burned my hand.

"Ms. Willson…what are you doing here? And what is that awful smell?" he asked, then sniffed the air. I glanced at the boys to see Carter and Aidan duck behind the desks while Blake stood stiff as he glared at me.

"I was just cleaning the board, sir. Don't want to leave ugly marks now, do we?" I nervously laughed.

"I suppose…I'm terribly tired, and since it's Friday and there's a game on tonight, I'll let you two leave early," he said as he stood up.

"Thank you, Mr. George. Enjoy your weekend," I said as he walked out the door. Aidan and Carter came out from under the desks, then clapped their hands. I dusted the ash from my hands and threw the cigarette in the trashcan.

"I've taught you well, young one," Aidan said as he wiped a fake tear.

"That was incredible, Lana. Not only did Mr. George let you two go early, but he also walked out with a penis on his face!" Carter laughed as he took out his phone. He showed me, and I smiled as I saw Aidan doing a duck face next to Mr. George, who had marks on his face.

"Now we have plenty of time before the game," Aidan said as he walked out of the room. Carter and I followed, but someone stopped me. I looked down and saw Blake's hand on my arm. I glanced up and noticed his awe-struck look.

"Gotta hand it to you, Willson…not bad." His lips twitched up into a smile. I smiled back at him as he stepped forward. I stood still as he approached me, only then realizing how tall he was. I looked up into his dull brown eyes and ignored the red mark around them; his eyes screamed for me to come closer. We were so close that I felt his breath on my forehead, but it was soon replaced when he pressed his forehead against mine. He bit his lip again, slowly and seductively. I couldn't help it; I slowly licked my lips too. He looked at my mouth; I sensed his impatience as we stood there. We inched closer, yet he had a look of hunger on his face as I had a look of need.

"Come on, you two!" Aidan yelled from outside the room. We stepped back, and I looked down in embarrassment, then walked out. I asked Aidan to take me home, and he gladly said he'd pick me up again for the game. The whole ride home, I thought of what had occurred in the past two days. Ethan almost kissed me, Carter slept over, and Blake almost kissed me. I glanced at Aidan, who somehow interrupted both situations.

"Thank you," I mumbled. Aidan looked at me from the corner of his eye as he raised a brow.

"I don't know." I nervously laughed, then looked down. "Forget about it."

"I should be thanking you, Lana. I know I've pulled a few pranks on you and embarrassed you through the years, and yet you still gave m—us a chance." He licked his lips. "I know this is coming out of the blue, but you guys are my friends now. Parker Collins was the worst person I could've asked to be friends with."

I didn't know what to say. Parker was one of Aidan's friends who also pulled pranks on me, along with Austin. Parker was meaner, though, and he had a bad reputation at Jefferson High. I did not want to get on his bad side again.

"I promise, I won't let anything happen to you, Lana," Aidan said as he gave me a warm smile. "Neither Parker nor Benny will hurt you ever again."

***

"Enjoy the football game, honey!" Mom said as I walked out of the house. Mom and Dad were glad I finally went to support my school's football team. No way I told them that Ethan wanted me to wear his jacket. They'd freak and said I finally found the right guy, which was untrue. I mostly saw Ethan as a big, supportive brother than a boyfriend.

"Go, Jefferson!" Aidan yelled as I got into the car. I squinted my eyes at him and noticed that he wore the school's colors: blue and black. At least I wore black; the weather became cold and windy, so I decided on a gray sweater, jeans, and Converse. The rest of the drive consisted of a sing along to music. I realized Aidan would always be there to put a smile on my face and take my mind off things. I wasn't close to him or any of the guys now, but I knew that I'd come to him when I felt down. Also, the topic of Parker Collins always lingered in my mind as to what Aidan Rowley knew.

"There you guys are!" Carter exclaimed as he raised his arms. "The game is about to start!"

As we walked, I noticed Blake was nowhere to be found, which worried me. I shook the thought away and looked around the open field. I saw Ethan; he wore his football uniform as he glared at his teammates, Liam and Nick. Benny showed up, and everyone laughed at his red hair and shoved their phones in his face. Ethan and Benny glared at each other but soon shook hands. Maybe they didn't want to have tension through the whole game. Ethan's eyes met mine as he walked toward us. "You made it."

"Wouldn't miss it for the world." I smiled. He took off his varsity jacket and put it around my shoulders. I felt the stares of people as Ethan looked at me.

"Thanks," I mumbled as my cheeks warmed up.

"No, thank you," he said, then ruffled my hair.

"Good luck," I said as he walked off. He looked at me once more, then jogged off to meet with his team. I bit the inside of my cheek, then turned to the grinning boys who sat next to me. "What?" I hissed. Carter shook his head as he put his arm around my shoulder.

"People just have to remember that you're my date to Homecoming," he said with much confidence. I playfully rolled my eyes as I scanned the gym.

"Where's Blake?" I asked after a while.

"He said he'll be a bit late. I'm gonna get some snacks. I'll be right back," Aidan said as he got up. I watched him as he met up with some guys, and they did a bro hug. He pointed to me as the guys looked. I tensed up a bit, but he looked away. Austin said something that made Aidan laugh as he punched him. Parker looked up as his eyes met mine. I sheepishly turned away because I hated him.

"The game is starting," Carter announced as he kept his gaze on our school team. I glanced at the other school, which was Northwood High, and they were equally as tall and muscular as Ethan, Benny, Nick, and Liam.

Chapter Eight

Lana

As always, Jefferson faced another excellent win. Ethan was good, the way he scored and played fairly with his teammates even though they became enemies. When they won, I ran up to Ethan, and he engulfed me in his arms as people congratulated him. Blake didn't show up, which was no surprise, because Carter told me he wasn't into school sports…yet I thought about our almost kiss. It was on my mind all night when we went out for pizza to celebrate. I was glad we didn't kiss, because then I wouldn't have to face the feeling of rejection when he pulled away.

"Lana!" Miranda snapped her fingers in front of my face.

"Hmm?" I turned to her.

"We're here." She gestured to the shopping center in front of us.

"Oh yeah," I said, then got out of the car. Yesterday's events disappeared from my mind as we walked into the big mall. It was Saturday, and I spent it with my best friend as we searched for Homecoming outfits. We'd walked into three stores already and found nothing. Miranda decided we should go for lunch. We ate in silence as I stared at my drink—it was a can of soda—but my mind was elsewhere. I heard Miranda slam her can down on the table, and I glanced up.

"Okay…what's up? You've been spacing out all day," she stated as her eyebrows rose.

"Ethan tried to kiss me," I muttered as I chewed my food. "Then Blake."

"At the same time?" she asked as her eyes widened.

"No!" I exclaimed, and we laughed.

"So, at different times?" Miranda asked. I nodded, then returned to my food. "That's amazing, Lana!" she exclaimed as I gaped at her. Miranda's mouth pulled up into a smirk as her eyebrows wiggled. "You've got them wrapped around your little finger, Lana Willson. I mean your date to Homecoming is Carter hot ass Halls, and Ethan looks like he's falling for you, and now Blake!"

"Ugh, please, I bet it's just because I look like this…" I gestured to the clothing I wore today, which was a black leather jacket, ripped jeans, and ankle boots. It had become my regular attire.

"Yeah, but you're killing the look."

"What can I say?" The corner of my mouth rose as Keene and Levi appeared in my mind. "Keene Stoner and Levi Radcliff taught me the basics."

Miranda's jaw tightened as she looked down to her soda. I let out a sigh as I remembered that she wasn't a big fan of them, especially Levi. Keene was at least older than all of us, so he was responsible.

"And what about you, Ms. Stevens?" I tilted my head. "What's going on in your love life?"

"Marcus took me out on a date last night."

"And you didn't tell me!"

"It was short notice."

"So that's why you weren't at the game," I said, then wiggled my brows. Miranda playfully punched my shoulder, and we went back and forth as we talked about the recent events.

***

"Come on, get ready," Miranda said, then tossed clothing toward me. We were at her house, and I slept over since we'd come home late from shopping, but thankfully I got a beautiful dress.

"Why?" I raised a brow as I removed the clothes from my face. I looked at the mini skirt, black crop top, and a sleeveless denim jacket.

"We are going to a party, my lovely friend," Miranda said as she walked out of the bathroom with a robe on.

"Whose party?"

"Ethan's party, of course! Since Jefferson won last night, we must celebrate, young one," she said, then poked my nose. I glanced at the clothes again and realized that it wasn't such a bad outfit. Naturally, I'd find Blake and Carter at the party because it was at Ethan's house, so it'd increase my chance to win the bet. I put on the clothes, and to be honest, they fit me perfectly. I had second thoughts when I put on the crop top, but when I put on the jacket, it looked cute. I walked out of the bathroom and saw Miranda in a long sleeve pink Bodycon dress. She looked amazing; the dress fit her so well and showed off her long legs. She straightened her hair as she sat down in front of the mirror. I stood awkwardly in the back as I watched her long blonde hair fall to her hips.

"There you are!" Miranda said as she looked at me from the mirror. She put the hair straightener down and spun around. She eyed me up and down, and I couldn't help but curl my toes up in a shy way. "You look amazing, Lana."

"You look hot," I said as her cheeks reddened. "Marcus better watch out tonight."

"Oh, your shoes! I have the perfect heels to complete the outfit," she said as she ran to her closet.

"Do I have to wear heels?" I groaned as she pulled out a pair of black platform heels. "Do you expect me to walk in that?"

"Lana, you will look amazing…plus, it's practice for when you wear your heels for Homecoming." Miranda winked. She walked back to her mirror, then did her makeup. I looked at the black heels in my hands, then set them down. I slipped my feet in cautiously and stood up.

"I feel like a freaking giant."

"But you look like a European supermodel," Miranda pointed out. I rolled my eyes as I turned around and walked into her room.

"No…I'm wearing Converse. You got me into a

106

skirt, Stevens, so at least let me wear some comfortable shoes." I huffed as I took a pair of black high-top Converse from my bag. I stayed over, so I packed an overnight bag with all my things.

"Fine! Now, come on, let me do your hair and makeup!" she said as she got up from her seat and gestured me to sit down.

Marcus came fifteen minutes later and complimented both of us on our outfits. He was quite the looker and recently joined the school's soccer team. It was a good decision, though, because he had a big build.

Ten minutes later, we arrived. Music blared from the house. I got out, and my jaw dropped at the mansion. Two floors and it was packed with drunken teenagers. We walked up the stairs, past the two mini fountains on either side of the door. A bouncer stood at the door with his lips drawn into a straight line.

"Name?" he asked, then looked at the clipboard in his hands.

"Marcus Sanders."

"No Sanders here."

I turned to Marcus, whose jaw clenched. He cleared his throat, which caused the bouncer to look at him. Marcus was shorter than the bouncer, but he was muscular.

"My name is Marcus Sanders, and I am on that list," Marcus stated in a neutral tone as he stared at the man. The bouncer's eyes widened as he eyed Marcus up and down, then looked at the clipboard again.

"Oh sorry. Yes, sir, my mistake. You can go in, and it says plus one," the bouncer said as he turned to Miranda and me.

"It's okay. You guys go in," I said.

"You sure?" Miranda asked. I nodded with a sad smile as they walked in. My smile vanished as I glared at the guy.

"Do you know who I am?" I dramatically asked as I put my hand to my chest.

"Am I supposed to?"

"I'm Lana Willson."

"Oh, I'm sorry, Ms. Willson. You're the first person on the list! Very sorry!" he said as he stepped aside to let me in. The corner of my mouth rose as I walked into the house, the smell of alcohol hitting me instantly. Drunken teenagers filled the room, the lights were dim, and people drank, made out, and smoked.

"There you are!" Miranda exclaimed. "What did you do?"

"I was first on the list."

"*Oh*...wonder why," she said with a grin.

"Lana!" a familiar voice yelled. I squinted my eyes as a tall figure approached us.

"Hey, Ethan," I said, then hugged him.

"Hi, glad you could make it. You look beautiful, by the way," he said, then eyed me up and down.

"Hey, Ethan," Miranda said as she awkwardly waved. Ethan greeted Miranda and Marcus, then turned to me. "We'll leave you two alone," Miranda whispered, then grabbed Marcus's hand. I watched them walk into the crowd, then looked at Ethan, who wore a white tee, black jeans, and black Vans.

"What's with the bouncer?"

"These parties can get a little crazy, so just keeping the unwanted ones away."

"So do you always hold the parties?"

"Sometimes Benny and Liam, but I heard Liam might be moving to the city."

"Are they here?"

"Yeah, they're somewhere around here."

"Look, Ethan, I don't want any tension happening between you guys because you guys are teammates and you see them every day."

"It's okay, Lana—"

"Let go of me, man!" a deep voice interrupted. Ethan and I turned to the noise to see two guys fighting.

"I'm sorry, Lana. I have to take care of this, but I'll see you later, though, right?"

"It's okay, I'll go look for the other guys," I said. Ethan sent me another apologetic smile then walked toward the fight. The bouncer came, and he and Ethan took the two guys and threw them out as people cheered. I felt thirsty as I strolled around the house. Somehow, I ended up outside as I looked around for a drink. I saw a table close by and walked toward it. It held all the different types of liquids. My eyes stopped at a familiar bottle that read Apple Juice. I smiled as I took the bottle and a Solo cup. I drank the liquid anxiously. It tasted good, yet strong. I poured another cup, then walked on as I tried to spot familiar faces.

"Boom!" someone yelled. I turned in the direction of the voice and saw a familiar blond playing beer pong with a few other people.

"Hey, Carter," I said as I tapped his shoulder. He looked over his shoulder, then down at me as his eyes widened.

"Lana!" he exclaimed, and I looked over his shoulder to see the other guys' stares. "You look a—"

"Sexy," the guy I didn't know said as he winked at me. I rolled my eyes as I looked at Carter.

"Close your mouth. A fly might go in."

"You look hot."

"Whatever," I said. I knew it was rude, but I've gotten upset lately that the guys only said that kind of stuff because I dressed up. It made me think back to when Levi didn't care what I wore. He wanted to show people what a nerd could do, but to be at a party dressed in attire that I'd felt uncomfortable in made me miss him.

"My name is Quinton, by the way."

"Lana. Happy to meet you."

"Wanna play, Lana?" Quinton asked as he bit his lip. I looked at Carter, who had his jaw clenched.

"Sure," I said, then turned back to Quinton as I took a sip of my drink.

"What is that?" Carter asked as he furrowed his brows at my cup.

"Just some juice," I said with a wink. Carter laughed as he set up cups with the guy from school, whose name happened to be Tyler. He was also on the team and was liked by many.

"You can be on my team," Quinton said as he wrapped his arm around my shoulder. The smell of alcohol fell from his mouth as he spoke. I nodded as I looked across the table to see Tyler's smirk as well as Carter's glare.

Eight cups of beer and three games later, I thought I stood, or leaned on the table, as Quinton threw the ball across the table and into the cup. Tyler groaned as he took the cup and downed the liquid. Carter threw, and it landed in our last cup. I looked at Quinton, who laughed.

"Go for it, babe," he said. Even though we lost, I still felt like a winner because I got free beer. I clenched the cup in my hand and let the beer run down my throat. I slammed the cup down and threw my hands up in defeat.

"Well, I'm done," I said as I attempted to walk but fell into Quinton's arms. "Oh no!" I exclaimed, and we laughed as he held me.

"You're drunk," he said after we cooled down. I raised my brow at him and scoffed.

"No way!" I gasped. "How'd you know?"

"Okay, seems like you had a lot of fun," Carter said as he took me away from Quinton.

"Hey! No fair…he was cute." I pointed at Quinton, who had a pout on his face. Quinton had beautiful sleek brown hair, he was tall and buff in his plain black shirt, yet I noticed his abs through his shirt.

"Lana, you're drunk. I'm taking you home," Carter said as he looked at me. I stared at him, then shook my head.

"Mommy told me never to go in a car with a stranger."

"Lana, it's me, Carter Halls? Sex God? Hot blond dude? Also known as your date to Homecoming?"

"Oh yeah!" I jumped into his arms then stroked his hair. "I love your hair."

"Lana, stay here. I'm gonna get my keys, then I'm taking you home, okay?" he asked. I quickly nodded as he put me on a sofa, then walked into the crowd.

After a minute of Carter being gone, I stood up because I got thirsty. A guy approached me and slapped my ass; I turned around and glared at him.

"What are you gonna do about it, babe?" he asked with a smirk on his face. I stared at the guy and pulled my tongue at him, and he laughed. I immediately walked off with my arms crossed. I passed a table and straightway stopped when I saw bottles. I scanned the bottles as I searched for the right one, Apple Juice. I took the bottle, opened it up, and drank from it. Nobody would drink juice at a party when there's alcohol.

"Lana! Whoa, slow down!" a familiar voice yelled. A hand wrapped around the bottle and pulled it away from my lips. My eyes narrowed at the person for rudely disrupting my beverage.

"Aidan!" I cheered, then wrapped my arms around his neck.

"You've been drinking," he said as he sniffed me.

"No!" I said and grabbed the bottle. "I've been drinking juice, like a good girl."

"No, Lana, someone just wrote Apple Juice on here. It doesn't mean it's actually apple juice!" Aidan scolded. He pointed at the bottle, then peeled off the label, which revealed the big word *whiskey*. I frowned and shook my head.

"I'm not drunk."

"Yes, you are! How many fingers do I have?" he said, then held up his fingers. I looked at them and said, "Five."

"No! I have three!" he said, then showed three fingers.

"No! You asked how many fingers you have. You have five fingers!" I looked at his hand that still held up three. He had a look of confusion, but it immediately changed as he laughed. "But the two are gone now...oh no! Aidan, what happened to your other two fingers?" I exclaimed as my bottom lip curled up. He laughed, and out came two other fingers. "Whoa! How did you do that?" I asked as I played with my fingers.

"Never mind that. The fact is you're drunk, and you need to get home," he said, then grabbed my hand.

"No," I whined.

"Why?" He gaped at me.

"Let's dance!" I said as I grabbed his arm and took him to the dance floor. "One Dance" by *Drake* played, and it seemed all the couples got on the dance floor. I grinned at Aidan, who hesitated at first, but when I danced, he quickly changed his expression into a smirk. I held his hands as I swayed my hips; I turned around and leaned on him as his hand went to my waist. Wizkid's part came on, and I continued to swing my hips against him. It was my favorite part of the song, so I almost forgot he was there. The song ended, and I bit the inside of my cheek as I skipped off the dance floor with Aidan behind.

"Okay, you're clearly drunk."

"What do you mean?"

"You wouldn't dance like that if you were sober. Damn, you would slap me," he said, then awkwardly rubbed the back of his neck. "Especially since I was friends with Parker."

"You're so funny, Aidan." I ignored the last part about Parker as I walked off. "I need more juice," I said as I grabbed the bottle. Aidan quickly snatched it before I could, and he shook his head.

"No more for you." I groaned. As I walked off, I heard him yell my name, but I continued to walk. I strolled around until I found the kitchen. It was huge, people made out on the island, and someone even did a body shot! I squinted my eyes to see who did a body shot, and my eyes widened when I saw Jennifer Brighton on the counter, and licking the salt from her stomach was Nick Byrne. I watched as people around them cheered as he took the lime from her mouth. He hopped off the counter, and they got back in a circle.

"Dude, that was epic!" Liam grinned as he high-fived Nick.

"Okay, okay, now, Benny, your turn. Truth or dare?" Kelly asked as she flicked her hair off her shoulder.

"Dare." He grinned. I walked to the drinks and took another sip of the Apple Juice. I didn't really care. I was already drunk, so what difference would it make?

"I dare you..." She trailed off as her eyes scanned the room. Kelly's eyes landed on me as the corner of her mouth turned up. "I dare you to do a

114

body shot with Lana."

Everyone in the circle froze as they looked at me. I drank the liquid as I tried to mind my own business, yet inside I was nervous.

"Hey, guys!"

"Willson, is that you?" Nick asked as he eyed me. I looked at Benny, who gaped at me.

"The one and only," I said as I walked to their small circle. Melissa, Kelly, Jennifer, Liam, Nick, Benny, and a few people I didn't know stood and watched me.

"You look—"

"Ouch!" Nick mumbled as Melissa stepped on his foot.

"Hot," Benny finished Nick's sentence.

"Err, thanks, I guess." I laughed as I struck a pose. Liam laughed beside me while Benny's mouth couldn't close. He approached me with his jaw tightened, then placed his hands on my hips. "That tickles, Benny!" I laughed as he lifted me up and put me on the counter.

"You're drunk," he stated.

"Well, duh," I said, then flicked my hair. Benny Nielson laughed as he ran his hand through his red strands of hair. He got on top of me, and I heard Liam and Nick cheer him on. Benny hovered over me as he licked a small area of my stomach, then sprinkled the salt. All eyes were on us, and from the corner of my eye, I saw Kelly whip out her phone. The next thing Benny did, I didn't expect. He took the lime and held it between his lips as he slowly bent down. His face was mere inches away as we looked into each other's eyes. I noticed his face still swollen as he leaned forward, the lime brushed over my lips, and he looked down at my lips. I opened my mouth and took the lime in between my teeth. I watched Benny as he slowly traveled down to my open stomach. I didn't even realize he took off my jacket. He took the shot of tequila and slowly put the cup between my breasts. I stiffened as he smirked. I looked down at him as he looked up, and our eyes met once more as he left a peck on my stomach. I closed my eyes and tilted my head as I felt him lick the salt off. My eyes snapped open as he took the shot of tequila from my breasts. He slowly came back up and grabbed the lime from my mouth. Our lips touched, but he climbed off before I thought any further. He helped me off, and we awkwardly stood side by side.

"That was fun." I giggled as I took another cup from the island.

"Yeah, err...I think you're drinking too much," he said as he slowly took the cup away from me.

"What's this? Benny Nielson is concerned about me." I dramatically put my hand to my chest. We laughed but were interrupted when Liam walked over. He gave me my jacket as he smirked at me.

"You look amazing tonight, Lana," he slurred with a cup in his hand.

"Thanks, I guess. Well, I'll see you guys later," I said. Benny smiled while Liam saluted. As soon as my back faced them, I let out a deep breath. I couldn't believe that Benny Nielson and I did a body shot.

"No, Lana!" I yelled to myself as I walked to the backyard.

"Hey, baby," a familiar voice said behind me. I turned around and looked up at the tall figure. The lights weren't bright, so I couldn't see his face.

"Hello?"

"Really tired of beer pong." He groaned as he wrapped his arms around my waist.

"Quinton?"

"The one and only, babe."

"You clearly played too much beer pong." I laughed as I got a bit uncomfortable with where his hands went.

"Yeah, I miss my old partner," he mumbled in my ear. His left hand held my arm tight as his right hand squeezed my butt.

"You're hurting me, Quin—"

"Mm, let's go inside, baby," he moaned in my ear. I tried to push him off, but his grip tightened.

"Ouch, Quinton!" I yelled as I tried to shove him away from me.

"Come on," he growled as he grabbed my arm.

"No, you're hurting me," I said as I tried to let go. Quinton cupped my cheeks as he smashed his lips onto mine. The kiss wasn't sweet at all, no passion, just need and pain. I punched him, but he was too strong as he pulled me closer. I felt him being pulled off, my eyes shooting open as I saw Quinton being punched.

"You fucking dick! Fuck off!" someone yelled.

"Who the fuck are you?" Quinton shouted. People gathered around us. Some even took out their phones. How typical. Quinton punched the guy, and he immediately tackled Quinton to the ground. I stepped closer to see who it was, and my eyes widened as I watched Quinton get punched multiple times.

"Hey! Break it up, you two!" Ethan yelled as he came into the circle, followed by the bouncer. Ethan ran to the guy on the ground and pulled him off Quinton. The bouncer grabbed Quinton and held him up. Quinton's face looked bad as I saw blood from his nose. "What the hell, Blake?" Ethan yelled as he looked at him. Ethan's eyes then spotted me as his jaw clenched. "What the hell happened?"

"This guy wanted to sleep with Lana, and she obviously didn't want to, but he kept pulling her." Blake huffed as he glared at Quinton. I looked at Blake, who had bags under his eyes, and his hair was messed up. Ethan glared at Quinton, then let Blake go.

"Get the hell out of here, Quinton. I never want to see you here ever again! And if you touch her, I swear to God I'll hunt you down and beat you," Ethan said. The bouncer and everyone else returned to whatever they did, then shoved Quinton out. "Lana, are you okay?" Ethan asked as he held my hand. I nodded as we walked back into the house.

"I feel sleepy," I mumbled as I leaned into his chest.

"Lana, don't sleep! Not here..." He trailed off. My eyes got weaker as they closed.

Chapter Nine

Lana

I opened my eyes and realized I was being carried down a hall. It was quiet, too quiet. I glanced up and saw Blake. We entered another room, and his pace reduced.

"Blake," I mumbled as I looked up at him. He looked down with a smile on his face as he set me on a bed. "Thank you."

"No problem, princess," he said, then sat at the edge of the bed as he took off my shoes. I fake-smiled because I didn't like that he called me princess as he undid my laces. He looked up, and our eyes met. I stared because I felt calm, and all my worries slipped away.

"Where are we?" I asked as I looked around the room. It seemed dull, white walls covered in band posters, a shelf full of things. There was a desk with a computer and some knickknacks.

"My house."

"How did we get here?"

"Ethan and I were arguing whether you should stay at his place or I could take you home, but then another fight started, so I took you quickly while he went to go sort it out." He chuckled, then ran a hand through his hair. "I didn't want to return you home like this, so I thought to bring you here."

"Thank you," I said. "Plus, I'm supposed to be sleeping over at Miranda's, so it's cool."

"Cool, well, you should get some rest, and I'll see you in the morning," he said, then stood up.

"Wait." I raised my hand. He looked tall by the door, his hair went in all directions, and to be honest, he looked sick. "Are you okay?" I asked. The words seemed to fall out of my mouth. I was concerned.

"Yeah," he mumbled as he grabbed the doorknob.

"Wait!" I repeated. This time, he let out a sigh as he looked over his shoulder. "Can you stay? It's terribly quiet, and I'm not used to such quiet places."

It was true, because it sounded like we were the only ones in the house and he didn't turn on the lights. Blake walked to the edge of the bed and stared at me; I scooted over and smoothed the spot next to me. He took off his shoes, then crawled in next to me. He laid on the bed as he stared at the ceiling. I laid on my side as I took in his features. His jawline clenched as he stared at the ceiling; his nose was pointy and cute. He had a few freckles here and there, but other than that, he seemed perfect.

"It's not nice to stare."

"Sorry," I mumbled, then turned around so my back faced him. I heard movement behind me as I felt Blake's arm around my waist pull me closer. My eyes were open the whole time. I couldn't sleep as I felt his breath on my neck from his humming, but I wasn't tired.

"One more week," he mumbled after a while. It took me a while to figure out what he meant, but I immediately frowned at the thought.

"I actually like it, you know," I said as I cupped my hand over his. "Not the ditching and stuff, but the clothing and the feeling of not being picked on a lot."

"Why don't you stay like this? You don't have to ditch but…hang out with us and stop letting people trip over you," Blake mumbled. "You're more than the sheriff's daughter."

"I don't know. I've always been like this, so I haven't quite thought about it."

"Are you scared?"

"No, why do you keep asking me that?" I said, then turned to face him. Our faces were inches apart as he let go of me.

"You look like it. I understand because of your dad and all."

"I'm sorry," I mumbled, then looked down. It was surprisingly hot under all the layers, even though I had on a crop top and a skirt.

"No need to apologize. We're all scared of this world," he said as he wrapped an arm around me again and brought me closer to his chest. I felt his slow heartbeat as I focused on it. The only sound to be heard was Blake's breathing as he rested his chin on my head.

"Goodnight, Blake."

"Night, princess."

"Please don't call me that."

"Whatever you say, princess."

***

"Oh no." I groaned as I vomited into the toilet. I knew for next time that alcohol and I didn't get along. I tossed and turned in the bed because my stomach hurt. I didn't want to wake up Blake because he looked so cute and comfortable beside me, and I was glad he was a heavy sleeper, so I ran to the nearest bathroom and puked. I felt a hand wrap around my hair as it was pulled out of the way. Then I felt another hand rub my back gently. Once I was done, I got up and flushed the liquid down. I turned to see a lazy-bed-hair Blake. He looked adorable in his long-sleeve baseball shirt. "Thanks."

"Err…here's some spare clothing. You can shower here, and there's an extra toothbrush in the cabinet." He handed me the clothing. I thanked him as he walked out of the bathroom.

After the shower, I felt refreshed. I brushed my teeth and slipped on the clothes that happened to be a maroon sweater and sweatpants. I put on my socks and strolled down the long hallway. It was still quiet except for the kitchen.

"Hey, breakfast is ready," Blake said as he placed two plates on the table. I took a seat as he set a bigger plate in the middle with pancakes. He put all different types of toppings and syrups around it.

"Gotta hand it to you, Gunner, you really know how to impress a girl while she's hung-over," I said as I reached for the syrup.

"I felt like spoiling you," he said with a grin. I blushed as we began to eat. I looked at Blake, who decided on whipped cream and chocolate syrup.

"Where is everyone?" I asked. Blake immediately froze as he stared at me. I stiffened as I looked at him. The last time I saw that stare was when he looked at me back at school when I gripped his arm.

"My mom is working, and I don't know where my brother is." He stared at me for a moment, then continued to eat. The rest of breakfast was spent in silence. We watched a movie on the sofa, and I got curious as to why Blake stared at me when I asked him that question earlier.

"I'm going to take a quick shower then we'll go," he said, then walked down the hall. I nodded as I flicked through the channels. When nothing was on, I decided to check my phone.

Carter (23:30): Where are you? I told you to stay!

Aidan (01:00): Yo where'd you go?

Miranda (02:30): Heard you're spending the night with Blake…enjoy. ;)

I winced at the last text I got from Miranda. How could she possibly think like that? Well, Miranda wanted the best for me, and now that she's with Marcus, she wanted me to be happy too, especially after what happened with Levi.

"Ugh," a deep voice groaned as I heard a door shut. My head snapped toward the door to see a tall figure walk in. He had keys in his hand but threw them on the sofa and collapsed on the couch next to me. I didn't think he noticed me yet. I took the time to look at him while he leaned his head back and shut his eyes. He had similar features as Blake but a couple of tattoos on his hands, and he was taller and very muscular. It must be his brother; I didn't know he had an older brother, but he looked older than Blake.

"Hello," I mumbled. His eyes shot open as he gave me a once over.

"Who the hell are you? And what are you doing here in my house?" he asked bluntly. I bit the inside of my cheek as I looked down.

"Err…I'm Lana."

"Willson?" His eyebrows rose as I slowly nodded.

"So you're the chick my little brother ha—"

"Axel, what are you doing?" I whipped my head around to see Blake in a shirt and some faded jeans. I glanced down at the many tattoos on his arms. I slowly stood up as Blake approached me.

"I was just introducing myself, Lil Bro," Blake's brother said. Blake heavily sighed as he stepped aside.

"Lana, meet my brother, Axel," Blake said, then raised his hand. "Axel, meet my friend, Lana."

"Still in the friendz—" Axel cut off when Blake

glared at him.

"Nice to meet you, Axel," I said as I held my hand out. His rough fingers entwined with mine as he left a kiss on my knuckles.

"It's a pleasure to finally meet you, Lana Willson," he said with a wink. "I've heard many things about you."

"Come on, Lana, go get your things," Blake said before I replied to Axel. I nodded as I walked down the hall and grabbed my clothes from last night that Blake put into a small bag. I quickly put on my Converse, then walked to the living room. Axel stood by the front door with a grin plastered on his face while Blake was nowhere to be found.

"Where's Blake?"

"He's waiting outside."

"Okay, well, thanks, and it was nice meeting you," I said as I tried to make my way out the door, but I felt a hand grab my arm.

"Don't get too close," Axel whispered in my ear. After he said that, he didn't let go. We stood there as I felt his breath on my ear. I finally pulled away and forced a smile as I walked to Blake's motorcycle. He handed me the helmet, and as I put it on, I noticed Axel watched us.

***

"We have an assembly tomorrow," Blake said as he puffed out smoke into the air. We sat in the cottage as we waited for the guys. After the weird encounter with Blake's brother, we didn't really talk.

125

"Oh, why?" I asked as I lit a cigarette. It was relatively rare to get assemblies. If there was one, it'd be long and tedious.

"Only for the seniors, probably about Homecoming or some shit," Blake said. I nodded and looked at him; he still had bags under his eyes, and he looked pissed. I didn't know whether it was from his brother or last night. I still couldn't remember much from last night, but I remembered when Blake punched the guy, whose name I entirely forgot. My gaze lowered down to his tattoos as I exhaled a cloud.

"When did you get your first tattoo?"

"Last summer. I kind of lost a bet and got this." He pointed to the feather on his right arm. It looked unusual and different from an average feather tattoo.

"Did it hurt?"

"When I fell from heaven?" he asked with a goofy grin on his face. I playfully rolled my eyes as I inhaled the smoke then blew it in his face. "A bit at first, but now I'm used to it."

"Do the rest of the guys have tattoos?" I asked, a bit curious since there was a rumor all of them had tattoos, but you'd only see them clearly if you slept with them.

"Yeah, it's sort of our thing."

"What's up, people!" a loud voice yelled. Blake and I turned our heads to the door to see Aidan, Ethan, and Carter.

"Hey guys," I said as I dumped my cigarette in the ashtray. They came to the sofa, and we greeted each other. After that, they smoked, but I refused. I already had two today, but Blake kept smoking; it was probably his fifth one.

"Awesome party last night," Carter said with a grin on his face.

"Yeah, bit hectic too. Are you okay, Lana?" Ethan asked as he turned to me.

"I'm great," I assured him.

"Do you even remember half of the stuff you did last night?" Carter asked as his eyes darted toward me.

"All I can remember is getting there, talking to Ethan, the start of beer pong, and then the fight." I mumbled the last part as I looked at Blake. He turned away as he continued to smoke.

"So you don't remember..." Aidan trailed off.

"What?" I asked. He shook his head with a smirk on his face. After that, the conversation of the party seemed to end, but Ethan and Carter talked about the girls they hooked up with. I blocked them out and looked away at Blake, who stared at me. I raised my eyebrow because I knew something was wrong, but he often shrugged it away.

"No!" Ethan yelled as he looked at his phone.

"What?" the rest asked. Ethan's eyes darkened as he stared at his phone, then shifted to me. Everyone looked at me as I furrowed my brows in confusion.

"Lana? What is this?" he demanded, then gave me his phone. Carter, Blake, and Aidan seemed interested too as they surrounded me. It was a YouTube video; the title was *Nerdy Bad Girl Whore?*

My eyes widened as I pressed play. Everyone focused on the phone, yet I glanced over at Ethan, who fidgeted. The video started with me in the school hallways with my glasses on, face down as I tried to make it to class, but I immediately changed into the clothing I recently wore. There were two people on either side of me, and I realized it was the guys. It showed me getting into Carter's truck after detention, Blake's motorcycle, then Ethan's car. I thought the worst part was over, but it showed the events of last night. I played beer pong with Carter and the guy Blake punched. It showed me in his arms, suddenly it stopped, and the words "party whore" surrounded the screen. It continued with me drinking by the table, then talking to Aidan. Out of the corner of my eye, I noticed Aidan stiffened next to me. I glanced back at the phone and saw me dance with Aidan. My eyes widened as I watched myself. Then the worst of them all came on. Benny and me in the kitchen doing a body shot. The video ended with Blake punching the guy whose name I remembered—Quinton. I placed Ethan's phone on the coffee table and stared at it. The words ran through my head as I played the past week's events in my mind. It was quiet; nobody talked. I was on the verge of tears as I looked down.

"Who did this?" I broke the silence as I stared at the phone.

"I just saw it on Instagram. The full video was on YouTube, so I don't know." Ethan shrugged.

"Did you really do a body shot with Benny?" Blake asked.

"Well, no, I…"

"Did you?" he demanded.

"Yes, but they were playing truth or dare, and

128

Kelly dared him to do it."

"Kelly," he hissed.

"They're the reason behind all of this," Carter said as he pointed to the phone. I nodded, then turned to Ethan, who scrunched up his nose.

"Of all people, you danced with him." Ethan huffed as he pointed to Aidan, who smirked.

"Why, you jealous?" Aidan cooed. Ethan shook his head and turned away.

"I hate them so much," I growled as the remembrance of Benny and Kelly's group entered my mind.

"We need a plan," Aidan stated. I stared at him with a malicious look as we nodded.

"Yep, and it starts tomorrow…at assembly," I said, then looked at Blake. For the first time since Friday, I saw a smile appear on his lips, but it was rudely interrupted when my phone rang. I took out my phone and looked at the caller ID. It was a number I didn't have in my contact list, which caused me to furrow my brows. They stared and waited for me to answer it. I looked at them and showed the phone. "Do you know this number?" I asked. Ethan told me to answer it anyway, and I knew they were curious too. I answered, then pressed the phone to my ear. It was quiet, so the guys heard the caller.

"Hello?" I mumbled. The next thing the person said caught me off guard as they all looked at me with daggers in their eyes.

"Hey, princess, can't wait to see you!"

Chapter Ten

Lana

After yesterday's phone call from a certain someone, the guys demanded to know who it was. I said it was nobody, but they didn't believe me. Eventually, they let it go. We spent the rest of the day removing the video from everywhere and anywhere. Thankfully, Carter and Aidan were experts in that field, so they got it off. Blake taught me how to ride his motorcycle, which was a fun experience, yet scary. I almost ran over him and Ethan while they had an intimate conversation. I wondered if it had to do with the thing that they'd do on Tuesday. I got frustrated, so I gripped the handle and went straight into them. Ethan moved, but Blake didn't while I yelled at him to run; yet he stood and told me to hit the brakes. I hit the brakes in time, but the motorcycle went up as my eyes widened. I was a few inches from Blake's face as he smirked at me, but I felt the bike go down.

"Do we have to go?" Carter whined as I pulled

his arm.

"Yes! It could be substantial," I said as we walked to the auditorium.

"Why you so jumpy today?" Miranda asked with a grin on her face. Last night when Carter dropped me at home, we talked on the phone for hours about what happened.

"I don't know, just feels like a good day."

"Your nerd is showing. Who likes Mondays?" Blake asked.

"No! I hate Mondays. I just feel like missing Calculus and going to the assembly," I said.

"People are staring," Miranda whispered in my ear. I looked around and saw people's sour looks. It was probably because the video was down. Then I heard the clicks of heels approaching us.

"Hi, Lana," Jennifer said as she stood right in front of me.

"Hello," I stated, and Jennifer handed me a pink envelope which smelled like perfume. "What's this?" I asked. The guys and Miranda surrounded us as Kelly and Melissa made googly eyes at them.

"You're invited to my sleepover," Melissa mumbled with a roll of her eyes.

"Well, it's our sleepover, but it's at her house, since she has a hot tub," Kelly said.

"Oh, why me?" I asked.

"Because only the prettiest girls in school get invited." Jennifer smiled.

"What about Miranda?"

"Oh well." Melissa shrugged as I squinted my eyes. I gave my invitation to Miranda, who crumpled it into a ball, then tossed it into the trash can nearby.

"Oh well." I faked a smile. Jennifer laughed, Melissa muttered something under her breath, and Kelly gasped. Jennifer and Melissa followed Kelly as she walked off.

"That was hilarious!" Aidan said as he put his arms around Miranda's and my shoulders. We laughed as Ethan high-fived Carter and ruffled my hair.

"It's weird. Yesterday, they uploaded a video calling me a slut, and now they want to invite me to a sleepover," I said as we took our seats. Aidan sat on my left while Blake sat on my right. Miranda decided to find Marcus while I stayed with guys. The auditorium filled up with all the seniors as we sat a few rows down from the back.

"It's a trap," Carter said in a flat tone.

"Yeah, I know. In sophomore year, they asked, and I was gullible enough to go. They made a complete fool of me, and I swore never to mix with them again."

"Hey, I'm proud of you," Blake said, then rested his palm on top of mine. I looked up and gave him a warm smile.

"So you're not going?" Ethan asked from behind me.

"No, they might egg Miranda and me," I said. We laughed as we continued to talk, but Principal West interrupted us.

"Good morning, Jefferson High seniors," West said into the mic. "As you know, Homecoming is this Friday." He scanned the audience. A few people cheered, but we stayed quiet. Out of the corner of my eye, I saw Carter lean forward and wink at me. I blushed as I thought about the beautiful dress I bought and how handsome Carter would look. "I'm sorry to say that, due to critical weather conditions, we cannot have Homecoming this Friday, since there will be a big storm, so we have—" Principal West was cut off when people protested. "We have moved it to this Thursday!"

People groaned, and I looked at the guys, who didn't look interested at all. I tapped Aidan on the knee, and he looked at me. I slipped my phone out of my pocket and showed him; he furrowed his brows in confusion as I grinned. Blake, Carter, and Ethan seemed interested as they looked at me.

"Now, explaining the night's event is…" He trailed off. People's expressions lightened up a bit and focused. "We'll have our Homecoming Committee President, Jennifer Brighton, take over."

Everyone shifted his or her gaze to Jennifer, who walked across the room. I quickly put in my password and went to settings. I tapped on Bluetooth and saw the device was already connected. Like any other teenager who loved music, Jennifer loved to carry around her Beats Pill in her bag. I went to my music and searched for *Nicki Minaj*. I glanced at Aidan, who looked at me with wide eyes. Blake, on the other hand, smirked. I glanced at Jennifer, who strolled to the podium. As soon as she faced the students of Jefferson High, I hit play on "Anaconda". Everyone's eyes widened as Jennifer froze. All eyes were on her as the music played. Sniggers and whispers erupted through the room as I grinned. Jennifer reached into her bag and grabbed the Beats Pill. Everyone laughed as I increased the volume. Out of nowhere, Melissa and Kelly ran up to her as they tried to help. I paused the song as they sighed in relief. Melissa and Kelly went back to their seats as Jennifer stood up on the podium. She cleared her throat as she stood up straight with a big smile.

"Now that we have confirmation on when Homecoming is, we can finally declare the theme!" she squealed. Everyone mumbled as I huffed, because I'd already bought a dress. "The theme will be Starlight Fairytale!" she cheered into the mic. Whispers and mumbles spread across the room as she tried to get everyone's attention again. I glanced at Aidan, who held my phone with a grin spread across his face. As soon as he hit play, we laughed. The auditorium went silent as we stared at Jennifer, who had a pissed look. She walked off the stage, grabbed the Beats Pill out of her bag, and smashed it to the ground. Aidan quickly disconnected it and turned my phone off before the song played from the phone. Principal West rushed to the podium as he adjusted the mic. It made a screeching noise that made everyone squirm.

"Who is behind this?" he demanded. Everyone was silent as we stared at him. "Teachers, lock the doors. Nobody comes in, and nobody goes out until our miscreant speaks up."

"Why is he so—?" Blake whispered.

"Kelly West...Principal West," I slowly said. He looked at me, jaw dropping as he shook his head.

"Daddy's girl," Blake muttered as he looked at Kelly. She stood next to Jennifer along with Melissa as they glared at everyone.

"Fine, since nobody will speak…you all have to come to school on Friday," Principal West said with a satisfied look. It seemed like it was the end of the world because everyone yelled. He wasn't serious, was he? If the storm from the previous night ended up being so bad, he wouldn't tolerate anyone coming to school the next day.

"Speak up, idiot!"

"Guys, just tell the guy who did it!"

"I don't want to come to school after Homecoming!"

"Screw this school!"

I glanced at the guys who already stared at me. I tensed up as I looked at Kelly, who eyed everyone to see who'd speak. I slowly got up, but someone gripped my thigh and shoved me back in my seat.

"I did it," Blake admitted. Students cheered. That should've been me they cheered on.

"Very well, Mr. Gunner, you do—"

"No, I did it!" I cut Principal West off as I pushed myself out of my seat. Turned out nobody cheered; instead, everyone gasped.

"I did it," Aidan chimed in.

"I did it," Ethan said from behind us.

"No, they're covering for me. I did it," Carter piped up as he rose to his feet.

"No, we did it," Miranda said as she and Marcus stood up.

"Who really did it?" Principal West asked through gritted teeth.

"Me," we said simultaneously.

135

***

"Lana, can I talk to you for a moment?" Mr. Bronx asked when I stepped into the room. After assembly, he asked if he could have a word with me. Lunch started, and I was supposed to meet the guys for a smoke, but they'd understand if I was a few minutes late. We waited for everyone to get out of the classroom as Mr. Bronx stood behind his desk. "I heard about your little doing at the assembly earlier."

"I'm glad. Do you think I could've chosen a better song like—"

"You're becoming really disruptive in my classes, and I do not accept you arriving late every day."

"At least I'm doing my work and keeping my grades up."

"I know, but why? Why now suddenly? Is it that Gunner guy?"

"No, it's complicated," I mumbled, then looked at him. Griffin Bronx had bags under his eyes but still managed to keep the "cool teacher" reputation with his smile and witty replies. "Are you okay, sir? You look exhausted. Does this have to do with a particular English teacher?" I asked with a smirk. Rumors went around that Mr. Bronx and Miss Rosa saw each other.

"Yes, but don't tell anyone," he said, then licked his lips.

"Wow, Uncle Griff, I'm happy for you, but why do you look like you haven't gotten sleep in days?"

"Principal West has a strict no teachers dating

136

policy, so we only meet each other late at night after doing the school work, and we just talk and talk…" He trailed off. A smile appeared on his face as he spoke about Miss Rosa.

"I'm happy for you."

"Thank you, Lana." He gave me a side hug. I walked out of his classroom and down the quiet hallways. I heard heels click behind me as I rolled my eyes.

"I know your little secret, Willson," the voice said behind me. I whipped around to see Melissa Singe.

"Which is?"

"You and Mr. Bronx. You're jealous because he's with Miss Rosa. Now you think you have a shot with him," Melissa spat as she eyed me up and down. I laughed and wiped the tears that formed at such a ludicrous thing.

"You're so funny, Melissa! I'd never see Mr. Bronx in that way. He's a cool teacher, but we're family friends."

"Whatever, Willson. Your secret will soon come out. Don't think I wasn't there last time," she grumbled. My eyes widened as she stormed off, leaving me dumbfounded in the hallway. I planned to go to the guys, but I had reminded myself to go to Principal West. After the assembly, he told us we had detention for the rest of the week and that we'd come to school on Friday along with everybody else. I couldn't let my friends take the blame for a stupid prank I decided to pull. So I decided to confess.

"Ms. Willson, what a surprise." Principal West

huffed as he slouched in his seat.

"Nice to see you too, Mr. West," I said as I took a seat. He raised an eyebrow as he gave me an odd once-over.

"Heard rumors about you that, that Gunner kid broke our only hope for a Yale-inspired student."

"Well, I can assure you, next week you'll see me back to my usual self, which includes getting my application for Yale ready—even though I'm early—and getting back into extra-curricular activities."

"What do you want, Ms. Willson?" Principal West sighed and closed his eyes for a brief moment. In that few seconds, my smile dropped, and so did my confidence.

"It was me," I stated. Principal West stared at me, then laughed.

"Please…I've heard it enough times today."

"No, I can prove it to you. Don't take it out on them. I'll be the guilty one in the back as they look at me," I whined as I pulled out my phone. I unlocked it and went to Bluetooth. "Look, my phone is paired with her Beats Pill."

"Still doesn't prove it was you. Maybe you used it a long time ago," he said, then pushed my phone away. I grabbed it and went to music.

"Look at the last song I played," I urged as I shoved the phone in his face.

"Ms. Will—"

"Look, I know why you don't really want to punish me. It's because my dad is the sheriff of this crappy town, and if I tell him, you think it'll cost you your job, but it won't! I just want to be treated like any other student!"

"Very well, then. I will inform the rest that there is no detention, but you will have to go on Wednesday and help set up for Homecoming."

"That's it?" I asked, then placed my hands on my hips.

"And you will have detention for a whole week starting next week." He glared. I couldn't help but smile as I thanked him, then walked to class.

***

"How smart, Willson." Blake chuckled as I sat on his motorcycle. We waited for the guys to open the cottage because Blake forgot his key at home, so we sat, face to face on Blake's bike. It was comforting, the events of the weekend never came up, and I didn't plan to bring them up, either.

"I know, right?" I flipped my hair because I told him about Principal West. I looked at Blake's hands, which rested on my knees. Occasionally he'd take his thumb and gently rub it against my jeans. I traced the ink on his wrist. Tattoos suited him well. I ran my fingertips along the smiley face he had, and when I raised my head, I saw his stare on me. "Sorry."

"No…it's comforting," he said, then rested his palm against mine. We stared at each other for what felt like an eternity. Our contest got interrupted when we heard a car honk. Blake and I snapped our heads to see Ethan's car right in front of us as Aidan climbed out and opened the cottage. I jumped off the motorcycle and walked inside. We sat on the sofa and smoked as the guys watched a soccer game. My eyes glanced around the room as I remembered Aidan and Carter's conversation a few days ago. Tomorrow's Tuesday. I wonder if we'd be here tomorrow this time.

"Hey, guys, I won't be able to hang out tomorrow. Miranda and I are going to the mall," I lied because I hoped for a reaction.

"That's great. Plus I have practice, so I won't be able to come," Ethan said, then turned to Aidan.

"Yeah, err...I got a ton of homework," Aidan mumbled.

"We'll find something to do," Blake said as he eyed Carter. Those answers right there told me they were lies. Ethan didn't have practice this week since last week was a big game and Homecoming was soon, so Coach gave the team a little break. Aidan never did homework, and Blake and Carter haven't been on speaking terms.

"Cool." I nodded. Everyone returned to the big television as I thought how the hell I'd get here tomorrow at four p.m. without the guys' consent. Apparently, they didn't want me to know what went on, but I was curious.

***

"Morning, beautiful family." I grinned as I walked into the kitchen. Dad sipped his coffee while Mom buttered toast.

"Hey sweetie, how'd you sleep?"

"Fine, I guess."

"Any plans for today?" Mom asked as she

handed me the toast.

"I think I'll be in the library after school, so don't worry about me," I lied. I had to find an excuse because they never knew I hung out with the guys after school.

"I'm staying late at the station. Got a whole lot of work to finish." Dad sighed as he sipped his coffee. A car's honk disrupted the silence as I stood up.

"See you guys later. Enjoy your day," I said as I walked out of the house. I got into Aidan's Subaru as his music blared through the speakers; I put the volume softer as I looked at him. "I didn't know you'd be coming today."

"Well, we figured whoever gets to your house first can take you." He shrugged with a grin on his face.

"Why can't you guys just take it in turns?"

"Where's the fun in that, Lana?" Aidan winked at me as I rolled my eyes. I gazed out the window as the trees passed by and thought about later today. I hoped my plan worked, because they were hiding something.

"You got a cigarette?" I asked, and Aidan looked at me with a frown.

"You should really slow down on those, Lana. After the bet, will you stop?"

"Will you?" I demanded. His eyes shot back to the road. The car went silent as he sighed heavily and handed me one.

"We just don't want you getting addicted to those," he whispered.

"Says the guy who smokes eight in a day." I

141

huffed then turned to the window. The car went silent again as he let out a soft chuckle. I glared at Aidan as he laughed uncontrollably.

"What?"

"I'm not a cigarette, but I find you smoking hot."

"Oh my god, Aidan, that's so lame."

"But it made you laugh, didn't it?" he asked as we pulled up into the school's parking lot.

"Aidan, you always make me laugh." I grinned as we got out of the car.

"I'm glad. It's amazing to watch you laugh," he said as he put an arm around my shoulder. We received a few looks, but I brushed them off.

When we came out of Calculus and switched classes, I met up with Miranda and Marcus. I had to tell Miranda before we reunited with everyone.

"Yeah, if my parents ask, just say you got me from the library and that we went shopping or something," I begged Miranda. Aidan and Marcus were talking together, and it was the only time I'd see Miranda until lunch. I couldn't help but feel Marcus's eyes on me the whole time.

"Okay, but why?" Miranda asked as she raised a brow.

"You'll see." I grinned as Ethan came up to us.

"Hey, guys," he greeted. The bell rang, and we strolled up the stairs. "What do you have now?" he asked. Blake and Carter were nowhere to be found as we walked through the busy hallways.

"Photography class." I grinned as we reached my locker. I noticed Miranda went with Marcus. Aidan disappeared down the hallway while Ethan leaned against the locker and reached into his pocket, and

142

out came a neatly folded paper.

"What's this?" I asked as he handed me the paper and I slowly began to unfold it.

"It's an appointment with the optometrist. Well, just call them up and say Baxter sent you. Everything from there's been taken care of. I know you've only been surviving with contact lenses."

"Ethan, this is too much…" I shrugged as he put a lock of hair behind my ear.

"No, it's not, Lana. Besides, the other ones were literally shattered. Take this as an apology gift for all the years I've bullied you," Ethan pleaded and covered my hand with his while I gripped the paper. My gaze traveled down to our hands and onto the paper. There wasn't any date, so I could make the arrangements while Ethan offered to pay. I didn't want him to, but either way, the optometrist would send his family the bill. I looked up into his puppy brown eyes, and I saw myself in them. Without my glasses, I fit the bad girl image more, but I couldn't always rely on contacts. If I didn't go, then I'd have to wear my old horn-rimmed glasses from my elementary days, which would be my last resort.

Ethan's signature smile showed but immediately disappeared when he looked over my shoulder. I turned around and saw Carter with a smirk as he flirted with some girls. Carter Halls was a charmer, but he could also be a player when he wanted to.

"Hey, cutie," he said as he put an arm around my shoulder.

"Hello," I stated in an ominous tone.

"Why you so happy? You finally get laid?" Ethan asked as I laughed.

"No! Well, yes, but I'm happy, Mr. Baxter, because after today, we'll be free men." Carter grinned then winked at Ethan.

"Why? What's happening today?" I asked. Ethan shook his head as we stared at Carter. I bet it had to do with what would happen at the cottage today.

"Well, err…we have a Trigonometry test today, and if we pass it, we immediately get an A on our report card," Carter said. Ethan shook his head again as he stared at the ground. I knew Carter Halls was the worst liar ever. He tried to cover it up by saying the lamest pickup line known to mankind.

"What's with you guys and lame pickup lines today?" I asked as we walked to my photography class.

"Well, at least you don't fall for it, because sometimes I used the lamest ones in the book and I still got laid," Carter said.

"Just go, you two." I laughed as we turned the corner. Carter and Ethan smiled as they walked to their classes. I went into the classroom and glanced around at the rest of the photographers. It was the only class where I'd relax. Everyone focused, and when they took photographs, it inspired me. I loved how the class was set up; one side had desks, and the other side was blank with the camera equipment. Mr. Dockwell was an excellent teacher, he's so laidback, but he's strict too. I decided to sit in the middle of the double desks, then took out my laptop.

"Morning, class. I'll be taking the attendance now," he said as he sat down. I glanced around the classroom to see Melissa nearby. She sat down in front of me, but I didn't miss the glare she sent.

"Blake?"

"Here," a deep voice said. I looked up from my laptop to see Blake Gunner walk into the classroom. Mr. Dockwell gave a stiff nod to Blake as he turned to us. He barely came to class, so to see him here was a surprise. Mr. Dockwell continued with the attendance as Blake came to Melissa's desk. She pulled out the chair beside her as he gave a small smile. He continued to walk as he took a seat next to me. I tried so hard not to laugh as Melissa stared at him. She had Nick Byrne as a boyfriend anyway; he was on the team.

"Okay, class, I have most of your photos from the previous assignment, and I'm happy to say that they were all beautiful. You've successfully used what is needed, and since everyone passed that task, we will be starting a new one," Mr. Dockwell said as he walked up and down.

"What's the topic?" Tyler asked.

"Well, since the previous assignment was about vintage, and you guys took some amazing shots with beautiful settings, I have decided to let you all make a decision on the topic." Mr. Dockwell beamed as a smile appeared on his face. Everyone cheered as people discussed among themselves. "But it will be due before spring break," Mr. Dockwell added. Everyone groaned as he playfully rolled his eyes. "That's your treat, if you pass this semester." Everyone went silent. "In the meantime, you can continue with your unique project." He went to sit back at his desk. For our unique project, we had to take pictures of what we thought unique was and explain why we believed it was. I'd started, but I might do something else. My mind had changed the past few days. I decided to go through all the pictures that I had taken; some were quite good, to be honest. A few had Miranda and me at the amusement park; she held a bunch of balloons while she posed by the pier. Then there was one of Miranda making googly eyes at something, but my focus was on her. She used to have a crush on Ethan when she first came to Jefferson High. I didn't know if she still did. She knew he was a sort of man-whore, but he was also a sweetheart. Out of the corner of my eye, I saw Blake grin as he held up a Canon camera. He snapped a few pictures of me, and I rolled my eyes, then looked at him.

"Like what you see, Willson?" he asked with a smirk on his face as he squinted his eyes behind the camera.

"You know we have to take pictures of something unique, right?" I asked. He lowered the camera and grinned at me.

"I think you are unique." I looked back at my laptop as my cheeks reddened. Blake laughed beside me, then put the camera down. "Is that you?" he asked, then casually leaned his head against my shoulder. I looked at the screen and saw a picture of a girl; I couldn't see her face because she angled the camera so that her face was covered, but I saw the rest of her body as she posed in front of a large mirror. Her long brown hair was in knots as she stood by the mirror in a tank top and shorts. The mirror ended at her thighs, yet the frame of the mirror was visible.

"Yeah," I breathed out.

"Who's that?" he asked and pointed to the person behind me. I didn't notice that anyone was there because the background was so dull, the white wall with a single painting hung up. The person's back faced the mirror, but I immediately made it out as a guy. His black hair was neatly gelled as he stood there. He had his left hand through his hair while his right arm hung loosely beside him.

"An old friend," I mumbled as I stared at Levi Radcliff.

"What happened?"

"Let's just say we moved on."

***

I was in Physics, the last period of the day before we went home. The teacher wrote formulas on the board as we copied them. Carter and Ethan were in this class as we sat in the back. I leaned on the desk as I slowly closed my eyes.

"Lana."

"Ugh."

"You okay?" Ethan asked as he touched my shoulder and rubbed it gently. I wanted to drift off to sleep at his touch, but I knew I couldn't. I nodded as I sat up and looked at Carter and Ethan. Looks of concern filled their faces as they watched me. I raised my hand as I did an awkward cough. All eyes turned to me as I slowly put my hand down.

"Can I be excused, sir?" I asked. He gave a slow nod as I got up. I gathered my things and rushed out of the classroom. I walked to my locker and put my books, along with my backpack, inside. I managed to catch up with all the homework, so I didn't have any. I walked out of the school and into the parking lot, where I saw the guys' cars. I leaned over Carter's truck and saw the blanket in the back that he kept when we'd ditch and hide in the back. He made it comfy as possible with two blankets and a few pillows. I climbed in the back and wrapped myself in the blankets. I shifted as far as I could so they wouldn't see me. The bell rang as I heard people rush out; I waited another ten minutes until I heard voices.

"Are we seriously gonna do this?" I made out the voice of Aidan.

"We have to. It's been going on long enough," Blake said.

"If we included Lana in this, she would have hated us," Ethan grunted.

"Yeah, so the sooner we get this done, the sooner we can just move on like nothing ever happened," Carter said as I heard him open the door.

"Whoa, Carter, didn't know you had so much junk in here," Aidan said as I felt a weight on the truck.

"Yeah, I should clean up soon," he said. I felt a hand hit the blankets, and I tried so hard not to squeal.

"Come on, guys, we gotta get going," Blake said as I heard his motorcycle roar. Carter started his truck as I held on for dear life. While he drove, it gave me time to think. I thought of what I'd say if they caught me. I didn't want to sound nosy, so I had to think of something. Plus, they're my friends, so of course they'd tell me.

"Oomph!" I groaned as the truck came to a stop. I heard Carter's door open, then slam shut. I waited for five minutes until I was sure they were inside the cottage, then unwrapped myself. I slowly looked up to see Aidan's car and Blake's motorcycle. Ethan must've gotten a ride with Aidan. I slowly got out of the truck and tiptoed to the cottage. I peeked through the open door to see them in a circle. They seemed to be in a deep conversation, as they spoke in hushed voices, so I walked to the other side. I peeked my head through the window and recognized the room. It was the one Ethan brought me to when Benny told me complete, utter nonsense. Thank goodness the window was open as I quietly slipped inside. I took my glasses off and stuffed them in my pocket as I scanned the room. It looked the same as last time, but the door was closed. I leaned against it as I heard shuffles from the main room.

"Okay now, let's get the others from the room," Aidan said. My eyes widened as the footsteps neared me. I ran to the bed and laid on it casually, but grinned as I posed on the bed like a model. The door flung open as they stood there, jaws dropped.

"I've been expecting you." I laughed as their eyes widened.

"Lana? What are you doing here?!" Carter demanded.

"That's not very nice." I pouted as I slowly sat up.

"I know, but we thought you'd be hanging out with Miranda today?" Aidan asked as I stood up. I looked over his shoulder and out the door. We weren't much of a height difference since we were the shortest ones. Ethan stood behind Aidan as he blocked the view of the living room.

"Miranda has volleyball practice, so she got Marcus to drop me here," I lied.

"Wait, you let Marcus come here?" Blake demanded.

"N-Not really. He dropped me off at the gas station, and I walked the rest of the way," I mumbled. I couldn't believe I made up so many lies in front of them. "And aren't you supposed to be doing homework? And you at practice?" I asked as I looked at Aidan, then Ethan. They looked away as I stared at each of them. I'd never seen Aidan look so nervous nor Carter so angry before, and it frightened me. A loud horn, which clearly wasn't a car, broke the silence.

"They're early," Aidan mumbled as he looked down at his watch.

"Who?" I demanded. Carter pulled me against his chest and pressed a finger to his lips. I slowly nodded as he slowly removed his finger.

"All right, we'll get the stuff in here, and Aidan, just stall them," Carter said, then forced me into the desk chair. Aidan walked out, then closed the door halfway. Blake emptied the drawers, and out came those weird parcels.

"What are those?" I whispered, because apparently, they didn't want me here. Blake ignored me as I looked at Ethan; he emptied the closet, and out came more parcels that he took into the living room. Carter grabbed more parcels from under the bed and carried them out.

"What the hell is going on?" I asked Blake, who passed the parcels on. He opened his mouth but cut off when a deep voice echoed throughout the cottage

"You got my coke, boys?"

My eyes widened as I stared at Blake. I wanted to yell or scream for what they did, and I couldn't believe I was so stupid as to ever get involved. I opened my mouth to speak, but it was immediately shut when Blake pressed his lips against mine.

Chapter Eleven

Lana

I was surprised at first as Blake's lips met mine, but I immediately let him take over as his upper lip sucked my bottom one. His hands wrapped around my waist as he brought me closer. My arms wrapped around his neck as we kissed. I heard movements in the room, but I knew it wasn't us. It didn't matter; all that mattered was Blake Gunner's lips on mine. A moan escaped from my lips as Blake smiled against mine. The kiss was passionate yet forced, but somehow I liked it, and I didn't want to pull away and neither did he.

"Wow, what a distraction," a familiar voice muttered from behind me. I pulled away from Blake as I saw Carter behind us with parcels in his hands, one of them slightly open, and I saw the cocaine spill on the floor. My eyes widened as I snapped back to reality.

"You guys are drug dealers?"

Carter looked down in disappointment as Blake

put a finger to his lip.

"Who's there?"

I gasped as a guy entered the room with a gun in his hand. Blake stood in front of me as he looked at the guy. I finally caught on and hid behind Blake.

"She's just a friend," Blake stated calmly. The big guy lifted his gun up as I stiffened. He motioned us to get out the room in silence, and we did as we were told. I quietly walked out of the room and down the hall into the central area. We were in the living room, where Ethan and Aidan stood with blank looks. Another guy stood next to them as a shorter, buffer guy stood in the middle. I glanced down at all the parcels of cocaine. We stood there as the shorter man, who I assumed was the boss, whispered to the other guy as they glanced at me. The shorter man walked closer to me as Carter held my hand. The shorter man had a grin on his face as he twirled a gun in his hand. Carter slowly let go of my hand as the guy stood right in front of me. I tried to keep my face neutral as I stared into his dark blue eyes.

"And who is this?" His voice was gruff as he eyed me.

"A friend," Ethan mumbled. As the guy stood in front of me, he slid the gun down my neck; I breathed uncontrollably as the corner of his mouth lifted.

"What's your name, beautiful?" he whispered. I bit the inside of my cheek, which only resulted in the gun being pressed against my chest.

"L-Lana," I stuttered, then sighed in relief when the gun was removed. He didn't seem phased by my name as he slowly nodded. He raised his gun and motioned toward the door.

"Count," he said, and the other men nodded. They picked up four parcels each and walked out of the room; the buff guy twirled the gun around his finger as he looked at us. Nobody spoke, yet I wanted to. So many questions ran through my head; however, nothing came out. We stood there as the shorter guy walked out of the room. Nobody moved or talked; I was surprised and confused that they'd be involved in such a thing. So many scenarios ran through my head that I didn't even hear the guy come back. I raised my head and noticed how his jaw tightened as he glared at us. This time the gun was in his pocket as he clenched his fists, his eyes darkened as he turned to Aidan.

"Two hundred and fifty."

"Excuse me?" Aidan asked.

"Two-fifty!" He raised his voice. "There's supposed to be two-fifty. There are only two hundred and forty-eight parcels!"

Everyone froze for a moment as I turned to the door. An engine roared, and I tilted my head to see a big truck. From the corner of my eye, I saw the guys running, probably in search for the two parcels. I wanted to help, heck, I tried to run away and never come back because I was scared, but something urged me to stay; something told me to stay put because if I didn't, then the man in the suit would shoot me. I stood there as I tried to register everything that happened in the last hour. The short guy took out a phone and typed. He did a hand signal to the other two guys outside. A few seconds later, they walked in.

"Wha-what are you doing?" I asked. By his appearance, it was clear that he was dominant and that people feared him. He wore a slick gray suit and shiny brown shoes; his hair was gelled, which defined his jawline. He was taller than me, probably Ethan's height, but the other two guys were the tallest in the room.

"Your friends have failed to do their duty, Lana Willson," he said, then walked outside. It took me a moment to realize that I hadn't told him my last name. It might be the reason as to why he wasn't surprised when I told him my name. I glanced up and followed him. My jaw dropped as I walked outside; there were two trucks filled with parcels. I couldn't believe two hundred and forty-eight parcels filled with cocaine came out of the cottage. I heard footsteps of the guys too as we looked at the men. One of them was still in the cottage. The one with the blue eyes came over to me again. He took my hand and left a gentle kiss on it. "Until we meet again, Lana Willson," he said as we locked eyes. He gave me such a comforting smile that made his features look similar, yet his smile disappeared when he glared at the guys.

"Now you'll face the consequences, boys," he said as the other guy came out of the cottage and gave the nod. I pulled my hand away, which only made him smirk. The three men approached the trucks and locked everything. We could just watch as they climbed in and drove away. The trucks got smaller by the second, and once they were out of sight, I looked over my shoulder. I kept my mouth in a straight line as I stared at the guys. I was worried, scared, but most of all confused. My thoughts were interrupted when Blake walked over to me. Something about their appearances made me afraid. I really didn't personally know them.

"Willson, you need to go now," he demanded as Aidan nodded in agreement.

"What? No! What the hell just happened? Who are they? Are you guy's re—" My hard questions got interrupted by Ethan.

"Lana, please, just go. We'll explain later," he murmured. I shook my head, then turned to Carter. He looked down as he slowly shook his head.

"Ethan, get her legs," Blake commanded, then pointed to Aidan. "Grab her arms."

I furrowed my eyebrows in confusion as I watched Ethan and Aidan walk over to me. Ethan grabbed me by the legs while Aidan took my arms; they hoisted me up in the air. "What the hell do you think you're doing? I demand answers!" I yelled as their grip on my arms and legs tightened. I heard Blake's motorcycle start, and I moved frantically. They forced me on the seat as Carter took the helmet and put it on me. "Carter…" I mumbled as I looked at his blue eyes filled with fear and sadness. The Carter Halls that held a smirk on his face, ready to become a free man, was gone. The sarcastic jerk that always made fun of me in English wanted to help me by not getting into trouble. I gripped my hands on the handles then turned to see Blake's stare.

"Go, Lana, please," he begged as he rested his hand on my thigh. His eyes were dark, and he had the same look as when I asked him about his parents. I didn't know what possessed me, but the look in Blake's eye told me not to question it. I was confused and knew they wouldn't let it go. I looked straight ahead and winced at the impressive noise as I kicked the side stand in. I sped down the road, although I didn't know where I'd go, but I drove. I looked back one last time to see why they dragged me away. Blue and red lights approached the cottage. Dad got out of the car, along with the rest of the police force. I looked back at the road to see it clear, but I couldn't help but look back again. They were pushed to the ground by the police officers as their hands were forced behind their backs. I looked back at the road with tears in my eyes as I went faster. I glanced at the rearview mirror to see they got smaller by the second.

I couldn't take it anymore. The longer I drove, the guiltier I felt. It would be my fault. If I wasn't there, maybe they could've gotten away with it or they could've found the other two parcels. I couldn't believe they were drug dealers and that they'd hide it in Ethan's dad's cottage. However, I shouldn't be quick to judge. I didn't know the full story, so I shouldn't jump to conclusions. I stopped Blake's motorcycle on the side of the road and looked over my shoulder. They're probably at the station already, and something inside me told me to go there. So, me being me, I turned around and sped to the location.

I arrived at the old building and parked in the visitors' area. The last time I was here was when I was twelve. A guy robbed a bank, so my dad thought it'd be fun to show me how it worked.

I got off the motorcycle and placed the helmet on the seat. I shoved the keys in my pocket as I walked to the front doors. I looked at myself in the glass and shivered at my appearance. I grabbed the hair tie that was around my forearm and put my hair up into a high ponytail. At least today I wore a big sweater, black jeans, and black Converse, so I looked at least presentable when I entered the sheriff's station. I opened the double doors to see people walk up and down, and none gave me a second glance as I strolled to the front desk. I recognized a few faces as I looked behind the counter to see Ms. Jackson on the computer. She was a middle-aged woman who worked here for years. When I came to the station, she'd always keep me occupied while I waited for my dad.

"Hi, I'd like to talk to the Sheriff, plea—"

"Sorry dear, he—oh, Lana! It's you! Hello dear, how are you?"

"I'm good, Ms. Jackson."

"Long time no see. Where have you been?"

"School, I guess." I shrugged, then tilted my head down the hall to my dad's office. "Can I talk to my dad, please?"

"I don't know. He's kind of busy, and I don't—"

"I'll be quick," I cut her off then walked around her desk.

"Good luck!" she yelled before I turned the corner.

"Hey, Paul," I said to the Deputy.

"Afternoon, Lana. What brings you here?" he asked while he scribbled on papers.

"Just here to talk to my dad."

"He's actually busy. We finally got those miscreants." He huffed, then looked over his shoulder. I followed his gaze, only to be met by the interrogation room. A glass separated us, and I squinted to get a better look. Dad stood while the guys sat opposite him. They looked guilty while my dad shouted at them. I felt sorry for Ethan, because he was my father's favorite, and Dad never thought Ethan Baxter would do such a thing.

"I'll be quick," I begged the deputy. He rolled his eyes and motioned me to go inside. As I pushed the door open, I managed to force a smile. It was a square room with four chairs on one side, where the guys sat, and one chair on the opposite side, with a table that separated us. "Hey, Daddy how ar—" I cut myself off as I looked at the guys. "What are they doing here?"

They each had a different expression on their face. Ethan frowned, Aidan grinned, Carter looked surprised, and Blake smirked.

"Lana, they were—"

"Daddy, do you know Carter helped me get an A in History, and Ethan helped me with this boring assignment we had? Without them, I wouldn't understand," I sighed as I tried to avoid eye contact. I didn't want him to say those words. I wouldn't believe it.

"That's…very kind of them," Dad mumbled, then walked to the door. "Lana, can I talk to you…alone?"

I eagerly nodded as I skipped out the room with my dad. He closed the door. I noticed Deputy Paul was gone, and we were the only two in the hall.

"Lana, we got a call from an unknown number saying that four teenagers that I've been trying to get for the past few weeks were spotted. We traced the call to a cottage where we found some drugs; they were outside, looking as if they were going to leave. Thankfully, we got there in time," Dad said, then sighed heavily.

"You don't think…" I trailed off. That's why the guy was on his phone and why he nodded to one of his men. Probably to put parcels back on purpose because they didn't finish the job. My mind told me not to do it, to go home and let them suffer alone, or maybe even go to juvie since they had so much. Yet my heart said to do the right thing. They'd been there for me and showed me the fun side of life instead of putting my face in books all the time. If they were gone, my life would return to normal, and I didn't want it to.

"We've done some tests, so we're waiting on the results. Other than that, they not saying anything." Dad sighed then turned to the glass.

"Can I talk to them?" I asked. They stared at us but immediately looked somewhere else when I caught them.

"Lana, I don't think that's a good idea."

"Please, Dad, they're my friends, and I don't think they'd do something like this. There must be a logical reason."

I'd known Carter, Aidan, and Ethan for more than five years, and even though they're cocky and annoying, I couldn't picture them doing stuff like that. As I got to know Blake, I noticed there's more to him other than the narcissistic bad boy attitude he's known for.

"Okay, but remember, I know and see everything." He motioned to the computer by his desk. It had a monitor of all the rooms in this section of the building. I saw Deputy Paul flirt with Officer Jackson as she stared at him in amusement.

"Yeah, Dad," I said as I grabbed the box of doughnuts from the desk. Before I walked inside, I took a deep breath. I closed the door as I kept my face down, not daring to make eye contact with them. Out of the corner of my eye, I saw their stares as they watched me. I placed the box of doughnuts on the table and slid it across. Surprisingly, it stopped before it fell, yet they didn't move. I thought food would get them to talk. I sat down on the other end of the table and stared at them.

"What was that?" I whispered. They avoided eye contact. I waited as I saw Aidan move his arm to reach out for a doughnut.

"Nuh-uh...speak. Or should I introduce you to your prison cells?" I tilted my head, then grabbed a doughnut. The guys exchanged looks, and Ethan sighed.

"It all started in sophomore year," he said. I put the box down as Aidan grabbed the glazed doughnut and devoured it. "Blake always came to Illinois for the summer because we were close when growing up. One day we walked in the city, and this guy came out of nowhere and shoved a bag in my hands. He yelled out, 'I don't want to do this anymore,' and 'please,' then ran off. We looked at it and found the same parcels in the bag with a small note attached to one of them. It had the address to where the parcels needed to go," Ethan said, then turned to Carter.

"We went to the address and found two guys by the door. We showed them the bag, and they immediately let us in. We were confused by it all and didn't know it was drugs. The one guy led us to a room where we waited for over an hour until the man in the suit walked in. He asked where we got the bag and if we knew what's in it. We told him, and he didn't take the bag. Instead, he said to keep it safe and that there's cocaine in it," Carter said as he played with his fingers. Blake continued, but this time he stared at me as if he were waiting for a reaction.

"He threatened us if we didn't do as he said. We went back to Ethan's place and talked about it. The guy didn't ask our name, and we didn't ask his name. The next day, we went back to the address, but there was nobody there, not a soul in sight. When we got back to Ethan's place, there was a box that was delivered. No address and no name on it, so we opened it and saw more cocaine. We freaked out on how he found us and knew where we lived, so we did what he asked. It was too risky to have it at Ethan's house or move it all to Carter and Aidan's houses because we got more parcels every second day. We decided to go on a road trip in the middle of summer to my state, where we hid it all," Blake said. I don't think he blinked once while he said that, but I continued to look at him to see if there was any sort of hesitation. Nothing. They told the truth.

"We stayed for a week, and surprise, surprise, more arrived. The weird thing was they didn't even know that Blake lived in Minnesota. We drove back to Illinois, and when summer break ended, we thought it would too, but it didn't. Blake got a guy who came once a month to check up on the cocaine. Thankfully he didn't do anything, so we carried on with our lives until Blake had to move here," Aidan said as he chewed the doughnut. I glanced at Blake, who kept his head down while everyone else ate doughnuts. We waited for him to continue as I took the box that had two doughnuts left.

"Again, they drove up to help with the moving of some of my stuff and the drugs. By then, Ethan's dad told us we could have the cottage and make it into our man cave, so we put it to actual use and stored all the cocaine there. We didn't see the men for six months, and we didn't hear from them until last week. He told us in two simple words, it's time, and we knew what it meant," Blake said.

"So, for the past two years, you guys have been dealing with drug dealers who you don't know, but they know everything about you guys, and now suddenly, they want the cocaine," I said as I tried to digest all the information they had told me. They nodded in unison as I tapped my chin. "And it's all because this one guy who worked for them had enough and decided to just shove the bag to you?"

"Yeah. Could've just stayed indoors that day," Ethan said as he rolled his eyes. I was about to ask another question but froze when my dad entered the room. He stared at me, then the guys.

"The tests came back," he said, then placed his

163

hands on his hips. "You won't be allowed at the cottage anymore. It's under investigation until further notice. Deputy Paul and I shall take you guys home. We've called your parents, and we have negotiated on something."

A small smile formed on my lips because I knew my dad heard the whole thing, and he's not an easy one to crack, so there must've been something that made him click. I wonder what they had negotiated on, since they won't get away that easily, maybe a fine. The guys got up, but we kept our distance as they walked out the door. I stopped Blake and looked him in the eye as I shoved his keys into his hands. He mouthed, "Thank you," then left the room.

We sat in the cop car in silence. My dad drove, me in the passenger seat, while Aidan and Carter sat behind us. Blake and Ethan drove with Deputy Paul even though Blake's motorcycle was in the parking lot. He didn't want to make a scene, so he said he'd come back for it in the morning. The car was silent as I looked out the window. We were in a modern neighborhood and stopped at a two-story home. It looked cozy and hospitable as my dad got out and took the cuffs off Aidan. I watched the two walk up the driveway. My dad knocked on the door as Aidan turned around to us and gave a thumbs up. My dad flicked his head, and he straightened. I laughed as I shook my head; even though he almost got thrown in jail for cocaine, he still managed to lighten the mood.

"Thank you," Carter said. I got a fright, as I'd forgotten he was in the car. I looked at him through the rearview mirror and raised a brow.

"For what?"

"For coming back…for saving us," he mumbled as he looked out the window.

"I couldn't just leave you guys there. You guys showed me to not be so serious about life and take risks. It's something I haven't done in a while."

"Do you think it's safe to tell your dad that I slept with his daughter and watched her shower?"

"If you wanna die in this real cop car, then go ahead."

Before Carter answered, Dad got back in the car. We drove for another ten minutes, then arrived at an average house that was like Blake's, but a bit bigger. Dad got out of the car first, then Carter. He still had the guts to say, "Goodnight, beautiful," and walk off with cuffs on. I watched as Carter stood tall by the door while my dad spoke to his mother, who glared at him. My father took the cuffs off Carter's wrists. Dad got in the car, and we drove home in silence.

"How did you know they would be there?" Dad asked as we pulled up our driveway. It was only then that I noticed Carter lived five minutes away from me.

"I didn't. I was just out with Miranda, and I told her to drop me off at the station," I lied again. If he knew I was there, I might as well cuff myself to the car while my dad lectured me.

"I don't want you hanging out with them so much anymore."

"What? Why? You heard them! They didn't—"

"I don't care! I just don't want anything to

165

happen again."

"Dad, that was just…"

"A mistake? Ha, just listen to me, Lana. I'm only doing this because I am worried about you. You should be focusing on your last year of school and getting into university. We don't want—"

"Is that what you think of me? That I'll go off doing that again since I'm hanging out with the opposite sex? They are my friends, Dad."

"Just please, when the Radcliffs come, be what it used to be seven years ago."

I didn't give him enough time to talk again as I got out of the car and slammed the door shut. I walked in the house and didn't bother to close the door because I knew he'd be right on my tail.

***

"So? Where were you?" Miranda asked as we walked through the hallways. Last night when we got home, Dad told Mom we had father-daughter time, which my mother bought since I was quiet for the rest of dinner. This morning I decided to walk and think about things clearly as I took in the breeze of fall.

"Err…just out with the guys," I mumbled as we walked into the cafeteria. We took a seat at our regular table to see Marcus already there.

"Hey, babe," he said as Miranda sat next to him. I sat opposite them as they kissed. I scrunched my nose up as they shared saliva.

"So you two are together now?" I asked after they pulled apart.

166

"Yeah, and I couldn't be happier." Marcus grinned as he winked at Miranda. I playfully rolled my eyes as I saw Miranda's cheeks redden. I took my pasta out and ate it immediately as Miranda and Marcus got into their conversation. My thoughts went back to this morning when I had a talk with my dad. Apparently, the guys gave a description of that guy, and turned out it matched with a case that was opened two years ago when this guy came to confess to my dad that he worked with a drug dealer yet didn't know his name. It was the same guy who stuffed the bag into Ethan's hands after he confessed to the cops; two days later, he was reported dead. No doubt by that scary man. Each of the guys had to pay a fine or spend a long time in the juvenile detention center since they held cocaine for the past two years. They weren't going to get away that easily. Hopefully, they'd take the wiser option and pay the goddamn fine.

"Right, Lana?" Miranda snapped me out of my thoughts, and I glanced up.

"What?"

"They gonna get us at your house tomorrow night, yeah?" she asked with a look of concern.

"For?"

"Tomorrow night is Homecoming," Marcus said.

"Oh. Sorry, I forgot," I mumbled.

"Don't worry." Miranda waved off as she looked up. So did Marcus as I stared at them.

"Hey…can we sit?" someone asked from behind me. I looked over my shoulder to see Carter, Aidan, and Blake. Aidan had a tray full of food; Carter had a sandwich and a box of juice, while Blake had his hands shoved in his jeans.

"Sure," Miranda said. Aidan and Carter sat on either side of me while Blake sat next to Miranda. Out of the corner of my eye, I saw Marcus scoot closer to her protectively. We ate in silence as Aidan passed a slice of pizza to Blake, who ate it slowly as he stared at me. My eyes diverted to the empty spot beside him, and I wondered where the big jock was. I looked around the cafeteria and saw Ethan with Kelly and Jennifer. Ethan gripped his tray as Jennifer stroked his bicep, a look of annoyance spreading across his face as she talked. Kelly stood next to her and put on the best smile she could. Ethan raised a brow as his face shifted toward our table. He sighed heavily and nodded. The girls clapped as he rolled his eyes and walked toward our table.

"Hey, guys," Ethan greeted.

"Hi," I mumbled. His eyes were red, and he had rings under them; I noticed a short stubble formed as he stared into space. I glanced at Blake, who continued to eat the pizza. "Did you get your motorcycle?" I looked at the brown-eyed boy. Today he wore his usual attire, white muscle tee, black jeans, and combat boots. The muscle tee showed his beautiful tattoos as well as his biceps.

"Yeah, thank goodness that deputy and your dad weren't there yet. I would've been screwed," Blake said as he licked his bottom lip.

"Are you okay?"

"Never better, sweetheart," Blake said as he winked at me. I rolled my eyes, thinking there's the Blake Gunner I knew. I looked back at him to see

Ethan talking to him. Blake let out a scoff as his jaw clenched. "No."

"We have to. You know what he said," Ethan mumbled as he looked at me from the corner of his eye. Blake looked at me then nodded.

"So what happened last night when you guys got home?" I asked, then turned to Miranda; she was in an in-depth conversation with Marcus, who had his lips glued to her ear. Although I didn't think he was whispering to her.

"Ma yelled at me and told me I have to work to pay off the $2000. So for the next week, I'll be working." Aidan cheered.

"Why you happy?"

"Well from the amount the guy paid us for keeping the coke, I'll probably work for a few days…just to get experience or some shit." He waved us off.

My brows rose, because I didn't think they'd earn so much from cocaine.

"My mom took my truck away, so now Eth is my ride for the rest of the year." Carter grinned as he looked at Ethan. He raised his eyebrows, then shook his head.

"Nuh-uh, get your own ride, dude," Ethan scoffed.

"Okay then, lend me one of your fancy-looking cars," Carter said. Ethan and Carter stared at each other for another two minutes until someone spoke.

"When you two are done with your staring contest, I'd like to explain my punishment." Blake smiled sarcastically. Both glared at each other as we turned to Blake.

"You didn't get yelled at?" Aidan asked as Blake grinned.

"Nope."

"How come?" I asked. I knew Blake had a mother, so naturally, she would've shouted at him at least.

"Momma wasn't home, so Deputy Do Da spoke to my bro, who couldn't give two shits about me." Blake grinned.

"What did Axel say?" Carter asked.

"He shook his head and promised not to tell Mom if I didn't tell on him." Blake shrugged like it was no deal.

"What did he do?" Aidan asked. We were suddenly interested now as the dark-haired boy looked at us.

"Things…some awful things." He grunted as his fist clenched the can.

"Well, my dad grounded me, so you won't be seeing me on the weekends for the next few weeks other than school," Ethan said, then rolled his eyes. I felt sorry for them, except Blake; it seemed like he didn't care, but I wondered what would happen if his mother was home.

"You in, Lana?" Aidan asked.

"What?" I asked.

"This girl has been spacing out the whole day," Miranda said as everyone laughed. I rolled my eyes as I lightly kicked her under the table and earned a glare in return.

"We're going to that new diner that just opened up near the city," Aidan said.

"I heard it's a kind of fifties theme, looks kinda

cool," Carter said.

"We're heading there after school. You in, nerd?" Blake asked.

"Sure, why no—oh wait! I have to help for tomorrow night." I sighed heavily.

"Why?" Ethan asked as he raised his brow.

"Either that, or we all spend the next week in detention," I said as I looked at everyone.

"Oh yeah, and I don't want to fall asleep with you in the room. I'll wake up to the smell of cigarettes and have a penis drawn on my face." Aidan laughed as he took out his phone. We laughed as he showed us a picture of when Blake and I were in detention, and I drew a penis on Mr. George's face.

"I saw him that night at the game—he still hadn't noticed as people around him laughed," Carter said, his blond locks bouncing as he laughed. "You're lucky Mister Bronx noticed and sort of wiped it off his face and he's a cool teacher, otherwise you guys would've gotten into serious trouble."

"But thanks, guys, for getting into trouble with me," I said after we recovered from the laugh. I looked at each of them as they smiled.

"No problem. That was gold, by the way," Marcus said as he high-fived me.

"Yeah, someone recorded it, and the video went viral!" Aidan exclaimed as he scrolled through his phone. We watched the video as we saw Jennifer walk up the stage and "Anaconda" by *Nicki Minaj* played. We laughed as we watched mash-ups of the video—it was hilarious. The video already had eighty thousand views. I looked around at everyone; this was how it was supposed to be. I wouldn't say eighteen hours ago they were on the verge of going to prison. They looked like their typical idiot selves who fooled around but didn't let anyone in too deep.

Chapter Twelve

Lana

Note to self: never get into trouble with Principal West again. Jennifer and Kelly went overboard. I had to sweep, set up, lay tables, decorate, and Jennifer even had a rehearsal for when she'd win the Homecoming queen. Kelly and Jennifer fought as they played with the crown and almost fell off the stage; I wished I'd recorded it. I looked at my watch to see that it was four p.m. I walked out of the school building and got ready for a long walk home.

"Need a ride?" a familiar voice asked behind me. I turned around to see Blake Gunner as he leaned against his motorcycle. He had a cigarette between his lips as he stared at me. "Admiring my beauty?" Blake smirked as I walked closer. I rolled my eyes as I watched him get on the bike; he scooted to the front to make room for me to sit.

"Aren't you supposed to be at the diner with everyone else?" I asked. He didn't start the motorcycle yet; instead, he put his hands on his lap. He threw the cigarette to the ground and crushed it.

"I thought I'd wait for you," Blake mumbled as he put the key in the ignition.

"So you waited for a whole hour? What if they're already gone?" I yelled as he started the engine. He ignored me, and I locked my arms around his waist as the bike sped off.

Ten minutes later, we arrived at the diner. Blake got off the motorcycle and motioned me to stay where I was. I didn't know what he was up to, so I stayed seated. Five minutes later, he came out of the diner with a brown bag. I assumed it was takeout since the bag had the diner's name and logo on it. He also had two drinks in his other hand. I got off his motorcycle and set the helmet on the seat.

"What's this?" I blurted out.

"We're going to have a little picnic." Blake grinned as he walked past me.

"In the fall?" I asked as I caught up to him. The trees were already a lovely shade of red and brown, and some leaves were on the ground. "Where?" I asked. He didn't say anything as he looked straight. I followed his gaze to the park; it was one of those parks where it's built for everyone. It had a playground, skate ramp, picnic area, and a pond. It was my favorite park to come to as a kid, and since there's a diner in place now opposite the park, it would always be busy. We walked for another five minutes until Blake stopped under a big tree. It was in the middle of the park and not too far from the playground. Thankfully, the grass was soft as we sat down. He reached inside the large bag, and out came two burgers along with a box of fries. "You didn't have to," I explained as he set out the burgers. He took the burger paper and put it on the grass and used it as a plate. Blake placed our burgers on the papers and the box of fries in the middle.

"I figured you'd be hungry. You barely ate lunch." He smiled, then held up two cups with straws. "Chocolate or strawberry?"

"Strawberry." I grinned as he handed me the strawberry milkshake.

"Okay, Gunner, tell me about yourself," I blurted out as I took a fry. Besides the fact that he had a mother and an older brother, I barely knew him.

"Okay, I'm eighteen years old, I have brown hair, brown eyes, a lot of tattoo—"

"I know all of that! I mean, like what your favorite movie is? Or hobbies? Favorite band?"

"What about you, Willson? I barely know you, yet you're here eating burgers with a guy you barely know."

"Fine, my favorite movie is *Mad Max*. My hobbies are reading, swimming, painting, doing math for fun, and my favorite band is *My Chemical Romance*," I stated, then took a bite out of my chicken burger.

"You do realize *My Chemical Rom—*"

"Don't! Speak of it!" I raised my finger as I glared at him. He threw his head back and laughed, then sipped his milkshake.

"Wow, I've never met a person who enjoys math."

"Well, since I have Mr. Bronx, he makes it fun."

"How old is he? He looks twenty-two."

"He's thirty-eight, you idiot!"

"*The Breakfast Club*, listening to music, pool table, and *The Killers*," he said after a while.

"What?" I looked at him in confusion as he smiled.

"You wanted to know more about me, so now you know," he said, then traced the tattoos on his arms.

"How do you know the guys?"

"Aidan's my cousin."

"He's your…cousin?" I breathed out as my eyes widened.

"Yeah, we grew up here, but I moved," he stated. My urge to laugh soon disappeared, as it was a chance to find out more about him.

"Why did you come back?" I asked as I looked at him. Blake got up and threw the rubbish in the trashcan.

"My dad passed away a few years back; we couldn't afford to live in Minnesota anymore, so we moved back here. Aidan is my first cousin since his mom and my dad were siblings. My dad's will helped us, but only for a while, because one day all that money just…disappeared. So we moved back here and started again. My mom works for this company, and Axel is wasting his life," Blake mumbled. We walked in silence then sat down on swings. I twirled my milkshake in my hand, then turned to him.

"I'm sorry for whatever happened to your dad."

"It's all right, Willson. It isn't your fault."

"Yeah, but I'm sorry that you're sad and that

he's gone," I whispered. I'd experienced death in my family, but none of them were close to me.

"I miss him. I miss him so fucking much, Lana," Blake croaked as he shut his eyes. I got off my swing and stood in front of him. I noticed he tried not to look affected by it as it'd ruin his whole façade. Blake looked up at me, and I saw how his eyes darkened. I crouched down on my knees to face him. Blake must not cry; I couldn't handle people who cried. It made me want to cry too, plus I'd never imagined him crying in front of me.

"Hey, there's a reason why things happen, Blake. I'm sure he was a very nice man, but remember he's always with you in here," I said, then pointed to his heart. I stared into his eyes. They might look dull and boring, but they were filled with loss and emptiness. He blinked a few times to get the feeling away, and a blank expression filled his face.

"Thanks, Willson." A forced smile appeared on his lips as he stared at me.

"Why do you stare at me?" I asked as I returned to my seat.

"You're beautiful, Lana. How can anyone not get hypnotized by your beauty?" he asked. My cheeks flushed as I sheepishly looked away.

"Whatever, Gunner," I muttered, then stood up. I threw my cup in the trash can, and so did Blake. As we walked back to his motorcycle, he lit a cigarette, and we shared it.

"How do you know how to smoke?" he asked. I knew that question was bound to come up sooner or later.

"I watch a lot of movies, I guess." I shrugged. I

wasn't ready to tell him why, because that'd lead to many other questions, even though the guy almost cried in front of me. I took one last drag of the cigarette and threw it on the ground. I crushed it with my foot then followed him.

The whole drive home I thought about what he had told me. I was surprised Blake and Aidan were cousins and even more surprised that Blake almost cried in front of me. He must've really loved his father if that topic made him sensitive. We arrived at my house, and Blake helped me off his motorcycle.

"So I'll see you tomorrow?" he casually asked as we walked up to my porch. Dad wasn't here, so it was safe for Blake to at least walk me to the door.

"Yeah, I guess," I mumbled as I stuffed my hands in my jacket. Blake did the same, but he shoved his hands in his jeans. We stood at my door and waited for one another to speak. I looked up to see him stare, but this time I felt comfortable as I stared back at him. It must've been a while as I stared into his chocolate brown eyes, because I didn't notice my mother by the doorstep.

"Evening, Mrs. Willson." Blake turned to her.

"Hi, Blake. Returning my daughter in one piece?" she asked with a stern look on her face. I let out a sigh as I bit the inside of my cheek.

"Yes, ma'am," he said, then turned to me. "I'll see you tomorrow, Lana. Have a good night, Mrs. Willson."

We watched him get on his motorcycle and put on the helmet; the engine made that loud noise that could wake up the whole neighborhood. I watched him speed down the street until he was a tiny figure.

"Tattoos, huh?" Mom wiggled her brows as we stepped inside.

"Ugh, Mom!"

"I'm not against it! He looks fierce and brave in tattoos; I'm just confused, dear. You said that you have that blond boy, Carter," Mom said as we entered the kitchen. I opened the fridge and took out a can of soda.

"I don't 'have' anyone, Mom. They're friends. Plus, Carter is my date to Homecoming."

"Oh no, dear, Blake isn't a friend. You two had matching outfits! And the way you two looked at each other—inseparable," Mom cheered as she came next to me. She shoved her phone in my face like a teenager who showed her friend that her boyfriend cheated on her. I glanced at the picture and saw Blake and me walk up the porch steps. I watched in amusement as she swiped to the next image. That one was worse because it was moments ago when Blake and I stared at each other.

"Really, Mom?"

"Lana, sweetie, all I can say is you'll be breaking and fixing hearts before you graduate!"

I rolled my eyes as I walked upstairs and into my bedroom. I didn't have time to clean up yesterday because I was too tired, so my room looked like a mess. I collapsed on my bed and groaned. Tomorrow was Homecoming, and the bet would come to an end soon. I wondered what would happen after that if I lost...there's a chance we'd still be friends since I'd be their puppet the rest of senior year. If I won, we'd be friends since they'd protect me from Benny and Kelly. My thoughts got interrupted when I felt something under my pillow. I grabbed it and pulled it out, only to reveal a pack of cigarettes. Not any pack of cigarettes, Blake's pack of cigarettes. I'd become so addicted lately that I couldn't help myself last night when Blake kissed me. My hands went behind his back and pulled out the box; thankfully, the guys always kept two packs of cigarettes because they shared with me. He didn't ask any questions or notice that his pack was gone. My dad confiscated all their cigarettes, and he probably went to buy new ones this morning. I couldn't help myself; I knew if my parents found it, they'd blame the guys and I'd be homeschooled for the rest of senior year. I immediately got up and searched my room for the perfect place to put it. I went to my desk and shoved it between my workbooks; Mom knew not to touch them because I liked them in order and neatly placed on my desk. Afterward, I took my books and put them into one of my drawers.

That night we had dinner together, but it still felt a bit awkward as Dad glanced at me. Mom talked about the Radcliffs coming for Christmas, which only made things more awkward.

***

We didn't do much work because people talked about the upcoming dance tonight so much that the teachers gave up. I barely talked to the guys today except for Carter, who was incredibly excited and couldn't wait to see me tonight. Blake, on the other hand, was distant.

"Come on, Lana! My dress is already in the car," Miranda exclaimed as she dragged me out of the school building. My best friend was extremely excited for Homecoming, yet I couldn't wait for it to be over. Miranda forced me into the car as she got into the driver's seat. I looked behind to see her Homecoming dress, makeup kit, and heels. Marcus and Carter would pick us up from my house, so we decided to get ready there. I suggested Miranda's house, but she said her mother wasn't in a good state, so it wasn't a good idea to go there. I didn't question it since I knew her mother drank. For the next two hours, we got ready. I sat in front of the mirror while Miranda did my hair. She was ready; all she had to do was put on her makeup. She looked beautiful with or without makeup, and Marcus was a lucky guy.

"Okay, since your dress is a closed neck and opens in the back, I'll try this," she said. I felt my hair being pulled, combed, dried, and even curled. "Okay, here's the result." She picked up the mirror and held it behind me so I could see what she had done to my dead hair. I wasn't even sure it was my hair; it looked so elegant and cute. It was a little bun made into a French plait, a few strands of hair stood out, but it seemed right. I stood up, being ever so careful with my dress. I stood in front of my full-length mirror and gasped. Even though we went shopping for the dress before they announced the theme, I felt a bit too formal for a Starlight Fairytale. Yet Miranda said Carter and I would stand out.

"Wow, Miranda, thank you," I exclaimed as she stood next to me. My sleeveless light pink dress hugged my chest, a floral belt around my waist as it flowed from there. It was long and elegant yet matched my hairstyle perfectly. Miranda stood beside me in her silver dress. She looked like a princess with her blonde hair curled. Her dress was also long, but hers was a long sleeve that outlined her body well.

"Aww, you look beautiful," Mother cooed as she came into the room. Miranda and I smiled at each other as Mom sat on my bed. Miranda finished her makeup while I put on my shoes. Miranda said I should wear heels, so I did…nothing fancy, just a pair of silver heels. We heard the doorbell ring, and I immediately got nervous. I turned to my mother, who smiled as she walked downstairs. I looked back at Miranda, who stuffed things into her purse; I didn't want a bag tonight, so I gave her my phone to keep. She slipped on her red heels, and with a last look in the mirror, we strolled downstairs. Miranda walked down the stairs first, and all eyes were on her as she walked down. I saw Carter, then Marcus, who stood nervously and commented on her. I slowly walked down as I gripped the rail. I wasn't used to heels, so I raised my dress and walked down. Once I was downstairs, I greeted Marcus, who had his arm around Miranda; he wore a black tuxedo and a bow tie, his brown hair styled. He grinned. I glanced over to my date, Carter Halls, and he looked gorgeous. He wore a blue jacket, black bowtie, white shirt, black trousers, and shoes. The blue coat blended into his eyes as an illusion of never-ending waves.

"You look beautiful, Lana," he breathed out as he held my hand.

"Thanks, you too." I grinned as he rubbed circles on my hand.

"Pictures, you lovebirds!" Mom cheered as she brought out her phone. I blushed as I stood next to Miranda. After a group photo, my mother took one of Carter and me, then of Marcus and Miranda.

"Okay, Mom, let's go," I urged, then took Carter by the hand.

We arrived at the school gym and saw couples go in. The place looked amazing, a real fairy-tale theme. The entrance door was decorated as an entrance you'd go to when entering a castle. Girls dressed as Sleeping Beauty, Cinderella, and Snow White surrounded the place. I was glad we didn't come as a Disney couple; we stood out. We entered the gym, and it was packed with people.

"I'll get us some drinks," Carter said over the loud music.

"I'll come with you," Marcus said.

"Isn't this place amazing?" Miranda exclaimed as she squeezed my hands. The stage had two large chairs to make it look like thrones for the Homecoming king and queen; it seemed like a *Frozen* theme with its blue lights and white decorations.

"It's beautiful," I mumbled. I felt a tap on my shoulder and spun around to see Aidan. He wore a full black suit and had a smirk on his face.

"Hey, Lana, you're looking lovely tonight."

"Thanks, Aidan, you look good too. Love the

black."

"Thanks. So where's Halls? He's not a very good date, so I suggest—"

"Beat it, Aidan. She's mine," a deep voice grunted beside us. I glanced up to see Carter as he held two cups. "Where's your date? She finally realized how ugly you are and ran away?" Carter asked as he put an arm around my waist.

"Hilarious. She's right over there," Aidan said, then pointed across the gym where a girl and guy spoke.

"Your date is Tiffany? Isn't that her overprotective twin brother, Tommy?" I asked. It looked like Tiffany and Tommy were arguing.

"Yeah, but I've known Tommy since fourth grade. He trusts me with his sister." Aidan waved off as Tiffany walked toward us. She wore an elegant white ball gown, her red hair curled and bouncing as she walked.

"Hey, Aidan, Carter, and…whoa, Lana, you look beautiful," Tiffany said in her southern accent.

"Thanks, Tiffany, you look gorgeous as well."

"Wanna get something to eat? I heard people are scooping up the shrimp!" Tiffany motioned to a bunch of jocks devouring the food table.

"Let's go!" Aidan cheered as he locked arms with Tiffany.

"Would you like to dance, Miss Willson?" Carter asked in a failed British accent.

"Why, of course, Mr. Halls." I smiled as I put my hand out. He chuckled as he took my hand and led me to the dance floor. RnB music played, and we joined Miranda and Marcus. I couldn't dance, but it didn't matter; Carter and Marcus made us laugh by making silly dance moves. I had such a good time that I didn't notice that Miranda stopped. She put her hand on her hip as she looked past me.

"That can't be right," Miranda said as she raised her brow. We followed her gaze, and I bit the inside of my cheek as I looked at the front doors. Jennifer and Kelly entered the building, accompanied by their dates, Ethan and Blake.

***

Blake

"Let the night begin," Ethan mumbled as we got out of the limo. I locked arms with Kelly West as we entered the building. She looked pretty with her midnight dress and black heels. Her hair bothered me, as it was styled to stand out, literally, because as I stood next to her, it fanned my face. Ethan's with Jennifer Brighton; she wore a pastel yellow dress with her brunette hair curled. She looked like Belle, and Ethan was the Beast. Kelly got me a suit and said it was a designer label. It looked the same as my other suit, but I didn't care; it was a simple black suit, white shirt, and bow tie. My hair was styled into a quaff as always, but Kelly sprayed it because she said my hair tended to get messy. The moment we entered the gym, all eyes were on us; Melissa and Nick came over and chatted. Melissa, Kelly, and Jennifer talked about their outfits, while Ethan and Nick spoke sports. I glanced around the room at the many teenagers; it'd be a good night if

Kelly wouldn't annoy me. My smile dropped as I saw Lana. She danced with Carter, and they laughed at something Aidan said. Lana looked beautiful in her pink dress, her hair bouncing as she danced. She looked breathtaking as she laughed. I wish I danced with them; I wanted to dance with her.

"Blake!" Kelly exclaimed as she snapped her fingers. I turned to her as my lips drew in a straight line. "Let's dance." She smiled as she grabbed my hand and led me to the dance floor. I tried my best to dance a fair distance away from Lana, but Kelly moved closer to them. I bumped shoulders with Aidan, and he turned to me with a grin.

"Hey, dude."

"'Sup?"

"So how's the lady keeping you?" Aidan asked as he winked at me. I glanced at Kelly, who stared at us; I was about to answer Aidan when Kelly spoke.

"Hi, Carter." She smirked and looked past me. I followed her gaze to see that Carter and Lana held hands.

"Hey, Kelly," he mumbled as he glanced at me. Carter let go of Lana's hand as we hugged. I was about to greet Lana but noticed she was gone when I pulled away from Carter. I frantically looked around the dance floor only to see her leave with Aidan. I looked back at Carter, who had an awkward conversation with Kelly. I rolled my eyes because I didn't care about my date; I had to do it. I walked off the dance floor and searched for Lana. I saw Miranda and Marcus with people; hopefully, she knew where Lana was.

"Miranda, hey, you look pretty tonight," I said as I glanced at her dress. She smiled at me.

"Thanks, Blake, you look quite handsome too!" she said, then poked my side. I raised a brow as I looked at her; only then I noticed the cup in her hand. A weird smell came from it, and I shook my head.

"Someone spiked the punch?" I grinned as she took a sip. Marcus came beside her and swung his arm around her shoulder.

"Yeah, dude, all thanks to Benny." Marcus cheered as he shoved his cup in my face. Clearly, since they're drunk, thanks to Benny Nielson, they wouldn't know where Lana was. I scanned the gym for a brunette with a pink dress until I found her with Ethan. My fists clenched as I walked to them; they were at the food table, feeding each other like a happy couple. It disgusted me as the jock played with the nerd, my nerd.

"Hey, guys."

"Hi, Blake. You cleaned up nicely," Lana said as she gave me a once-over.

"Thanks, you look beautiful in that dress."

"Thank you."

"Aren't you guys supposed to be with your dates?" a familiar blonde asked as he popped out of nowhere. Ethan and I groaned in unison as we watched Kelly and Jennifer approach. Carter wrapped his arm around Lana's waist and whispered something. She giggled.

"Hide me," Ethan mumbled as he raised the tablecloth. We laughed as Ethan attempted to duck under the table.

"Blake, come on. Let's go in the photo booth!" Kelly whined as she gripped my arm.

"Do we have to go now? There's a long line," I said as we looked at Aidan, who got in with his redhead date.

"Yeah, but we're popular, so they'll let us pass," Jennifer said as she grabbed Ethan's arm. As our dates dragged us to the photo booth, I got one last glance at Lana and Carter, who laughed.

After a half an hour of pictures in the photo booth with Kelly, Jennifer, Ethan, Aidan, Benny, Nick, Melissa, and Liam—the photo booth almost fell over with all the people inside it—Kelly said she had to go to the bathroom. I was glad because I could finally speak to Lana. She sat with Miranda as they talked; I took this as my chance and walked toward her.

"Hey, would you like to dance?" I asked as I approached her. She looked up at me, confused at first, but then her lips turned up into a warm smile.

"Sure."

"Let It Go" by *James Bay* played. Everyone seemed to get the idea as we walked to the dance floor. Guys got their dates while I was with Lana. Our partners were nowhere to be seen. I gently placed my hands on her hips as she put her hands around my neck. We moved in sync with the music; I looked at Lana to see her eyes were closed. I couldn't believe she managed to forgive us, even though she knew we were dangerous. Lana knew she'd get caught by her dad if she didn't go that day, but she did. Yet she came back and helped us; all my worries were gone, everything that went on seemed to vanish when I was with Lana. I thought when I sent her on my motorcycle that she wouldn't come back and that she'd never speak to us, but she did, and she took a significant risk for us. I'd learned a few things from Lana, and that's to never judge a book by its cover and always give people a chance even though they didn't seem to deserve it. There's still a second chance. Yesterday's conversation seemed to be on my mind a lot; I never shared my dad's death with anyone except the guys. I almost cried in front of her; I never cried in front of anyone except at my dad's funeral. Fuck, she got to me. Even though I only knew Lana for two weeks, it seems like we've known each other for years. Lana glanced up. The dress she wore brought out the color of her eyes. We stared at each other for what felt like an eternity until she placed her head on my chest, and I rested my chin on her head. I wrapped my arms around her as the song played. The song ended, and I felt emptiness as she pulled away. Lana smiled at me as she walked off the dance floor. She spoke to Carter as she rubbed her arms furiously. He took off his blue jacket and put it on her. Another party song came on. I was thirsty, so I walked off the dance floor over to the food table. I got myself a drink and went to stand by the guys. Aidan talked, and Carter and Ethan laughed.

"So when is it finished?" Parker asked, who I've conversed with before.

"Well, she has Friday, Saturday, and Sunday, which I doubt she'll handle, because we're taking her out, right, guys?" Ethan asked as he looked at us. I looked at him in confusion as Carter mouthed

Lana's name.

"Sure."

"Man, you guys are lucky you get to use her like that," Austin said. "You show up late to class, and you have Willson covering your ass. Mind if we tag along?"

"I don't know how she does it, coming up with excuses like that every time. It's gold!" Carter laughed.

"And Gunner, congrats on getting her wrapped around your finger. The bad boy and the sheriff's daughter," Parker said as he sent me a wink.

"Whatever, dude. After we win the bet, and she breaks, she'll just be another one." I shrugged. I didn't want them to bother me with Lana; Aidan already knew how I felt about her. The guys laughed as they looked at the four of us.

"So which one of you got hold of the sheriff's handcuffs?" Austin smirked.

"None, even though I was so close. Her dad was downstairs, and she has thin walls." Carter smirked as he looked at me. I rolled my eyes as I remembered that night; I was so pissed at Carter when he sent us a picture of Lana in the shower.

"But man, underneath those glasses, she's hot as fuck," Parker said as he bit his lip. The guys nodded in agreement as I watched them with my jaw clenched. From the corner of my eye, I noticed Aidan lowered his head.

"Blake, have you seen Lana?" a familiar voice asked. I looked to my side and saw Miranda with an anxious look on her face.

"No, we haven't. Why?" Ethan asked.

"I need to give her phone back. It's been going off like crazy!" she exclaimed as she held Lana's phone in her hand.

"Last I saw her was when you two were dancing," Aidan said as he pointed to me. Parker and Austin had left, and it's just us five.

"Miranda, come on!" Marcus yelled over the loud music; he dragged her away and left us. By their lopsided movements, they must've been drunk already.

"Yo, what's up with Willson?" Nick asked as he made his way over to us.

"Why? What happened?"

"She ran out of the gym covering her face," he said. As soon as those words fell from his mouth, we walked out of the gym.

"Ladies and gentlemen, it's time to announce the Homecoming king and queen!"

We heard strange noises from outside, and I seemed to get annoyed as we walked out of the building to rain pouring down on us. Principal West moved Homecoming a day earlier because of the rain, but it rained anyway.

"There!" Ethan yelled as he pointed. I followed his gaze to see a tiny figure in the distance. No doubt it was her. We ran into the open parking lot where we saw Lana, her back to us as she held onto Carter's jacket.

"Lana, what the hell are you doing out here?"

"You're going to get sick!"

Lana Willson turned around, and even though it rained and she was soaked, I saw her face. She was crying.

"Y-you guys were using me?" Lana croaked out as she looked at us. Right then and there, we stopped to look at her. I glanced down and felt guilt take over me; she must've heard our conversation with Austin and Parker. "*Answer me!*" Lana shouted as she looked at us. Aidan stepped forward as he held out his arms, but she backed away. "Don't touch me!"

"Lana, just let us explain," Ethan mumbled as he looked at her.

"Explain what? How you guys have been using me to get away with things? When I loaned you guys my homework, I thought that's what friends do, and when I covered for you when we were late, I figured it was out of kindness, but no, you filthy bastards were using me!" she yelled with a pained look in her eyes. "Oh my God, what if you guys were just using me to get away with the drugs because you knew I would be gullible enough to come back?" Lana mumbled as she covered her mouth.

"Lana, I know you're scared right—"

"*I am not fucking scared, Blake!*" She cut me off, and we stared at each other. Her mouth moved, but no words came out.

"Lana, come on, we—"

"No, leave me alone. You've all put me through so much hell the past few weeks. Just leave me the fuck alone!" she shouted as she turned around to walk.

"Willson, you can't walk in this weather!" I yelled over the rain. Lana stopped; her back faced us as she slowly spun around. A sigh of relief went through me as she walked back. At least we could take her home and explain to her. As Lana walked, she ripped off Carter's jacket, eyed him the whole time, then shoved his coat in his chest.

"I fucking hate you!" She pointed to each of us as she yelled. Lana spun around and walked away, but none of us went after her.

Chapter Thirteen

Everyone stood where they were as they watched Lana storm off. The rain dripped and clung to their wet suits. They tried to process what had happened. Part of it was correct—they did use Lana in a way to get what they wanted.

"Fuck!" Ethan screamed as he ran his hand through his damp hair.

"What are we going to do now? Lana's running around not knowing where to go in a fucking dress, and it's our fault!" Aidan yelled as they walked closer to each other. Suddenly, Carter, Ethan, and Aidan turned to Blake.

"I don't fucking know! Are your cars still here?" Blake asked as he looked at Ethan and Aidan. They'd left their cars and got a ride with Marcus. They'd become friends with him, so they went out to the diner after school and left their vehicles at school.

"Yeah."

"Okay, Ethan, you go and drive around her neighborhood. Aidan, take Carter, and you guys

194

drive around town, and I'll grab my motorcycle and look around here," Blake ordered.

"Call us when you find her!" Carter shouted as they ran to Aidan's car. Blake and Ethan gave the nod, and they went their separate ways.

***

Lana

Lana cried while she attempted to run in heels. She finally gave up and ripped them off her feet. She didn't know where she'd go, but anywhere was better than the school. She was upset that they used her in the hope that one of them would get to sleep with her in the end. Lana thought they were friends. The part that hurt her the most was that Blake danced with her a while ago, and now she ran away from him. While she danced with him, she thought of the connection they had. They didn't talk much, but when they did, they talked about anything and everything. How they listened to each other with interest and comforted each other. It all ran through Lana's head as she walked with her heels in her hand. While Lana shouted at them, she looked at Blake; she couldn't believe she fell in his trap. Literally and figuratively, she fell for him. Hard. But she didn't know what to think. Tears streamed down her face as she ran near a couple of buildings; she went into an alley for cover from the rain, but she knew she wasn't alone.

***

Ethan

Ethan drove around her neighborhood. He must've driven around ten times already with his headlights bright. He couldn't believe what he'd done. Ethan knew something would happen when Blake asked about Lana, how he watched her every day as girls threw themselves at the guys while she sat back and laughed. Ethan made it worse when he offered a ride to Lana; he wanted to be nice to make up for hitting Miranda with a ball, and he knew she was Lana's ride home. Then the next day when Blake asked to bring Lana to him, Ethan saw it coming. He tried to protect her in a way, not wanting Blake to use her. She was kind and beautiful; girls like that you didn't use then throw them aside. You kept them, were friends with them, gained their trust, and watched them open up to you. Ethan wished he could've taken back all the times he teased and bullied her; he only did it because he was influenced by Benny. All Ethan ever wanted was to be friends with her. He'd known her since second grade, and he still remembered when they spoke about what they wanted to be when they grew up.

"Ethan, what do you want to be when you grow up?" Ms. King asked as they sat in a circle. Ethan shyly sat next to Lana.

"I want to play football!" he cheered as he waved his hands. Everyone laughed at what he said.

Seven-year-old Ethan frowned but felt a hand on his shoulder.

"You can be anything you want, Ethan. You just gotta believe in yourself," Lana said with a bright smile. Her big glasses covered her face but still managed to bring out her big blue eyes.

"Thank you, Lana. You're a real friend." Ethan smiled with his chubby cheeks.

He remembered that day and what she had said. Now look at him. He's team captain and played toward a scholarship, and everyone liked him. All thanks to Lana, who encouraged him. He drove around her neighborhood once more. Every time he passed a house, his nerves shot up. The rain got worse, it was close to winter, and she could be anywhere in Illinois. Ethan drove faster, and since he drove a sports car, he had to put it to its actual use. The way the car drove swiftly down the streets, his eyes flickered left and right as he searched for Lana. The feeling of going fast got interrupted when he saw the familiar blue and red lights flash behind him. Ethan cursed as he stopped the car. The vehicle behind him came to a stop too as the woman got out of her car.

***

Carter and Aidan

Carter and Aidan drove in silence for the first five minutes. They drove everywhere in search of the girl in the pink dress. They grew impatient as they drove on. Carter decided to open the window as far as it'd go.

"What are you doing?" Aidan yelled as Carter stuck his head out the window.

"Looking for my Homecoming date...properly!" he shouted as he leaned out the window. "Lana!" Carter yelled as they slowly drove down the streets. He didn't care that he was soaked; he took off his jacket and threw it in the backseat of Aidan's car. Carter thought back to when they fought in class and corrected the teacher.

"And if you see here in the textbook, it says William Shakespeare was born in April 1564 in Stratford and died in May 1616," Mr. Goodman, *their tenth-grade teacher, said as he read from the textbook. "Yes, Miss Willson?" Mr. Goodman asked Lana, who had her hand up. He glanced at Carter, who stared at Lana too. Mr. Goodman knew what would come.*

"Actually, sir, William Shakespeare died Apr—"

"April 23rd, 1616, sir," Carter cut Lana off. She glared at him while he smirked at her.

"Thank you, Mr. Halls and Miss Willson..." Mr. Goodman sighed.

Aidan was lost in his thoughts as he glanced at Carter, who hung out the window as he shouted. He remembered when he used to play pranks on Lana with Parker and Austin.

"She's coming!" Parker said as he rushed in the hall. "Good...everyone make way, make way!"

Aidan shouted as Austin set up.

"You guys are going to be in deep shit." Ethan laughed as he watched Aidan, Parker, and Austin remove their clothes.

"Here she comes!" Austin grinned as he stood beside Aidan. Lana entered the hallway to see a big slip and slide run through the corridor; her eyes widened as Aidan and Austin took her by the hands.

"What are you guys—" She cut off when Parker ran and slid down the hall as students poured buckets of water to make it slippery.

"Come on, Willson!" Aidan said as the three of them stood in front of the slip and slide. Austin shoved her down to the ground and pushed her. She noticed Aidan held her hand the whole time.

"Aidan, I'm going to kill you!"

Aidan smiled at the memory along with the rest of the pranks. "Where are you, Lana Willson?"

***

Lana

"What's a pretty thing like you doing on this side of town?" a deep voice asked. Lana turned her head toward the deep voice. It was a man, more like a perverted homeless guy. He had a ginger beard and a long nose and wore an old beanie and a big sweater. Lana realized she was in an industrial area. Even though all the buildings were locked up for the night, there were still creeps that lurked around trying to find shelter.

"I...I..." Lana mumbled as she swallowed the lump in her throat. The guy stepped closer, which only made her nervous. "Please, I..." she stuttered as the man stood right in her face. Her back hit the wall as the man breathed on her neck. He took his hand and gently stroked her cheek. She used all her energy and pushed him off her, but he was fast and gripped her arm. "You're hurting me," she said as she tried to pull away. Lana didn't need this; she was angry and devastated that her friends used her, and she didn't need the man to cause trouble.

"Oh, baby, I didn't get to that part yet," the guy whispered in her ear. She took the chance and slapped him. He shoved her, which made her land into a puddle; her dress was ruined. "You bitch!" he yelled as he came closer to her. She quickly got up and picked up her stiletto heel. She didn't know where the other one was. Her dad had taught her self-defense. Lana hit the man with her heel; the end was sharp as she repeatedly moved her arm. Her grip tightened as she thought about the past two weeks. Everything came out as she used all her energy on him. "You're hurting me!" he shouted as he tried to take the heel from her hand.

"That's the whole point, you asshole!" Lana shouted as she shut her eyes. She hit the guy repeatedly as she held his one arm; the other arm he used for cover but failed. Lana heard a scream and a weird sound. Her eyes shot open, and she wished didn't open them. The guy had blood sprout out from his head; she didn't realize she hit him that hard. She looked down to see blood all over her wet, soggy dress. Her hands were covered in blood

200

too as she looked at the shoe.

"I'm gonna—" the guy shouted, but Lana picked up her dress and ran off with the heel in her hand. Tears streamed down her face as she ran. Lana couldn't believe she stabbed the guy. It was their fault, she thought as she ran. She felt blisters on her feet, which made it worse. After ten minutes, she stopped to catch her breath. A car stopped beside her, and the driver stared at her in horror as she did the same. Lana collapsed to the ground as her legs buckled; she knew her body would be sore tomorrow. She felt two arms scoop her up. She was carried to the car and placed in the passenger seat. The heel was still in her hand as she observed it; it had blood all over it. She glanced down at her dress to see it was ripped, wet, and crumpled.

"What happened to you?" Benny asked as he looked at her. He didn't start the car, so Lana knew she had to tell him. She saw him at Homecoming. He still wore his suit, but she couldn't wrap her head around as to why he was here.

"Nothing," Lana mumbled as she looked anywhere but at the boy who bullied her yet saved her.

"Bullshit, Lana. You have blood everywhere. What the fuck happened?" Benny asked as he reached for her hand to comfort her. Lana pulled away, and Benny awkwardly did the same.

"I was defending myself," Lana whispered as she referred to the chipped heel. "Please, Benny, take me home." She trembled. He nodded and started the engine. They drove in silence, clouded in their thoughts.

***

Blake

Blake didn't move; he was still at school. He sat on his motorcycle as he smoked a cigarette. So many thoughts ran through his mind. He wanted to look for her, but he didn't know where to look. Even if he did find her, what would he tell her? He knew she'd find out somehow, but he didn't want her to find out and run off. Especially when she wore a stunning dress and big heels. He thought of how he danced with her an hour ago, how everything was perfect and no worries seemed to linger in the air. It was weird that one moment everything would be perfect, next moment everything crumbled. Lana seemed to brighten up his life in a way. He always had girls throwing themselves at him, but she seemed to sit back and watch. He couldn't take his eyes off her, especially in P.E. She was a nerd, but she was better than half the class, the way she was so focused and determined. Blake went home every day and thought about Lana, how she managed to pull off an innocent look, yet she was anything but innocent. He knew that she needed a push and a little encouragement to show who she really was. Blake wouldn't rest until he figured her out. How she smoked so well, was a good liar, a good athlete, and the one that seemed to bother him the most—that she wasn't a virgin. He asked the guys, but they didn't know, and it was a shock to them too. Blake's mind traveled to when she was drunk. How innocent and clumsy she was. He was surprised when she asked to sleep with him; if she were sobered, then she'd care, but she didn't. He remembered the talks they had, how close their bodies were. She still had her outfit on, which turned Blake on even more. He adored when she got nervous, and her glasses fell to her nose, how her cheeks turned red when she blushed, her sassiness but also her kind-heartedness. The kiss they shared that night of the drugs, how she gladly kissed him back. All the things that happened the past two weeks made Blake realize that he'd fallen in love.

Chapter Fourteen

Lana

"Thank you," I mumbled as we approached my house. I looked at my home as I thought what lie I'd tell my parents, because they'd obviously have questions as to why I looked like I'd got hit five times then forced to run into the woods.

"No problem. So are you going to tell me what happened?" Benny asked as the car came to a stop. I looked at the guy who tortured me for the past eight years. I had so many questions to ask him, but it was already late.

"Not today, Benny." I sighed as I gripped the door handle.

"Okay, well, good night, and I'm not letting this go, Lana."

"Good night," I said. I got out and shut the door. I didn't look back as I walked up the porch. I gripped the heel in one hand and picked up my dress with the other. I glanced back to see Benny was still there. The windows were tinted, but I knew he looked at me. I opened the front door as quietly as I could and walked inside. As I closed the door, I heard footsteps. I cursed as I turned around.

"Lana, dear, how was your—" my mother said as she walked closer to me. "Baby, what happened to you? You look horrible!"

"Just some prank one of the guys pulled."

"But your dress is ruined and your shoe—"

"Mom, I'm tired. Can we deal with this tomorrow?"

"Lana, you look like you've just been dragged through woods and stomped on by giants, not attending a school dance."

"I fell, Mom," I lied, even though the tilt of her head and pout told me she wanted more than that. "I broke my heels and scraped my knee. When I tried to regain myself, I just made it worse by getting the blood on my dress."

"Where did you fall? Where was Carter or Miranda? Do you want me to take a look at it?"

"I'm fine, Mom," I mumbled and grabbed the railing, pushing myself up the stairs before she could get to me. "It's not that bad, so I can manage."

Once I got to the top, I ran to my room, then shut the door. I wanted to scream and pull my hair out. We started to become comfortable with each other after the drug situation, but it felt like a truck had hit me. I slouched down and brought my knees to my chest, then looked at the heel. It wasn't even silver anymore; the end of the heel was chipped with blood on it; the rest of the shoe was blood red. I couldn't believe that I had done that…I still remembered his face clearly when I stabbed him. It looked like someone shot him in the forehead and the blood oozed down his face, but no, I stabbed the guy.

All because of them, everything was a lie. From the start, I knew something was fishy. Suddenly, they dragged me to the end of the school to make a bet with me—why me? Couldn't they choose Kelly or Melissa? Not now, in senior year, when it's the most crucial year of my life. I should focus on school and college.

I glanced up to see the poster on my wall; it was the Red Hot Chili Peppers. I still remembered Blake bought that for me since I was a big fan. At the corners of the poster, I saw an outline of something. I got up and walked closer to it. I remembered when he gave it to me, that I didn't have anywhere to put it, so I put it on another poster. It was a quote that I put up before senior year started; it was one of my favorite quotes. I slowly pulled off the Red Hot Chili Peppers poster and read the quote that I lived by for the past ten years.

I observed my room; it looked horrible. I always had everything in place, but it currently looked like a nuclear bomb exploded in my room. Makeup on the table, shoes out of the closet, books everywhere, clothes sprawled on my bed. I walked to my clipboard that hung above my desk. It had a few knickknacks, but what really caught my eye was the picture of Carter, Aidan, Blake, Mr. George, and I when we were in detention. Carter and I pulled funny faces, and Aidan grinned while he looked at Mr. George, who had the penis drawn on his face.

Blake smiled with the cigarette between his teeth, but his gaze was on me. I shook my head and turned the picture around, so it didn't face me.

I cleaned up my room while I thought where to put the heel. I couldn't throw it in the trash because Dad emptied it out every Friday, so I had to find a way to get rid of it or at least clean it.

I sat on my made-up bed as I stared at the quote again. It made me realize something: I didn't need a bunch of guys to define who I was. I was Lana Willson, and I wanted to be a nerd. They couldn't change that because I was supposed to be one, and I'd always be one no matter what happened because I grew up as one, and I chose to be one. I didn't want to enter that part of my life again—even though I knew the bad was stronger than the good. That the good wasn't good; they're damaged. I didn't need a bunch of teenage boys to change me or tell me what to do and what not to do, because when I graduate, I'd never see them again. I should focus on college and my future. None of this would matter in a couple of months. It'd be another chapter of my life ending.

I walked to my drawer, opened it, and rummaged through my stuff until I found the case to my old pair of glasses. With everything that happened, I still hadn't gone to the optometrist, the one Ethan suggested. How ironic, the paper sat right on my desk and stared back at me. I picked up my glasses and slowly put them on, then walked to the mirror. My pink dress looked like vomit, my hair went in all directions, my bloody hands were cold, and my face looked like I hadn't slept in days.

"This is me."

***

"Lana dear."

"Ugh."

"Listen, your dad won't be home until late afternoon, and I have to go to the hospital. Will you be okay here alone for the rest of the day?" Mom asked. I turned my head to my door and saw my mother's shadow underneath. I looked at my window and hissed as the sun shone through the curtain.

"Yeah, Mom."

"Okay, dear, see you tonight," my mother said. "By the way, Carter called this morning to check if you're okay."

"Okay," I mumbled as I got up and walked to the bathroom. I yelped as I saw myself in the mirror. My hair stood in all directions because I didn't bother brushing it out last night and the bags under my eyes darkened by the minute. I glanced at the small clock on the sink and noticed it was almost eleven a.m. I walked to my desk and took something out of the drawer, then unlocked my door and walked out of my bedroom. It was quiet as I walked through the house. My parents' room was clean as ever, and the guest room looked ordinary, waiting for its regular guests. I walked downstairs and into the kitchen. The dishes laid in the sink, and my mother's tea was half finished, since she had to rush out. I was barefoot as I walked to the abandoned cupboards in the kitchen corner. I opened it and saw a bottle of whiskey. I smiled as I grabbed it and ripped the lid off, then took a few sips. The liquid burned my throat. I walked to my dad's office and searched his drawers as I set the bottle on his desk. "Yes." I cheered as I grabbed the lighter from the drawer. I opened Blake's pack of cigarettes, took one, and lit it. I stuffed the lighter in my bra, then walked around the house with the cigarette between my lips and bottle in my hand. "Thank you, Carter Halls, Ethan Baxter, Aidan Rowley, and especially Blake Gunner for ruining my life."

I leaned against the wall and sipped the vicious alcohol. I thought back to last year and everything that had happened after that. A single tear rolled down my face as I remembered them. I bit my lip to prevent a breakdown, since Aidan was friends with him.

"You too, Parker."

***

Carter

"Did her mother say anything else?" Aidan asked as we arrived at Lana's house.

"No, just that she looked horrible and tired from the prank some guys pulled."

"Prank? What prank?" he asked as we got out of the car. Blake and Ethan arrived too, and we stood on her lawn.

"I don't know."

"Are you okay?" Aidan asked Ethan, who had

bags under his eyes. Ethan's hair wasn't brushed, his shirt was wrinkled, and he didn't have matching socks.

"Well, considering we were looking for a girl in a dress last night and I drove too fast, leading to a cop taking me to the station and my dad bailing me out...I'm peachy," Ethan grumbled as he forced a smile.

"What cop?" Blake asked.

"A female, don't worry." Ethan waved us off as he walked up the porch. We followed behind him as he pressed the doorbell. "Lana! We know you're in there."

"Come on, we just want to talk, Willson," Blake shouted.

"G-guys look," Aidan mumbled. We turned to see his stare by the window. We followed him and stood in front of the window which displayed the living room. There stood Lana Willson with a bottle of whiskey in her hand and a cigarette between her lips.

"What the fuck?"

"Lana, open the fucking door!"

"Is that dried blood?"

"Where did she get that cigarette?"

We looked like crazy people. Blake and Aidan banged on the door, Ethan yelled at her through the window, yet I stood with my arms by my side. A part of me wanted to break that door down, but something told me to stay put.

"What the hell?" a familiar voice shouted. We whipped our heads to see Miranda. Her blonde hair was still curled from last night, she wore a sweater, jeans, and brown boots, and she had a look of confusion on her face. "What are you guys doing here?"

"We want to talk to Lana. What are you doing here?" I asked.

"Bringing her phone. She forgot it last night," Miranda stated as she held up Lana's iPhone. We backed up and cleared the way for Miranda to enter. Clearly, she'd let her best friend in. "Lana…" Miranda trailed off. "Please open the door."

We went to the window as we watched Lana take another sip of whiskey. Miranda raised a brow as she looked at her best friend. Her face paled as she rushed back to the door and banged on it continuously.

"Not again," Miranda whispered. We exchanged looks at what Miranda had said. "Lana, open the fucking door right now!" she yelled. "Please, Lana, don't…"

Miranda leaned down and shoved the phone under the door; she came back up and leaned her head against it. Ethan went beside her and gave her a comforting hug; it was quiet as we watched Miranda cry into Ethan's shoulder.

"This is all your fault," I spoke up as I pointed to Blake.

"What the fuck? How is it my fault? You're the one who asked her to Homecoming!" Blake raised his voice at me.

"Well, if we didn't have to drag her out to the other side of the school that day for you, we wouldn't be here," I yelled as I stepped forward.

"Ha, if it weren't for this jackass giving her a

ride, none of us would be here!" Blake shouted as he gestured to Ethan.

"Excuse me, you're the one who gave her a cigarette that day!" Ethan yelled, then pulled away from Miranda and shoved Blake against the wall. Blake adjusted his leather jacket, then threw himself at Ethan. I didn't know why, but I jumped in and tried to break them up, but I made it worse.

"*Shut up!*" Aidan yelled. We stopped to look at Aidan, who had a grave look on his face. Aidan was never the type of person to get angry or take anything seriously, so to see him this way frightened us. The only time he'd be serious was with the guy with the drugs. "It's all our faults, okay? Ethan's fault for picking her up, Carter's fault for asking her to Homecoming, my fault for bringing her to the cottage, and Blake's fault for offering her cigarettes. *It's all our fucking faults!*" Aidan yelled, and I noticed how he'd clenched his fists. It was quiet, nobody talked after a while, everyone tried to register what Aidan had said, and he was right. It was our fault. We took the bet too far. We ruined her.

"I suggest we give her time to think and I'll check on her tomorrow, okay?" Miranda suggested as she wiped her tears away. We nodded in agreement, then walked to our vehicles; I climbed in with Aidan since my truck was gone. The whole drive home was quiet, yet the radio played softly as we were trapped in our thoughts.

Chapter Fifteen

Lana

"How was Homecoming?" Mom asked as she put a plate of lasagna in front of me. It was Saturday, and we had lunch. After yesterday's fiasco, I decided to ignore my parents. I heard her, Miranda's soft weeps on the other side of the door when I took my phone. I couldn't stand to listen to it anymore, so I went up to my room to finish the bottle of whiskey. I heard their yells, then everything went quiet; I thought they murdered each other, but then I listened to their cars drive off. I showered and cleaned up before my parents came home, and I made sure to use air freshener around the house to get the cigarette smell away. I washed the dress and hung it up on the line to dry, then went back to my room. No questions were asked, especially when I asked Mom to take me to the optometrist because she noticed I had on my old pair. She asked where my other pair was, and I lied again when I told her I lost them at school. I did what Ethan said, even though I was mad at him, and told the optometrist Mr. Baxter sent me. He was delighted even though he didn't ask if it was Ethan or his dad. Mom and I were home by sundown, and I walked through the house in a pair of Ray Ban eyeglasses; I wanted to take the most expensive one, but I couldn't do that to Ethan, even if I hated him at this particular moment.

"Lana?"

"Hmm?" I turned to my dad; he wore a plain black sweater, loose jeans, and sneakers. I rarely saw him in casual wear since he's always at the station.

"Your mother asked you something," he said. I shifted my gaze to Mom, who looked at me in a concerned way.

"It was great, Mom," I mumbled, then continued to poke my food.

"Carter seemed quite concerned yesterday," my mother challenged me. She bothered me and wouldn't stop until she got the answers she looked for.

"Why? What happened?" Dad demanded.

"Err...these guys played a prank, which caused my dress to get ruined," I lied. Thank goodness, I remembered what I had told my mother.

"Assholes," Dad muttered.

"Honey, not at the table. Since the storm came out of nowhere, why was your dress ripped?" my mother asked as she glared at my dad.

"Err...Carter's vehicle broke down, and we were close to home, so I walked. The dress must have gotten hooked by a branch or something," I muttered as I tried to avoid eye contact.

"I thought Carter couldn't drive?" Dad pointed out.

"Why can't he drive?" my mother asked as she looked at dad. His eyes widened as I grinned. Way to go, Dad.

"How was work, honey?" Dad changed the subject as he gently took my mother's hand in his.

"Harry Bobby Willson, do not alter the subject," Mom scolded as she pulled away from my dad's side. I snorted at Dad's middle name; Bobby sounded like a fun, humorous person, which was not my dad.

"Something happened at work, and he was involved along with his friends, so his mother took his truck away." My father sighed as he rubbed his forehead.

"So how did his car break down if he didn't have one?" Mom turned to me.

"He borrowed one of Ethan's cars; Carter wouldn't show up to Homecoming in a truck anyway," I lied.

"But you guys left here in a limo with Miranda and Marc—"

"Can we stop with the questions, please? It happened. It's in the past," I exclaimed as I cut my mother off. They looked at me with a worried look their eyes but continued to eat. "Thanks, Mom. It was delicious," I mumbled when I finished my lasagna. I picked up my plate and empty cup, then put them in the sink. "I'm going to do some homework." They gave a nod, and I raced up to my room. Everything was back to normal, my room spotless, my glasses on all the time with my focus on Yale. Since I didn't plan to go anywhere, I wore a gray hoodie, boyfriend jeans, and Converse. I collapsed on my bed and took my phone from the bedside table. It had two hundred messages and a few missed calls, mostly from Miranda, asking what happened. I wasn't ready to tell her everything. It's not that easy to tell your best friend, "Hey I stabbed a guy with a heel, and I found out that my so-called friends only wanted me to get laid, a bet introduced by Parker Collins himself." To hear Miranda's cries behind that door broke my heart. The worst part was I made her cry. I broke our promise. I remembered the day when Benny got a hold of me. Ethan almost kissed me, and Carter slept over. I remember the intimate conversation we had...

"I promise...you will never get hurt again," he mumbled as he hugged me tightly.

"Don't make promises you don't tend to keep, Carter Halls," I whispered to myself as I stared out the window.

"Lana, dear, you have guests!" my mother sang. I heard the excitement in her voice as I rolled my eyes. I didn't want to see them.

"Coming, Mom!" I replied as I got up. As I made my way down the stairs, I heard Dad's voice.

"You guys on the football team, right?" he asked. I reached the bottom of the stairs. I looked up to see Dad's back facing me.

"Yes, sir, proud Jefferson Eagles!" a familiar voice exclaimed. My eyes widened as my father stepped aside.

"B-Benny? What are you guys doing here?" I

stuttered as I looked at Nick, Benny, and Liam.

"Wanted to know if you'd like to hang out today? If that's okay with you, sir?" Nick asked as he looked at my dad. Nick Byrne was needless to say the less harsh one; since he dated Melissa Sing, he wasn't violent. He had wavy blond hair that made him look like he surfed, crystal blue eyes, a long nose, and plump lips.

"I don't see why not." Dad smiled at me. He noticed my discomfort, then turned back to Benny. "Where will you be going?"

"To the mall, then to get a bite to eat." Liam grinned as he winked at me. Liam Sanchez was the annoying one, always found ways to irritate me. He ran a hand through his brown hair, his eyes looking at me as he played with his lip piercing. Liam wore a red flannel with a white tee underneath it, black jeans, a gray beanie, and Converse, which entirely gave the whole skater look. I've seen him with glasses before, but I'm not sure if it's for style or if he wore a pair.

"I have a history essay to—"

"Oh, Lana dear, you'll finish that in no time. Go have fun." Mom cut me off.

"Okay, err…I'll grab my phone, then we'll go," I added, then spun around. I approached my room and walked to my mirror. I looked like a mess. I quickly ran to my makeup table and put some eyeliner on, along with lip gloss. I jumped up when I heard a knock; my head shifted to see Benny with his hands shoved in his pockets. His hair was still red from the dye, yet it made him look like an anime character. He wore a long crewneck with slim-fit jeans and Vans; his brown eyes looked tired with the bags under them.

"Does it take that long to get a phone?" Benny joked as he cautiously stepped into the room.

"Well, sorry for thinking I had a whole weekend to myself," I blurted out as I took my phone. We stared at each other for a moment. I tried to register that he was in my house and not teasing me but wanting to hang out with me. "What are you doing here, Benny?"

"I told you I wouldn't leave it, Lana."

"Why couldn't it wait till Monday?"

"I couldn't sleep for the past two nights; I couldn't get the image of you standing there all ruined, in the rain, in that area. Those big buildings always attract people, sometimes the wrong ones. I don't know why it bothered me so much, then it hit me that for once it wasn't my fault, but every time that it was, I didn't care up until now, seeing you all shattered and broken. Lana, you're like a fragile piece of glass that I broke but never bothered to fix, but now I'm willing to put the pieces back together slowly."

"Benny, I—"

"That's when I called Liam and Nick and told them. So I guess we're here now wanting to apologize but also wanting to help you," Benny continued as he stepped toward me. Next thing I knew, Benny slowly wrapped his arms around me. I stiffened at the sudden contact. Never in my life would I have thought Benny Nielson would pull me into an embrace. After a few seconds, I finally put my arms around his shoulders. We stayed like that for a few minutes until someone interrupted us.

"Lana, just a little warning that Benny likes to lick people's ears when hugging," Liam said. Benny and I pulled away, and I felt myself go red. Liam and Nick stood at the door as they chuckled.

"Shut up, ass," Benny mumbled.

"You ready?" Nick asked as he leaned against the doorframe. I looked at them, then let out a deep breath.

"Ready."

***

Liam belted out the lyrics to "Close" by *Nick Jonas* as we drove in Benny's car. We were on our way to the new diner where Blake and I got food for our picnic. I sat in the front while Benny drove, and Nick and Liam sat in the back. Nick groaned as Liam continued to sing.

"You sound like a dying cat," Nick hissed.

"Whatever, this is one of my favorite songs from *Nick Jonas*," Liam pointed out as he reached over to turn up the volume. I scrunched my eyebrows as I swatted his hand away.

"Thank you, Lana. You've saved our ears from bleeding." Nick sighed in relief.

"Humph, I like *Nick Jonas* better than someone else named Nick," Liam muttered as we heard a thump. "Ouch! Benny, he hit me!"

"Would you two shut the hell up?" Benny roared as he glared at them through the rearview mirror. They shut up as I let out a soft giggle. I felt Benny's gaze on me.

219

"Are you guys always like this?" I snickered as I turned to look at them. Liam bobbed his head to the music while Nick typed on his phone.

"Yeah, it's fucking annoying with these two," Benny mumbled.

"Speak for yourself, Nielson," Liam responded. I chuckled as I turned to look at Benny, who shook his head in amusement. The light turned green, and Benny drove as he tapped the wheel to the beat of the music. "Aww yeah, here's my favorite Jonas brother!" Liam cheered as he began to sing along to "Cake by the Ocean" by *DNCE*.

"Ugh," all of us groaned as we continued to listen to Liam.

***

"Finally," I mumbled as the car came to a stop in front of the diner. We piled out of the car, but I felt someone open my door. As I got out, I saw Nick smile at me. "Th-thanks."

"No problem."

We entered the diner and took in the smell of deep-fried oil and milkshakes. The place was themed as a classic diner with baby pink and blue colors that sprouted everywhere. The seats and walls were blue along with the bar, and the tables were pink; the floor was a classic black and white. Posters of famous old singers and bands were plastered everywhere. "Sh-Boom" by the *Crew Cuts* played from a massive jukebox on the other side of the diner.

"Lana, you coming?" Benny asked. I smiled as I

slid into the booth and sat next to Liam. Benny was opposite me, and Nick sat next to him.

"This place is sick," Liam exclaimed as he looked around. I nodded in agreement as we looked around at the many teenagers, young adults, and old people who enjoyed the atmosphere. Everyone seemed happy, even the waiters. The women wore baby pink dresses with white Converse, and the men wore little blue polo shirts, black jeans, and Converse. Yet one specific waiter caught my eye as he approached us, his eyes locked on me as he twirled the pen between his fingers.

"Hi, I'm Aidan. I'll be your waiter for today," he said, then looked at the guys. "Oh hey."

"I didn't know you worked here," Benny hissed as he stared at Aidan.

"Yeah, just started a few days ago. What are you guys doing here?"

"We're here to catch some Pokémon. What do you think we're doing here?" Liam motioned to the people around us.

"What are you doing here?" Aidan turned to me. "With them?"

"We wanted to hang out with her. Is that such a crime?" Nick snapped as he glared at Aidan.

"Not if you threatened Lana to hang out just so you could beat her up later," Aidan said through gritted teeth.

"She wanted to!" Liam barked as he got up from his seat and stood in front of Aidan. Liam was taller, being a football player, but Aidan didn't mind as he held his head up high confidently. "Right, Lana?" Liam demanded. I glanced at Aidan, who looked at me. Hurt filled his eyes, but it was mixed with disappointment.

"Yeah," I breathed out, then looked down at the menu. It's like everything went silent after I had said that word. I continued to stare at the cardboard in front of me. Out of the corner of my eye, I saw Liam sit down. I sighed in relief as I pushed my glasses back up and turned to Aidan.

"So what the hell do you guys want?" Aidan demanded as he flipped open his notepad.

"Liam, I don't believe a waiter should talk to a customer like that, do you?" Nick asked as he flipped through the menu.

"Hmm, I don't think so; the waiters should talk with respect to their customers. Otherwise, they don't get a tip." Liam sang the last part as his eyes flickered to Nick, then Aidan.

"What would you like to order?" Aidan sighed.

"Oh, we're not ready. Give us a few minutes." Liam waved him off as he looked at the menu. Aidan threw his arms up in exasperation as he walked off.

"Would you guys please not start? I don't want world war three happening," I said.

"The dick started it," Benny mumbled, then looked at the menu. I rolled my eyes as I thought back to a month ago. They were friends, laughing at me, but now they're enemies. Last week Aidan, Ethan, Carter, and Blake beat up Liam, Nick, and Benny, and they hated each other. It's my fault. They'd be friends, but I had to come between their friendship. On the other hand, if I didn't come between their friendships, they'd still bully me.

From the bruises Benny had from Blake beating him up, I wouldn't want to see what he'd do to me.

"You guys ready to order?" Aidan came back with a much better look on his face.

"Have you gained manners while you waited?" Nick asked.

"Hehe, get it, cause you're a waite—" Liam giggled.

"Shut up," Aidan demanded then forced a smile. "Now are you guys ready to order?"

"Yeah, burgers and strawberry milkshakes all around with a side of onion rings," Benny said, then closed his menu.

"Right away," Aidan muttered as he took the menus. Liam and Nick started to argue about which Jonas brother was better. Out of the corner of my eye, I saw Benny's stare on me. I sat up straight as I looked at him.

"What?"

"I still want an explanation."

"Me too," I stated. He knew what I meant as he glanced at Nick. He looked at me then back at Benny.

"Let's go to the jukebox." Nick sighed as he looked at Liam.

"What? Why? I love this song—ow! Okay." Liam groaned as we heard a kick from under the table. The boys got up and walked to the other side of the diner where the jukebox was.

"Do you remember back in second grade when the teacher asked us what we want to be when we grew up, and Ethan said a football player?" Benny started. I slowly nodded but wasn't clear on how that explained why he bullied me. "Well, I remember seeing you guys always talking and watching him on the playground, playing football. He continued to play until middle school, when he joined the team. I joined too, but he was always better. Everyone loved him," Benny said as he let out a scoff. "Then do you remember that dance class we took, and we were partners?" he asked. I nodded as I shivered from the memory. "Ethan danced with Ashley Baker, and they were the best in class. I got jealous because I couldn't dance. You told me I could do it; I just needed a bit more practice. Everyone always focused on them when dancing, but nobody took a second look at us. I became angry that he'd always win, so I had to take my anger out on someone—" He paused, then looked away. "And the right person was you, Lana Willson, the girl who encouraged him back in second grade. The girl with the big glasses and braces. The girl who had a sheriff as her father.

"After the first time, it sorta became a habit. Yet I hated myself for it. I told the guys, and they'd laugh because you didn't do anything, never told anyone, so naturally, we took advantage of you.

"As the years went on, more people bullied you. Ethan started too, which surprised me, but hey, you had to take your anger out on someone, right? Especially after their girlfriend cheated on them."

"You kissed Zoey back in freshman year while she was dating Ethan?" I asked.

"Nope." He pointed to Aidan. Wow. "But now when you show up to school looking all hot and badass with that Blake guy, it was kind of hard to tease you, but before he'd always watch us while we teased you. I haven't done anything to you in a week now, and to be honest, it feels so good. I don't know what was wrong with me back then, but I'm sorry, Lana. Seeing you the other night made me realize something. Every time I hit you, you looked like that, and when it wasn't me, I sort of just…I felt like a jerk for using you like that. I'm so sorry for putting you through hell these past years, and it's okay if you don't forgive me, I get it, but please can we just…start over?" Benny cried. I saw the tears in his eyes, and they were real genuine tears.

"You fucking asshole," I said after a while.

"I think I deserved that," he mumbled, and I couldn't help but let out a dry laugh.

"That's fucking ridiculous. Just because you couldn't handle someone being better than you?" I raised a brow. "Ethan Baxter's not all that, y'know. He's fucking pathetic, just like the rest of them."

The silence stretched as Benny blinked away his tears. I glanced up and noticed how he'd pull his sleeves down continuously. We locked eyes, and I stared at the guy who tormented me because of his jealousy. He must have hated himself. When he'd talked to me, he'd say a whole lot of nonsense, but I understood now. He cursed himself for what he did to me.

"Do you forgive us, Lana?" a familiar voice asked. I looked over my shoulder to see that Liam had his head down while Nick shoved his hands in his pockets.

"I-I don't know," I croaked out. My voice felt raspy as I looked at Benny. He wiped his tears away as Nick and Liam took their seats. I thought back to when the guys apologized to me; if I gave them a second chance, then it'd be fair to give them too. Even though Benny was the worst out of everyone, he saved me the other night. I'd at least give them a chance.

"But everyone deserves a second chance, and I'm willing to give you guys one last chance," I mumbled. Small smiles appeared on their faces as Liam pulled me in for a hug.

"Thank you!" he cheered like a seven year old. Aidan appeared with our food, but he didn't even glance at me.

"So, Willson, tell us why were you running around like Cinderella when she left her shoe?" Nick asked with a mouthful of food. I took a deep breath and told them everything from the day when Miranda went home early to the night of Homecoming. They already knew about the bet, since they overheard Marcus and Ethan talk about it in the locker room. Obviously, I didn't tell them about the cocaine and arrest situation yet; I was angry with the guys, but I wouldn't tell anyone of that night.

"So you didn't sleep with Carter?" Liam asked after I finished.

"Out of that whole story, the only thing you got was whether I slept with him?" I asked, then flicked his temple.

"Ouch! Well, you weren't very specific." Liam coughed.

"We never slept together. We fell asleep in the same bed, then I woke up alone," I explained as I

226

took a sip of my milkshake.

"And then you went to shower and found him in there, so you guys decided to save water," Nick said as he wiggled his brows.

"What? No! You guys are just so immature!" I muttered as my cheeks turned red.

"But are you okay? When I found you, you looked..." Benny trailed off as he searched my face.

"Yeah, but the...I...the man in the—" I stuttered.

"Hey, hey, hey, don't worry. You were just using self-defense, plus he was harassing you. It's okay," Liam said as he put an arm around my shoulder. I rested my head against his chest as I silently cried. Out of the corner of my eye, I saw Aidan as he wiped the counter. As he raised his head, he looked at me, and I sheepishly turned away.

***

"My house is that way," I said as I pointed at the sign for my town. We drove past it as I looked at Benny.

"Dude, where are we going?" Liam asked from the backseat. Benny kept quiet as we looked at him for a response. Seeing as we weren't going to get one anytime soon, I looked in front to see where the car would take us.

"Wh-what are we doing here?" I stuttered as I began to recognize the place. We entered the industrial area, the same one I ran into that night. Since it was a Saturday afternoon and all the business people went home, others decided to come. Gangs looked at us, which made my nerves shoot up. The car came to a stop in front of a building, we got out, and I gasped from the familiar surroundings. "Benny, what are we doing here?"

"Which alley was it?"

"W-why?" I stuttered and looked at the dark alley that I was stupid enough to go to for cover.

"Lana, you said you lost your other shoe. If we don't find it and that guy reports what happened, you're gonna get into trouble," Benny muttered as he gripped my arms.

"D-down there," I pointed out. They followed down into the alley with me behind. It was darker than I thought; it seemed like a never-ending pathway.

"Lana?" Nick mumbled.

"Hmm?" I turned to Nick. His wavy blond hair was tied up as he crouched to the ground. Liam and I saw a trail of blood. My eyes widened in horror as we slowly followed the path. The trail ended by a dumpster where Benny stood, his hands shoved in his pockets. We followed his gaze to what he looked at, and the lump in my throat grew.

"Lana, what have you done?" Nick whispered. My face paled as I looked at the homeless man with the ginger beard lying against the dumpster. His face was covered in blood as he held something against his chest. His eyes were wide and bloodshot, as if he watched us. I looked at his temple and noticed the dry blood.

"That's your other shoe, right?" Benny asked. I slowly nodded as I looked at them; they stared at me for a response to the deceased man in front of me.

"I'm a murderer."

Chapter Sixteen

Lana

"Oh, man, we're so dead," Nick muttered, then he turned to Liam. "No pun intended!"

"What are we going to do?"

"We're gonna get caught."

"I don't wanna go to jail…I don't look good in those orange jumpsuits!"

"This is all my fault."

"Everyone calm down!" Benny yelled as he hit the wheel.

"How the hell are we supposed to calm down? We have a dead body in the trunk, blood on our hands, not to mention the murder weapon at Lana's house, and you're telling us to calm down?" Nick shouted from the backseat.

"The worst part is your dad is the sheriff," Liam mumbled.

"Oh, thanks, Captain Obvious," Nick yelled, clearly irritated with Liam since it was his idea.

"I'm so sorry, guys. This is all my fault. I should

go and confess," I cried, then looked down at my hands. They trembled as I stared at the dried blood.

"It's not your fault, Lana. It's those assholes. They did this to you," Benny muttered as he gripped the wheel. Our hands were covered in blood because we dragged the guy out of the alley. All the evidence was there: my shoe and ripped pieces of my dress. We tried our best to remove most of it; at least the footprints were thankfully already washed away from the rain. As we did so, we tried not to leave any evidence, but it was hard because there was so much blood. "Nick, how far is your house from here?" Benny asked. Throughout the years that I'd known Benny Nielson, he wasn't one to show much emotion—well, except anger, naturally. I glanced at Benny in the alley, and he was calm while the rest of us freaked out. Other than being a big jerk, he was acutely reserved.

"Twenty minutes, why?" Nick asked as we turned to Benny. He anxiously licked his lips, then glanced at Nick through the rearview mirror.

"Your dad still a builder?"

"Yeah."

***

"Here," Liam said as he gave me a shovel. We were in the forest far out from anywhere. Benny drove to Nick's house, where we got a few shovels from his dad's garage. I never thought I'd bury a body, especially since I killed the man.

"Okay, here's good," Nick said as we stopped. We'd walked for ten minutes. Nick and Benny carried the body by the arms and legs while Liam and I held the shovels. They placed the body on the ground as I handed Benny a shovel. We dug where the ground wasn't too hard, but not too soft. None of us spoke as we dug.

"All right, that's deep enough." Liam sighed as he wiped the sweat from his forehead with the back of his hand. The hole was dark as I bent over to glance down, perfect for a middle-aged man. I watched as they picked up the guy and gently put him in the hole. They dug as I stood there. I dropped to my knees as the tears fell. I cried as I watched them, and Liam turned to look at me.

"I can't believe I did this," I croaked out as I slowly backed away. He cautiously approached me with a smile.

"Hey, don't worry—everything's going to be okay," Liam said as he crouched down to wipe my tears. His brunette hair fell on his face as he smiled at me.

"No, it won't! I'm a murderer! A killer! Lana Willson, the geek, nerd, the loser of Jefferson High, killed someone," I exclaimed, then looked over Liam's shoulder to see Nick's and Benny's stares. "I'll never be able to look my dad in the eye ever again."

"Sshh...ssh...Lana, please, you're scaring us. It was only self defense. We'll get through this," Liam mumbled as he brought me in for a hug. We stayed in the position for a while until I pulled away and looked at Liam.

"If it's self defense, then why can't we tell somebody?" I whispered.

"Where's the fun in that?" Liam tilted his head, then slipped his hand into mine. "Let's finish up."

"First drugs, now this," I mumbled to myself as I picked up the shovel.

***

"Why did you help me?" I asked as we got back into the car. We were covered in dirt. My hair was a mess, and there were blisters on my hands from the many times I gripped the shovel.

"We had no choice, Lana. We couldn't let you face this on your own. Even though we've been dicks to you for the past years, we're here for you," Benny said.

"Plus, our footprints were there so…" Liam trailed off, which got him a slap from Nick.

"But remember, Lana, you can't tell anyone about this. We all have blood on our hands." Nick sighed, then looked out the window.

"We gotta get cleaned up," Benny said as he started the car.

"And the car," Liam added.

"Then let's get to the car wash." Benny grinned as he looked at me.

***

"Lana, baby, why are you so filthy?" my mother asked as she opened the front door.

"Err…we went go-karting," Liam said as he stood beside me.

233

"It was dusty outside," Nick added.

"Oh well, it looks like you guys had fun."

"Yeah, had a blast," I muttered.

"Thank you, boys. You can go home now," my father said as he appeared behind my mother.

"Oh, don't be so rude, Harry. Would you like to come in? I just made a pie!"

"Sure!" Liam said as he stepped forward. My parents opened the door further to let us in.

"It's still cooling off, so why don't you get cleaned up?" my mother suggested.

"Yeah, may we use your bathroom?" Benny asked as he turned to my father.

"Sure, but be down in ten minutes," Dad responded with a fierce look on his face. I rolled my eyes as we went upstairs. I walked into my room and showed them the bathroom while I walked to my bed.

"Where is it?" Nick whispered as he guarded the door. I went down on my knees and grabbed the heel along with the other one that I had in my jacket.

"Here," I said as I held each of them with my sleeves. They surrounded me as we stared at the murder weapon. Both shoes were full of dried blood, but I'd quickly point out that the left was the evidence of the crime. It was chipped on the end with the heel almost broken from all the force I put into it.

"Wow, who knew a heel could kill a guy?" Liam said. "Yet from what we saw, it looked like you put a lot of force into it, Lana."

"We need to get rid of these quick," Benny

mumbled.

"There's a junkyard not too far from my house. We can dump them there," Liam suggested.

"Yeah, now err...you keep that one—"

"Why do I get the bloody one?!" Liam argued as he stepped back. Benny covered his hands with his sleeves, then took the heels.

"They're both full of blood, you idiot!" Benny groaned as he shoved the heel into Liam's chest. Benny stuffed the one heel in his jeans as Liam did the same.

"You know I can give you guys a bag—"

"No, we're cool." Liam waved off. I glanced down at their jeans as I tried not to laugh.

"That looks wrong." Nick chuckled as he walked back to the door. I laughed as Benny and Liam looked at each other with the heels in their jeans.

"I'm getting you a bag," I said, then walked to my desk. I took out a plastic bag and gave it to Benny and Liam.

"Pie's ready!" my mother yelled from downstairs. We rushed downstairs after we cleaned up; thankfully from all the digging, the dried blood was barely noticeable. We sat in the family room and ate pie while we watched TV. I sat in the middle of the sofa with Nick on my right and Benny on my left. Liam sat on the other sofa with my parents as he munched on the pie. I glanced at the bag by Benny's feet. I couldn't help it; I was nervous.

"Nick, dear, would you please turn the volume up?" my mother asked. Nick had the remote placed next to him. I glanced at the television to see why my mom wanted to watch rather than talk.

"Jack August, local citizen, has been missing over a week now. He was last seen at his place of employment, the Maple Tree Café. He had recently been let go. Jack didn't have any contact with family or friends, and his co-workers weren't very fond of him. He worked in the city and is thought to still be in Chicago," the reporter said as she held the microphone. In the background, I noticed she was in front of a building. "The police believe that they have found Mr. August," she added. A picture of the man showed up, and I almost choked on my pie. I saw Benny shift uncomfortably as we stared at the television. There he was, the man with ginger hair covering his face, but in the picture, he looked innocent. He had sad blue eyes, a flat nose, thin lips, and a beard. "Here in the back alley of the café he worked in, residents have noticed blood and belongings." The reporter gestured to the front of the alley. There was a box with all kinds of strange things like hairbrushes, books, lighters, candles, toys, and a Chinese takeout box. I paled as I stared at the television. "Signs of blood are everywhere from the wet ground to the wall. Witnesses have said they heard shouting and yelling a few nights ago, but it was not safe to go and see due to the critical weather conditions. Tire tracks, as well as many footprints, are also seen." The woman showed the blood on the wall, the witnesses I recognized from when we drove past them, the tire tracks of Benny's car, and our footprints. "Blood tests have been done, and it is certain that it is Mr. August, but now the real question is: Where is he and what happened?" the blonde reporter dramatically asked. It changed to the weather, which got my parents' attention. I got up and walked to the kitchen with my plate in my hands. I heard footsteps behind me as I placed my plate in the sink.

"We need to get rid of our shoes," Nick whispered as I turned around. All three of them were in the kitchen as they held empty plates.

"But I just got these brand new Chucks." Liam frowned at his black high tops.

"Forget about the shoes. We have to get rid of the car," I grumbled as I looked at Benny, whose eyes widened.

"No, not my baby."

"Dude, we have to. It's got our footprints, fingerprints, and not to mention we put a dead body in the trunk!" Nick hissed.

"Fine, we'll find a way, but Lana, hand me your shoes," Benny said.

"What are you going to do them?" I asked as I took my shoes off.

"I'll dump it with your other shoes as well as ours."

I stared at my favorite pair of Converse. They were my first pair, yet they looked worn out. I'd worn the black and white sneakers for three years.

"Goodbye, my friends," I said dramatically as I handed Benny my sneakers. Liam came up beside me and put an arm around my shoulder as we watched Benny put them in the bag.

"It was a good few years." Liam sniffed as he wiped away his fake tears.

***

"*You what?*" Miranda yelled through my laptop. It was Sunday evening, and I was busy with my essay, but Miranda wanted to chat, so we used FaceTime. "Lana, I just wanna come hug you right now. Stay strong, girl." She pouted as she hugged her laptop. I'd told her everything from the night of Homecoming up until now. Well, except for the part about Jack. I hadn't heard from of any of the guys since yesterday when they left. We'd exchanged numbers, but there wasn't a need to talk. They said they'd be busy at the junkyard. "I hate them," Miranda scoffed as she rolled her eyes.

"Hate is an unyielding word."

"Yeah, and so are real friends."

"That's two words."

"You know what I mean! So, on the other side of the wall, you made up with Benny?"

"Yeah, they're not so bad." I smiled.

"You forgave him that quickly? Lana, look, I know you're a softy bu—"

"I never forgave any of them." I cut her off as I thought about Benny and Blake's groups. "I gave Ethan and them a second chance, and they fucked up. Now I'm giving Benny a chance."

"Lana, you're giving too many chances. Even though I think they don't deserve it, you're always gonna offer them another chance," Miranda rambled on. I knew she was right. I was a softy, and I always gave people a chance even though I got fooled half the time.

"I'm sorry."

238

"It's okay, but will you ever forgive them?"

"I don't know, but not now."

"Understandable, they're a bunch of sexy douchebags."

"Ooh, by the way, who won Homecoming?" I asked. A smirk grew onto her lips as she stared at me.

"Kelly and Carter."

"What's so funny?"

"We waited for Carter to show up, and when he didn't, she got angry." Miranda snickered. I shook my head because he should've stayed. "Wait, here's the best part. Since there was no king, Jennifer got on the stage and snatched the crown from Mr. Bronx. Let's just say it was a cat fight like never before."

For the rest of the evening, we caught up with each other's business. With the bet, I didn't have time for Miranda, but since Them were out of my life, I'd go back to my best friend.

***

"Still the same car," I mumbled as I crossed my arms.

"Well, good morning to you too," Benny muttered as he opened the passenger door. Since the guys didn't take me to school anymore and Miranda would be late if she took me, I had no other choice but to call him. A few weeks ago, I'd slap myself silly to call Benny Nielson for a ride to school, but I guessed things were perfect one minute, then suddenly falling apart the next. "I'm getting a new car tomorrow, so this is my last day with her." Benny pouted as he hugged the wheel.

"What did your folks say?"

"Told them I needed an upgrade. Believe or not, this car has broken down once or twice."

"What about the shoes?"

"Yesterday we literally watched them go through that machine where it was dumped, pressed, and burned; it was awesome!" Benny grinned as he started the car.

After that, we didn't speak for a while as we drove. Benny turned on the radio to make it less awkward. I glanced down at my clothing, thinking this was me. My striped sweater, dark blue jeans, and ankle boots fit me correctly. Even though I missed the badass look, I knew it wouldn't suit me; I tried too hard. I wanted to be me. "Do you think people will find this weird?" Benny asked after a while.

"I don't know."

"The bully and his nerd," he mumbled as I raised a brow. "I don't care anymore. If people can see you with Blake, they shouldn't be surprised."

"What will happen?"

"People will stare, tell each other, and then by lu—"

"No, I mean like would you still be the Benny you are now in public?"

"Yes, I said I'll do everything in my power to let you forgive me, even if it means showing it to the whole school," he stated. We stared at each other for a few seconds until a honk behind us broke our gaze. I took a deep breath as we reached the school.

The bell hadn't rung yet, which made me uneasy. Benny parked in his regular spot. As he hopped out, I gripped the handle and slowly opened it. Benny was right there with a smile on his face. "Come on." He motioned me to follow him. I slowly followed as I kept my head down. I felt the stares as we walked.

"Hey, guys," Nick greeted. I looked up to see his arm wrapped around Melissa.

"Why did she get out of your car? Did you find her on the way to school?" Melissa gasped as she stared at me.

"No, we're all friends now, baby. We made up," Nick awkwardly mumbled. Melissa did a double take as she looked at Benny and me.

"You two made up? As in you're not going to make fun of her anymore?"

"Yeah," Benny mumbled as he shoved his hands in his pockets. Melissa stared in shock but immediately took out her phone and typed.

"'Sup, guys?" Liam yawned as he approached us.

"What happened to you?" I asked. Liam still had bed hair as he chewed on his stud; he wore a big hoodie, sweatpants, and Vans.

"Couldn't sleep last night from the junkyard," he said as he rubbed his eyes.

"What were you doing at the junkyard?" Melissa asked. Liam's eyes widened as he only noticed her.

"Throwing junk…in the…yard?" Liam stuttered as we glared at him.

"See you guys later. I gotta get to Calculus," I mumbled as I held the straps of my bag.

"I'll walk with you. We do have Calculus

241

together," Nick suggested as he let go of Melissa.

"But you always walk me to Literature." Melissa frowned as she gripped her boyfriend's arm. Nick turned to me, then Melissa. I smiled, then waved him off.

"It's okay, Nick. I'm heading to my locker anyway," I said, then walked off. I felt the constant stares as I headed to the building. I stopped and spun to look at a pure sports car. They stared at me with sad looks. I glanced at Aidan and scowled. I bet he told the guys that I was at the diner on Saturday. I gained all the courage and approached them. Carter seemed taken back, as he avoided eye contact. Blake leaned off Ethan's car as he stood up straight. My eyes locked with his as I stood right in front of him. Nobody spoke for a while as we stared at each other.

"You ditched us for your bullies? That's low, Willson, even for you," Blake muttered as he looked at me.

"Shut up, you jerk!" I yelled, then shoved him. Blake staggered backward but regained his balance quickly.

"What the hell are you doing, hanging out with them?" Ethan barked.

"At least they want to hang out with me, unlike some people who do it to get laid."

"Lana, let us explain—" Carter sighed, but I cut him off.

"I don't wanna hear it. Now what must I do?" I asked. They looked at each other with confused looks on their faces as I rolled my eyes. "I cracked. I lost the bet, and if I lost, I agreed to be your puppet for the rest of senior year. I am a person of my word, so what must I do?"

Chapter Seventeen

Lana

"Lana, you don't have to do this." Carter sighed as we walked along the hallway.

"No, I lost the bet, fair and square. It's fine," I muttered. With our little argument outside, they saw I wasn't in the mood, so they let me carry their bags. I took Aidan and Carter's backpacks, Ethan's gym bag, and my own, since Blake didn't have a bag with him.

"Can we at least help you?" Ethan begged as he tried to take one of the three bags on my back. I turned to him and raised a brow.

"Are you implying that I am not strong enough to carry four bags?"

"No, no, I just…"

"Well, look who we have here. Geeky Lana back in her natural habitat, serving her purpose in life," Austin announced as he stood in front of me.

"I thought the bet was over. Well, now we know the results." Parker laughed as he stood next to

Aidan. Word got out by last Wednesday about the bet. So far, I'd been told I was going to lose. It turned out that everyone was right.

"Told you she couldn't last. Pay up." Austin grinned as he looked at Parker.

"You guys bet on me?" I yelled, then dropped the bags; I saw a crowd forming around us.

"Yeah, if anything, you're just an attention seeking wh—" Austin laughed as he towered over me. He's tall, probably Blake's height, but he was skinnier. I cut him off when I gripped Ethan's bag and hit him. "You bitch!" he yelled as I continued. I felt two arms around my waist pull me away from Austin. I saw Aidan approach us as he tried to get the bags from me.

"Lana, just leave him!" Blake growled in my ear. I looked down to see his tattooed arms around me. I glanced up again and noticed Austin used his arm for protection. Flashbacks of when I hit Jack with my heel entered my mind as I stopped. I froze and looked around me; everyone stared at us as looks of horror filled their faces. I dropped the bag into Aidan's hands and fell to the ground.

"They're assholes," Blake whispered. I realized he still had a good grip on me. I jumped up to see everyone's stares. Phones and cameras were out as the hallway went quiet. I looked around to see Austin pressed against the lockers. I cautiously stepped closer, which frightened him, but eventually, he straightened. Off to the side, I saw Aidan glare at him. I stood right in front of Austin, his heavy breathing making me sigh.

"I'm sorry," I croaked out and waited for an

answer as we stared at each other. His eyes pulled away from mine as he looked around for help. I didn't know what happened behind me as I looked at him, but he slowly nodded then returned his gaze.

"Me too. I'm sorry, Lana." I gave a firm nod then turned; all the bags were still on the ground as I picked them up. As I collected them, I felt everyone's eyes on me. I walked to Aidan, who held the gym bag. I looked at him, then the bag. He didn't say anything as he handed it to me. A sad smile formed on his lips, yet I wished it were the one that made the corner of his eyes wrinkle. The bell rang, which signaled the first period, but nobody moved; after the bell, it fell into a profound silence. I began to walk down the hall, and people cleared the path for me as they watched Lana Willson fulfill her side of the bet.

***

I sighed in relief because it was finally lunch. I'd carried the guys' books for the day, but only if we had a class together. Each time we'd have a class together, they'd try to talk to me, but I ignored them.

"If you're mad at us for using you to do our homework, then why are you doing our class work?" Ethan asked as I took his books. For the first few times, they said they'd carry their books, but I insisted, so they finally gave in.

"Because I thought I was doing it out of kindness, and y'know, I thought that's what friends do, but now I must do it," I stated as we walked to his locker.

"Lana, please, let us explain—"

"There's nothing to tell, Ethan. I heard you guys loud and clear that night. See you in P.E." I sighed as we stopped by his locker. He frowned as I walked away, but I didn't care. I got my lunch from my locker then walked to the cafeteria. Miranda and Marcus sat at our regular table in the middle of the cafeteria. I slammed my lunch on the table and took a seat.

"Are you okay? I heard what happened earlier. Parker and Austin are assholes," Miranda mumbled as she looked at me from across the table.

"I'm okay, Miranda. Please, can we not talk about any of them for once?"

"Sure...how was your weeke—oh, never mind." Miranda cut herself off as she remembered our conversation from last night.

"You don't have to be their puppet, Lana. They already feel bad. Heaven knows why, but don't do this to them," Marcus added as I looked at him. Marcus Sanders was the only one who didn't know the full story. He knew about the bet, but he didn't know everything. I was glad I had Miranda as a friend; she wouldn't tell him until I was comfortable with it. I felt a weight on my side of the bench, and two figures plopped themselves down on either side of me, then one next to Marcus.

"Bonjour," Liam sang.

"Jock table is that way," I grumbled and turned my head to see a confused Marcus in front of me. Nick sat next to him while Benny was on my left.

"Take a chill pill, girl," Liam replied as I rolled

my eyes.

"Plus, why would we want to sit with him?" Benny hissed as he looked at the jock table. The rest of the team sat there, but I thought he motioned to Ethan and Austin. "Can't believe you're their puppet."

"I lost fair and square, Benny. Lana Willson is a girl of her word."

"Still, after what they've done to you—"

"What did they do?" Marcus demanded as he looked at us. I glanced at Miranda and gave her a nod.

"Babe, we need to talk," Miranda mumbled as she took Marcus's hand. We watched the couple walk out of the cafeteria. As soon as they were out, Nick sighed.

"Have you watched the news this morning?"

"The news comes on at six in the morning. Who the hell in their right mind would wake up that early for news?" Liam asked.

"Well, considering we were almost on it!" Nick spat as he glared at Liam.

"Wha-what happened?" I asked.

"At first they thought it was a suicide, but then the tire tracks and the many footprints led to more questions. I saw your dad there too," Nick mumbled.

"That's why he left early this morning. He didn't say anything because my mother doesn't like it when Dad has that kind of business to attend to," I mumbled.

"Why the heck was he there? He better not be taking this on. He's a damn sheriff, not a detective,"

Liam scolded.

"I'm going to pick up my new car tomorrow. Nick, you come so you can drive the old one to the junkyard, and we can dispose of it," Benny explained as his eyes shifted around the cafeteria.

"I'm coming too."

"No, Lana. It's too ris—"

"Please, I don't want you guys to get into trouble."

"And we won't. You can stay and watch Liam practice. By the time we come back, he'll be done." Benny gestured to Liam's football practice. I nodded, then ate my chicken salad. As I glanced around, my eyes locked with his. Even though they sat in the corner of the cafeteria, I knew Blake had his eyes on me. His eyes filled with mixed emotions as I sat with my past tormentors.

***

"What do you think we'll do in Phys Ed?" Carter asked as we walked to the gym.

"Coach is in a bad mood, so guess we'll be doing laps," Ethan replied.

"So what's been going on with you and Benny?" Aidan asked. I turned to look at him and noticed his jaw tightened.

"We made up."

"You made up with those assholes, yet you can't forgive us?" Blake asked.

"I'm giving them a second chance! Unlike some people, who just blew theirs." I rolled my eyes as we got to the locker rooms. Blake stared at me as he opened his mouth, but Carter beat him to it.

"How can you give them a second chance? They basically ruined your life!" Carter yelled as he raised his arms in exasperation.

"Like you didn't already!" I screamed, then tossed the bags by the door. They stared at me with guilty looks. I almost gave in, but thankfully I didn't. I knew I was a softie, but they influenced me, and to get hurt by them was the worst feeling in the world. "You don't know what the hell I've been through after that night!"

"What are you talking about? What happened?" Blake asked.

"Lana, come on, we're gonna be late," Miranda called from the girls' locker room. I sighed as I walked into the locker room to change.

"Thanks for that."

"No problem." Miranda grinned. "Now hurry up."

For the whole period, I ignored them. No way I'd tell them what happened. For the next few days, it was the same. Benny was my ride to school, me carrying the boy's bags and doing their work, then driving home with Miranda. Things got back to normal as days turned into weeks. None of us started a conversation because we knew the regular routine. Marcus got comfortable with Benny, Nick, and Liam. It wasn't hard since Marcus recently became captain of the soccer team. Jack August's body was never found, but the case was always open. It still frightened me to think I killed him. Every time someone touched me, I'd flinch as I thought he wasn't dead and came back to get his revenge. Benny got a Toyota 86 that was spacious so we'd all hang out. We were at the cinema with Liam, Miranda, Marcus, Nick, and Melissa.

"Are we being third wheeled?" Liam asked as we watched Nick, Melissa, Marcus, and Miranda walk into *Me Before You* theater. The past few weeks when we hung out, Nick had to bring his girlfriend, Melissa Singe. Obviously, Miranda and I didn't like it, but we got along with her because we wouldn't want to be a killjoy. She was the less bitchy out of the three girls, but she always gave us sneaky glances.

"I think so. Besides, who wants to watch a boring romance movie anyway?" Benny groaned as we walked.

"Me," I mumbled.

"Ooh, let's watch *Finding Dory*!" Liam cheered as we stood in line for the tickets.

"We already saw that last week," I groaned. His eyes lit up as he bit on his stud excitedly. The first week *Finding Dory* came out, Liam and Miranda dragged us to watch it.

"Fine, who's up for a little action? Purge anyone?" Liam smirked as he glanced at *Purge: Election Year.*

"I'm down." Benny grinned as he turned to me.

"Yeah, have you guys watched the first two?" I asked as we approached the ticket booth.

"Yeah, I was hooked from the moment those masks came out." Liam smiled as he took out his wallet. I quickly fished out the money that Mom gave me and placed it on the counter. They'd paid for the past things we'd done or eaten, so it was my turn.

"Three tickets to *The Purge: Election Year*." I smiled at the lady behind the counter. She could be in her mid-thirties, curly blonde hair with bright red lipstick. A look of boredom spread across her face as she looked at the three teenagers.

"Yes, please," Liam said as he waved the money in front of my face. We argued for about five minutes while the lady stared at us.

"Liam, you pay for the tickets, Lana pays for snacks, and I'll pay for pizza afterward," Benny suggested.

"Well, now we know who's the smart one here," the lady behind the counter commented.

I rolled my eyes as Liam teased me the whole way of how Benny was smarter than me. We entered the theater and sat right at the back so that we got a view of everyone.

***

"How was your guys' movie?" Marcus asked as we entered the pizzeria.

"Eh, the first one is always the best." Benny shrugged as he gestured to Nick to help push tables together to make one long table. After we rearranged the furniture in the restaurant, we finally sat down. Miranda sat on my left with Liam on my right and Benny in front of me.

"*Me Before You* was amazing! Lana, there was this par—" Miranda gushed.

"Don't spoil it for me!" I cut her off as I took my glasses out of my pocket and put them on. We got into our own conversations while we waited for the pizza to arrive. The most prominent topic was that today was Halloween.

"Hey, anyone going to the party tonight?" Nick asked.

"Heck yeah. Parker throws one of the best Halloween parties ever." Marcus grinned as he whispered something into Miranda's ear that made her giggle.

"Do you guys have costumes already?" I asked. I'd heard of Parker's awesome parties but didn't bother to talk about it since I was never invited. Even if I was, I'd never step foot in Parker Collins' house ever.

"Yeah, can't wait to see you, cat woman." Nick smirked as he kissed Melissa.

"Hmm, kinky," Liam joked as we laughed.

"What are you going as, Lana?" Benny asked. I let out a shrug and sipped my drink.

"I'm not in the party mood."

"Yeah, we don't want anything happening like the last time." Liam wiggled his brows at Benny and me. Memories of when Benny and I did a body shot went through my mind as I punched Liam. Even though Parker and Austin weren't in my good books, I didn't want to spoil everyone's fun. Other than hanging out with the guys, I'd focused a lot on my work. I'd applied to a few colleges, which Mom and Dad helped with.

I got home and watched a random series. Mom was at the surgery while Dad was in his study. In the second episode, the doorbell rang. I placed the hot bowl of mac and cheese on the table, wrapped

253

the blanket around me, then rose to my feet. There was a bowl full of candy by the front door, and I grabbed it on the way.

"Coming!" I yelled as I heard the doorbell again. When I opened the door, I was met by Mickey and Minnie Mouse.

"Are you wearing that to the party?" Marcus asked as he looked at my panda pajamas.

"I'm not going. What are you guys doing here?"

"I'm sure there's a costume store ope—" Miranda cut me off as she whipped out her phone.

"Good to know, but I'm not going. I thought I made myself clear earlier."

"You can't keep yourself isolated here all the time, Lana. If you moved on, then you wouldn't care if they were there," Miranda said.

"So going to Parker's party and getting drunk off my ass will make me feel better? Err…no thanks, Miranda. Just go and enjoy."

"All right, but I gotta use your bathroom quick," she said, then sprinted upstairs.

"Will you ever forgive them?" Marcus asked as he leaned against the doorframe.

"Marcus, I—"

"They're not the same anymore. Ethan is continuously on the court nonstop, Carter is quieter in class, Aidan barely smiles anymore, and Blake…"

"Wha-what about Blake?"

"He's become violent," Marcus muttered. I deeply sighed, as I knew there was something up with them. I heard Blake got into a few fights, but I didn't bother to ask. "You've changed them, Lana.

You have an effect on them," Marcus whispered. "They don't even talk to each other that much. Since Carter has no truck for heck knows what reason, I give him a ride. Every morning I watch him come out his house slouching, no smiley sarcastic Carter Halls in sight."

"Trick or treat!" a familiar voice boomed from the open front door. I looked up to see Jack Sparrow, Dracula, and a mouse. I picked up the bowl with candy and thrust it into Liam's arms.

"Cheap ass." Benny grinned as he looked at the candy.

"Excuse me, Nielson?" a deep voice asked behind me. I kept in a laugh as Benny's face paled. "Now what the hell are you supposed to be?" Dad asked as he looked at Nick.

"Err…a ma-mouse, sir."

"That's Sheriff to you, and you look like a rat."

"Mr. Willson, stop scaring them. It's Halloween!" Miranda said as I heard her footsteps behind me.

"Where you kids heading?" Dad asked as they stood by the door.

"A party."

"What are you supposed to be?" Dad asked as he turned to me.

"I'm supposed to be on the couch watching a vampire jump out of a plane."

"So you're not going, honey?" Dad asked as the corner of his mouth raised.

"Nope. Now buh-bye! Enjoy the party!" I smiled, then pushed my friends out the door.

"Wait, should I stay?" Benny asked, but I cut

him off when I shut the door.

"You need more female friends," Dad muttered. My jaw dropped as I followed him into the kitchen.

"I don't need more female friends, Dad. I have Miranda, and she's genuine."

"I know. Listen, I'm on duty since there's going to be a bunch of Halloween parties on tonight. I gotta go." He grabbed his jacket. "Your mom will be home after one, but in the meantime, I've got you a babysitter."

"I'm too old for a babysitter. Besides, who on earth will be free tonight?" I asked as we walked to the front door. The person behind it knocked as I grew curious.

"Griffon." Dad smiled, then opened the door for Mr. Bronx.

"Hello, sir," I mumbled since I was jaw dropped.

"Hey, Willsons, happy Halloween!" Griffon exclaimed, then hugged my dad.

"Lana, you know when we're out of school, it's Uncle Griff." Mr. Bronx smiled as he pulled me in for a hug.

"Sure, Uncle Griff," I mumbled. Griffon Bronx had different attire; he wore a casual sweater, jeans, and sneakers. "I'm gonna get my phone," I said. I don't think they heard me because they conversed. I walked upstairs, and I opened my door to some déjà vu. "Not again," I mumbled at the teenage boy who sat on my bed. He didn't look at me; he stared at the wall where my poster was placed. He decided to make himself comfortable since he was sprawled out on my bed with a cigarette between his lips. As he exhaled the tobacco smoke, he pointed to the poster.

"You're not into them anymore?" Blake asked.

"I put it in the drawer."

"I like the song, *California*—"

"Blake, what are you doing here? Aren't you supposed to be at the party?" I cut him off. The moon seemed bright as it glowed into my room and outlined his figure.

"Not in the party mood," he replied and stood up. I watched as he dumped the cigarette in my trashcan then covered it with a blank paper. "I need to talk to you."

"Blake, I don't want to tal—"

"Then don't! Just listen, Lana!" he muttered, then gripped my arms. I looked up to see his eyes darken; he didn't wear his usual attire. He wore a baggy hoodie, sweatpants, and sneakers.

"You do realize my dad and our math teacher are downstairs," I muttered, then pushed him away. I didn't want them to catch me with Blake in my room; they'd naturally think the worst.

"I don't care. I need to talk to you. Things just aren't the same anymore." He groaned in frustration.

"Blake, I'm not going to listen to you while they're downstairs, so I suggest you quit being a pussy and get the hell out that window and knock on the door like a man!" I hissed, then pointed at the window. Blake stared at me while I glared at him. His blank expression changed into a smirk.

"Nice pajamas," he pointed out as he looked down. My cheeks reddened in embarrassment as I met his eyes. "See you soon." He winked and walked toward the window. I rolled my eyes, then walked downstairs to see Uncle Griff in the living room.

"Hey, that's mine." I motioned to the mac and cheese he ate.

"I'm the adult here, so—" he said with a mouthful of macaroni but cut off when the doorbell rang.

"Expecting anyone?" I asked since Blake wouldn't ring the doorbell.

"No, are you?" he asked, then opened door. There stood Blake Gunner with a flustered look on his face.

"Blake? Aren't you supposed to be at Parker's party?" Uncle Griff asked. Mr. Bronx knew all the parties that happened, and the cool thing was that if it were on a school night, he wouldn't pile work on us the next day because he knew most of us suffered from a hangover.

"Err…no, I came to speak to Lana," Blake insisted as he tried to walk into the house. Griffon looked at us a few times, then gave a short nod and motioned Blake to come in.

"I'm gonna make some popcorn," Griffon said, then walked into the kitchen. I invited Blake into the living room and sat down as I watched him.

"I'm listening."

"That night when you heard Parker and Austin talking like that, you heard wrong. I admit that at first, it was about who'd get to sleep with you first, but then you became our friend, a person we trust, and that night back at the cottage, I knew this was more than a bet."

"Then why did you say once the bet is over I'll just be another one?" I whispered. Blake stepped closer, then crouched down; he placed his hands on my thighs as I looked at him.

"I said that because I didn't want them to suspect anything," Blake mumbled. "I miss our talks that we used to have, arguing over whose safety is more important when riding my motorcycle, sharing a cigarette, how your glasses fell to your nose when you got nervous...I miss us."

I didn't know how to respond because even I missed those things. As I opened my mouth to speak, Blake lowered his head and rested his forehead against my knees.

"Have you talked to the guys lately?"

"Now and then. We just give each other space," he mumbled into my lap. I took my hand and ran it through his hair. It was quiet, too quiet, so I knew Uncle Griff eavesdropped from the kitchen. "You never gave me a second chance," Blake blurted out. I stopped as he looked up.

"What?"

"You never gave me a second chance. I never hurt you." He whispered the last part. He mentally hurt me many times, but I guess he was right since those things were silly little arguments. "I'm not saying you have to, but please forgive me, Lana Willson. I've been a jerk, coward, arrogant asshole, but somehow you managed to make me look at things differently. I only said that stuff that night because I didn't want them anywhere near you. I care about you a lot, Lana, and through the weeks of becoming drunk and getting into fights, it made me realize that no matter how many times I do that stuff, it won't bring you back, so here I am, skipping one of the best Halloween parties in Illinois to apologize to a person I really care about."

"Who's up for a mov—" Uncle Griff said as he came into the room. He stopped mid-sentence when he saw our position. We stood up immediately, and I tried so hard to avoid eye contact with either of them.

I never thought I'd watch a horror movie on Halloween with my godfather and Blake. We sat on the same sofa, but there were significant gaps as I sat in the middle. Thankfully, I'd watched *Insidious 1, 2* and *3* so I knew when the scary parts happened, but it still didn't help when I'd cover my face with the blanket. After the movie, Uncle Griff ordered Chinese food, so we sat in the dining area.

"Let's play a game," Uncle Griff spoke up.

"What game?" Blake asked as he struggled with his chopsticks.

"It's where we each ask a question, and the other people have to answer and remember we're not at school, so you won't get into trouble." Griffon winked. "I'll go first. Have you ever lied to a person you cared about, but it was for a good reason?"

"No. Yes." Blake and I replied at the same time. We stared at each other and thought over what lies we've told.

"Interesting. Blake, you're up."

"Which person here knows something about you that nobody else does?" Blake immediately asked like he knew his question already. Griffon and I pointed at each other then laughed. Blake raised his eyebrow and slowly bit his lip.

"Err…if you were stuck on an island, who'd you take within this room?" I asked because I didn't know what question to ask. It's like the questions they'd asked meant something.

"You," they replied. Griffon raised a brow at Blake, whose jaw tightened.

"My turn," Uncle Griff said as he rubbed his hands together. He looked at Blake with a look I hadn't seen since he was young. He used to sleep around and drink all the time. Dad had to arrest him a few times, then Dad got fed up and gave him a whole lecture. So he built himself up and became a high school teacher. "When last did you get laid?" Griffon asked, and I noticed how he turned to Blake first. I choked on my food as I looked at them. There was the young Griffon Bronx I first knew.

"A few weeks ago," Blake bluntly stated. They stared at each other for a while, and on cue, they looked at me and waited for an answer.

"Err…" I stuttered. Blake's eyes seemed to darken as Griffon stared at me.

"I'm home!" a familiar voiced echoed through the house. My head snapped to the door to see my mother. I got up and walked over to her, then engulfed her in a hug. "Baby, you seem happy." Mom giggled. Thank goodness I didn't have to answer; I hated Griffon's games.

"Ahem," someone coughed. I pulled away to see Blake and Griffon behind me. Before the game started, I went to the bathroom and overheard them, which could be the reason why Blake was so quiet.

"Evening, Griffon. Thanks again for looking

after her. Hi, Blake," Mom said.

"Hi, Mrs. Willson."

"Evening, Angie." Griffon smiled and hugged my mother. He kissed my forehead then took a sneaky glance toward Blake. "I have to get home, but I'll visit soon."

"Bye," we said as I watched him walk out the door.

"Have you kids eaten?" my mother asked as she walked to the kitchen.

"Err…yeah, Mom, there's Chinese food if you want," I said as I walked into the living room while Blake trailed behind. We sat on the sofa and stared at each other.

"You didn't answer the question," Blake grumbled as he looked at me.

"The game is over."

"Yeah, but—"

"Blake, honey, are you planning to stay? If you are, the guest room is ready," my mother yelled from the kitchen.

"Thank you, Mrs. Willson," he shouted. Before he said anything else, she came into the room.

"You can call me Angie."

"Thank you for your hospitality, Angie."

"I'm going to call it a night, but I just want to make some tea. Any of you want some?" Mom asked as she looked at Blake and me. We shook our heads as she walked out of the room again.

"So will you give me another chance?" Blake asked.

"I suppose, but don't think things will go back to normal, Blake. It's not that easy," I mumbled. He drew his lip between his teeth and nodded.

"Do you forgive the guys?"

"I-I don't know."

"We can meet up and talk things out if you want, but if you need spa—"

"Perfect." I cut him off with a smile. Somehow, I missed when we'd meet up and joke around. The silence seemed to follow as I looked around the room; I noticed the kitchen light was still on. Mom was either on the phone or eavesdropped. "Blake, do you miss it?"

"What?"

"Me. I mean when I dressed like that and acted like that…do you think I should be that person?" I asked. I'd thought about it lately because I didn't know what to do with most of the clothes.

"No. The whole purpose of the bet was to bring out the best in you. I didn't mean for things to go overboard, but it didn't matter what you wore or did. What was important is that you had fun and experienced things. You don't need leather jackets and a bitchy attitude to impress other people. You are Lana Willson. Nothing will ever change you from being you. I know you hate living under the nerd stereotype, but if you want to be like that, nobody's stopping you. Just promise me you won't act in a certain way to impress someone. The most attractive thing is to always be yourself."

"Promise," I whispered as my lips formed a smile.

"Well, you two enjoy and don't—" Mom said as she came into the living room but cut off when we heard a knock from the front door. "Expecting anyone else?" Mom asked. We shook our heads as I got up and went to the door. I told Blake to stay in the living room as my mother followed.

"Hell—whoa!" I cut myself off when someone leaned against me.

"Lana."

"Benny? Are you drunk?" I asked as he raised his head.

"Yeah." He giggled.

"Bring him in," my mother called. I followed her instructions and dragged him into the living room.

"Wait! I gotta tell you something!" he exclaimed as he looked at me.

"What is it, boy?" my mother asked.

"I...I...luv choo," he slurred, then fell into my arms again.

"Oh, my...take him out," Mom said as she pointed to the door. I sent her a glare as I helped Benny stand up again. Out of the corner of my eye, I saw Blake walk in.

"And Mrs. Will...Smith? Willson! Yeah, that's right." Benny snapped his fingers. "Can I have permishon to marry your daughterrr?" He giggled like a seven year old. Mom's eyes popped as she looked at him.

"He's drunk." Blake huffed beside me.

"What gave chu—hey, what the hell are you doing here?" Benny asked as he spun around. Once he spotted Blake, he pulled me away. "Stay away from my woman!" Benny growled and pushed me behind him as he stood up to Blake. They were the same height as Blake scowled at Benny.

"She's not your woman. You're not thinking

straight, dude," Blake warned Benny as he stepped closer.

"What about that quote? Drunk words are sober thoughts?" Benny asked as his eyelids drooped.

"Screw that shit!"

"Boys!" Mom yelled.

"You're not in love with her. You can't be. You've hurt her emotionally and physically," Blake said and shoved him.

"Oh yeah? Well at least I'm not the one who just used her to get la—" Benny replied but cut off when Blake punched him.

Chapter Eighteen

Lana

It amused me to watch a drunken Benny Nielson fight Blake Gunner, who seemed monotone and exhausted half the time. Benny was tough, but I'd never seen Blake punch someone before except at the party. That was a random guy, but I knew both of them this time.

"Not in my living room!" Mom yelled as she tried to pull them apart. I snapped out of my thoughts and jumped in. I held Benny back while Mom stood in the middle of them. Blake glared at Benny while he huffed. Blake had a swollen eye while Benny had a bruise on his cheek. "Now I don't know what the hell is going on between the three of you, but you better sort it out before my husband gets home. I'll be upstairs, and if I hear any furniture breaking or yelling, I'll kick you out myself," my mother warned. She stared at the three of us for a moment, then took her cup of tea and walked upstairs. Once my mom's door shut, I spun around to see the glares they sent each other.

"Blake, he's drunk. He doesn't know what he's doing."

"What is he doing here? Wanna cause more shit?" Benny asked.

"Fuck off," Blake grunted, then shoved Benny down.

"You dipshit!" Benny groaned as he tried to get up, but Blake was quick as he pinned Benny to the floor. Blake overlapped Benny and punched him.

"Stop it!" I hissed as I tried to pull Blake off Benny. "Blake, please stop."

As Blake raised his fist, I watched how his knuckles hardened. He swung his arm one last time, and that was hard enough to knock Benny out. I backed away and stared at the scene in front of me. I knew Benny was going to be knocked out from all the alcohol he'd consumed but not from the punches Blake gave him. Blake slowly rose to his feet, then looked down at him.

"Had to find a way to shut him up." He shrugged, then collapsed on the sofa. I stood and watched as Benny's chest rose. I glanced at Blake, who had a look of boredom written across his face as if nothing happened. I had no choice but to sit next to him as we watched Benny on the floor, face bruised, as he laid in his Dracula costume and worn-out Converse. "What time is it?"

"Almost three in the morning," I replied as I looked at the clock on the wall. I let out a deep sigh and pictured myself in the warmth of my bed, but unfortunately, I'm here.

"If he was drunk, how did he get here?"

"Parker doesn't live too far from here. He must've walked."

"Can I crash here for the rest of the night? I don't trust him."

"Sure, but it doesn't look like he's going to wake up anytime soon."

"I'll wait."

As Blake continued to observe Benny, I took the time to look at him. His brown hair stood up; I watched his nostrils flare out his nose ring as he exhaled deeply. I glanced down to his sweatpants and noticed the faint outline of a square in his pocket. First, I thought it was his phone, but then it hit me. A smile formed on my face as I looked up, yet he already had his eyes on me.

"Please?" I pouted, then looked at the pack of cigarettes.

"No," he instantly replied as if he knew I'd ask.

"Oh, come on, just one. We need it now," I blurted out as I took off my glasses and set them on the table.

"Lana, your mom is upstairs, your dad could walk in any minute, and this guy will freak out if he wakes up," Blake complained as he pointed to the unconscious Benny.

"Then can we share? It'll go quicker," I said, then moved closer to Blake. He immediately got up and stood beside Benny.

"No, you're not going to do that thing where you touch my tattoos and look at me with those mesmerizing blue eyes of yours. No, not here!"

I pouted as I watched him pick Benny up and cautiously put him on the sofa beside me. He sat down again, but this time, he folded his legs to make a barrier.

"I've been craving one for a few days now."

"I don't care. It's not safe to do it here."

"Says the one who just did it in my room."

"You took your time. I got bored."

"Wow, what an excuse," I said, then playfully rolled my eyes. I got up and strolled to the kitchen. I got an ice pack from the freezer, then walked back. I gave it to Blake, and he muttered out thanks. He pressed the bag against his swollen eye. I bit my lip as I saw a bruise on his forehead. I pushed his hair out the way and observed it. He squirmed from the touch but quickly recovered his forehead with a laugh. His eyes seem to meet mine as I quickly moved my hand away.

"So what excuse did he tell for you to forgive him?" Blake asked as we looked at Benny.

"That's another story for another day." I sighed then leaned my temple against his shoulder.

"Okay, sum it up in five words."

"Okay, err…young, jealous, attention, stress, and alone." I mumbled the last part as I looked at Benny. He was alone most of elementary school. I felt sorry for him as I watched him get picked last for the team, but now here he was. In my living room drunk, confused, on the team, popular yet unconscious.

"Some very descriptive words."

"Yeah," I said then let out a yawn. "How's your brother?"

Even though I'd only met him once, somehow I felt like I should know him. The first time I saw him, he seemed shocked, then he changed into that Gunner Sibling Smirk and played it cool. It still bothered me that he said I shouldn't get close.

"He's okay, just being Axel and shit," Blake mumbled as he put his arm around my shoulder. I leaned into him. I sat with my eyes closed and my back against his chest. I didn't even notice that the light was off because of the moonlight that shone through the living room window. My eyes got weaker until they finally closed. The last thing I saw was Blake throwing a blanket over us and kissing my forehead.

***

"What the hell happened here?" a familiar voiced yelled as my eyes fluttered. I sat up and realized I'd fallen asleep on Blake's lap. His feet were propped up on the coffee table as we stared at my dad.

"Dad, I…" I mumbled as I looked at Blake, who didn't seem phased by my father's appearance. "I—we—Blake came over last night, but Uncle Griff allowed him to! Then Uncle Griff left when Mom came back, then Benny came from the party."

"Yeah, and he was drunk and didn't want to go home, so we looked after him," Blake continued, then stood up. He approached my father, who stood there all official in his uniform. Dad observed Blake as he raised a brow.

"And you ditched a party on Halloween to stay with my daughter?"

"I wasn't in the party mood, sir."

There was an awkward silence as I watched the

270

two, staring at each other. I glanced at Benny, who was still asleep. I hoped that he wouldn't vomit when he woke up. I looked at the window and noticed it was morning, since the sun glistened through the window. The silence broke when loud footsteps emerged from the stairs. I sighed in relief as my mother walked into the room.

"Harry, you're home, dear." She smiled.

"Yes. Angie, did you know about this?" Dad asked as he pointed to Blake, then Benny.

"Yes, I did, and I told them they could stay since it was so late."

"Okay, but next time I want you to tell me this. Wake him up." Dad pointed to Benny. I nodded as I watched my parents go upstairs.

"Benny."

"Mm."

"*Wake up!*" I yelled, then gave him a slight push.

"*Did they find the body?*" His eyes snapped open as he fell off the sofa. My eyes widened as I watched Benny. I heard Blake chuckle.

"Not funny," I scolded, then helped Benny. Once he was on his feet, his eyes narrowed at me.

"Lana, I thought you weren't coming to the party?"

"You're at my place."

"How did I get here?" Benny asked as he looked around the room. His eyes landed on Blake, and they suddenly widened. "Did we?" he asked as he pointed to the three of us.

"What the fuck? No!" Blake finally spoke as he stood next to Benny. "Gross, dude."

"Then what the hell are we doin—" Benny cut

himself off as he covered his mouth. My eyes widened as I pointed toward the stairs. He sprinted out of the room, and I sighed as we heard his loud footsteps.

"Weirdo," Blake commented as we heard Benny puke.

"He's not a weirdo. He's just confused," I pointed out as I put my glasses on. My parents came downstairs with Mom still in a gown, while Dad wore a sweater and jeans.

"Lana, go help Benny clean up," my mother said. I nodded. I walked upstairs and into my room. I got a hoodie that Levi forgot here for Benny and clothing for me, then walked into the bathroom. I sat on the edge of the bathtub as I watched him lower his head in the toilet.

"Why is he here?" Benny asked after he flushed the toilet.

"Just came to talk," I mumbled, then gave him a paper towel. "There's a spare toothbrush in the cabinet."

"How did I get here?" he asked as he took out the toothbrush. Benny spun around and leaned against the sink as he applied the toothpaste. I noticed his eye was bruised and his lip was cut.

"I don't know. I assumed, since my house is the closest to Parker's, you decided to come here," I said as he brushed his teeth.

"Probably made a wrong impression on your mom." He groaned.

"Oh yeah." I laughed, then looked down at his costume. "Err, do you want to change? There are a few vomit stains on your costume."

"Yeah, thankfully I'm wearing clothes underneath." He chuckled as he washed his mouth. Once he was done, he took off his costume. I watched as he pulled it over his head and got a peek of his muscles. He stood in a black tee and jeans. I tossed him the hoodie. "I assume you want to shower now?" Benny asked as he looked at the rest of the clothing in my hands. I nodded and he walked out. "I'll be waiting downstairs then."

I quickly took a shower, then put on black jeans, red flannel, and white Converse, brushed my hair as fast as possible, then walked down to the kitchen. Eventually, Benny would remember what happened last night, and I didn't want to take the chance of Blake and Benny in the same room. We sat around the table and had breakfast. For once I was glad that we had a rectangular table rather than a square. Benny sat next to my dad; in front of him was Blake, and my mom sat next to him. I sat on the end as I watched my food, pancakes with all the toppings in the center of the table. It reminded me of the morning at Blake's house. He made perfect smooth pancakes with many toppings. It's weird because I recovered from a hangover, but now Benny was.

"Lana, dear, are you going to eat?" My mother snapped me out of my thoughts, and I realized all eyes were on me.

"Yeah."

"How was patrol?" Mom asked as she looked at dad, who read the newspaper. I glanced at Blake and Benny, who were in front of me. They glared at each other, and I rolled my eyes at their behavior.

"Same as every year, drunk idiots running through the streets naked wanting to get arrested."

"Err...sorry for entering your home drunk, Mr. and Mrs. Willson," Benny mumbled as he avoided eye contact.

"Just be glad I didn't catch you on the way, son," Dad said as I scoffed. Blake, on the other hand, found it funny and chuckled.

"What my husband is trying to say is it's okay. Our home is always open to Lana's friends."

"He's not considered a friend," Benny muttered as he glared at Blake.

"Neither were you," Blake hissed.

"I'm tired. See you tonight; hopefully they're gone by then." Dad mumbled the last part as he stood up. I glared at Benny and Blake as my father walked out of the room. He was probably annoyed as much as I was.

"I should probably get going," Blake mumbled as he picked up his plate and put it in the sink. I watched as he stood by the table and smiled at my mother. "Thank you for letting me stay, Mrs. Willson." He nodded then turned to me. "I'll see you later."

"Benny, do you have a ride home?" my mother asked as Blake walked out.

"Err...no, Mrs. Willson, but I'll call Nic—"

"Oh, Lana can take you. I'm sure Nick is also recovering from a hangover," my mother joked as we stood in the hallway. My eyes widened as she grabbed her car keys, then held them out to me. I grabbed the car keys then went into the kitchen while Benny trailed behind. I gave him a glass of water along with aspirin before we went to the car. I sat in the driver's seat and stared at the wheel as I waited for Benny. I usually didn't drive since Dad had his Jeep and Mom had her Ford. Besides, I always got rides from Benny or Miranda.

"Lana?"

"Huh? Sorry, just daydreaming." I shrugged, then started the car. The garage opened, and we gently drove out.

"Do you still think of it?" Benny asked. It took me a while to figure out what he meant. The thought of Jack August entered my mind as I sighed.

"Think of it? I have nightmares." I responded as my grip on the wheel tightened. He was a poor homeless guy who lost his job; he didn't know he'd get stabbed. The way I ran on foot in a dress that night, not having the intention to kill someone. How I let all my anger out on Jack as I continuously hit him with the heel. "Do you?"

"Yeah. Never thought I'd find a body. I only had a few nightmares. It was mostly when Jack would be in my room covered in dirt. Just lying there on the ground, waiting for me to return him back to his hole," he mumbled, then looked out the window.

"I'm really sorry, Benny, sorry you have to go through all of this." I sighed as we pulled up his driveway.

"It's okay, Lana. We'll get through this together."

"Thanks." I smiled. He took my hand in his, which was soft as his thumb rubbed circles on the back of my hand. I looked into his brown eyes and

275

noticed a hint of pain. All he ever faced was jealousy. He was a great guy, but I knew that nobody took him seriously. "If you ever need something or just wanna talk, I'm here, okay?" I blurted out. I didn't know why I said that, but something in his eye made me worried.

"Thank you." He smiled then pointed to his house that looked like a mansion. "Do you wanna come in?"

"Oh, no thanks, you should get some rest."

"Okay, be safe, and see you tomorrow," Benny said as he gave my hand one last squeeze, then got out of the car. I glanced down at my phone to see that I received a message from Blake.

Blake: All right, we're meeting at the diner for lunch. Should I get you?

Lana: Nah, I'm driving today. :)

I started the car and watched Benny walk into his garden. He looked over his shoulder, so I lowered the window.

"And thanks for everything!" he shouted, and I smiled as I drove off. As I drove to Blake's house, I couldn't help but wonder that Benny didn't only mean for last night.

I arrived at the Gunner household. It was the same as last time, but there were cars in the driveway. I parked in front of the house, then approached the front door. I rang the bell twice as I bit the inside of my cheek.

"Can I help you?" a feminine voice asked.

276

"Err…I'm here for Blake," I mumbled as I observed the woman. She could be a few years old than me; her long brunette fell to her hips as she stared at me. Before she responded, a tall figure appeared behind her and grinned at me.

"Lana, happy to see you again," Axel said with a mischievous smile on his face.

"Err, yeah, you too, Axel. Where's Blake?"

"I didn't know you wear glasses."

"Well, now you do." I awkwardly chuckled as I entered the house.

"Oh, where are my manners? This is Tamia. Tamia meet Lana, Lana, Tamia."

"Nice to meet you," she said as she gave me a once over.

"Nice to meet you too."

"Blake's in the shower, came home pretty late, right, Tamia?" Axel asked as we entered the living room.

"Yeah, and what happened to his face?"

"I…I don't know," I lied as I sat on the sofa.

"He looked really pissed, if you ask me. Wouldn't be surprised if he got into another fight." Tamia sighed.

"Lana, does he always come to your house with a black eye?" Axel asked.

"N-no."

"So he did come to your house." Axel smirked as he looked at Tamia. She wouldn't stop looking at me to even acknowledge him.

"Quit interrogating her, you guys." Blake huffed as he came into the room.

"Just concerned about you, brother."

"Come on, Lana. The guys will be there soon," Blake demanded as he put his hand out for me. I accepted it as he pulled me up from the sofa. Our hands were still interlocked as Blake pulled me to the front door.

"Oh, come on, bro. We're just worried about you."

"Whatever, Axel. You don't need to worry about me," Blake scolded as he opened the door. I turned around to see Axel and Tamia behind us.

"Bye." I waved as Blake pulled me to the car.

They waved back, but I heard Tamia say to Axel, "She looks oddly familiar." Tamia sighed as they walked back into the house. Axel whispered something in her ear that made her giggle. I got in the driver's seat as Blake got into the passenger seat. I put the key in the ignition, then drove out of their street.

"I didn't know you could drive."

"Err…yeah, but I don't drive a lot."

"Sorry about my brother and his friend. They're just annoying."

"It's cool." I laughed, then turned on the radio. "How's your eye?"

"Happy to see," he grumbled, then took a cigarette from his pocket.

"Nuh-uh, this is my mom's car," I whined as I tried to get the lighter.

"Oh, come on, you have perfume. Girls carry that shit around, right?"

"No, I don't even have a bag with me."

"Eyes on the road, Willson!" he yelled. My head snapped to the road, and I swerved, since we almost drove into a pole. Once I knew the road was clear, my eyes flickered to Blake.

"You're not smoking in the car."

"Not even if I share it with you?"

"No!"

"Ugh, you're no fun," Blake replied as he put the cigarette back in the pack.

Minutes later, we arrived at the diner and noticed Ethan's and Aidan's cars. Blake and I walked side by side as we entered the little restaurant. It wasn't full since it was a Sunday. I looked around and saw the guys at a booth. Blake walked ahead as I slowly followed. I hadn't had much of a conversation with them, so it got awkward.

"'Sup, guys?" Blake greeted as he slid into the booth and sat next to Aidan. I pulled a chair from another table and sat on the end.

"Hi, Lana," Ethan said as he gave me a warm smile.

"Hello," I muttered. It was awkward, we saw each other every day at school, but it was the first time in weeks that we'd had a proper conversation.

"I thought you worked here," I said as I turned to Aidan.

"Oh, err…I got fired."

"What'd you do?" Carter asked.

"Flirting with the customers and waitresses," he mumbled, then lowered his head. I laughed and shook my head.

"How was the party?" Blake asked.

"Same as every year, wild and crazy." Ethan chuckled as he read the menu.

"Liam was so drunk he jumped off the roof and

into the pool," Carter said. I laughed as I thought of Liam Sanchez in his Jack Sparrow costume.

"Where were you guys?" Aidan asked as he looked at Blake and me.

"Wasn't in the mood," we said in unison. The guys stared at us because they wanted to know more, but the look Blake had said he wasn't in the mood for questions.

"Hi, I'm Lindsey, your waitress for today. What would you like to order?" A squeaky voice broke the silence.

"Burgers and milkshakes please—all chocolate, Lindsey."

"Right away, and no, Aidan, you don't get a discount because you don't work here anymore," she snapped, then walked away. We laughed as we looked at Aidan. He had that smile on his face that I barely saw; it was big and bright as he looked at us.

"I missed this."

"Me too," Carter mumbled as his blue eyes sparkled. They suddenly turned to me with guilty looks.

"Are we cool?" Ethan asked.

"No, we're not cool. You guys didn't explain why." I snorted. Blake licked his lips as he turned to Aidan.

"What?"

"It was your jackass friends who started this. You explain," Blake scoffed as Lindsey placed our milkshakes on the table.

"But we were talking. You're the one who eavesdrops," Aidan said as he pointed to me.

"Well, sorry for trying to find my Homecoming

date!"

"I'll explain! Goodness, you guys are annoying." Carter sighed. "Parker and Austin said whoever sleeps with you first is supposedly the 'King Player' for breaking the nerd's virginity, but when we found out you weren't a virgin, it made things harder."

I rolled my eyes as Carter continued but bit my lip as I thought about Parker. It didn't make sense that he made a bet, since he did those things to me last year.

"As we got to know you, we sort of forgot about that and focused on actually being your friends. Lana, we didn't mean to hurt you like that."

"Yeah, we're sorry for putting you through all this shit," Ethan murmured.

"We only said those things because we didn't want you to get hurt." Aidan frowned. Well, I certainly got hurt. I should've given them a chance to explain—then we'd be friends, and I wouldn't have run off and stabbed someone. I wouldn't sit at home and stare at the picture of us in detention. I wouldn't have nightmares and wake up in the middle of the night, then cried myself to sleep.

"I'm sorry too. I wish I never ran off like that," I mumbled then stared at the table.

"Wha-what happened? You looked destroyed the next day," Blake said as I raised my head. I wanted to tell them, I really did, but it wouldn't be fair to Benny and them. I didn't say anything to them about the drugs, so it'd be fair to not tell them about Jack August.

"It was storming that night. I fell and stuff." I

shrugged it off. Lindsey brought our food, and I dug in to avoid further questions. I stared at Ethan; the blond streaks in his hair faded into his dark brown hair. He wore a Nike sweater as he ate his burger. His brown eyes met mine as I stared at him. "What were you going to do that would make me lose the bet?" I asked since I remembered what he said at Homecoming.

"Oh." He awkwardly chuckled. "We were gonna go to a monster truck show, a club, do graffiti in the city, go bungee jumping, then get matching tattoos."

Blake grinned as he lifted his sweater, which displayed a small tattoo. It was a 3D box that was sealed; I looked at him in confusion. Ethan raised his sweater that showed a tattoo of the same box, but his box had a small hole in it. Aidan had one on his bicep, but the box was wide open, while Carter had a square.

"You guys are crazy. At least two of those things would've gotten me killed." I laughed as I shook my head. "What do the tattoos mean?"

"Well, mine is wide open because I'm an open person and not very secretive, but you see there," Aidan said as he pointed to his tattoo. "There's a line there. That's supposed to be a mirror, so if a person looks into the box they see nothing because the mirror will reflect to show an empty box." He smiled. "The people who notice the mirror would know I have secrets."

"Mine is just a square because there's no way around it. What you see is what you get," Carter said.

"I have a small hole in my box because

somehow, someone always manages to look inside of me," Ethan mumbled, and I smiled at their explanations.

"Mine is sealed, nothing to it," Blake muttered.

"Really, Gunner? It's sealed because you don't let anyone in," I whispered as the guys got back to their food. He smirked at me while I drank my milkshake.

"Lana, we don't want you to be our puppet anymore," Carter said as we finished our food.

"Why? I lost the bet, and it said to be your pu—"

"No, we feel bad, especially for what we put you through. Please don't; besides, you don't want to spend the rest of senior year doing our work when you have to focus on yours," Ethan begged as he put his hand on my arm.

"But—"

"If you do one last thing for us, you don't have to do anything for the rest of the year, and we can all be friends again," Aidan cut me off.

"Err...okay, what is it?" I asked as I looked at them.

"We want you to find out the guy's name who sent us the drugs."

Chapter Nineteen

Lana

"Hey," I greeted, then got into Benny's car. When I put on my seatbelt, I noticed that we hadn't moved yet.

"Morning," he breathed out as he stared at the road.

"Are you okay?" I asked. He wore a hoodie with a pair of jeans, but the thing that caught my eye was the bags under his eyes.

"Yeah," he mumbled, then started to drive. We drove in silence as I tried to remember what happened last between us.

"Did you have another nightmare?"

"Maybe."

Okay, that's not it. Besides the fact that Benny was drunk and we talked about nightmares, I didn't know what was wrong with him...unless he remembered what he said when he was drunk. My eyes widened as I glanced over to Benny. Maybe he didn't remember.

"Are you okay?"

"Yeah, just stressing over mid-year exams."

"We still have Thanksgiving, then a few more weeks till midterms."

"Yeah," Benny said. I bet he didn't even hear; there's a difference with Benny when he's mature and when he's distracted. The rest of the drive to school was awkward as I stared out the window. The radio wasn't on, and it was windy…another typical Monday morning in Illinois. I got out of the car and noticed Benny rushing ahead of me as he entered the building, entirely disregarded his friends. I let out a sigh and approached Miranda, Liam, and Marcus.

"What's up with him?" Liam asked as we watched Benny walk in.

"He was quiet the whole ride," I mumbled, then looked at them. "How was the party?"

"Amazing," Miranda slurred as Marcus whispered in her ear.

"A night to remember," he added. I rolled my eyes at the clingy couple and looked at Liam.

"Heard you got drunk off your ass."

"I wasn't that drunk."

"Yet you jumped in the pool from the roof and kept yelling out Marco!" Marcus laughed.

"And nobody said Polo." Liam frowned, then looked at his feet.

"If I were there, I would've said Polo," I said, then patted his shoulder.

"Yeah, but you were too busy with a certain someone," Miranda spoke up.

"And that someone starts with a B," Marcus

sang.

"Nothing happened between Benny and me, okay?" I snapped with a roll of my eyes. They stood, jaw dropped, as I rose an eyebrow.

"We were talking about Blake," Liam said as he gripped my arms. "What did you do to my best friend?"

"Nothing!" I shouted as he repeatedly shook me.

"I remember Benny leaving the party; he kept saying I need to tell and all that." Marcus shrugged.

"So they were both there? Lana Jane Willson, what happened?" Miranda demanded.

"They slept over," I mumbled.

"Oh, way to go, Lana!" Liam cheered as he raised his hand.

"Not like that, you idiot!" I said as I scrunched up my nose. Liam lowered his hand but kept his grin. The bell rang, and I sighed in relief as I began to walk into the building. When I walked into Mr. Bronx's class for Calculus, I saw Aidan grin. I turned my head to see Nick. I usually sat with him in Mr. Bronx's classes.

"Morning." He grinned as I sat down.

"Hi," I mumbled. I sat in the middle with Nick on my right and Tyler, who's always quiet, on my left. Out of the corner of my eye, I saw Aidan approach Tyler.

"Scoot," he demanded. Tyler looked up from his phone, and his eyes widened as he quickly gathered his stuff and walked to the back. Tyler was the golden boy of the school, sporty and smart, yet he was quiet at times. He often conversed more with the guys on the team.

"What's up, peeps?" Aidan asked as he sat down in Tyler's seat.

"What is he doing here?" Nick glared at Aidan.

"Oh, haven't you heard, Nicky boo? We made up," Aidan mocked when Melissa called him that.

"What? Lana, is this tr—"

"Good morning, class," Mr. Bronx said as he walked into the room.

"Morning, sir," I said, trying to ignore the glares sent from each side.

It was a rough morning, and I was glad it was lunch. Through the period I had with Blake and Benny's groups, I decided to ignore all of them. When I walked into the cafeteria, I saw the long line and sighed, then looked at Liam, who waved at me like a five year old that saw the ice cream truck.

"Lana!" a familiar voice yelled. I turned my head to see Carter, who motioned me to sit with them. I looked back and forth between the two tables. Benny kept his head level as everyone glared at the other table. They seemed too busy arguing with each other, so I trailed out of the cafeteria. I walked as fast as I could, then stopped by Mr. Bronx's classroom.

"Lana, I wanted to talk to you," Uncle Griff said as I shut the door.

"Err...is this about Aidan distracting me in class? I have been paying atte—"

"Not that, and I know you've been, so it's fine. About Saturday."

"Oh, err...what about it, sir?" I asked as I noticed the grin he sent.

"You still haven't answered the question that I

287

asked you on Saturday night, Miss Willson," he sang, then folded his arms. "The answer should be something along the lines of Saturday night when I left or even Sunday."

"No, Uncle Griff!" I whined as I felt my cheeks warm up.

"Just playing with you, Lana, but if that boy did, you come to me, okay? That conversation you guys had was deep."

"Yeah," I muttered, but the corner of my mouth rose as I thought of his love life. "So how are things with you and Miss Rosa?"

"Not good. I fucked up," he said, then lowered his head.

"What happened?" I asked. Uncle Griff barely swore in front of me, but when he did, it was serious.

"Just little arguments, and now she's mad at me. I like it when she's upset with me because she looks cute, but this time it's the real thing."

"You care about her," I stated. Griffon talked about Miss Rosa on Saturday night like she was a goddess. He never spoke about anyone like that before.

"I do, and I don't want to lose her."

"I have her subject tomorrow; maybe I can throw in a good word or two about you," I suggested, and I noticed how the corners of his mouth turned up.

"Would you?"

"Anything for you, Uncle Griff. You've always been there for me, and now it's my turn to be there for you."

"Thank you, Lana!" he exclaimed, then wrapped

his arms around me.

"Okay," I breathed out as his grip tightened. Uncle Griff let out a chuckle as he let go. With one last smile, I walked out the door and into the hallway. Out of the corner of my eye, I saw movement. As I looked over my shoulder, I noticed Kelly West and Melissa Singe against the lockers.

"Told you she goes to him at lunch," Melissa said as her eyes flicked to me.

"So sad, wait till everyone knows who's really behind those glasses," Kelly said. I watched the girls as they walked off, confusion written all over my face as the bell rang.

***

"Why couldn't I just drop you off at home?" Miranda asked as she stopped at the sheriff's station.

"My mom isn't home until midnight, so Dad asked me to come here," I said as we stared at the building in front of us. I couldn't believe how many lies I'd told, yet it was for a good cause.

"What's up with Benny?" she suddenly asked.

"I don't know."

"He was silent today. Lana, if you guys have a thing going on, you can te—"

"No! What? No! I honestly don't know what's up with him."

"Did you guys kiss on Saturday?"

"No, Miranda, plus Blake was there."

"So that's why they both had bruises on their faces." She wiggled her brows. I let out a scoff, then got out of her car.

"Thanks for the ride. See you tomorrow."

"See you, Willson."

Once Miranda was out of sight, I spun around and stared at the building that I hadn't been to in weeks. Dad didn't even know I was here, and as far as I knew, Mom was at work. It's not easy to tell your best friend you're here to find out information, because that'd lead to many questions.

I walked into the building and took in the full aroma of a station. Dad was the Sheriff of the small town we lived in, but the police department in the city of Chicago was much bigger and often dealt with more significant crimes. Since the drug situation and Jack August took place in this town, there was bound to be something I could find out.

"Hi, sweetie. What can I do for you?" Ms. Jackson asked as I approached her desk.

"Just here to see my dad, Ms. Jackson."

"Go on in; he's been in there since lunch."

"Thanks," I muttered, then walked past her. Deputy Paul sat at his desk and typed.

"He's in there," he said as he pointed to my dad's office.

"Thanks," I mumbled, then walked in. In my father's office, there were papers and files scattered everywhere. "Hey, Dad," I murmured as I sat in front of his desk.

"Hey, sweetie. What are you doing here?"

"Miranda dropped me off," I said, then took a book out of my bag. "I won't disturb you."

He nodded, then proceeded with his work. I noticed a crime board behind him. I stared at it as I saw the investigation of the cocaine. A picture of Ethan's cottage was there, along with the guys' photos. Each had a form beside it with their information. Then there was a clear picture that connected the rest of the images with string. It had a big question mark on it and small text below.

"I want my lawyer!" a loud voice echoed throughout the building. I looked through the glass and saw a man in handcuffs being dragged into the interrogation room by two police officers.

"They never learn," Dad said as he shook his head.

"What did he do?"

"Accused of murder," my father stated. My eyes widened as I dropped my book. "You okay?" Dad asked as I let out an awkward chuckle and picked up my book.

"Yeah, peachy," I said as I covered my face with the book. The blood on my hands, shoe covered in blood, Jack by the dumpster, then the others. I wish they never got involved, because we'd all end up like that man who was still shouting!

"Dad?"

"Hmm?"

"Whatever happened to Ja-Jack August?" I asked as I lowered my book.

"Not our case. All I know is they haven't found him yet."

"But what if they do find him?"

"They'll continue their investigation, even if he's dead or alive," Dad responded as he stood up. "Is there something I need to know, Lana?"

"No, just curious," I mumbled, then leaned back

in my seat.

"Sheriff, robbery on Flinders Street," Deputy Paul yelled as he knocked on the door. I turned to my dad and watched as he collected his gear. He took the paper from the clipboard and rushed out of the room. I looked over my shoulder to see Ms. Jackson by the door.

"Look after her," Dad said to her. I threw my hands up in defeat because I knew I had to come back if I wanted to know the identity of the drug dealer.

***

"See you in the cafeteria," Benny said as I walked to Miss Rosa's classroom. It was Wednesday, and yesterday was a fail since my dad was out on patrol, so I had to try again. I didn't have time to talk to Miss Rosa earlier, so now was my only chance. Benny returned to his usual self, and so had everyone else. Yesterday I sat in the library instead of the cafeteria and researched on crime, because not only was I anxious, but guilty too.

"Miss Rosa," I said as I tapped her shoulder.

"Yes, Lana?" she asked. A bright smile filled her features as she stared at me.

"Y'know, Mr. Bronx told me what an excellent teacher you are."

"Is that so?"

"Yes, Miss, he was at my house the other night, and he went on and on about how amazing you are," I exclaimed. Behind me, I heard Aidan and Liam snort.

"You had Mister Bronx as a babysitter? How did that go?" Aidan laughed.

"Did he only put you to bed if you finished your math?" Liam added. I rolled my eyes and looked at Miss Rosa.

"His compliments, Lana, they honor me, but I don't want to talk to him," she said, and I frowned as I turned to the two brunettes.

"You know, Miss Rosa, since you're a teacher...sometime you can teach me a thing or two like you do with Mr. Bronx." Aidan winked at her.

"Excuse me?" she asked as her cheeks turned red.

"You're excused, and it is Miss, right? No ring mea—" Liam smirked as he leaned over the desk.

"Thank you, Miss Rosa. We have to go now." I cut him off then backed away. Without a word, we stumbled out of the classroom. As we walked, I huffed and turned to them. "Why?"

"Why not? She's magnificent." Aidan sighed as he rested his palm on his chest.

"Well, she's off limits now," I said, then turned the corner for the library.

"Nuh-uh, nerd, you're coming with us," Liam joked as he linked his arm with mine.

"I-I have studying to do," I stuttered as Aidan linked his arm with my other arm.

"I'm sure you're smart enough," Aidan said, then playfully rolled his eyes. They dragged me to the cafeteria, which could be interesting, since they sat at different tables. I watched Miranda smirk at me as she looked at Blake's table. Aidan and Liam pulled me on either side as I cursed. "Lana, you're

293

coming with me."

"No, she gets to decide, and it's with us, right?"

"Stop!" I yelled. They dropped my arms with guilty looks. I walked to the back table that was on the other side of Blake's table and far away from Benny's. Nobody sat at the table, which made me smile as I sat down. I took out my lunch and licked my lips at the delicious potato salad. From the corner of my eye, I saw two figures approach.

"There's no escape," Blake whispered in my ear as he sat down on my left.

"The one time you choose a big table." Benny huffed as he sat on my right. I looked up and noticed that everyone from both tables sat down. Benny was right; it was the biggest table. Miranda and Marcus sat in front of me, and only then I noticed we were the only females.

"You don't have to be here if you don't want to," I blurted out.

"We always wanna be with you, Willson." Blake put an arm around my shoulder. Out of the corner of my eye, I saw Benny's stare. "What, Nielson? If you wanna say something, say it to my face," Blake barked as he lowered his hand from my shoulder and rubbed my back. The strange feeling made me shift, which made Blake drop his hand.

"You're an asshole," Benny said.

"Like you're better…beating a girl," Blake replied as he glared at Benny. I leaned against the wall. Everyone waited in anticipation to see what the next would say.

"Sad that's the only thing you can come up with, man-whore," Benny laughed. "I can go on and on about how big of an asshole you are, but I don't waste my breath on useless things."

"You want me to knock you out again?" Blake demanded as he stood up.

"Stop!" I yelled. The whole cafeteria went silent as I turned to Blake. "I am sitting here because I don't want any favoritism, so I suggest you all get your shit together or go back to your fucking table."

Blake stared at me; his lips twitched up as he nodded. I sat down and looked at Miranda, who had a smirk on her face as I rolled my eyes. She enjoyed this because she's friends with all of them, but wherever I went, she went.

"Home or station?" she suddenly asked.

"Station."

"Speaking of the station…did you get his name?" Ethan asked. Before I could answer, Nick asked another question.

"Did you watch the news?" he asked as he looked at Benny and me.

"What's with you and the news lately?" Liam asked.

"Why would she watch the news?" Carter asked as he raised a brow.

"Whose name must she get at the station?" Benny demanded. I looked at the guys beside me. They were so stupid. I swear sometimes I was the only smart one at the table.

"What guy?" Nick asked. He squinted his eyes.

"I can't seem to remember; Ethan, what man do you speak of?" I asked with a bit of annoyance. His eyes widened as everyone stared at him. "And what did I miss on the news, Nick?" I asked. He ran his hand through his blond locks while he tried to avoid eye contact.

"Err…" Nick stuttered as he looked at us.

"The cat!" Liam piped up.

"The cat?" Blake asked as the corners of his eyes wrinkled.

"Yeah, he was…stuck in a tree," Nick continued.

"They had that on the news?" Aidan tilted his head.

"Yeah, but the twist was that the cat…wore a tutu," Liam added as he bit on his lip stud nervously. Benny shook his head in disappointment at his friend's weak attempt to cover up for Jack August.

"Now tell us who was the guy at the station?" Benny asked as he looked at Blake. This should be interesting.

"Ethan got a ticket the other day and just wanted to know the cop that gave it to him," Blake said as he tapped his fingers on the table. I glanced at the team captain to see his jaw dropped.

"Didn't you see his name tag?" Marcus shrugged. I almost forgot that he was there.

"There's a reason why I got the ticket. I was drunk…couldn't read anything," Ethan muttered, and I noticed how Blake grinned. My eyebrows rose since I was impressed at the lies they made on the spot.

"Okay, those are some interesting stories." Miranda sighed as she leaned onto Marcus's shoulder.

"How's your community work, guys?" I asked as I turned to Carter. Dad wasn't going to let them off the hook that easily, so they had a bunch of community work to do.

"Community work? What did you guys do?" Liam asked.

"I don't remember. Willson, tell us what did we do again?" Blake asked with a wink.

"They ran into a gay club naked." I smirked. I saw Carter's jaw drop while Ethan did a double-take. "So they have community work to do since they got arrested."

"What must you do?" Liam asked as he laughed at Aidan.

"They had to cut the whole neighborhood's lawns…with a scissor." I shrugged. We laughed, but Miranda quieted us down.

"Okay, since we're all being big mouths here…" She trailed off, then turned to me. "Who keeps calling you princess?"

"I don't know what you're talking about."

"At Homecoming, your phone piled up with messages. Most of them said princess."

"Oh yeah, I remember that one day, he said 'can't wait to see you, princess.' Ugh. Who is he?" Aidan asked.

"I can't remember."

"Come on, Lana."

"Fine, it's just a friend," I muttered as I avoided eye contact.

"Was that so hard?" Blake cooed into my ear.

"So what are we doing this weekend?" Benny asked. The past few weeks we spent the weekend together, every time it was different.

"Nuh-uh, Lana and I are having a girl's day on

Saturday," Miranda said. "We haven't had one in a while since horny bastards surround her."

I let out a snort as the guys glared at her. She clasped her hands together, then let out a squeal. "You guys are going to have a sleepover!"

"What?"

"Yes, so you guys can get along with each other better. All of you are going."

"Whose house?" Carter asked.

"Ethan Baxter is kind enough to invite a couple of dudes to his house to, y'know, drink beers and all that man stuff you guys do."

"What? Why my house?"

"Your house is the biggest."

"I'm not coming." Benny huffed.

"Yes, you are, because if you care about this girl, you'll do this for her. I mean, look at her. No offense, Lana—" Miranda said.

"None taken."

"—she has to come into the cafeteria every day to decide what table to sit at. Since she's so sweet and stuff, it leads her to sit in the library or restrooms."

"Eww, you sit in the restrooms?"

"It was one time!" I groaned. "Besides, you guys used to be friends. Please don't let some loser come between your friendship."

"How will you know that we showed up?" Nick asked as he looked at Miranda.

"That's where my beautiful boyfriend comes in. He's coming too, and he'll tell me if you show up. If you don't, I'll kidnap you and throw you into Ethan's pool."

"Whoa, okay." Ethan smirked.

"Yeah, and baby, keep an eye on these two bad boys," Miranda said as she pursed her lips at Benny, then Blake.

"Haha, get it? Because both of your names start wit—"

"Lame, dude," Aidan cut off Liam as he threw a grape toward him.

"Okay, we will, and you ladies get your girls' night, but don't be surprised if you see one of us." Carter smirked.

***

"Dad?" I asked as I looked up from the book I read. Today was the day I finally asked him about the name, and I hoped that I wouldn't get interrupted. Dad looked up from his computer. The bags under his eyes formed as he licked his chapped lips. I glanced at the board with Blake's picture, along with the rest of them on it. He followed my gaze and awkwardly coughed.

"They're gonna be okay."

"What about the guy?"

"Still looking."

"Do we know his name?"

"Lana, that's classified information."

"Knowing his name? Dad, maybe I know the guy."

"You know a drug dealer?"

"No! But Daddy, please, I won't tell anyone," I begged as I clasped my hands together. He deeply sighed and straightened in his seat.

"His name is James Cornelius."

"Cornelius?" I snorted. "I thought his name would be badass and evil, but Cornelius? Cornelius Fudge from *Harry Potter*?"

"Lana," my dad warned as I laughed.

"Wow, so is he still in Illinois?" I coughed awkwardly.

"Yep, we have the whole country looking for him. James is a clever man and very hard to find."

"I know you'll get him, Dad," I said, then leaned forward and rested my palm against his hand.

"Other than keeping that cocaine for almost two years, they're not that bad."

"So you like them?"

"I never said that, but they barely come to the house, for which I'm glad, but now it's those weird guys who look like they surf, but I like them because they play for the team," Dad said, then looked at me. "What happened?"

"Those two groups don't get along well, but hopefully they will sooner or later."

"What about Miranda and her weird boyfriend?"

"Us three get along with both groups, so we're cool." I shrugged, then leaned back in my seat. I looked at my dad and tilted my head. "What's with the questions, Dad?"

"Nothing."

"Dad."

"Just that guy with the tattoos looks oddly familiar."

"Which guy?"

"The one with that nose ring…" He trailed off.

"Dad, there's a lot of people with nose rings that

we know," I pointed out.

"With the damn bike and looks like he's on his period most the time!"

"Blake Gunner?"

"Yeah, that guy," my dad grumbled as he squinted his eyes. "He looks like someone we know."

"Yeah, he does."

"Both are quite something."

"Yes, they are."

***

"And make it nice and wavy," Miranda said to the guy behind me. It was Saturday, and as Miranda said, we had our girls' day. The guys were at Ethan's house while we were at the salon.

"Mm, maybe little trims too," he added as my hair got yanked. At the start of the school year, I meant to cut it, but I never got around to it. My hair was at my waist, and it seemed to bug Miranda a lot since I hardly brushed it. Most of the time, I either tied my hair up in a ponytail or bun or kept it hidden under a beanie.

"How are the guys doing?" I asked Miranda as she sat in the seat next to me.

"Marcus said they were acting childish at first, but now they're in Ethan's basement hanging out."

"Hope they get along,"

"Yeah."

An hour later, I stared at myself in the mirror. My eyebrows rose at the shiny dark hair. "Wow."

"Even though your hair is below your shoulders,

it brings out the color in your eyes more," Miranda commented as she stood beside me.

"All better!" the guy cheered as he clapped his hands.

"Thank you."

"Ugh, no problem, you look beautiful!" He smiled as we paid. We walked out of the salon and got into Miranda's car. She sat in the driver's seat and smiled at her phone.

"Do you want me to drive?" I asked as she put her phone down.

"Wha—nope, it's cool," she said and started the car.

"Where we going?" I asked. Before she'd answer, her phone rang. She glanced at me, pouting at me to answer. I groaned as I answered. It was a FaceTime, so I awkwardly stared at Marcus.

"Lana—whoa, you look different."

"I just cut my hair."

"Yeah, but you look…different."

"Hey, babe," Miranda greeted. I moved the phone so he'd see her.

"'Sup, err…we're going out now, making progress. We should be back late," he whispered as if someone heard him.

"Cool, so how's lover boy?" Miranda asked.

"Getting there."

"Who's lover boy?" I asked. Miranda and Marcus stared at each other for a moment, then looked at me. They laughed as I rolled my eyes.

"You'll find out sooner or later, Lana." Marcus grinned, then looked up. "We're going now. See you beautiful ladies later."

"Bye." I ended the FaceTime before he'd blow a kiss to Miranda.

"Yet I ask again. Where are we going?"

"Ethan's house."

"Why? The guys won't be there, so what's the use?"

"But first we gotta pick up somebody."

"Who?"

"Melissa."

"Wha—Why?" I asked, then looked at Miranda as if she'd grown a second head.

"Remember? She used to date Ethan back in Sophomore year."

"I thought she was over him."

"Yeah, but a little revenge won't hurt. Besides, it's nothing illegal."

"And your crush with Ethan?"

"Ugh, I have Marcus now."

"So whose idea was this?"

"Mine." She smirked as we pulled up Melissa's driveway. "Besides, we've been getting along. You should too."

"Yeah, but every time I talk to Uncle Griff, she's there, either with Kelly or Jennifer."

"They do know he's a family friend, right?" Miranda asked. "Your godfather."

Before I replied, we heard the back door open.

"Hey, guys," Melissa greeted.

"Hi," I mumbled and looked back and forth at the two and only noticed now that they wore black. "I didn't get the invitation."

"Oh, that's why we're heading over to your house, duh." Miranda smiled as she started the car.

"If both of us showed up at the salon in black, that guy would've noticed something. It's not like we're gonna rob a bank or something."

"Are you?" I nervously asked.

"Nope, just a rich bastard's house." Melissa smirked.

"His house is like a bank! Everything in there is three hundred dollars and up," I scolded.

"Even the toilet paper," Miranda added.

We arrived at a supermarket, and I couldn't help but squint. It's as if they planned the whole thing and I felt excluded.

"What are we doing here?"

"You ask too many questions, Lana," Melissa said as she got out of the car.

"Wanna come?" Miranda asked as she opened her door.

"No, I'll stay."

"Hey, if you can forgive all of them, you can forgive her," Miranda said, then playfully punched my shoulder.

"We'll see."

"See you soon, Willson; this is gonna be a long day." Miranda laughed as she climbed out of the car. I watched the two girls walk into the supermarket, talking and laughing like they're best friends, even though if it weren't for me they'd be pulling each other's hair out by now, but I was glad Miranda was friends with everyone. I pulled out my phone and went through old messages. I smiled at the group chat with Blake, Ethan, Aidan, and Carter. We barely spoke in there, but when we did, it was mostly to help each other out of class or detention. I figured they made one on their own since we haven't talked in the group since the bet.

Lana: I'm bored. :(

Worth a shot. I scrolled through my contacts and saw a familiar name. Since I had the confidence to send a message to the group, I should have a bit left to call someone. I hit call, then placed the phone to my ear and waited. It rang for a bit, then went to voicemail.

"Hello, it's yours truly, Levi. I haven't picked up because I'm out doing something really fun or just being a lazy ass. Leave a message and I might get back to you."

I sighed and didn't bother to leave a message. I looked down at my phone again and noticed that someone replied.

Aidan: Only boring people get bored.

Blake: I hate this.

Carter: Hi bored, I'm Carter. Nice to meet you.

Lana: -.-

Ethan: Where are you?

Lana: Somewhere...

Blake: I'm gonna get Miranda for this.

Lana: What are you guys doing?

Aidan: Your mom!

Blake: Dude…

Carter: Really?

Ethan: Now you scared her off.

Lana: Whatever, guys.

Blake: Aww Willson don't have a comeback.

Lana: Shut up.

Blake: Oooh me scared.

Aidan: We are sitting right next to each other.

Ethan: Yeah Benny's getting pissed. Lol

Carter: With his red hair he looks like a freaking tomato.

Lana: Shame on you, at least try to hang out with them?

Blake: We'll TRY.

Before I typed anymore, I received a call. I rolled my eyes at the ID caller but answered anyway.

"Hey princess!" Levi shouted into the phone. I

pulled it away from my ear as I huffed.

"You should stop calling me that."

"What? No hello, my knight in shining armor? Remember?"

"Yeah, when we were like eight." I laughed as I twirled my dark brown hair. "Now people think you're my boyfriend."

"Who? If they ask again, say that they're jealous that they don't have a princess."

"So funny I forgot to laugh," I hissed.

"Aww, tired of me already? I'm not even there yet." Levi laughed into the phone.

"You're so annoying. I don't even know why I called." I groaned, then glanced up to see Miranda and Melissa approach the car with two shopping carts.

"Cuz you love me," he cooed into the phone.

"Whatever, see you soon. Bye," I replied, then ended the call as Miranda opened the door.

"Who was that?"

"No one important."

* * *

"You lucky bitch," Melissa squealed as she observed my wardrobe. All the clothing and shoes that Ethan bought me for the bet finally came in handy, yet I still wore them.

"He bought all of this for you?" she asked, then pulled out a black top.

"Yeah, it was for the bet."

"Okay, here we go. This looks fashionable enough to break into a mansion," Melissa said as

307

she pulled out a long-fitted crew neck and Vans. I took off my blue sweater and put the crew neck on along with the Vans. I tied my hair up into a high ponytail and put my glasses in the drawer.

"Come on, you two!" Miranda called from downstairs. We walked out of my room, and as we walked downstairs, I noticed my dad with a cup of coffee in his hand.

"Gonna rob a bank?" he asked as he looked at our outfits.

"We're going to egg somebody's car; he emotionally hurt your daughter, so we're gonna help," Miranda lied, even though my dad was the sheriff.

"Use flour too, and don't let the police see you," Dad said, then sipped his coffee.

"Thanks, Mr. Willson!" Melissa smiled.

"Anything for my daughter," Dad exclaimed as we walked out of the house. We got in the car, and I bit the inside of my cheek as I digested what we're about to do. I didn't have time to see what they bought, but hopefully, we'd egg someone's car. I wanted to.

"What are you guys planning?" I asked as I sat in the back.

"Wait and see." Melissa winked at me from the rearview mirror. Miranda always used her mother's car, and as she revved the motor, I heard how old it was.

"Let's go get 'em, girls," Miranda cheered as we raced down the street.

Chapter Twenty

Lana

"How we gonna get in there?" I asked as we looked at Ethan's mansion. The gates were closed as the security guard smoked in his small booth. It was dark, and all the cars were there except Nick and Aidan's. They probably piled into two cars and went out.

"With this." Melissa smirked as she held a walkie-talkie. I tilted my head, then glanced at Miranda, who grinned. Melissa kept the walkie-talkie to her mouth and looked at the security guard. We parked opposite his house as we watched the security guard pick up his large walkie-talkie.

"We got a drunk man running around Fifth Avenue naked, seems to be heading into the Baxter residence," Melissa deepened her voice as she spoke. "Over."

We watched the security guard as he shook his head; he looked back at the big mansion as his eyes widened. He jumped up from his chair, grabbed the walkie-talkie and flashlight, and ran out. We giggled as we watched him sprint down the street, in search of a naked man.

"Okay come on," Miranda said as she started the car. She drove all the way to the gates and stopped. I climbed out and walked to the booth. I pushed the button and watched as the gates opened. I got back in the car, and we drove to park on the side. We got out of the car and stared at the enormous house in front of us.

"Should we do inside or outside first?" Melissa asked as she opened the trunk.

"Inside," Miranda whispered.

"Are his parents gone?"

"Yeah, but the maid or gardener could be here."

"How we gonna get in?"

"Ethan always leaves his bedroom window open," Melissa said as she looked up. I followed her gaze to an open window; thankfully, there was a tree.

"Someone will need to climb that tree, get into his room, then open the back door," Miranda said as she handed me a flashlight.

"I'll do it, leave him a surprise in his room while I'm there." Melissa smirked as she grabbed a few egg cartons. I watched as she took duct tape and stuffed it in her backpack, then walked to the tree and climbed.

"I never realized she was so…" I trailed off as I watched Melissa.

"Fun?"

"Yeah," I said, then squinted my eyes. "She's not that bad. I mean, Nick's a good guy. At first, you'd think why'd he go for a bitchy girl like her, but she's not bad. Did that make sense?"

"Sure."

"So what do I have to do?"

"You have to take all these sticky note packs and cover the whole basement with them since they'll be sleeping there," Miranda said as she handed me packs of sticky notes.

"Lame."

"Then you put this fish in one of their sleeping bags," she said as she held a bag. We scrunched our noses…ugghh.

"Come on, guys!" Melissa yelled. We looked to see that she was by the back door. We got the rest of the stuff, then joined her. As we tiptoed down the basement, I couldn't help but apply a sticky note here and there.

"That beer mixed with cologne," Melissa hissed as we walked downstairs.

"Eww." Miranda groaned as she turned on the light. There were pizza boxes on the table. All the guys' sleeping bags were on the ground, along with their overnight bags, and I couldn't help but smirk.

"Lana, you gotta cover this whole room, so I suggest you start now," Melissa said as she took more duct tape then walked upstairs.

"I'm gonna get something in the cinema room," Miranda mumbled, then followed Melissa. I turned to the four walls and sighed as I got to work.

***

"Whoa." Melissa's voice echoed through the

basement as she glanced around. "This looks amazing."

"Thanks," I said. The room was filled with sticky notes. They gave it a rainbow color rather than a man cave. With the leftover sticky notes, I covered the sofa and pool table. "What'd you do?" I asked Melissa as she giggled at her phone. She approached me with a mischievous grin. I laughed, since Ethan's room had eggs hung from the ceiling, thanks to the tape.

"Little help," a familiar voice asked. We looked at the stairs to see Miranda with a popcorn machine.

"What are you going to do with that?" I asked as we helped her.

"Fill this room with popcorn," she said, then held the big bags of kernels.

"But first we need to fill their sleeping bags," Melissa said as she held up a bag. She pulled out the fish, and we let out a gag. We filled some sleeping bags with the fish, others received cactuses, while the leftovers had tiny bugs. Yet I remembered that there was one sleeping bag short. After thirty minutes, we finished. I glanced down one last time at the basement filled with popcorn. Miranda shut the door, and we let out a sigh of relief. We walked out of the house, through the back door to see Miranda's car still parked where it was.

"Now we do outside." She grinned, then ran toward the car.

"Wait…we only filled six sleeping bags, excluding Ethan obviously," I spoke up.

"Blake seems the type to not bring one, so he must be crashing on the sofa. Although we got something special for your bad boy." Melissa winked, then turned to Miranda.

"What?" I bit my lip from excitement. Miranda opened her trunk again and took out a spray can; she handed it to me. I looked up and saw Miranda with eggs and flour, while Melissa had toilet paper. Melissa pointed to something behind me, and I followed her gaze to Blake's motorcycle. "Y-you want me to do graffiti on his bike?"

"Yeah. Don't worry, it's not permanent."

"What are you guys gonna do?" I asked as I looked at the supplies in their hands.

"As your dad said, egg their cars and add a little flour." Miranda grinned as she walked off.

"Tee-peeing his house," Melissa answered as if it were a regular thing to do. I watched as they began their stunts, their silhouettes jumping and running in the moonlight. I glanced down at the pink spray can and opened it.

"Well…you only live once." I sighed as I began to spray the motorcycle.

***

"Nice job." Melissa grinned as she took a photo of Blake's motorcycle. It was still black but had pink polka dots all over. I smiled because I was satisfied with my work even though my hands were pink too. I looked at Benny's car along with the rest and laughed. Their vehicles were covered in flour and egg. Some were even wrapped in toilet paper.

"I just need to do there," Melissa said as she pointed to a blank wall.

"We'll help," Miranda suggested as she took a few toilet rolls, then handed me some. For the next five minutes, we threw toilet paper at Ethan's house and cheered when it went on the roof.

"Goal!" Miranda cheered as she threw into his window.

"Freeze!" a deep voice yelled. I stopped what I was doing and raised my arms as the light flashed on us. I squinted as the bright light approached us. "Drop the toilet paper and put your hands up!" he yelled. The voice sounded familiar, and I glanced up to see who it was.

"Deputy Paul?" I questioned. He lowered the light and stared at me.

"Lana?"

"Daddy said don't get caught." I nervously laughed as he groaned.

"All of you...get in the car!" he yelled as he motioned to the car with his gun. We made our way into Deputy Paul's cop car. With the cage that separated us, I looked around. Miranda was covered in flour, while Melissa took out popcorn from her hair. I couldn't imagine how I looked. We drove in silence as Miranda played on her phone and Melissa looked out the window. They seemed calm for being in a cop car, while I died inside. I stared at the cage again. This was where I was supposed to be. I killed someone and got away with it and watched my friends deal with drugs, yet I didn't get into trouble.

After twenty minutes, we arrived at the station. Deputy Paul confiscated our belongings then handcuffed us. We walked in with guilty looks, yet

I didn't see any people that'd recognize me. It was all the people who took the night shift, mostly middle-aged people.

"You each get one phone call," he announced as we walked into the prison cell. There were a few in the station, most of them filled with drunk old men, but there was one empty in front of us.

"Come on, we've known each other for years," I groaned as he took off the handcuffs.

"That's Deputy to you," he said. I wrapped my hands around the bars and huffed as he walked away.

"I knew he never liked me."

"What gave you that idea?" Melissa questioned. I spun around to glare at the two. They sat on the bench that attached to the wall. Miranda glanced around the jail cell like it was a fantasy, while Melissa twirled her blonde hair.

"What are we gonna do?" I asked as I sat between them. I glanced around the small prison cell. It had squat toilets but no toilet paper. Could have told us to bring some.

"Y'know Liam always sang that ninety-nine bottles of beer on the wall, but since you're so worried, we'll change it to milk." Miranda waved off. I rolled my eyes and hoped that the guys had a better night than us.

"Ninety-nine bottles of milk on the wall, ninety-nine bottles of milk. Take one down and pass it around. Ninety-eight bottles of milk on the wall!" They began to sing.

***

"Fifty-seven bottles of milk on the wall, fifty-seven bottles of milk! Take one dow—"

"Shut up!" the middle-aged man shouted in his cell.

"Geez, just trying to kill time," Miranda said.

"Oh, I'll show you how to kill time," he roared, then hit the wall that separated us. Miranda yelped as she shut her mouth. In the distance, I heard Deputy Paul. "Of all nights, you rebellious teenagers choose this one to trash cars."

Behind him were tall figures. My eyes widened as I watched him open the prison cell opposite us. Out of the corner of my eye, I saw Miranda shift nervously.

"You get one phone call," he said as Benny, Nick, Liam, Marcus, Aidan, Carter, Ethan, and Blake piled into the prison cell.

"What? Why only one?" Nick asked as he shut the gate. Doing the same as I did, Nick wrapped his hands around the bars and peered his face through.

"Because there's so many of you," Paul said. Without another word, Deputy Paul walked down the hall. Nick showed Deputy Paul the finger as he walked away.

"Don't let them see us," Melissa whispered as she covered her face with her hair.

"They won't…there's barely any light in here," I replied. There was a window next to us, which made the night shine onto their cell. They were covered in red gooey stuff as they fought over the small bench.

"At least we got the job done," Carter said.

"Yeah, Principal West is gonna have a big

CAUGHT

surprise tomorrow before he goes to church." Aidan
chuckled.

"Thank goodness we did Kelly's car as well,
plastic bitch," Ethan muttered. I looked at Melissa,
who shook her head in disappointment. Even
though the whole school knew she was a bitch,
Melissa was still her friend.

"Fake is the new bitch," Blake added.

"Amen, brother." Benny chuckled.

"Hey, that's my girlfriend's friend you're talking
about," Nick blurted out. I saw Melissa smile.

"Remember back in sixth grade when Kelly
teased you for your bad acne and told the whole
school 'beware of NickZit?' She's evil," Benny
muttered.

"Well, remember when you started the whole
'Geeky Lana' thing?" Nick barked. Benny scoffed
and flipped him off. "It's called 'Fuck Off,' and it's
located over there," Nick replied as he pointed to
the corner.

"If that's what you want." Benny shrugged as he
approached the corner and unbuckled his belt.

"Really, dude?" Marcus groaned, to which
Benny tightened his belt. There was silence after
that. I couldn't see properly, but there was enough
light from the moonlight to look at their figures.

"NickZit?" the guy next door snorted.

"Yeah, puberty was a bitch, dude." Nick sighed.

"Wait, who said that?" Liam asked.

"All right, three musketeers, you're free to go."
Deputy Paul's voice echoed through the hall. We
stood up as Melissa covered her hair and I pulled
my beanie down. We glanced over at Miranda, and

317

I facepalmed because we'd get caught. She had flour all over her black clothing, and her hair was a mess. "Teacher bailing out his students. Not weird at all," Deputy Paul muttered as he unlocked the gate. We walked out, and from the corner of my eye, I saw Benny squint. His eyes widened as I quickly looked away. Up ahead, I saw Uncle Griff.

"Who called?" I asked him. Uncle Griff shook his head and motioned to his car. Deputy Paul gave us our belongings and a warning for next time. I shook my head because I'd never do something like that ever again.

We drove in silence as I stared out the window. Melissa and Miranda were in the back while I sat in the passenger seat of Griffon's BMW.

"Never thought I'd bail you out of jail."

"I know, right?" Miranda said as she popped her head between our seats. "Are you gonna tell our parents, Mr. Bronx? If you do, then you'll be the lamest teacher in the world. Just saying."

"I'll think about it."

"So…you and Miss Rosa?" Miranda wiggled her brows at Uncle Griff.

"Yes, and thanks for talking to her the other day. Don't know what you did, but now she's finally talking to me!" Griffon cheered as I raised a brow. I opened my mouth to tell him that I failed but noticed we pulled into Miranda's area. "All right, here we are. Now get lost, you rascals."

"Thanks, Mr. Bronx. See you Monday," we said, then got out of the car. I watched as his car disappeared around the corner, then walked to Miranda's door.

"Won't your mom shout at us?" Melissa asked as we watched Miranda unlock her front door.

"Nah, she's cool as long as the c—" Miranda shrugged but stopped before she opened the door. She snapped her head to the driveway and groaned. "*The car!*"

***

"Do you think someone bailed them out already?" I asked as we approached the familiar neighborhood. We walked for an hour all the way to Ethan's house. It turned out Miranda's mom knew we'd be out late; she wouldn't mind as long as the car was returned safely.

"Maybe…that's why we have to hurry," Miranda whispered. I looked ahead and saw the security guard back in his booth, and the gates were locked. "You two distract him."

Melissa strolled to the booth as I trailed behind. I looked over my shoulder and noticed Miranda climbing the wall.

"Help!" Melissa dramatically sighed as she stood by the door. The security guard stared at her but eventually got up.

"Can I help you?"

"Y-yes…this naked dude is running around the neighborhood and knocking on people's doors," I said as he towered over us.

"You've seen him?"

"Yes! He came knocking on my door and stuff," Melissa said as her eyes widened. Behind the security guard, I saw a shadow. I tilted my head and realized Miranda was on the other side of the gate. She ran to her car, then held out the remote. My eyes widened as the vehicle made a noise. The security guard turned around, but I quickly gripped his arms to look at us.

"You need to help! Before he goes off doing something crazy!"

"I'll contact the other guards in the neighborhood. What were your names again?" he asked as he took out his walkie-talkie. Melissa looked over her shoulder as her eyes widened. I followed her gaze to see Miranda with the car as she neared the gate. While the guy spoke in the walkie-talkie, we watched Miranda. She pointed toward something, and Melissa and I turned. I spotted the button and pointed at it, since Melissa was closer. She let out a gasp, then pressed the button. "Hey! What do you think you're doing?" the man yelled. As soon as the gates opened, Miranda sped through them. She stopped right in front of the booth, then opened the passenger and back door. "Hey, you girls!"

I ran to the car and climbed in the backseat while Melissa got in front. Miranda changed gears as we shut our doors.

"Go!" I laughed at the man who tried to chase us. Once he was a few yards away, I let out a sigh of relief.

Sunday was spent at the spa. Melissa got a discount from Jennifer, so she thought it'd be fun to go. After the spa, we went to the mall, even though I didn't buy anything. The weekend was fun since I spent it with my girlfriends. I didn't know if the guys got out of jail, but Dad came home Sunday night with a frown on his face. That must've meant something.

"You're a big girl now?" Miranda grinned as I got out of my mother's car. I decided to drive today since my dad took my mother to work.

"Sure." I chuckled as we walked upstairs. I glanced around the school grounds and noticed none of the guys were here yet. "Have you seen any of the guys yet?"

"Nope, that's a good thing." Miranda hummed as we laughed. Before we walked into the building, we heard a yell and a screech of tires. I spun around and saw Melissa walk out of Nick's car. She ran toward us with her eyes widened.

"Guys, who did that?" she asked as we stared at the damaged vehicles in front of us.

"N-not us."

"*Who the fuck did this?*" Parker yelled as he kicked his car, which was covered in tomatoes, yet it was evident that he had tried to take it off.

"Speak for yourself!" Kelly shouted as she got out of her car. The whole school suddenly went quiet as we heard a familiar engine roar. In between Parker and Kelly's cars, Blake pulled up. Everyone watched as he removed his helmet and got off. The look on his face intimidated anyone to talk. I tried to hold in a laugh as I looked at his pink polka dot bike. His leather jacket swayed as he walked. Parker snorted, and Blake snapped his head at him.

"What the fuck are you laughing at?"

"Your motorcy—"

"Oh yeah? What the fuck happened to your shit-ass car?"

Parker's jaw clenched as he looked down. Blake laughed, then walked toward us. From the corner of my eye, I saw Aidan laugh while Liam took photos.

"Was this you two?" Kelly hissed. They raised their arms as they shook their heads.

"I thought you said it wasn't permanent?" I whispered to Melissa.

"At least it'll fade," she said and gave an innocent smile. I watched Blake as he tramped up the stairs. I avoided eye contact as Blake neared me. Suddenly, he gripped my arm. I glanced up and noticed how his eyes darkened. His gaze shifted to my hand, and I bit my lip since I still had pink faded on it.

"Busted, my little nerd."

"At least it's faded," Melissa whispered beside me. I looked at the boy who gripped my exposed pink hand. I'd tried everything to get it out!

"How dare you accuse me of doing that to your death machine?" I asked, then pulled my hand away.

"Then why is your hand pink?"

"Err…I wanted to dye my hair." I laughed nervously. "And I am not your nerd!"

I spun around and walked into the building. I went to my locker first and grabbed my Calculus book. As I gathered my things, a weird scent lingered in the air. I raised my head and sniffed as I shut my locker.

"That was pretty good, right?" Aidan was beside me as he turned his head. I followed his gaze to see Kelly's and Parker's glares. The bell rang, and we walked down the hall. I played the recent event in my head and chuckled as I turned to Aidan.

"Couldn't you use eggs or toilet paper?"

"How do you know?"

"Know what?"

"Benny, Marcus, and Ethan's cars got egged and then floured." He smirked as we entered Mr. Bronx's class.

"Really?"

"Yeah, and the sticky notes were a classic!"

"What happened?"

"Someone trashed Ethan's house. It was awesome, if you ask me."

"Wonder who could've done such rebellious things?"

"Don't worry, GG, your secret is safe with me." He winked. I rolled my eyes, then looked up at Nick. He sat next to me, and I noticed how he scratched his skin.

"You okay?"

"I'm great," he quickly responded. Aidan spun around to look at Nick. A grin spread across his face as I sniffed the air again. Something smelled so familiar.

"All right, class, as we know, mid-terms are coming up," Mr. Bronx said as everyone groaned. "We will be doing a lot of review, but first..." He trailed off as he held papers. "Pop quiz!"

"Sir, do you hate us that much?" Aidan groaned as he took the sheet from Mr. Bronx.

"I hate all of you, from the bottom of my heart." Griffon smiled as he handed me my sheet. I rolled my eyes at his playful personality and got to work. I didn't think I'd spend time with my friends because of the exams. I'd spend most of my time studying. One of the universities I wanted to go to was Yale. "Austin, you're late," Mr. Bronx stated. I glanced up to see Austin walk in, his nostrils flared. He sat next to Aidan as Mr. Bronx approached his desk. "What's up with you? Got bitch slapped over the weekend?"

"More like Parker's car," Austin huffed then turned to Aidan. "And I bet it was you!"

"I wish humans would automatically shut up when someone tells them to." Aidan ignored Austin, which only seemed to annoy him more. I shook my head and turned to Nick, who looked anxious.

"I know I'm beautiful, but please no staring," Aidan spat as he looked at Austin.

"I'm trying to see things from your perspective, but my ego isn't far up my ass, unlike yours, Rowley."

"That's because you're full of shit!"

"Kiss my ass, baby!"

"Not until yo—"

"Both of you shut up!" Mr. Bronx shouted as he glared at the boys. We watched as he walked to the front of the class. He grabbed a paper from his desk and read it. I looked at the boys to see if they were still glaring at each other, but they kept their mouths shut, because nobody liked Mr. Bronx when he was angry.

***

324

"What is that awful smell?" Miranda asked as she sat at our cafeteria table.

"I don't know," Ethan and Aidan said in unison.

"I've taken ten showers, and I can't get this stupid fish smell away," Liam groaned as he sat between Nick and Benny. They scrunched their noses and shifted away.

"Fish?" Melissa asked as her eyes flickered toward Miranda and me.

"Some people thought it'd be funny to prank my house while we were gone Saturday. I walked into my room, and an egg cracked on my head," Ethan muttered.

"At least you don't have cactus thorns on your back." Benny huffed as he rubbed his back.

"Hey, at least you guys don't have bugs everywhere. I swear I'm itching like crazy!" Nick babbled as he scratched his arms.

"So what did you guys do?" I asked.

"We had to watch these two eat their way through the popcorn, and I thought that was the prank, but filling my basement with sticky notes made it worse!" Ethan groaned as he raised his arms.

"The popcorn was good, though," Aidan said as he high-fived Liam.

"Well, at least you guys don't have a pink polka dot motorcycle," Blake growled.

"At least it's not permanent," I said with a tight-lipped smile. Blake raised a brow and opened his mouth, but I cut him off. "Who's ready for mid-terms?"

"Ugh, don't ask." Marcus groaned.

"At least Thanksgiving's next weekend. So we have three weeks until we write."

"Yeah, what are you guys doing for Thanksgiving?" Carter asked.

"Eating," Liam and Aidan cheered.

"What about you, Willson? Going anywhere?" Blake asked as he nudged my shoulder.

"Nah, I have to study," I said as I thought of Yale.

"Boring," Miranda groaned.

"I am so going to fail Physics," Benny mumbled.

"I can lend you my study book," I suggested.

"Last time I took your book, Lana, I stared at it like it was another language," he replied. Blake snorted beside me, and I elbowed him. AP Physics was hard, but I got through it with the help of Mr. Bronx coming over on the weekend and explaining it to me. The rest of the students didn't have that advantage, so it was understandable.

"I can tutor you," I mumbled. Benny turned to me as he bit his lip.

"Okay."

"Now if you'll excuse me, I have to get to Debate," I said as I stood up. I felt their eyes on me as I walked out, yet I didn't care because I had to focus on school. I'd do anything to get into Yale.

Miranda offered Melissa and me a ride home, and I gladly accepted. I wished I could've taken it back. They talked and talked about their boyfriends while I spaced out in the passenger seat.

"What do you think, Lana?" Melissa snapped me out of my thoughts.

"Huh?"

"Do you like Blake or Benny?" Miranda smiled. "I think you and Benny are cute. I mean, in the cafeteria when you offered to tutor him…"

"Yet Blake is hot, and I sense a connection between you two," Melissa spoke up.

"What? I'm not even dating any of them; I want to graduate single because of Ya—"

"Yale is the perfect college, and once I get my degree, I'll look for a man," they said in unison as I raised a brow.

"We know you're a nerd and all, but sometimes you need to chill, have some fun being a teenager," Miranda whined as she turned into my neighborhood.

"I do! I've done it all!" I argued as I balled my fist. I remembered similar words from Blake.

"Even *it*?" Melissa gasped as she looked at me. I looked away, too annoyed to answer her question, but with the look on my face, she knew better. "Oh my God, with who?"

"An asshole, that's who," Miranda answered as she parked in front of my house.

"There's a lot of assholes at our school, and many of them wou—"

"Thanks for the ride, bye." I cut Melissa off as I stepped out of the car. My pace quickened as I walked up the porch. I didn't turn back as I opened the door. As the door creaked, I heard a shout, followed by footsteps.

"Well, maybe they shouldn't come!" The voice belonged to my father as I shut the door. I quietly walked down the hall and into the kitchen, where I saw my mother.

"Mom?"

"I'm fine, dear. Don't worry."

"Is this about the Radcliffs coming?"

"Yes, apparently something happened with Levi. They don't know how lon—"

"Wait—what happened to Levi?"

"Don't you guys talk anymore? I assumed he told you."

"We sometimes do, but we don't talk for long," I lied. Levi and I only spoke once a few days ago.

"Well, it's better if he tells you."

"How does this affect us?"

"Well, it mostly concerns them, but I think you'll be glad if he tells you." Mom smiled as she stroked my shoulder.

Breakfast was awkward. Dad barely spoke while Mom tried to lighten the mood. I still didn't talk to Levi. It was weird to ask him something that I wasn't aware of. I had a lot of questions to ask him. I walked out of the house and looked down at my phone. Benny was supposed to pick me up, and sometimes he'd come early so that we'd study.

"Washed it like a thousand times." I turned my head and saw Blake against his motorcycle as he stared at it. The pink faded, but with a few more washes, the pink would be out.

"What are you doing here?"

"I'm your ride for today," he said, then threw his helmet toward me.

"I'm not gonna ride with you," I said, then shoved the helmet in his chest as I approached him. Blake chuckled as he put the helmet on and got onto the bike. Once he was on, he turned to me.

"What's going on with you and Nielson?"

"Nothing, why?"

"Will anything be going on between you two?"

"You know, I can walk if you're going to interrogate me every time we talk."

He stared at me with a blank expression. I folded my arms and watched as he kicked the side stand. Ever since I started tutoring Benny, Blake's been moody and distant.

"Then walk!" Blake yelled as he started his motorcycle. The engine came to life as his grip tightened on the handles. I backed away as he drove out of my driveway.

"Screw you!" I shouted, but I didn't think he heard me. Blake drove off, and I let out a round of swear words as I began to walk. Then it started to rain.

***

I was ten minutes away from school, and I bet Blake was in class with a smirk plastered on his face. From the corner of my eye, I saw a familiar Subaru approach me. I smiled at Aidan as he opened the passenger door.

"Thanks."

"No problem. I thought Blake was going to get you?" Aidan asked as we began to drive.

"I never want to drive with that asshole again."

"What did my cousin do this time?"

"He's like my dad, questioning me every time we talk! It's just—he's the worst!"

"Well, you have been spending a lot of time with

Benny."

"I'm tutoring him!"

"Okay, geez! Don't get your panties in a twist, love."

"Blake Gunner is the biggest asshole on the planet," I muttered, and from the corner of my eye, I saw Aidan fiddle in his pocket. I turned to see that he held out his cigarettes.

"Looks like you need it," Aidan said as I took one. He gave me his lighter—I lit two cigarettes for us.

"Thanks," I said, then inhaled. I looked at the road and realized we'd passed the school. "Where we going?"

"I got a Chemistry test which I am going to fail."

"So we're gonna ditch?"

"Uh-huh. Don't worry, we'll be back for your little tutoring. Is there a problem?" Aidan asked as the corner of his mouth rose. I looked at Aidan, then at the cigarette between my fingers. A smile appeared on my lips as I looked at him.

"Nope. Not a problem at all," I said, then inhaled the only thing that exhaled all the stress.

Chapter Twenty-One

Lana

"Hope you got a killer excuse, Willson," Aidan mumbled as we walked through the school doors. It was the period before lunch, and I was nervous. I looked over my shoulder and raised a brow at Aidan.

"How do I know you're not just using me again?"

"Well, we just had Phys Ed, and I heard we played dodgeball again. You do not want to be in the same room with my cousin when we're playing that." He chuckled as we walked down the hall. "Ouch!"

I spun around to see that a door opened and hit Aidan in the face as he walked. I disguised my inner laugh with a cheekily hidden grin, yet that reaction disappeared as Parker Collins walked out.

"Well, well, well, look who we have here," Parker sang as he shut the door. He wore a reasonably long coat with combat boots. Since

331

every guy had his purpose in high school, Parker was the "go-to guy." If someone needed sold-out concert tickets, matches, knives, fake ID cards, or even condoms, Parker was the guy. Yet everything came with a price.

"What do you want?" Aidan glared at his ex-friend.

"You missed Chemistry."

"Does it look like I care?"

"Since you have such a clever mouth, I'll just tell Mis—"

"No!" I cut him off as I placed a hand on his chest. Parker looked down at my hand with a familiar grin as I stepped back.

"Dude, come on, it's Friday," Aidan whined.

"Well, I won't shut up for free."

"Name your price…"

"How can I when you haven't purchased anything?"

"You got gum?" I asked. Parker raised a brow as he approached me. I stiffened when he leaned in, and from the corner of my eye, I saw Aidan's glare.

"Wow, next time can I come?" Parker asked as he sniffed me.

"Do you have gum or even mints?" I groaned.

"Of course, I do!" he exclaimed and pulled out a box of mints from his pocket. I reached for one, but he slapped my hand away. "Being quiet comes with a price."

"Yet I ask again, what's your price?"

"You and Austin are fighting like cats and dogs, but we're still cool, right?" Parker asked as he looked at Aidan. He didn't reply, so Parker licked his lips and continued. "So I'm willing to give you guys a discount."

"How much?"

"Fifty dollars."

"Fifty just for mints?"

"And for keeping quiet. I'm nice. It's a generous discount," Parker said with a shrug. "But if you want to smell like tobacco for the rest of the day, I unde—"

"Fine!" Aidan said, then shoved the bills in Parker's chest. They were the same height as Aidan glared at Parker. "If I hear anything, I'll know who it came from."

"My lips are sealed, and you and Austin should make up some time. Just saying," Parker said as he gave me the box. I shoved a few in my mouth then handed it to Aidan. While he took a few, I turned to Parker, who winked at me as he turned the corner. There was still thirty minutes left until lunch, and since I didn't have anywhere to go, I decided to go to class. I cupped my hand over my mouth once more and smelled my breath. Once I was satisfied, I let out a sigh and walked in.

"Lana, you're late," Miss Rosa said as she turned to me.

"Sorry."

"Care to explain?"

"I had to walk."

"I didn't know it took three periods to walk to school."

"Me either, but hey, we're not all perfect," I said with a shrug. She gave me a skeptical look as I walked to the back of the class. I sat behind Carter and next to Benny.

"I thought Blake was gonna get you," Carter whispered over his shoulder.

"That guy is a fucking douche. I don't want to talk to him." I huffed.

"So you had to walk in the rain?" Benny asked as he pointed to the window. It drizzled, and I bit my lip as I thought of Aidan.

"I suppose."

"Bastard."

"He was pissed in Phys Ed, but someone seemed to brighten his mood," Carter spoke up.

"Who?"

"Kelly."

"No surprise there, being the man-whore he is," I muttered. Carter and Benny shared a look but eventually got back to work.

Twenty minutes later, the bell rang for lunch, and everyone rushed out of the room.

"Mr. Nielson," Miss Rosa called as Benny approached the door. He stopped, then went over to her desk as I gathered my things. "Thank you again for what you've done. I really appreciate it," she said as I walked to the door.

"No problem, Miss Rosa. Don't want to see my favorite teachers in a bad mood."

"Of course! It was a complete misunderstanding, but thank you again."

"Anytime, enjoy your weekend."

Benny gave one more smile then walked past me. I raised a brow at their conversation, but then it clicked when he mentioned teachers.

"It was you," I said as I caught up to him. Benny

smirked as I thought about Mr. Bronx and Miss Rosa.

"Liam told me that you knew Mr. Bronx for a long time and about the things he has done for you, so I just thought why not."

"Thank you!" I squealed as I gave him a side hug.

"No problem. Anything to make up the eight ruthless years I put you through," he said as he put his arm around my shoulder. I smiled as I thought how Benny had changed; he'd lived up to his second chance. "And since they're in a good mood, we don't have homework from either of them."

"You have done well, Nielson," I said as we entered the cafeteria.

"We can grab something to eat then head to the library," Benny suggested as he looked at the line.

"Sure, I'll be right there. You go ahead," I said, then walked to our table. "Hey, guys."

"Lana! Oh my god! I thought something happened to you!" Liam exclaimed as he pulled me down on the seat and hugged me.

"Why?"

"Blake said he'd pick you up, but instead he showed up alone with a murderous look on his face."

"Nothing new," Miranda joked.

"We just had a little argument, so he left me. I had to walk in the rain."

"And then her knight in shining armor came to the rescue," Aidan's voice echoed behind me, and when I turned, he winked while I forced a smile.

"You guys are lucky that you missed P.E. Blake

sent someone to the nurse," Carter said. Some found it funny and laughed, but I let out a scoff because he took out his anger on someone else. Everyone at the table suddenly went silent, and I followed their gaze to see Blake Gunner and Kelly West.

"Where were you?" he hissed.

"Again, with the questions," I pointed out as I stood up. He wrapped his arm around Kelly as I folded my arms. "I had a smoke with Aidan and only came back a half hour ago."

"Wow, no surprise there, and how ironic that you're always giving my middle finger a boner," he said, then flipped me off.

"Kelly told me it's the only boner you can get," I said, and everyone laughed.

"You better watch that smart mouth of yours, bitch. You don't know what's coming to you!" Kelly hissed as she pointed at me.

"Shock me, West. Say something clever for once."

"Lana," Blake warned, and I turned to him with my eyes squinted.

"Don't Lana me, you asshole!" I said, then shoved my index finger in his chest.

"Err…Lana," Miranda whispered behind me, but I ignored her.

"You just come into my life saying meaningful bullshit that makes me look at things differently, then take me on a ride just to treat me like shit in the end? But no, everything revolves around Blake Gunner. The only way to satisfy him is to send him to the queen bee herself!" I said, pointing at Kelly. His jaw tightened, and I noticed how his eyes darkened.

"Recall the moment when I said I cared? I lied," he declared. My lifted eye twitched, and I raised my fist to punch him, but Benny pulled me away. The corner of Blake's mouth rose as I backed away.

"Let's go," Benny mumbled. I spun around, but Blake decided to have the last say.

"That's right, walk away like you always do!"

***

"I hate him." Benny broke the silence. We were in the library, and I stared at him, then shook my head.

"No, you don't. You were all getting along. Don't let my stupid arguments with Blake make you pick sides."

"You guys fight like an old married couple."

"We're not even a couple! I swear I'd never go for a douche like him."

"Well, then, what kind of guy would you go for?" Benny murmured.

"I'm not too choosy, but any guy who wouldn't treat me the way Blake does," I said as I avoided eye contact. There were a few people in the library, most of them were on their phones, but a certain someone caught my eye. Parker was with someone behind a bookcase, yet I spotted them through the books. The guy handed Parker money in exchange for a packet. It had to be drugs.

"Is this right?" Benny brought me back to reality. I turned and looked down at his book.

"Yeah, but if you want to get more marks, write

the whole equation," I said. He nodded. I looked at Parker again and watched as he shook hands with the guy. I bit the inside of my cheek and pushed myself out of my chair. "I'll be right back. Just going to check for books," I said. Benny nodded. I walked to the bookshelf, then turned the corner. Parker had his back to me, which gave me a sight of his blond curls. "I saw you," I said, then folded my arms. Parker spun around and grinned.

"I saw you," he mocked as I thought of earlier. "What do you need, Willson?"

"Nothing."

"Then why'd you come here?"

"I don't know."

"I got cocaine," he said as he wiggled his brows.

"Where'd you get cocaine?"

"I know a guy."

"Does he go to our school?"

"Maybe."

"How much you got?" I asked as my brows knitted.

"Why, you interested?"

"Nope, just curious."

"I don't know. It's going quick, though, so probably around five hundred grams," Parker said as he stepped closer. I thought back to when James Cornelius got angry because there were only two hundred and forty-eight parcels and not two hundred and fifty. My eyes widened at the thought of Parker, who must've had them.

"Why so little?"

"It's my favorite time of the year. The money just rolls in since everyone wants to pass mid-terms and get on to winter break," he said as he eyed me with a smirk. "Especially people like you, Willson. They'd say anything."

"Wha-what do you mean?"

"To focus…they'll do anything," Parker whispered as he stared at me. "Cocaine is just one of them, and with the stunt you pulled in the cafeteria, it looks like you need it."

"I don—" I stuttered but cut off as he put a finger to my lips.

"What grades did you get last year?" he asked as he removed his finger.

"Straight A's," I whispered as I looked down in guilt.

"Straight freaking A's…all thanks to mwah." Parker gestured to himself.

"Yeah, but I've chang—" I cut off again when he put his finger back on my lips.

"No, you haven't changed. Think about it. You can't focus now with Benny and Blake on your case all the time," Parker said, then tilted his head. "None of them have made a move yet because they don't want to face your dad. If they do make a move, then that other guy is gonna be pretty upset. What's his name? I can't seem to get it, but he's friends with Keene."

My eyes widened as I stared at Parker. I was blank on how he knew Levi, let alone his best friend Keene, who I hadn't seen in ages. "This will make you focus and even pass finals," Parker whispered as he walked around me. His chest pressed against my back as he held out the familiar bottle. The same pills inside that made me pull an all-nighter before.

"Take these, and you'll even get a scholarship to Yale," he whispered as I stared at the bottle. "Any friend of Aidan is a friend of mine; thus, you get a discount. So what do you say, Lana Willson? Wanna become my favorite customer again?"

Chapter Twenty-Two

Lana

I pulled the sheets closer as I stirred in bed. I couldn't sleep again. I twisted and turned until I stared at the ceiling. I stared at it for what felt like an eternity until I saw movement from the corner of my eye. I snapped my head in that direction only to hear my desk chair squeak. *It's the wind*, I repeated to myself as it turned. After a while, the chair stopped, but the feeling of not being alone didn't. Again I saw movement, and when I glanced at my door, there he was. My eyes widened in horror as he stood at the edge of my bed. His ginger hair the exact same as the last time, he wore the same worn out clothing as he watched me. I sat up as I observed him; it was only then I noticed the item in his hand. Not any item, my shoe. The silver heel looked brand new as Jack raised his arm.

"No please…" I cried as he stabbed himself in the head with the heel. The blood spat out like a volcano as I cried. With both hands on the shoe, he

341

put more force into it. The blood ran down his face as I watched. "I'm sorry, please!" I begged as the familiar nauseous sound erupted in my ears, aware that he had gone too deep.

"Lana!" Jack yelled.

"Please, I didn't mean to!"

"Lana!"

"I'm sorry!"

"Lana!"

My eyes snapped open as I rose from my bed. My chest rose and fell as sweat dripped from my forehead. I felt two hands on my shoulder and shook as I looked up, only to be met by my dad. I let out a sigh as I tried to relax. Dad sat next to me as he rubbed my shoulder for comfort.

"That's the fourth night in a row," Dad muttered. I glanced up and noticed the tiredness took over his features.

"I'm sorry." I sighed, then looked down. The nightmares had gotten worse, and it seemed like they were here to stay. Every time I closed my eyes, I pictured Jack August.

"Do you wanna talk about it?" Dad asked.

"No—" I cut off when a knock came on my door. Dad and I turned to see my mother enter with a tray and three mugs on it. The smell of hot cocoa spread through the room as she placed the tray on my desk. She handed Dad and me a mug, then took hers. I watched as she sat on the edge of my bed and glanced at my father. They kept eye contact for a few minutes while we sipped our hot cocoa. It's as if they talked to each other with their eyes.

"I've changed your sheets already…" Mom said.

"Thank you."

"Do you want to talk about it, dear?"

"It's my last year of school. Just a lot of stress."

"You'll get through it, kid," Dad assured me as he got up from beside me. He placed his mug on the tray, then stood next to my mother.

"Besides, Thanksgiving is soon. You'll have a nice break." Mom smiled.

"I guess."

"Try to get some sleep. We'll be right across the hall, okay?" Dad stated as I nodded. My parents walked out as I smiled. I watched as the door closed, and the shadows under it disappeared. I sat in my bed for a while and watched the light on the ceiling. I couldn't go to sleep. I didn't want to worry my parents again and be questioned. I couldn't let them know what I dreamed of. Only Benny knew about the dreams. We studied at my place after school in the kitchen. I got out of my bed and looked across the room at my bag. I reached for it, then unzipped the bag. I searched for the bottle until I found it. As I read the description, I sighed, because I'd never thought I'd be back on it.

***

As I walked through the halls, I blinked away the tiredness and saw Benny against my locker. With a smile, I approached him, yet when he saw me, his face lit up.

"Hey," Benny said as he stood against the locker next to mine.

"Hi," I mumbled as I opened my locker.

343

"You okay?"

"If waking up at two in the morning and worrying your parents terribly is normal, then yeah, I'm all right."

"I'm sorry," he breathed out, then looked down. I turned to him and noticed he covered his head with a hoodie.

"It's okay...how are you?"

"Been better," Benny muttered as his brown eyes met mine. "You ready for the test?"

"Yeah, I studied all morning," I admitted with a smile on my face. I expected a smile back, but Benny squinted his eyes as I raised an eyebrow.

"All morning?" he repeated, and I nodded. "How many hours of sleep did you get?"

"Enough."

"Lana, your mom told me abou—" Benny cut off when Carter came up beside him.

"Cool kids, ten o'clock." Carter chuckled as he looked over my shoulder. Benny and I followed his gaze. There were no more Them; it was a mix of Blake, Kelly, Jennifer, and Austin. Blake and I hadn't spoken since the fight last Friday in the cafeteria. He'd still hang out with the guys, but we ignored each other. A rumor was going around about him and Kelly dating. It irked me that he despised them, but they walked around like they owned the school. Blake still had that look of "I don't give a fuck," even though he walked with an entirely new crowd. We looked at each other, but he'd be the first one to look away. He made me feel so much pain these past few weeks that I couldn't even think straight anymore. I didn't know what possessed me to put my leg out as they walked past, but I was glad I did. Austin fell for it as he leaped forward and landed into Kelly. She tumbled over into Blake's arms as Jennifer stood speechless. Benny and Carter snorted as I smirked. The four of them glared at us, but we turned away. Once they were all steady, they walked away as if nothing happened. "Okay, that just made my day." Carter laughed as he high-fived me. "See you at lunch." The bell rang. We watched the blond boy skip down the hall, and being the typical guy he was, he stopped to greet a few girls. I smiled, then turned to Benny, who raised his arms at me. I raised a brow, and he laughed.

"Come on," he cooed as he motioned me to hug him. I playfully rolled my eyes as I stepped forward and accepted his hug. He wrapped his arms around me as I buried my head in the crook of his neck. We stayed like that for a while as he gently rubbed my back.

As I walked into Photography class, I groaned. The test was hard, which meant that the examination would be even harder. Mr. Dockwell wasn't here, so I glanced around the classroom and saw Melissa in the back. I smiled as I sat next to her, and we began to chat. I was talking about Thanksgiving when Melissa tuned out. I followed her gaze to see Blake and Kelly walk in. Blake and I locked eyes as he slowly approached us, but he sat in front of us with Kelly next to him.

"Is she even in this class?" I whispered to Melissa. She shrugged as we watched the two. Blake whispered to Kelly as she giggled. He kissed down her jawline as I shivered. Mr. Dockwell entered the class and took the attendance. Afterward, we were told to do our assignments. I immediately set out to work on my laptop. I stared at the screen with its brightest on, so I'd focus. It didn't help that my eyes drooped.

"Who's that?" Melissa asked as she pointed to the screen. I opened my sleepy eyes to see a little girl and boy. I smiled at the pictures of Levi and me when we were seven and eight years old on Halloween. We went as ketchup and mustard, because Levi's mother forgot to order our Cinderella and Prince Charming outfit, so those were the only ones left. "Is that your long-lost twin brother?"

"No, he's just a friend." I laughed at the thought of Levi and me being related.

"Well, you guys do look alike…same hair color, same blue eyes, and whoa—" she babbled, but cut herself off when she saw the next picture. "Puberty!" she squealed as everyone turned to us. Melissa gaped as she stared at the picture of me in the mirror and Levi's back turned to the mirror. It was the same picture Blake asked about.

"You can barely see him."

"Yeah, but look at his back muscles, and his hair…is that tattoo—"

"Miss Singe!" Mr. Dockwell scolded Melissa. I kept in a giggle as she apologized.

"I'll be right back," Melissa assured me as she got up and walked to the other side of the classroom. As I went through old pictures of Levi and me as kids, I smiled. My happy moment got interrupted when I heard giggles in front of me. I looked up and saw Blake with the camera in his hands. I rolled my eyes as I tried to focus, but I couldn't with Kelly. I sighed and looked around the classroom before my hand reached down for my bag. I quickly took out a pill and popped it into my mouth before anyone noticed.

"Blake, you're supposed to be doing your unique assignment," Kelly whispered.

"You're unique," Blake said as he lowered the camera and looked at her. I choked on the tablet as soon as those words fell from his mouth. Everyone turned to look at me as I tried to breathe, and instead of helping, they watched!

I raised my hand, and Mr. Dockwell ushered me out. I sprinted down the hall and into the restrooms. I leaned on the sink and looked into the mirror. My eyes were bloodshot as they surrounded my dark blue iris. I had bags under my eyes, but I was thankful for my glasses. While I licked my chapped lips, I stared at myself in the mirror. I looked down at my bag and regretted what I'd do next. As quickly as I could, I took out the bottle and stared at it. I only had one pill left, so I placed it in my mouth and drank water. Afterward, I took my glasses off, washed my face, then tied my hair in a high ponytail. When I put on my glasses, I tried to smile, but anyone could tell it was fake. I shook my head, then walked out of the restrooms. As I walked down the hall, I saw Parker stuff something in a locker. I slowly approached him and raised a brow.

"What can I do for you, Willson?" he asked once he was done. Parker turned to me with a grin on his face.

"I need more," I mumbled, then looked to see if anyone watched us.

"Whoa, I just gave you a bottle on Friday." He raised a brow. I rolled my eyes as I took the money out of my pocket.

"Yeah, that was just one bottle. I need more for this weekend," I said, then shoved the money in his chest.

"All right, don't say I didn't warn you."

I tapped my foot impatiently since he took his time. I groaned as I retrieved my lunch money and added it to the other money. I knew that if I didn't have money, Parker would threaten to tell the whole school about the pills, or he'd find another way for me to make it up. I learned my lesson from last year; Parker Collins was a selfish asshole who didn't care about anybody. He didn't care who got hurt as long as he got his money.

"Make that two," I said once he gave me the one bottle. He gave me a weird look as he glanced down at the money.

"Lana, are you sure? These thin—"

"Yes, I'm sure! So much shit is going on in my life, Parker, and the only way I'll get through it is if you give me those pills!" I demanded. "Besides, when has Parker Collins ever cared about someone? Especially girls."

Parker was silent after that as he handed me the second bottle. He spun around to walk away, but I called after him. He turned to me.

"I fucking hate you, you know that?" He let out a sigh as he ran his hand through his dirty blond curls.

"Yeah. I fucking hate me too, Willson," he admitted, then walked away. The bell rang as I let out a sigh and put the bottles in my bag. I decided to skip my locker and hold onto my bag as I walked to the cafeteria. Since I was early, there were barely any people, so I joined the line.

"Lana." I looked to see Ethan beside me.

"Oh hey, Ethan." I smiled.

"Are you okay?" he asked. I nodded as we took food, then approached the cashier. Even though the exchange between Parker and I happened five minutes ago, I completely forgot that I gave him all my money. "I'll pay," Ethan said as he eyed me suspiciously. I looked down at my tray and sighed in relief, since I didn't have much food on it.

"Thank you." I smiled at Ethan as he paid. Once he was done, we walked to our table.

"What happened to you in Photography class?" Melissa asked as she approached our table, a tray in her hand. She sat next to Nick.

"I just felt a bit nauseous."

"Yeah, from the couple in front of us sucking each other's faces off."

After she said that, the table fell silent. The only sound to be heard was the rest of the cafeteria, as well as the clatter of our utensils. Blake never sat with us anymore. He was a jerk, but he wasn't an idiot. He still talked to everyone whether it was during school or after school, everyone except me.

"Melissa, come on." I glanced up to see Kelly's forced smile. She walked away in her knee-high boots and topped the look off with a white coat. Melissa looked at us, and I gave her a small smile.

Even though Kelly wasn't on the list of my most liked people, she was still Melissa's friend.

"Baby, please come with me?" Melissa begged Nick as she stood up with her tray. Nick looked over his shoulder to the other table and saw Blake, Jennifer, and Austin. He groaned.

"One day I'm gonna kill that bitch," Nick muttered as he stood up and walked with Melissa.

"Call us if you wanna get rid of the body." Liam grinned as he gave Nick the thumbs up. Benny spat out his soda, then glared at Liam. "Too soon?"

"And then there were eight," Aidan said as he observed our table. There was a total of eleven, but the other three were at another table.

"We don't need him. He only came to this school a few months ago. All of us have known each other for longer than three years," Miranda said as she turned to Blake.

"Yeah, and if he wants to hang out with them, we shouldn't stop him. It's his life. He should just know who's been there for him and who his real frie—" I babbled while I looked at Blake. We locked eyes, but I turned away when Benny rested his hand on my back.

"Lana, it's okay, relax."

"Sorry, it's just he's so unreasonable and chil—"

"Jefferson High students!" Kelly cut me off as she stood on top of the table. Everyone quieted as I looked down at Nick, who glared at her. "As you know, there's been some confusion going on these past few weeks," she said, and I noticed how her eyes flickered from me to everyone else. "Plenty of rumors have been going around ever since that table has been occupied," she said, then pointed to us. Everyone turned their gazes to our table as Benny dropped his hand. "Geeky Lana thinks she's cool now. Having everyone adore her behind those glasses—a bit too innocent, don't you think?" Kelly pouted as she walked up and down the table. Austin stood up with papers in his hands and handed them out to everyone. "Little did we know she preferred older guys." I looked at the people who received the papers, how they'd gasp. "Students of Jefferson High, our sweet little Lana here has been seeing Mr. Bronx."

My eyes widened as the paper landed in the middle of our table. It was that time Mr. Bronx kissed me on the forehead in his classroom, but only because he was worried about me. I glanced at Melissa and thought how she'd always be there when I came out of the classroom; maybe it was her idea all along. A look of betrayal spread across my face as I glanced at Blake. He knew Mr. Bronx was a family friend; maybe he was in on it, too. I stared at the paper on the table; the whole cafeteria was quiet as everyone tried to process what they've heard. I looked up to see everyone at the table staring at me. Miranda's nostrils flared as she glared at Kelly's table. She turned to me with a look of pity that I hated. Most people in these situations ran out and cried, but nothing came out. Wow, maybe the tablets did have an effect on me. Whispers and murmurs spread through the room. It was tiring to listen, so I stood up and grabbed the photograph. I felt all their eyes on me as I approached Kelly. She was on the ground with her hands placed on her

351

hips. Off to the side, I saw Blake stare as Melissa frowned.

"Not so perfect now, are we?" Kelly tilted her head. I gripped the paper, then shoved it in her chest.

"Fuck you!" I yelled, then raised my hand and slapped her. Everyone watched as Kelly's jaw dropped. She leaped forward to hit me as I did the same. We fought like cats and dogs as people howled and cheered. I felt two arms around my waist pulling me away from her. Blake did the same with Kelly, but he held her wrists. I glanced back to see Benny. I turned back to Kelly as she slapped me. Benny's grip tightened as he picked me up. "No!" I yelled, then raised my legs. Apparently, they went too high, and I kicked Kelly in the face. Everyone's jaws dropped as they took out their phones and recorded. My eyes widened as she ripped herself off Blake and launched at me. Marcus came out of nowhere and tried to stop us, but I somehow kicked him in the crotch. Liam came next but was immediately punched by Kelly; both groaned from their injuries as they backed out.

"Hey!" We froze and whipped our heads around to see Griffon Bronx. He looked at Kelly, and his eyes diverted to the paper on the table, then me. Mr. Bronx quickly snatched it and read it; he scrunched his nose up and groaned. "Oh fuck."

I did what any sane person would do in that type of situation. I released myself from Benny, then got my bag. As I swung my bag over my shoulder, I felt everyone's stares. While I thought of another pill, I pushed the double doors open. I froze as the doors banged against the wall, and I gasped at the sight in front of me. Pictures everywhere of Mr. Bronx and me from our past encounters. I sprinted and pulled them off before any teacher saw. Principal West didn't allow relationships with teachers. What would he think when he found this?

I looked at the paper, but I couldn't read it because it wasn't clear. I was going to adjust my glasses when I felt nothing on my face. Well, except the sting from Kelly's claws on my cheek. My glasses must've fallen off when we fought. I sighed, then continued to rip off the papers. Once I was done, I shoved them in a tiny trash can. The sound of heels clicking against tiles made me stop, and I looked over my shoulder to see Melissa.

"Lana, I'm so sorry!"

"No, I trusted you! That explains all the times when I walked out of Mr. Bronx's classroom you would be there."

"Kelly made me do it! Plus, that was all before we became friends. I didn't know she was going to do it today."

"You knew she was going to even do it?"

"I completely forgot, Lana, please. If I knew that Mr. Bronx was a family friend, I would've told her." Melissa rushed out as she placed a hand on my shoulder. Before I could answer, the bell rang, and I had German. Without another word, I sighed, picked up my bag, and walked to class.

I spent the rest of the day in silence. I didn't have the energy to talk to anyone. People looked at me in disgust, but I didn't care. I didn't see Mr. Bronx or Kelly for the rest of the day. The weirdest thing was that I wasn't called to the principal's office yet. It was the end of the day, and I stood by my locker and took out books. My phone buzzed in my pocket, and I checked to see that Miranda said she was waiting by her car. I put my phone back and glanced up at my locker. I noticed that it was fuller than usual. When I pulled a book out, all the papers fell—more pictures of Mr. Bronx and me. I sighed as I picked them up and spun around to put them in the trashcan. Someone must've shoved the rest in my locker. I walked back to my locker and looked at the small bottle that contained Adderall. Considering everything that I've been through today, I had to reward myself somehow. I quickly swallowed one, then returned to my locker. Once I was done, I shut it, but someone decided to visit me.

"Argh!" I yelled at Blake. His jaw clenched as he closed his eyes for a moment, clearly annoyed by my shout. "What do you want?"

"Again with the questions," he mocked with a sly grin on his face. "What did you just swallow? I swear that was a big ass gulp you took."

"None of your business!"

"Are you on drugs, Willson?" he asked. My eyes widened as he smirked. "Didn't know you could fight like that."

"You don't know a lot of things about me," I said as I tried to remember our last conversation. "What's your problem, huh? You knew Mr. Bronx was a family friend, but you still let that bitch do that to me!"

"Like I said last week, I don't care. So what if he's a friend? You can still ba—"

"That's wrong! He's with Miss Rosa!"

"You're eighteen. It wouldn't matter."

"It's like you want me to do something horrible." I tilted my head at Blake. "Do you expect me to go back to being a 'bad girl' for you? Will that please Blake Gunner for him to become less of an asshole?"

"No! You don't fucking get it!" Blake suddenly snapped as he slammed the locker next to me. My eyes widened as I stepped back. He saw my frightened eyes and lowered his fist. After he'd calmed down, he took a cautious step closer. "You dropped this," he whispered. I looked down to see that he held my glasses. I stared at it. Frustrated, Blake tilted my chin up. He slowly put on my glasses for me as I closed my eyes; I felt his hand put a lock of hair behind my ear, and I shivered from his touch. Once I felt the glasses on the bridge of my nose, I opened my eyes to see that he was gone.

When I got a ride home with Miranda, she told how the guys roughed up anyone who spoke about Mr. Bronx and me. It made me think that Blake was one of them. I got home and studied, as well as helping Mom clean the house for Thanksgiving. Needless to say, I was excited about a break.

The entire team was in Physics class. All students who played a sport had to keep their grades up, so it was either AP Physics or two other subjects. After I spoke to Ethan for a while, I turned to the front, yet our teacher was nowhere to be found. That reminded me of Uncle Griff, because I hadn't seen him all day.

"Is Mr. Bronx at school today?" I asked. Everyone shook their heads. I looked at the curly brunette in front of me and grinned. I tapped Liam's shoulder; he slowly spun around and glared at me. "Whoa!" I cupped my mouth. Ethan snapped his head to look at Liam, and he laughed. Benny looked up from his paper, and he shook his head. "I'm so sorry," I bit my lip to prevent a laugh. Liam had a swollen eye from yesterday's doing.

He rolled his eyes. "It's okay, but damn, you girls can fight."

"Yeah, you girls are worse than guys," Nick said as he sat next to Liam.

"Marcus is still recovering from that kick," Ethan joked as we laughed. My thoughts went back to the empty desk in front, and I frowned, because I knew something was wrong. I didn't care about the Physics teacher. I cared about Mr. Bronx and what yesterday meant for his career.

"Did you get called to the principal's office yesterday?" Nick asked.

"Nope."

"Weird. I just saw Mr. Bronx walking in that direction before I came to class."

"What?" I demanded and rose to my feet.

"Yeah, when I picked up Melissa this morning, she said Kelly's still taking things too far, whatever that meant." He shrugged. I rushed out of the classroom and ignored the guys' frantic calls. Principal West probably saw the pictures, so maybe he might fire Mr. Bronx. It was my fault. I had to fix it. I opened the door to his office and was met by Mr. Bronx, who glared across at Kelly. She had a bandage on her forehead. I raised a brow because I didn't kick her that hard.

"Lana Willson, I was just going to call you in," Principal West said as he sat behind his desk.

"Look, I can explain," I rushed out as I shut the door and sat next to Kelly.

"There's nothing to explain. This video shows it all," West said as he turned his laptop to us. It showed Kelly and I fighting, but the middle when I pulled her hair.

"She started it with the—" I cut myself off as I quickly glanced at Mr. Bronx.

"This is illegal, and it's overstepping the relationships in this school. Griffon Bro—"

"No! He's a family friend! My freaking godfather! The only reason he was comforting me was because your stuck-up daughter bullied me all the time!"

"Well, this video shows a completely different story."

"Then call my dad."

"Why on earth would I do that?"

"Because if it's illegal, call him. He's the sheriff. Show him the video while you're at it."

"No! Dad, I want a lawyer then!" Kelly shouted as her fingernails dug into the chair.

"Kelly, sweetheart, get back to class," Principal West said. We watched as she stood up and ripped off the bandage from her forehead. She sent me one last glare, then stormed out. I could see Griffon sit next to me. We looked at Principal West, who squinted his eyes at us.

"How long have you known Mr. Bronx?"

"Ever since I came out of my mother's womb," I replied. "He knows me better than I know myself."

"Lana, you have become very disruptive these past few weeks, and Mr. Bronx can agree with me on that, right?" he asked, and we turned to Mr. Bronx, who nodded. I looked down in guilt because I knew my behavior at school had changed. "Very well then. Since this was all a misunderstanding, I won't fire you, Griffon, but you two are not allowed to be near each other during school hours. I reconsidered changing your schedule so that Griffon wouldn't be your teacher but thought against it since we're in the middle of a semester and you're doing so well.

"I am sorry for my daughter's inappropriate behavior, and I don't think there's a need to call Sheriff Willson in," he added, then adjusted his tie. "But Lana, you will not get away with your behavior—"

"But Kel—"

"If you answer this simple question, you'll only get a detention, but if you don't, I'll suspend you!"

"Mr. West, come on, don't you think that's a bit harsh?" Griffon asked as he rose to his feet. Principal West stood and glared at him.

"A little harsh is kicking my daughter in the face! Now answer the question, or he's gone!"

"But I thought you sa—"

"Answer the goddam question!"

"You never even asked the question yet."

"Oh," he mumbled, then leaned on the desk, so we made eye contact. I saw Griffon sit down. "When you answer this question, you'll tell the

358

truth and only the truth. If you don't, then he's gone forever, got that?" he asked. I saluted him as he rolled his eyes. "What imbeciles decided to cover our cars in tomatoes?"

Chapter Twenty-Three

Lana

Detention wasn't how I planned to start Thanksgiving. Today was the worst because all the delinquents and rebels of the school went to that detention. When I stepped into the room, my eyes widened. Girls dragged their nails along the board and desks, guys did spit takes, couples made out, and others jumped on desks. I swallowed the lump in my throat, then walked to the back of the class. I avoided the weird looks I got as I sat down. A guy who I saw in the hallways spun around. He wore a gray hoodie with black stud earrings. He took in my appearance and raised a brow.

"You in the right place?" he asked as I pushed up my glasses.

"Yep," I said. He squinted his eyes then snapped his fingers. A girl with bright red hair appeared next to him. She's in my German class, but we barely talked, so I didn't know her name.

"She looks familiar."

"She's the one who bitch slapped West's daughter and covered both of their cars in tomatoes," the girl stated.

"Damn." The guy grinned as he eyed me up and down.

"What did you guys do?" I asked.

"Got caught smoking weed at lunch." He shrugged as if it were a regular thing to do. I turned to the girl, who smiled.

"I just come here because he's here."

"All right, listen up!" I glanced up and saw Coach Harris enter the room, which made everyone scramble to their seats. "You are all a disappointment to this school! Vandalizing the school and giving it a bad name…like why the heck do you still come here?"

"We're forced to come here," one guy replied.

"It's not like we have a choice," a girl with short blonde hair added.

"Whatever, now you'll spend the rest of the day writing out how sorry you are for being such idiots. Why can't you be like Max?" Coach Harris asked as he handed out the papers.

"Who's Max?"

"My pet fish," he answered as I snorted. Coach Harris looked down at me as his eyes widened. "Willson? What the hell are you doing in here?"

"She slapped Kelly West." The guy in front laughed. Everyone turned to look at me, an impressed look on his or her face. Coach's eyes widened as he raised his hand.

"That's awful," he mumbled, but I noticed the sudden twitch of his lips.

"Finally, someone had the balls to do it," a girl muttered.

"Okay, enough. Last one to finish their five hundred word apology will have to do laps," Coach announced. I sighed to myself as I began to write, and the strangest thing was, I had a lot to say sorry for.

***

"Are you sure you're okay?" Benny asked as he cupped his hand over mine. It was morning, and I had another nightmare. The first thing I did was call Benny; it made sense since he's the only one that knew. Dad was asleep as Mom made us coffee. I didn't say he should come over, but he insisted. Benny caressed my hand.

"I'm all right," I mumbled, then looked up at him. "Sorry for disturbing you,"

"It's okay. I was gonna laze around the whole day anyway." He shrugged, then removed his hand as my mother placed two cups in front of us.

"What about Thanksgiving?" Mom asked.

"Oh, my family drove to Wisconsin to visit some relatives," Benny said.

"Why didn't you go?" I asked.

"Mid-terms, plus it'll be boring anyway. Just my little brother with my little cousins and adults," Benny answered as he sipped his coffee.

"You're welcome to stay here!" Mom spoke up. I gaped at her as Benny almost choked on his drink.

"Err, I don't thi—"

"It's a splendid idea! Benny dear, you're always

362

coming here during the week, and we barely have time to talk because of you two studying. It'll be a great opportunity for Harry and me to get to know you better!"

"T-thank you, Mrs. Willson, looking forward to it."

"Plus, you're the only one who knows about these scary nightmares my daughter's been having, so any help is needed!" Mom added, then walked out of the kitchen.

"I won't let you down, Mrs. Willson!" Benny exclaimed. He turned to me with a goofy grin on his face. I looked away and thought about how the rest of the day would turn out. Benny scooted next to me and put his arm around my waist while he drank his coffee with his other hand. "This is gonna be an awesome weekend."

When my father shuffled in, Benny immediately dropped his arm and slid to the end of the counter. "Morning, Mr. Wil—"

"When did you get here?" Dad asked as he squinted his eyes at Benny. Even though Benny came to the house often, Dad was still overprotective, but slowly he was beginning to trust Benny.

"Fifteen minutes ago, sir," Benny answered as he avoided eye contact.

"Benny's staying over for dinner," I spoke up.

"Hmm, well, you're early." Dad eyed Benny suspiciously.

"He's just a good friend, Dad. Come on, Benny," I said, then grabbed his wrist as we walked out the kitchen. Benny immediately pulled away, but I didn't turn back as we walked upstairs.

"Keep that door open!"

"Y-Yes, Mr. Willson," Benny called as we entered my room. I quickly made my bed up as Benny played with the things in my room. Once I was done, he collapsed on the bed.

"What now?"

"Take a shower. Then we'll head over to my place so I take a shower, then we can chill till dinner," Benny suggested as he hugged my heart pillow.

"Okay cool," I said. I took out a cream sweater and blue jeans from my closet. I spun around. "Didn't you take a shower already?"

"Nope, plus do you really think I'd show up to the dinner table in this?" he asked, and I glanced down to the casual attire that he topped off with Converse. I laughed, then walked into my bathroom and shut the door. I took a quick shower because I never had Benny alone in my room before. Once I was done, I walked out to see him in the middle of the room with his back to me.

"Benny?" I whispered. He whipped around with a pained look in his eye.

"What is this?" he demanded as he held the cigarette pack. My mouth opened and closed, but nothing came out. "Are you using it?"

"No, it's not mine. It's Blake's," I croaked out as I reached for it, but he stepped back.

"I thought it was only for the bet!" he exclaimed as his grip tightened on the pack. "He got you back on these?"

"N-no, I took it from him because I was—"

"How many did you take?"

"Benny, I'm keeping it for him. Please, you have to believe me. I don—"

"I believe you, but give it to him as soon as possible, or even better, get rid of it," he muttered, then tossed the pack on the bed. I went after it like a dog and picked it up. Blake didn't know I had them. Why would he care? He used one pack in two days, and I barely smoked. There was an awkward silence as I put the pack in the drawer. I quietly sat on my bed and looked up at him. Benny had his arms folded as he stared at the ground. I noticed when he was mad or frustrated he'd yell then be silent. "You ready?" he asked after a while. I slowly nodded. I was shocked because he walked out as if nothing happened. I told my parents that I'd be back in the afternoon to help with dinner and they were okay with it. We got into Benny's car and drove in silence to his house.

I followed him into his house; it was similar to mine but looked like it had more rooms. The front door creaked as Benny pushed it open. Inside it seemed very modern; the furniture had the basic brown, gray, and black colors.

"Benny, I'm sorry," I mumbled as we walked upstairs. He looked over his shoulder with an expressionless look.

"It's okay, I just…"

"I'm fine, there's nothing to worry about," I assured him, then rubbed his arm. He gave me a sad smile, then led me to his room.

"Make yourself at home," he stated, opening the door. I took in the room of the guy who had bullied me for years. Gray walls covered with posters of football players and musicians. A cluttered desk with a laptop in one corner, and opposite that a TV with two beanbags. His bed was in the center of the room with a black headboard and bedside tables.

"Nice room," I commented as he typed on his phone.

"Thanks, err...I won't be long." I didn't know what to do, so I laid on his bed. I was tired. Benny's cologne mixed with fresh scent came from the bed. I smiled and took a deep breath as I absorbed his smell. Afterward, I took out my phone and scrolled through my contact list. My finger stopped at a name. I heard the shower run, so I had enough time.

Lana: Thanks for picking up my glasses on Thursday.

I waited for a reply as I sat on the bed. Maybe he's busy with his family. I stood up and gripped the phone in my hand as I paced the room. It caught me off guard when it vibrated and played only a few seconds of my ringtone until I answered.

"Hey, you finally answered!" a familiar husky voice erupted through my phone.

"What do you want?" I barked, not in the mood to talk him, of all people.

"Are you still mad, princess?" Levi cooed.

"Yes! And don't think when you come here, everything will be perfect, because I want an explanation...from the start!" I muttered into the phone. There was dead silence at the other end of the line as I took sharp breaths.

"You breathe loud," he said after I calmed down.

"Goodbye, Levi," I hissed and ended the call before he could reply. I was about to throw my phone against the wall until it buzzed.

Blake: It's okay.

Lana: Okay.

Blake: You starting some fault in ours stars shit?

Lana: Do you have to swear?

Blake: Sorry.

Lana: It's okay.

Blake: Okay.

Lana: Happy Thanksgiving.

Blake: Thanks, you too.

Lana: Okay.

Blake: Are you home?

Lana: No, why?

Blake: No reason.

Lana: Okay.

Blake: Okay

Lana: Enjoy. the rest of the weekend.

Blake: You too.

I put my phone on the table and sighed. Who knew two guys could cause such stress when they weren't even here? I heard whistles from the hall, followed by a shadow. Benny entered the room with a towel draped around his hips. Make that three guys. His eyes widened as his cheeks flushed.

"Oh, sorry, I forgot…"

"No, err…it's okay," I said, turning to his window. I heard shuffles on the other side of the room, then hops. I slowly turned my head and saw Benny in a pair of black jeans and black Vans. He was shirtless as he dried his wet hair with the towel. I glanced down to his toned chest, then back at him. I watched as he picked up two button-up shirts and held them in each hand.

"Okay, which one?" he asked. I tapped my chin as I pictured him with each of them on.

"That one." I pointed to the gray shirt. Benny smiled as he spun around to put the other one back. His back muscles flexed as he did so. I bit the inside of my cheek as I balled my fist. His muscles flexed as he put on the shirt. He spun around and moved through the room as he buttoned it up. "You look good," I said as he sat beside me.

"Thanks." He lightly chuckled. I rested my hands behind me as we stared at each other; his hair was wet from the shower as it covered his face. I didn't know what came over me, but I leaned forward and brushed it out of his face. He bit his bottom lip as our faces were inches apart. I looked into his dark brown eyes, then at his mouth. My hand was on his cheek as we stared at each other. I couldn't take the awkward silence anymore, so I leaned forward and kissed him. His soft, warm lips filled me as he kissed back. It felt like time froze as I sat there, his lips tugged on mine for entrance, and I let him. I tilted my head as he cupped my cheeks and deepened the kiss.

"Any Nielsons home?" a familiar voice echoed through the house. Benny pulled away from the kiss and cursed under his breath. I panted from the long kiss as I tried to avoid eye contact. He got up from the bed and walked out of the room as I trailed behind. One thing I knew was that kiss caused trouble. I didn't know why I did it, but I enjoyed it.

"Hey, dude, wanna hang?" Liam asked as Benny entered the kitchen. I took my time as I thought about his lips against mine.

"What the hell are you guys doing here?" Benny hissed as I entered the kitchen.

"We know you're alone today, so we wanted to keep you company," Nick said. His eyes landed on me and widened. "But seems like you already have company."

"It's Thanksgiving," I spoke up.

"Yeah, well, I only have to be back before dinner." Liam shrugged.

"And I just don't want to help. That's why I have other siblings," Nick added.

"You didn't even call." Benny huffed as he

folded his arms.

"We did, but no one was answering," Liam said as he looked at us.

"Not to be rude or anything, but what are you doing here, Lana?" Nick asked, but his gaze was on Benny.

"Her mom invited me for Thanksgiving dinner," Benny mumbled.

"Wanna get ice cream before dinner?" Liam asked. I peeked over at Benny, who scrunched his nose up.

"It's almost winter."

"Almost," Liam remarked.

"I'll take my car," Benny sighed as Liam listed flavors.

"I'll go with Liam," I stated as I walked to the other side of the room. Nick gave us weird looks as he followed Benny to his vehicle.

***

"Finally," Liam sighed as we entered a coffee shop in a small suburb. We drove around for an open place; most of them were closed because it was Thanksgiving. When we sat down, I made sure not to sit with Benny. Tension seemed to surround us after the kiss. Since it was almost dinner, we decided on two big waffles. I shared with Liam while Nick and Benny divided the other one.

"How does one recover from bad dreams?" Nick asked. I stared at him in confusion, then glanced at Benny. He must've told him about my dreams.

"I don't know," I mumbled, then continued to

eat.

"Your mom said your nightmares are getting worse," Benny scoffed.

"It'll go away."

"Your mom found you in the corner of your room crying one morning!"

The café went silent as everyone looked at our table, Liam apologized, and everyone got back to what they were doing. Benny huffed as he poked his waffle. One thing I'd learned over the years knowing Benny Nielson was that he had a quick temper. It actually scared me when he'd be quiet one minute then roaring like thunder the next.

"I had a dream the other night," Liam mumbled as I pushed the plate toward him. I watched as he devoured the rest of the great waffle. Once he was done, he looked up.

"What was it about?"

"Nightmare, actually. That creepy dude that we buried walked into our Physics classroom and caught us. Long story short, we ended up in jail and Nick became gay."

"Dude," Nick groaned as he kicked Liam's leg under the table.

"Scary and weird at the same time," I said, then looked at my phone. "Crap, we gotta go. Mom needs help, and I still need to get ready."

Nick paid for our food as we went our separate ways. I climbed into Benny's car and sighed. It was going to be a long night. As he drove, I stared out the window. None of us spoke, yet I had so much to say.

"Sorry," Benny mumbled after a while. I turned

to look at him; he had no expression as he drove. "Just really worried because you come to school with bags under your eyes, yet nobody says anything because you have such—" Benny cut himself off as he took a deep breath. "You have such a beautiful smile that it's hard to ask you something that will make you frown."

I didn't know what to say. We arrived at my house, and I watched as Mom paced up and down while Dad was nowhere to be found.

"Lana, go get changed!" Mom scolded as she placed something in the oven. I gave Benny one last look, then bolted up the stairs. There was a beautiful white dress on my bed. I grazed my fingers over it as I thought of my mother. It was a sleeveless dress that ended above the knee. I put on my camel-colored boots, then slipped on a maroon cardigan to give off an autumn look. I decided to leave my hair loose while I put on makeup.

When I walked downstairs, I came face to face with my father. He wore a dark blue sweater, black jeans, and brown shoes. He eyed me up and down and gave me a warm smile and raised his arms. I approached him and let him engulf me.

"You look gorgeous, honey," he mumbled in my ear.

"Thanks, Dad, you look good too," I said as we pulled apart. He gave me a small smile as he ruffled my hair. As I fixed it, I walked into the kitchen and saw Benny with the salad. He seemed concentrated as he squinted his eyes with his tongue stuck out. I leaned on the doorframe and watched him cut the tomatoes, then add it to the salad. I walked next to him and leaned on the island.

"Didn't know you could make a salad," I joked. He laughed as he looked up but immediately stopped when he took in my appearance.

"You look beautiful—"

"Lana, finally! Come help set the table," Mom ordered as she walked in. I gave Benny an apologetic smile as I strolled into the living room; it was the most significant room in the house since it had an open area on one side and the sofas on the other. There were six plates out as well as the cutlery. As I set the table, I heard laughter. When I looked over my shoulder, I saw Mom and Benny walk in.

"And this is when she went trick or treating," Mom cooed as she pointed to her phone. I looked over her shoulder and saw the photo of Levi and me when we were dressed up.

"He looks oddly familiar," Benny said as he squinted his eyes. I playfully rolled my eyes as I thought of Benny and Levi when we were little. It was in fourth grade, and Benny, Nick, Aidan, Ethan, Jennifer and I were in the same class. Levi was in the fifth grade, but he was well known as the clown of elementary school, along with Aidan. Levi left the following year, so he became another face to remember.

"Oh, that is Mrs. Radc—" Mom began but was interrupted by the oven. She bolted into the kitchen and left her phone in Benny's hands. He approached me with a confused look as he stared at the picture.

"You remember him." I grinned as he swiped to the next image, which showed Levi and me at the beach at eight and nine years old.

"Don't tell me. I know him. It's on the tip of my tongue." Benny would've remembered if he'd seen an older image of Levi. The doorbell broke the comfortable silence, and Benny set my mother's phone down. "I'll get it." He smiled as Mom came into the living room. My mother stood next to me as she took in my appearance and I took in hers. She wore a long-sleeve dress that ended below her knee, her hair up in a tight bun as she smiled at me.

"Where'd you get the dress?" she whispered.

"I thought you got it for me." I raised a brow. Before she replied, Benny came into the living room with an embarrassed look.

"Look who arrived," he said through gritted teeth. I looked over his shoulder and saw Griffon Bronx enter, but he wasn't alone. Benny stood beside me as we put on our best smiles for our two favorite teachers. "This is gonna be a long night."

Chapter Twenty-Four

Lana

"Did you know they were coming?" Benny mumbled as he helped me set the table.

"I sort of forgot, but I didn't know that he'd bring a friend." I grinned at the adults. Miss Rosa had a bright smile on her face as my mother chatted with her. Mr. Bronx and Dad caught up, while the two awkward teenagers set the table.

"It'll be awkward, though, with the whole Kelly pictures thing," Benny said.

"What gave you that idea?" I asked sarcastically. Benny looked at me with an annoyed expression. I pulled my tongue at him, and he playfully rolled his eyes.

"Benny." I glanced up to see him stiffen. I rolled my eyes and motioned him to approach them. He nodded, then left the cutlery and walked toward Griffon and my dad. I looked over my shoulder and saw the three men talk. There was a challenging look on my father's face as he spoke to Benny.

Thankfully, being the open guy Griffon was, he lightened the mood. I went to the kitchen to get the salad, along with the passion fruit. I heard laughter from the living room, and I smiled to myself. Tonight wouldn't be so bad. My thoughts were interrupted when I heard footsteps enter the room as I took a cucumber. Miss Rosa entered the room. Her dirty blonde hair was curled, and she wore a floral dress that ended at her knees and white heels.

"Caught in the act," she joked as I swallowed the cucumber. I sheepishly smiled as she walked to the sink.

"Miss Rosa, I'm sorry for what happened on Tuesday with Kel—"

"It's okay, Lana. I got the full story." She chuckled as her gaze shifted to the living room, then me. "I thought I'd never see the day that Benny Nielson and Lana Willson would be in the same room together, getting along."

"Well, he apologized for everything he's done in the past, and everyone deserves a second chance."

"He's quite something."

"Uh huh…how did you get the full story?"

"After school, I was packing to go home then someone came into the classroom. He explained how Kelly is such a, and I quote, 'bitch,' to you. Then you would always run off to Griffon, since you knew him longer than anyone in the school," she began. "He also said that you took full responsibility for ruining Principal West's car even though he doesn't believe you."

"Who told you?"

"You'll find out soon."

"Thanks, Miss Rosa."

"Anytime and please, call me Jenny."

***

"So, Harry, how's work?" Griffon asked as he cut the turkey. I sat next to Miss Rosa with Benny opposite her. Next to him was Uncle Griff, and at the ends were Mom and Dad.

"Same old. A few weeks ago, Deputy Paul said some teenagers were arrested and you bailed them out?" Dad turned to Uncle Griff. My eyes widened as I looked at Benny, then Griffon. He froze from cutting the turkey as a smirk crept up on his face.

"Oh, yeah, just a few students of mine getting up to nonsense."

"Thank goodness I wasn't on duty. Paul said they were annoying."

"Yeah, thank goodness these two aren't like them," Miss Rosa added as she looked at Benny and me.

"Yep." Benny winked at me. As Uncle Griff sat down, I noticed his gaze shifted from me to Benny.

"But wait...you were one of them." My eyes widened as Dad glared at Benny.

"Err...yeah, they dragged me into it. I was stupid, Mr. Wil—" Dad and Griffon exchanged a few looks, then laughed.

"We're just pulling your leg, kid." Griffon chuckled as my mother scoffed.

"Don't torture the poor boy like that," Mom added as she hit Griffon with a napkin. I saw Jenny Rosa look up in surprise.

"You'll get used to it," I muttered as I stuffed my mouth with carrots.

"He's like an older brother to Lana," Mom assured Jenny.

"If you don't mind me asking, what did you and your friends get arrested for?" Jenny asked Benny.

"We were just fooling around. Pulled a prank on the principal's car and got caught while doing his daughter's." He shrugged. Griffon Bronx and Jenny Rosa glanced at me as they tried to process what they'd heard. The whole school already knew that I did it, but now they'd hear Benny's story.

"Funny, that's the same night that Lana and her friends pulled a prank too," Dad said.

"Oh, come on, Harry, it's not like you haven't got arrested before." Griffon beamed.

"Whoa, Dad got arrested?"

"But they dropped the charges."

"Still, I wanna hear the story!"

"Yep, it was the first summer we had together. Your dad had the whole Mohawk thing going on and everything!" Griffon joked as everyone laughed. "We were in this cabin for the summer along with a bunch of other guys. One night there was a bonfire, and we played truth or dare. Your dad had two truths already because he was scared, so it was either another truth or a dare."

"So what did you choose?" Benny asked.

"Dare."

"Because you didn't want to answer the truth about Misty Taylor," Griffon added. Mom squinted her eyes at Dad.

"Misty Taylor?" she grumbled.

"This was before I met you, honey!" Dad exclaimed as he glared at Griffon.

"I know, because I wouldn't go for a guy with a Mohawk," she hissed as Jenny, and I laughed.

"Okay, but what was the dare?" Benny asked.

"Skinny dipping in front of the hot Misty Taylor!" Griffon cheered as he and my dad high-fived each other.

"And whatever happened to this Misty Taylor chick?" Jenny asked as Griffon whispered something to Benny and they laughed.

"Oh, she's, err…she's married now," Dad said, then raised his brows. "Five kids."

"Wow, but what do you expect? Who wouldn't want to—"

"Griffon!" my mother scolded as Benny and I laughed.

"Sorry, Angie." He apologized like a four year old.

"So you got arrested for that?" Benny asked.

"Yeah, apparently, they don't like it when drunk guys run across their cabin in their birthday suit and into the lake," Dad grumbled.

"Don't forget the Mohawk," Griffon added.

"All right, Sheriff Willson!" Benny cheered as he raised his hand. Dad stared at it and slowly shook his head. Benny lowered his hand.

"So, Benny, what are your plans?" my mother asked after a while.

"Well, since I'm next to take over the family business, I'll probably do that for a few years, but apart from that, I'm looking to go into physiotherapy."

"Wow, that's brilliant," my dad remarked as he gave Benny a smile.

"It'll suit you." Jenny smiled.

After that, conversation died down as everyone ate. I was glad that nobody asked about my plans. I wasn't ready for that question yet. Griffon started another random topic again as I cleared off the table. Mom and Jenny talked as Benny watched me; I raised my eyebrow at him as he looked away.

"Okay, Benny, you into NBA?" Dad snapped his fingers.

"Of course, Chicago Bulls all the way!" he cheered. I rolled my eyes and walked to the kitchen. As I cleaned up, I heard footsteps behind me.

"What's on your mind?" I looked over my shoulder to see Uncle Griff.

"Nothing," I mumbled, then looked down at the dishes. Yet my mind was on the kiss.

"It's written all over your face, Lana. Come on, tell Uncle Griff what's the matter," he cooed.

"I kissed Benny."

"*What?*" he yelled. I snapped my head to peek at the living room; thankfully, nobody heard Griffon's scream, and I sighed in relief. "So are you two—"

"No!" I yelled in a whisper.

"Phew!" He sighed in relief. I watched as he quickly recovered, and the familiar smirk appeared on his face again. "Do you have feelings for him?"

"No…I don't…ugh! I don't know. I mean, why would he go for a girl like me? I don't think I'm his type. He's sweet and all, but I—"

"You're letting your past get to you," he cut me off. "If you really like him, you'll look past all the bad things he's done to you and look at the good stuff. You're changing him for the better, and I never thought Benny Nielson wanted to become a physiotherapist!"

"What if I'm not good enough and peo—"

"Lana, you're beautiful, inside and out," Uncle Griff said as the corners of his mouth raised. "Any guy would want you. Some of them haven't made a move yet because they know if they don't play their cards right, they'll end up with Sheriff Mohawk."

We laughed, and I shook my head in amusement as he walked off. I heard laughter from the living room and frowned. I wish I were there, but Mom found out about the detention, so I had to clean up. Benny came into the kitchen with a few dishes in his hands. I watched as he placed them in the sink. We stared at each other until I spoke.

"Seems like they adore you."

"Just being myself, didn't know your dad was such a huge fan of sports."

"Yeah, when Ethan was here, they used to bond a lot."

"Hopefully when I come to your house again, your dad won't look at me like I grew a second head."

"Yeah, very soon you guys will be best friends." I smiled. Benny chuckled as he looked down. I noticed that his gelled hair had one strand out of place and stuck to his face. I wanted to fix it, but I knew where that'd lead to.

"Lana, look, I—"

"I have the recipe right here!" My mother's voice cut off Benny as she and Jenny entered the kitchen. I didn't think she even noticed we were in the kitchen as she spoke about Jamie Oliver. I glanced at Benny, who had his lips drawn into a straight line. I opened my mouth to speak, but nothing came out, so he shook his head and exited the kitchen.

The rest of Thanksgiving break was spent with my parents. I wanted to talk to Benny, but every time I looked at my phone, I'd overthink our friendship and back away. I didn't tell anyone, and it ate me inside. Monday came around, and I slipped on something warm since the weather didn't look too good. It was also the start of mid-terms, so I had to focus. I had breakfast, then heard a honk from outside. I greeted my parents, then hopped to the front door. My jaw dropped as I saw the familiar GMC truck in my driveway. Carter must've gotten his truck back.

"Don't wanna be late for the first test, Willson!" Aidan exclaimed from the passenger seat. The back door flew open as Liam hopped out and held the door open for me. I raised my eyebrow at their weird behavior as I walked to the truck.

"Morning, Mr. Willson," Liam greeted as he got into the car. I looked out the window and saw my dad by the porch. He sipped his coffee as he stared at us. We watched as he placed his other hand on his holster. Aidan made an awkward cough as he hit the dashboard.

"Go now, he's gonna shoot!"

Carter hit the gas pedal as I sunk in my seat. Once we were around the corner, he let out a sigh.

"Damn, one of these days I'll need to come with

a lawyer," Liam commented.

"He's just a protective parent," I said as I took out my history book. The guys got into their own conversations as I tried to review the work. My thoughts went back to Benny. Yesterday I studied all day and had not one text from him.

"Lana, I'm madly in love with you," Carter blurted out.

"What?"

"That got her attention." Nick chuckled beside me.

"Sorry, just reviewing," I mumbled.

"You're reviewing a closed book," Liam pointed out. I looked down to see that I hadn't even opened the book yet.

"You got a haircut!" I squinted my eyes at his lovely brunette hair.

"That's what's different about you," Aidan said as he turned to us.

"No duh, what gave you that idea?" Nick sarcastically asked.

"Was it the missing mop on his head or the fact that we can finally see his forehead?" Carter asked as I snorted.

"Hey, it was a phase!" Liam argued as he folded his arms.

"Okay, diverting the topic of Liam's new haircut and onto something more important...how was everyone's Thanksgiving?" Aidan grinned.

"Mine was good. My cousin Bethany was there. She kept on eating the cheese and talking to them," Liam said as he nodded. "My cousin is weird."

"Wonder where she gets it from," Nick

mumbled.

"My sister made this fabulous pudding, like oh my ga—"

"Benny and I kissed," I blurted out. Carter hit the brakes, I flew forward, but Liam held me back.

"What?" Aidan demanded as he turned back to us.

"Carter, just drive." I sighed as he looked at me through the rearview mirror, but eventually he drove.

"Finally, he had the balls to do it," Aidan spoke up.

"Hehe, well, I sort of kissed him," I said. As soon as those words flew out of my mouth, Carter hit the brakes again.

"*Carter!*"

"Wait, so you locked lips, made physical contact, and shared saliva with my best friend?" Nick asked.

"Well, if that's your definition of kissing, then err…yeah,"

"Damn."

"How? When?" Aidan asked.

"Well, on Thanksgiving, Benny came over because of the nigh…I mean to get something," I murmured since Aidan and Carter didn't know about the dreams. "And then we decided to hang out. So, we went to his place, and he was showering—" I cut off when I flew forward, and my head hit Aidan's seat. I dug my nails into Carter's shoulder as I glared at him.

"In the shower?" Carter raised his voice.

"Do that one more time, and I'll take that steering wheel and shove it up your ass sideways!" I growled, then leaned back. "Just let me finish."

I explained to the guys the whole situation at Benny's house yet left out the fact that Levi called. It wasn't important, and we were already close to the school. As they processed, I looked out the window and saw the many raindrops.

"What a nice way to start exams," Aidan scoffed as we arrived at the school. We hopped out of the car as Nick went to Melissa. I hugged my study book against my chest as I soaked. The rain soon disappeared as I looked up to see Carter trying to cover me with his umbrella.

"Thanks," I said, then snuggled next to him.

"How was the kiss?" Aidan asked as he played with his umbrella.

"Good, I guess." I shrugged.

"What did his breath smell like?" Liam asked as he tried to snatch Aidan's umbrella.

"I don't know," I replied as I raised a brow. Carter and I watched in amusement as they fought over the umbrella. Liam was a bit taller than Aidan as he tried to reach over his shoulder to get it.

"Wait for it…" Carter trailed off. I squinted my eyes as I watched them pull on the umbrella. They pulled too hard, and we watched as it broke.

"There you go." Carter laughed as the rain dripped from their hair. The bell rang, and Carter and I walked to the building while Aidan and Liam trailed behind us.

"Lana!" I looked over my shoulder to see Miranda walking up the stairs.

"Thanks, I'll see you later," I said to Carter as we walked into the building.

"Liam told me everything. How was the kiss?" Miranda asked, and I turned to glare at Liam, who smiled.

***

Blake

"Pleasure doing business with you, Gunner." Parker grinned as he handed me the pack of cigarettes.

"Whatever," I muttered as I gave him the money.

"So how's the female population been treating you?"

"Good, I guess."

"And your good girl who you tried unsuccessfully to turn into a badass?" Parker asked as he leaned against the lockers. We were in an empty hallway as everyone was at lunch.

"Screw you, and I didn't fail because she isn't a good girl."

"Uh huh, definitely," he said as I raised a brow. "You know there was this party last year and goddam she was hot. She was with this guy, and you wouldn't even say it was her. It's like he also tried to change her…"

"What are you talking about?"

"I'm saying that your little nerd isn't a good girl. Yeah, she has the glasses, does her work, and kisses up to Daddy, but that guy taught her a few things, and it seems she never forgot them." He spoke in a bitter tone. I got frustrated at Parker, so I pushed him against the lockers. I held him up by his collar as he smirked at me. "Wait, let me rephrase that. Not your little nerd or Benny's."

"What the hell does Benny got to do with this?" I demanded then backed away.

"Didn't you hear? They kissed."

"Bullshit."

"Bull fucking true!"

"And what do you mean she never forgot them?"

"Oh, you know what I mean," he said, then looked down. I followed his gaze to see the pack of cigarettes in my hands.

"She's buying from you?"

"You'll have to pay," he sang. I rolled my eyes and walked away, but Parker wasn't finished.

"She's got a killer body, though...love to bang it ag—"

I pushed the doors open to block the rest of his comment as I walked. I scoffed as I walked out of the school and into the parking lot. I took a cigarette out of the box, lit it with my matches, then stood next to my motorcycle. Axel took my lighter, so I was stuck with matches. I've learned over the past few weeks that cigarettes have gotten quite expensive; Aidan introduced me to Parker, so I go to him. This Parker dude gave off a weird vibe. Not saying that because he came up with the bet and sold stuff, but something else. Like how he knew things and how Lana reacted when she found it was him who started the bet. He spoke about a guy I'd heard about quite a few times. Parker knew something or at least did something. Yet it explained how Lana knew how to smoke when I first offered her a cigarette. It must also demonstrate her love for rock and alternative music.

"Hey," a soft voice interrupted my thoughts. I glanced up and saw Lana. I noticed that she wore a leather jacket, black jeans, and black Converse. She must've noticed when she spoke. "It was cold, and this was the only clean thing I had in my closet."

"What brings you here?" I asked as she leaned against my motorcycle. A weird sound came from the bike as it tilted to the side and fell.

"Oh, crap, sorry," Lana mumbled as she hurried to the other end of the vehicle. I watched as she tried to pick it up but hopelessly failed. She stood up and let out an exasperated sigh. Without a word being said, I reached down for my bike and swiftly picked it up, then kicked the side stand out. Lana rolled her eyes as she sat on the damp curb. "Thank you," she mumbled after a while. I turned to look at her a gloomy expression as she stared at the building. "Miss Rosa told me on Thursday, and I figured it was you."

Not knowing what say, I stared at the cigarette in my hand and took a drag. I exhaled the smoke and noticed her stare when I sat down beside her. "Why? I thought you and Kel—"

"Because it was the right thing to do. Why do you always want an explanation? Maybe I did it because I wanted to." I cut her off.

"Well, thanks."

"Rumor's going around that Nielson and you kissed."

"Yeah," Lana said, then turned to me. "Heard you and Kelly are going out."

"Yeah." I looked into her dark blue eyes; she had

circles under them as she pushed her glasses up. "It's depressing to hear that you're hooking up with your bully."

"We're not hooking up! And he *was* my bully, Blake. Everyone deserves a chance." Lana groaned as she pushed herself up.

"You're giving them too many chances."

"Ugh, please, Blake. How many chances have I given you?"

"Exactly!"

"Ugh, just go back to being a narcissistic bad boy player." She huffed and spun around.

"There's a difference, you know," I called after her. Lana froze, and I noticed how she clenched her fists as she spun around. "Between a player and a bad boy," I said then stood up.

"And you're a combination of both."

"Take Carter and Ethan for example." I ignored her, tilting my head. "How many girls do they flirt with in a day?"

"I don't know…eight, maybe."

"And if you ask half of the juniors and seniors in this school who they lost their virginity to, your answer will be…"

"Them."

"Uh huh, and since we've met, how many girls have you seen me with? Besides you, Miranda, and Melissa."

"One."

"That is correct! Now, like a bad boy, they don't go for any chick; they observe and watch. Once they have their prey, they go for it!" I let out a dry laugh. "Besides, bad boys are much more fun when it comes to riding a motorcycle, jumping off a cliff, getting a tattoo, and don't forget to go to prison with one." I winked, and she rolled her eyes. "Players, on the other hand…you'll always need to watch them like little kids. They see a toy and immediately drop the one they have to get a new one."

"You're really something, aren't you, Blake?"

"A special something," I said as she laughed, but it was gone when she sighed.

"I'm sorry about—"

"No, it's me who should apologize. I've been a dick these past few weeks because I was silly and immature. Not really good with apologies, so yeah." I trailed off. We studied each other as we stood there. Her blue eyes were full of mixed emotions as she stared into my dark brown eyes. After a while, she broke her gaze and laughed.

"What?"

"We're always fighting…it's so weird."

"Well, that's just us and our weird friendship."

"One question: is it true that you sold your kidney for an upgrade on your motorcycle?"

"Wha—No."

"So you got all your organs?" Lana raised a brow as I laughed. Before I answered, a familiar voice rang through the parking lot. I looked over my shoulder to see Miranda. "Coming! See you in class," Lana said as she jogged toward Miranda. I forced a smile but thought back to her question.

"Not really, someone stole my heart."

Chapter Twenty-Five

Lana

Mid-term examinations weren't so great. The past few days had been exhausting. I stared at my locker and sighed because we'd have Calculus in a few minutes. At least I had a pill with me, but I needed a refill. I gulped down the pill then shut my locker and threw the empty bottle in the trashcan. The sound of the bell deafened me as I groaned. As I strolled to class, I saw Parker approach me in his camel-colored coat and lace-up boots.

"Hey, Lana."

"Err…hi, Parker."

"You okay?"

"Yeah, I just…ran out. I need more."

"You sure? It's like the fourth bottle you bought."

"Please! Just a few more days and I'll be out of your hair," I begged. Parker anxiously bit his lip as he thought. He looked down the hall, over his shoulder, then took out two bottles. "I'll pay you as soon as I get cash."

"How can I trust you?" He squinted his eyes as his grip tightened on the bottles.

"Come on, we've known each other for a while. You should trust me by now. Plus, I'm friends with Aidan, so…"

"Okay," he sighed. I quickly snatched the bottles and twisted a lid open. I popped one in my mouth and swallowed. From the corner of my eye, Parker bit his lip as he gazed at me. "Lana, I'm sorry for what happened junior year. I'm really fucking sorry, and I get that you hate me."

"Whatever, Parker." I rolled my eyes. "No one must know, okay? It happened. It's in the past."

"Heard that Radcliff is coming."

"Yeah."

"He's gonna cause shit, you know?"

"Yeah."

"Him and his friend are gonna find out."

"Yeah…Levi Radcliff always finds out."

"Just go easy on those…"

I ignored Parker as we went our separate ways. I stuffed the bottles in my bag before I entered Mr. Bronx's classroom. Everyone sat at their desks as they got ready for the test. Mr. Bronx was in the middle of the classroom as he spun around.

"Lana, you're late."

"Sorry," I mumbled, then walked to the back of the class. Everything seemed so blurry as I approached my desk.

"Whoa," Nick mumbled as I tripped over my feet.

"Sorry," I apologized as he gently pushed me up.

I stumbled to my seat and sighed.

"You okay?" Aidan whispered as Mr. Bronx handed our papers. I gave him a short nod as I took the test paper. The words seemed to jump around the page as I groaned. I felt agitated as I tapped my fingers against the desk. I noticed Austin's gaze. For the past few days, he watched me, in the classroom and the hallways. I raised a brow at him, and he looked away.

***

"How was the test?" Miranda asked as I came out of the classroom. She held hands with Marcus as they gave me warm smiles.

"Fine, I guess." I shrugged because I wanted to sleep.

"You okay?"

"Yes, I'm fine," I snapped. Miranda rolled her eyes at my behavior and spoke with Marcus. We walked into the noisy cafeteria, and I immediately regretted it. My head pounded as I took my time to walk to our table. I lost my balance and almost fell, but someone caught me. I opened my eyes and looked up to see Ethan Baxter, secured in his arms.

"Lana, are you okay?" he asked. I squinted my eyes.

"Yes! Stop asking me that!" I hissed, then pushed myself up. With an annoyed look, I slumped down on the seat. I placed my bag on the table and rested my chin above it. Blake no longer sat next to me; he sat opposite me. Benny was perched on the right side of the table, while Miranda was on my left, and Ethan was on my right. Everyone else slid in wherever there was space. Melissa explained and apologized for Kelly. Even though I forgave her, she always said sorry. Benny and I returned to normal; not once had the topic about the kiss come up. Nothing felt the same. There'd still be the awkward tension that surrounded us. We no longer studied together since it was the actual exams.

"So we're gonna be together, Willson," Blake stated as I glanced up.

"What?" I asked.

"After winter break, all the classes will be changed," Ethan said beside me.

"Why?" I asked.

"Mr. Bronx's tired of you," Carter joked.

"How do you know that we'll be together?" I squinted my eyes at Blake.

"I just know. I'm in Mr. Hill's Physics class, so I might join you guys."

"How fun...more players in the class," I grumbled. Ethan and Carter glared at me as I gave a fake smile.

"There's a difference," Blake sang. I rolled my eyes. He raised a brow, and I flipped him off. Some people at our table noticed, yet no one said anything. A shiver went up my spine as I felt a pair of eyes on me. I looked up and glanced around the cafeteria to see Austin. He was the only one at his table who looked at me.

"You coming to the game on Friday?" Ethan snapped me out of my gaze.

"Maybe."

"Hey." He nudged my arm. I looked into his

394

chocolate brown eyes as he smiled at me. "If you need someone to talk to, I'm here, okay?"

I gave a curt nod, then turned to Aidan. He had a cheerful smile on his face as he shared his fries with Carter. I sighed, then turned back to Austin. No surprise there that he still stared. Aidan turned his head and followed my gaze.

"What's his problem?" Aidan glared at Austin, who turned away.

"I don't know. He's been staring at me a lot. It's creepy," I replied. Aidan shook his head and dropped the fries he was about to eat. We watched as he stood up and stared at Austin's table.

"Dude, stop staring. It's creepy. Chicks don't dig that!" he yelled from across the room. The cafeteria suddenly went silent as they stared at the two boys. Austin let out a dry laugh as he stood up.

"Nothing to see here. Nobody will be punching anyone," Austin shouted, and the cafeteria returned to normal. "Not today at least." He muttered the last part as he approached our table.

"Quit being a stalker, dude," Benny hissed as Austin, and I locked eyes.

"What do you want?" Melissa asked, yet he ignored her and smirked at me.

"Do they know?" he questioned.

"Know what?" Blake demanded.

"Ah, you'll find out soon, Gunner." Austin winked, then strolled back to his table.

"Know what?" Nick repeated as everyone turned to me.

"I don't know," I mumbled as I avoided eye contact.

"We should have a party," Miranda piped up. Everyone at the table chatted as if it were going to happen. I sighed and buried my face into my bag.

"Count me out."

"Do you sleep?" Carter asked. "I swear, every day you're like this. Even in class after you do work, your head hits that desk, and you're out cold."

"So?" I growled then rose to my feet. "If you guys are going to pick on me the whole time, then don't even bother talking to me," I grunted, then grabbed my bag. I must've left my zipper open, because all my things fell out. I crouched down and threw things into my bag as fast as I could, yet someone decided to help me.

"Lana, what the hell is this?" Miranda asked. I whipped my head to see her with a bottle in her hand. Everyone stared at us as Miranda glared at the bottle like she wanted to crush it.

"Nothing," I said as I snatched the bottle from her hands then ran out.

***

The following day, I decided to take my mother's car to school since I didn't speak to anyone after the incident in the cafeteria. I had to focus to get into Yale even if I didn't have a test today. Miranda knew how stressful I got with school, so she left me, but I don't know now since she saw the pills, as well as everyone else. I was early at school and thought to go to the library before the bell rang.

396

"You're early."

I spun around to see Parker and Austin, who held mischievous grins.

"What do you guys want?"

"We know," Austin stated.

"What the hell is that supposed to mean?" I demanded. Austin's eyes darkened as he darted toward me. He took both my arms and trapped me against the nearest wall. I looked around for help, but there was barely anyone at school; the sun wasn't even out yet.

"Don't act dumb, Lana."

"I don't know what you're talking about!" I stated as he neared me. Austin let go of my one arm, and it hung loosely. He squeezed the other one as I cussed and looked at the ground. I saw combat boots in front of me. Parker took his index finger and thumb and gripped my jaw, so I was forced to look up at him.

"If you tell any of this to Aidan or the other guys, we're coming for you," he warned.

"Like you're going to get away with it!" I yelled as Parker backed away.

"You think just because you have the team captain, co-captain, and jackass bad boy for friends along with the other idiots, you think people like you now." Austin laughed dryly as he dropped my wrist.

"There are still people in this school who wish to be in your position, Lana," Parker stated.

"And being the innocent sheriff's daughter, you use it to your advantage and do dru—"

"*No!*" I cut Austin off. He and Parker shared a

397

look as I rested against the wall. Austin twirled his wrist, then looked over his shoulder to see if anyone witnessed us. Once he spun around, he gave me one hard slap.

***

"Is it safe to enter the personal space of Lana Willson?" a recognizable voice asked as I shut my locker. I turned my head to see Carter, Blake, and Ethan.

"Yeah," I mumbled, then turned my back to them as I walked.

"What was that stunt you pulled yesterday?" Blake asked as he caught up to me.

"Nothing," I muttered, because I wasn't in the mood to talk after being slapped, even though I thought I deserved it.

"What happened on your cheek?" Carter stopped me in the middle of the hallway as he caressed my cheek.

"Nothing," I replied, then swatted his hand away.

"What crawled up your ass and died?" Blake asked, but I ignored his question and continued to walk.

"So are you coming to the game tomorrow night? Could really use your encouragement," Ethan asked. I turned to look at him with a sad smile.

"Sure," I said as I slowed down. I looked down each hallway but saw Austin and Parker at the end of the second hallway. "I'll catch up with you guys later."

"All right, and if you're not there in five, we're sending our troops!" Carter joked as they walked the other direction. I watched as they took their time to walk down the hall then turned the corner. When I turned my head, I was met by an empty hallway. I crept down the hall and looked over both shoulders. A door opened. Everything happened so fast as Austin pulled me into the janitor's closet and pinned me against the wall. I looked into his dark eyes as a shiver ran down my back. The room was dim but bright enough for me to see his face.

"I know about the drugs," he stated. I looked over his shoulder to see Parker, who seemed pissed. A familiar feeling whirled inside of me since we were in the janitor's closet. I swallowed the lump in my throat as a million scenarios ran through my head as to what someone like Parker Collins would do to me again. I was snapped out of my senses when Austin stepped aside and made way for Parker. His jaw tightened as he approached me.

"Where's my fucking money?" Parker demanded. The exact same words Parker asked me the last time ran through my mind. I feared what he'd do next. Yet he wouldn't do anything with Austin in the room. Last time Parker asked once, and that was it, then he used me. Did Austin even know what a monster Parker was?

"It's in my locker," I whispered. Parker let out a groan as he spun around and walked toward the door. Austin eyed me up and down, then followed. "Wait…" I trailed off before Parker reached for the doorknob. Both turned back to me as I squinted at Austin. "What do you mean you know about the drugs?"

"We know that you know about the cocaine we stole," Austin grunted.

"I knew it!" I said, then raised a brow. "But how? Why?"

"Money," Parker replied with a grin.

"But Aidan's your friend! How could you do that to him?"

"Because we wanted in!"

"In what?"

"The money," Austin replied as he looked down in shame, but Parker didn't seem phased.

"Wow." I rolled my eyes. Austin stared at me, then threw his arms up in exasperation. "What am I supposed to do about it? They don't have it anymore."

"Yes, but they do have the money," Parker said as he stepped toward me.

"No, no, no, I'm not going to steal for you guys!"

"Either we get the money, or we're telling the whole school what you've been doing," Austin threatened as he pointed to Parker.

"Like you haven't done it before," I remarked.

"You have until Monday," Austin said, then walked to the door. I watched as he twisted the doorknob and thrust the door open. I strolled behind him as I avoided eye contact with Parker.

"Ouch," I grumbled as I bumped into Austin's back. Once I looked up, I paled, since Aidan, Melissa, and Liam stood in front of us. It looked bad to come out of the janitors' closet. To make matters worse, Parker walked out as if nothing happened. "Aidan," I trailed off. A deceived look crossed his face as he glanced at the three of us. Austin and Parker spun around and walked off as if nothing had happened. I watched as Aidan stormed off. "Aidan, wait!" I called after him. He marched into a classroom as I chased after him. I walked in, out of breath as I shut the door. I spun around to see Aidan's back to me as he ran his hand through his hair in frustration. "Aidan, just let me exp—"

"Explain what? How my two ex-friends were makin—"

"It wasn't like that! I'd never do that to you!" I rushed out as he glanced up at me.

"Then what was it like, huh?" he demanded. I felt the agony in his voice as he spoke.

"I-I can't tell you."

"Are they bullying you? Is Parker a perv again? What did Austin say yesterday?" he questioned, then rested his hands on my shoulders. "Lana! Talk to us! We can't help you if you don't talk!"

"Pa-Parker has been giving me these pills—" I stuttered as I took out the bottle.

"No, no, no," Aidan repeated as he dropped his hands and stared at the bottle.

"And they've been helping me get through everyt—" I cut myself off when the door opened.

"What the hell is going on?" Blake demanded. Aidan snatched the bottle from me and threw it at Blake. I watched as he read the bottle with a confused look. Aidan paced backed and forth as he mumbled to himself. "Lana, what the he—"

"You don't need those!" Aidan cut off Blake as I bit the inside of my cheek. "You are one of the smartest, bravest people I know. Lana, you don't need this to keep you awake and alive," Aidan yelled. I felt like a little kid being scolded at for writing on the walls or something. It frightened me to see Aidan Rowley, of all people, freak out. I've never seen him like that before. Even if he did tease me he'd laugh and smile, I felt like since I've been around him, I made him worry a lot. "Why Parker? Of all people?"

"He came to me."

"Why was Austin in there?"

"I-I don't know."

"Come on, Lana, tell us," Blake demanded.

"He was threatening me, and this morning he warned me. That's how I got this bruise on my cheek," I mumbled as I stared at the ground. From the corner of my eye, I saw Blake grip the bottle so hard I thought it'd break. He used all his strength and threw it across the room. I winced as the pills fell out.

"That little fucker," he growled, then barged out of the room. Aidan followed behind him, but I tugged on his arm. He turned to me with a saddened look as I stared at him.

"Aidan, I'm sorry, I didn—"

"It's okay."

"There's something else you should know," I mumbled as I let go of his arm. "Remember back at the cottage when that James guy said two forty-eight? Austin and Parker stole the other two bags," I whispered. Aidan's brows rose as he processed the information.

"That would explain why they were acting so

weird the one day when they left my house. Probably excited about how much money they'd make," he muttered. "But how does he still have it?"

"He only sells cocaine twice a year."

"How do yo—"

"Chill, dude!" A recognizable voice cut off Aidan's next question. Aidan quickly rushed out of the classroom. I was about to follow but stopped and spun around. I picked up the pills, then shoved the bottle in my bag. I walked out of the classroom and down the hall where I heard the commotion.

"Don't you ever lay a hand on her again!" Blake roared as he held Austin by the collar then shoved him against the lockers.

"Or what?" he spat. Blake let out a dry laugh as he let go of Austin's collar and backed away. He flicked his wrist, and for the first time, Benny punched Austin. Ethan and Carter held Parker by each arm as he watched in amusement. Blake hit the locker next to Austin as he glared at him.

"Or else I'll cook your testicles for breakfast!"

"Told you not to touch her, dude," Parker added. I slowly approached the scene as Blake kneed Austin in the balls. He fell to the ground and groaned. Benny pulled him up by the collar and was ready to punch him again.

"Blake, Benny, stop," I yelled before they went all ape on Austin again. They turned to me as they held their fists in the air. I approached all the boys with a depressed look. "Just let them go."

"What? Lana, you can't be—"

"Just let them go!" I repeated, then looked at

Parker. He winked at me as Ethan and Nick dropped their arms. Austin slowly stood up with a smirk plastered on his face as Benny and Blake glared at him. Parker folded his arms as he watched me.

"I still want my money."

"What money?" Aidan asked before anyone else could.

"Your little princess over there owes me some money! I don't give out stuff for free!" Parker added. "She knows what happens if I don't get my money."

"Ethan," Blake said as he pointed to Parker. With a huff, Ethan took out his wallet and gave Parker money. Benny snatched the wallet from him and took out more money, then shoved it in Austin's chest.

"None of this happened," Benny said as Austin nodded.

"I-I don't think this covers everything. Those pills are rare," Parker hinted as he counted the money. Ethan grabbed his wallet again and took out fifty dollars.

"We hear anything, we'll know who said it," Ethan grunted.

"Our lips are sealed." Austin winked at me.

"Pleasure doing business with y'all," Parker exclaimed as they walked down the hall. Once they turned the corner, it was only us. Not one person dared to make eye contact. I felt guilty to put them through all that, especially Ethan, since he gave two hundred dollars away.

"Thank you," I blurted out. The bell rang, which broke the awkward tension; I looked up and noticed their stares. Then one by one, they walked off and disappeared into the crowd.

Friday was spent quietly as everyone talked about the game tonight. We sat at our regular lunch table as everyone yammered excitedly. I felt like a burden to all of them. Every time I caused problems, and they had to rescue me.

"You coming, right?" Miranda snapped me out of my thoughts as she smiled. "Take your mind off things."

"Sure," I mumbled, then glanced around the table and noticed Ethan, Benny, Liam, and Nick were gone. Blake and Melissa decided to sit with Kelly, so it was Carter, Aidan, Marcus, Miranda, and me. Aidan and I hadn't spoken since yesterday, but he looked okay. He still joked and laughed as if nothing happened. My phone vibrated as I stared at the table. I reached into my pocket then pulled it out.

Meet me half an hour before the game near the restrooms - P

"Did you get any sleep?" Carter asked. I turned my phone off and shoved it in my pocket.

"Yeah."

"Really?" Aidan demanded. I rolled my eyes as I stared at the brunette boy. He had no expression as I looked at him. I reached down for my bag and picked it up, then slammed it on the table. I ripped the zip open, then took out the small bottle and flung it across the table.

"There. Happy?" I growled. He caught the bottle

with ease and examined it. Everyone stared at me. Aidan let out a dry laugh as he played with the bottle. I raised my brow at him as he turned to me.

"You still dared to pick it up and take four more."

"What?"

"Yesterday I counted how many pills were in here; there were eighteen, now there's only fourteen," Aidan hissed as he handed the bottle to Carter. Miranda leaned over Marcus as she tried to read what's on the bottle. I watched Carter anxiously as his face turned to a look of confusion, then horror. He glanced at me, a look of disappointment on his face. Miranda grabbed the bottle from Carter's grasp.

"Lana, please, promise me you won't take these ever again," she begged. I stared at her with an anxious look. I wanted to say yes so bad, but nothing came out.

"How long has this been going on?" Marcus asked.

"Since the beginning of junior year," I mumbled and looked down in shame.

"How did we not know about this?" Aidan demanded as he hit his hands on the table.

"Well, considering you only came and messed up my life, no—"

"You're blaming us?" Carter raised a brow at me. I let out an exasperated sigh and glanced at Kelly's table. She and Blake kissed as Melissa conversed with Jennifer. Austin sat on the end, quietly eating his lunch, his eye bruised. I turned back to Aidan and Carter, who waited.

"No…him," I mumbled, then looked at Blake. Both looked over their shoulders at Blake, who grinned at Kelly as she spoke. He looked so engrossed in what she said that I scoffed. Marcus stood up and walked to the trashcan. I watched as he dumped the bottle into the bin.

"It's for your own good, Lana," Miranda said as she gently held my hand.

"Miranda, it's only until next week, then I'll—"

"No! It's a drug! You've become so addicted to it that you don't know what you're doing anymore!"

"Yeah, I mean, when last did you get some actual slee—" Aidan babbled on.

"*I can't sleep!*" I cut him off as I slammed my hands on the table.

***

I paced back and forth, then let out a sigh. The game began in half an hour, and I already heard people in the gym.

"Told you she'd come." I spun around to see Aidan and Blake against the lockers. Aidan held his phone in his hand as he scrolled through it. I glanced at Blake, who stared at me. I tried so hard not to look at the smudged lipstick on his lips.

"What are you guys doing here?"

"Should be asking you the same thing," Blake replied. Before I answered, I heard shuffles from around the corner.

"You guys are fucking annoying now…hey, hey! Watch the jacket; this is genuine leather!" I watched as Benny dragged Parker around the corner. He was

407

in his football uniform as he shoved Parker toward me. "Lana?"

"Parker?"

"Aidan!" Aidan beamed as he raised his arms in exasperation then rolled his eyes out of annoyance.

"What's going on?" I questioned.

"We knew that you'd fall for that text. It's not easy getting over something so addicting," Blake answered.

"So what do I have to do with this?" Parker asked.

"You are going to make sure that she does not buy from you. No matter how much money she offers you, you're gonna say no," Benny said as he towered over Parker.

"Or what?" he scoffed.

"Or we call the cops and tell them you stole cocaine and that you're selling on school property," Aidan replied with a fake smile. I snorted at what he said. None of them found it amusing as they stared at me.

"You do realize that if he's arrested, my dad, the sheriff, will question him. And there's a big chance that he'll ask who Parker stole the cocaine from. Leading it back to us." Aidan looked down in defeat as Blake shook his head.

"Just don't fucking take the pills. Like what the fuck?" he asked with an annoyed expression.

"Other than using it to focus, why else do you take it?" Benny asked out of the blue.

"I don't like sleeping." I shrugged. Everyone else stared in confusion, but he understood what I meant.

"Yeah, you made that clear at lunch," Blake

mumbled.

"Can I go now?" Parker asked. "I'd like to go encourage our school's football team."

"Whatever," Benny muttered. As Parker strolled past us, Aidan put his hand out and tugged on his arm. He whispered something to Parker that made him smile.

"Thanks, old pal," he stated, then ruffled Aidan's hair. I quietly tip-toed the other way to escape but failed when I heard whistles.

"Where's the rest?" Blake demanded. I groaned as I pulled out the pills from my pocket. Parker gave me two bottles yesterday, and I always had a few in my pocket. Blake trudged toward me and grabbed them out of my hand.

"Blake, no. Please!" I begged as he walked toward the trashcan. I beat him to it then threw my hands up.

"Out of the way, Willson," he said through gritted teeth. I shook my head continuously, and he shrugged, then forced it into Aidan's palm when he walked past. I sprinted toward Aidan as he ran down the deserted hallways.

"Aidan!" I called after him. He went into the first open door he laid his eyes on, and no surprise that it was the girl's bathroom. I entered the bathroom, out of breath as I searched for Aidan. I heard footsteps behind me and knew that Blake and Benny followed us. "Come on, Aidan, you don't have to do this…" I trailed off as I walked past each cubical. I stopped at the second to last one where I saw him loomed over the toilet as he held the pills in one hand and fingertips pressed down on the lever with the other.

409

"N-No!" I stepped forward but was pulled back. As if in slow motion, I watched the pills go down the toilet. Blake stood by the door as he stared at me. "You asshole!"

"Look at what it's doing to you!" Aidan yelled as I tried to release myself from Benny's grip. Blake squinted his eyes at me, then walked closer. I watched as he ripped my bag off of my shoulders and zipped it open.

"Blake don't you dar—" I cut myself off as he turned my bag upside down and out came everything. He shook the bag until it was empty. I glanced at all my belongings on the floor as Blake picked up the last bottle I had.

"This," he held up the bottle, "is just going to fuck up your life even more."

"*No!*" I screamed as he tossed the bottle to Aidan. Benny's grip on me tightened as I fought to get closer. My legs buckled as I felt tears in my eyes. I dropped to my knees as I watched Blake and Aidan take out the pills.

"You'll thank us later," Benny whispered in my ear as I cried.

"No, please!" I sobbed as I watched Blake drop the pills. "*Fuck you! Please!*" I bawled my eyes out as I watched Aidan flush the toilet. Benny pressed my head against his chest as I sobbed. The only thing that kept me going was gone.

***

My heart raced as I breathed in and out. I stared at the wet sheets draped around me. I was used to waking up from a nightmare, taking a pill, then studying, but now it was hard. It was the fourth time I'd woken up. I frantically searched for my heart pillow so that I could snuggle into it and try to get back to sleep. From the corner of my eye, I spotted it against my door. I forced myself out of bed to get it. When I crouched down to pick it up, I heard voices from the other side of the door.

"She usually sleeps in on Saturday." That was my mother. I glanced around and noticed a little light through the curtains. I tossed the pillow on my bed and opened them. I squinted as I was met by daylight. I opened the door and walked out, since I was hungry.

After the incident in the girls' bathroom, we went our separate ways. Benny got ready for the game while Aidan and I took our seats. Throughout the match, I sat with Miranda and Marcus. Aidan sat on the other end with Carter while they flirted with a few girls. I didn't see Blake or Kelly at the game, but I knew it wasn't his thing.

I headed for the stairs and walked down. My eyes were shut as I tried to recover from the light. My body collided with somebody else, and their arms instantly wrapped around me. I must've missed a step or tripped, which led us to tumble down the stairs. Thank goodness, I landed on top of somebody, so I wasn't badly hurt. I couldn't say the same thing about the person underneath me as they groaned. My eyes shot open, and I went pale as we made eye contact.

Chapter Twenty-Six

Lana

I watched as he shut his eyes and cursed under breath. His Adam's apple commenced to bob up and down as he moaned out, "Your knee."

I raised a brow as I glanced down and realized that my knee was lodged in between his thighs. Looking around, I saw two feet in front of me. When I glanced up, I was met by my dad. I immediately got up and put on an innocent smile. Dad's eyes diverted to Axel, who groaned on the floor. We watched as he got up and leaned on the staircase for support as he looked at us.

"I'm good, thanks for asking," Axel retorted sarcastically.

"Is this going to happen every Saturday that a random guy comes to our house? If so, let me know so that I can load my shotgun," Dad grunted.

"Err...Dad, meet Axel; he's Blake's older brother." I pointed to Axel, who was hunched over.

"I know who you are," Dad stated, then sipped

his coffee as he walked into his study.

"Nice to see you again, Sheriff Willson!"

I was confused as to why Axel was here and how he knew my dad. Maybe he had been arrested before. Without another word, I strolled down the hall and hoped that he'd follow. I caught a glimpse of how I looked in the side mirror and winced—my hair was a mess. Once we reached the kitchen, I spun around and squinted at him. He took his time to walk as he rubbed his thigh in discomfort. It was easy to tell that he and Blake were brothers: same brown eyes, pointy nose, sleek dark brown hair, olive skin, and tattoos. Axel wore a leather jacket, so I only saw the tattoos on his hands.

"What are you doing here?"

"It's practically one in the afternoon, and you look like a squirrel attacked you," he pointed out. I rolled my eyes and folded my arms. He let out an exasperated sigh, then stuffed his hands in his pockets. "You know that blonde chick with the ombre highlights?" I stared at him in confusion, yet the first person to pop into my head was Kelly. "My brother's girlfriend."

"Yeah, what about Kelly?"

"Oh, that's her name. Well, it's her birthday today, and she's having a party tonight. Being the delayed son of a bitch that my brother is, he didn't get her anything yet."

"This still doesn't answer as to why you're here," I hissed, but he ignored me.

"So he asked me what girls like, and I'm like, 'How the hell am I supposed to know? Does it look like I have boobs and va—'"

"Just get to the point!"

"Calm down, pumpkin." Axel raised his hand. "As I was saying, he got pissed because he didn't know what to get, and I made him angrier. We got into a huge fight, causing him to break Mom's favorite vase, so he kicked me out and told me to come back when I have a present for Kim."

"Kelly."

"Whatever."

"That still doesn't answer my question."

"Well, I don't know what chicks adore. Plus, you're Blake's friend, so you can help."

"Why couldn't you ask your friend Tamia?"

"She's busy with college and shit."

"And what makes you think that I will help you?"

"Because you're are a true friend who'll help a friend in need." He pouted.

"We're not friends. I barely know you."

"Yeah, but you and Blake are friends…" He trailed off. "With benefits."

"What?" I glared at Axel as the corner of his mouth rose.

"Nothing," he sang, then gave me a once-over. "So get ready."

"Why?"

"So we can go to the zoo," he mocked. "So you can help me get this chick a present!"

"Can't he take a bunch of flowers?"

"Lame."

"Isn't he her present already?"

"You got a point there," he stated. "But I'm sure she'll be pissed if he shows up to the party and be like, 'I'm your birthday present!' Then they'll maybe break up."

"Not such a bad idea."

"What?"

"Nothing," I responded with a grin.

"Clock is ticking…" He trailed off, pointing to his wrist that had no watch on it. I let out a huff as I trudged down the hallway and up the stairs. I tried my best to get done as quick as I could. I didn't trust Axel downstairs with my father. Since it was getting close to winter, I decided on a flannel, jeans, and boots. I brushed my hair out as quick as I could, then slipped on my glasses. I grabbed my phone, then walked downstairs.

"Hope everything is okay now," my mother said.

"Yeah, we're getting there," Axel responded. I raised a brow as I walked into the living room to see my parents on the sofa, while Axel sat opposite them. When Mom noticed me, she sat up, and everyone turned to look at me. I was intrigued as to how Axel knew my parents. "Well, we better get going. The mall can get full on a Saturday," Axel said as he stood up. I glanced at my dad, expecting him to protest, but got nothing. He gave us a small smile and nodded.

"Take care of her, Axel," Dad stated as he rose to his feet.

"Don't worry, I'm sober," Axel joked as he winked at me.

"You kids have fun," Mom added as she placed her hand in Dad's. I watched as the crazy people I presumed were my parents walked into the kitchen. Once they were out of sight, I turned to Axel with a puzzled look.

"What just happened here?"

"I don't know." He shrugged and walked to the front door. I trailed behind as I tried to think of a reason why my parents let me go with Axel so smoothly.

***

"Why do we have to go buy her something if Blake is her boyfriend?" I asked while we drove down the road.

"Again with the topic." Axel laughed.

"Well, you just ruined my whole Saturday worrying about what to get Kelly West for her birthday."

"What were you going to do the rest of the day?" He glanced at me. "Sleep." He answered his own question, which was accurate. "So think of it this way: you're helping Blake and yourself by doing something constructive on a Saturday."

"But sleep is the best."

"Not gonna argue on that one." He chuckled as he reached into his pocket. I watched as he took a cigarette out of the pack, then a lighter from his other pocket. He lit the cigarette and inhaled the tobacco. I think he noticed my stare, as he held out the pack. "Come on, I know you wanna." Axel wiggled his brows. I let out a dry laugh as I took a cigarette and the lighter. I noticed it was Blake's lighter. I placed the cigarette between my lips and lit it. As I inhaled the smell of tobacco, I shut my eyes because it was a substitute for the pills. I leisurely opened my eyes as I exhaled and blew the smoke into the air. I glanced over and noticed Axel's smirk. I tilted my head at him, and he shook his head and smirked. "Not gonna lie, that was hot."

I didn't know what to say, so I smiled and turned up the volume of the radio. I finally turned to Axel and watched as he dumped his cigarette out the window.

"How come you're not in college?" I asked. Axel's jaw clenched as he stared at the road in front of him. He gripped the wheel and intently licked his lips. I realized I wouldn't get an answer, so I remained silent. Earlier I asked if we could make a quick stop before the mall. Axel parked the Mitsubishi in front of the store, and we got out. I hadn't been here in almost two months. I stared at the entrance. It's where it all started.

"You coming?" Axel broke my gaze. I straightened my posture as I scurried behind him. As soon as we entered the store, we went our separate ways. I searched for Rodney as Axel went through the types of vinyl. We decided to stay on the bottom floor so that we wouldn't have to look for each other.

"Hey, Rodney," I greeted as he placed some posters in a box. He glanced over his shoulder and gave me a warm smile.

"'Sup, Lana? What brings you here?"

"Here to pick up those records I ordered."

"Oh yeah! They arrived last week. I'll just go and get them." I watched as he walked to the back of the store. Once he was gone, I whipped my head around to look where Axel was. True Gunner genes

417

right there. I shook my head in amusement as I watched Axel play the electric guitar in front of girls. Blake and Axel were roughly the same height, and it looked like they shared the same style. Same leather jacket, ripped jeans, and combat boots…or was it a Gunner thing? I wouldn't be surprised if their mom was a rock star. "*Alt-J* and *Mayday Parade* vinyls." Rodney's voice snapped me out of my thoughts as I spun around and saw him with a box. "If there's any issues, or one of them is cracked, just bring it back, and we'll figure it out from there." I gave him a warm smile as he reached under the table. From the corner of my eye, I saw Axel and his friends laugh. Beside them were a few tables and chairs filled with people who listened to music or used the free Wi-Fi. A light bulb appeared above my head as I gazed back at Rodney. "Just sign here and here," he instructed. I did as told, then handed him the money.

"Are you open during the week?"

"Yep, weekdays nine a.m. to six p.m."

"Is it okay if I hang out here after school?"

"No problem. You'll just have to buy something," he joked as Axel approached us. I chuckled as Axel took the box without my permission. He walked out of the store, and I said bye to Rodney, then caught up to Axel. He placed the box in the trunk and walked to the driver's side and got in without a word. I sighed. His mood reminded me of Blake…it must run in the family.

***

"How about we go in there?" Axel asked as we strolled past a few stores. For the past hour, we've been stuck at the mall, trying to find "someone's girlfriend" a present. It hadn't been going so well since Axel thought of such useless things to buy her. I glanced up, and my eyes widened at the store's name. "Come on, haven't you ever thought of having a pair?"

"No! Well, yes, but I'm sure there's something else for Ke—"

"Come on, Lana. Kaitlin will love this." He sighed as he yanked on my arm.

"It's Kelly!" I groaned as we entered the store. I felt uncomfortable entering a store like that with Axel. Girls with designer bags and looks of maturity gaped as we entered. I squinted up at Axel and noticed a grin take over his features. He enjoyed it; girls drooled over him as we walked.

"Hi, may I assist you today?" A squeaky voice snapped me out of my thoughts. A girl who seemed a few years older than me stood in front of us. Her light brown hair was up in a high ponytail that swung as she tilted her head to the side.

"Yes, I'd like to see the cutest lingerie you've got." Axel beamed as he smirked at her.

"Aww…you're so lucky that you have a cute boyfriend buying you Victoria Secr—"

"He's not my boyfriend," I said, then stepped aside. The girl gave us a confused look as she glanced at Axel. He let out an awkward chuckle as he swung his arm around my shoulder.

"She's really shy," he said. I scoffed and pried him off as the girl directed us to the lingerie.

"Take your time. Just shout if you need help." She winked at Axel. Once she was out of sight, I snapped my head back to him. He slowly walked down the aisle and rubbed his chin as he eyed the lingerie.

"Just pick one and let's get out of here," I said. He pulled out a set and placed it in front of me. I glanced down to see black lacy lingerie. I squirmed away as he raised his hands in confusion.

"You and Kimberly are basically the same, so just hold on, woman," he snapped, then placed the lingerie back in front of me. I let out a huff as he continued to hold up other pairs that looked the same but were a different color. "This one is perfect." He eyed me. "Let's just take a size bigger…just in case."

"Do you think Blake will like it?" I raised a brow as he searched for a bigger size.

"Please, I bet you my brother is worrying his ass off right now."

***

Blake

I glanced at the bottle of beer in my hand, then to the broken vase on the table. Axel was the most frustrating person in the universe—he was worse than Liam and Aidan. You'd think, him being the first-born, he'd be mature and responsible, but those kinds of words didn't appear in his vocabulary. I believe he dated my girlfriend more than I did. He especially woke me up and reminded me that it was her birthday. Whenever Kelly and I hung out, Axel came in the room and spoke to her.

I knew it was her birthday, and she was planning a bizarre party. I sent her text, and her response was thanks, and she couldn't wait to see the gift that I got her. Wasn't I enough? I'd slept around a few times, but I'd never committed myself to anyone other than Kelly. With her, it felt exciting yet desperate. Whenever I was pissed at someone, she appeared. Whenever Lana and I fought, she emerged. The first few times she stood and watched me. Afterward, we seemed bored, so we took it to the next level. I didn't know what to get her. I'd been to her house, and it's massive. She showed me all the things in her room, so that made it harder. I wanted to loaf around the whole day, but Axel nagged me. I got so annoyed that we fought and knocked down Momma's vase again. Instead of being the responsible one, he left and said that he'd get her a present since he's invited too. That took me by surprise, so I gave him money to buy a gift while I cleaned up. As always.

I placed the beer bottle onto the coffee table and got up. I approached the sound system and hooked up my phone, then hit shuffle. How ironic that "Happy Song" by *BMTH* came on. A smirk molded onto my face as I remembered my first encounter with Lana Willson. She surprised me there. That's where it all started. I shook the memory away as I glanced down at the broken pieces on the coffee table. I increased the volume as I sat down and held a glue gun in one hand and a glass piece in the other.

Half an hour later, I was down to the last two pieces. Nirvana blared through the speakers as I bobbed my head to the beat. Everything went silent as I heard shuffling behind me. I hastily got up and spun around, only to be met by my annoying brother.

"Look, Nirvana is amazing, but you don't have to deafen the neighbors," Axel sarcastically said as he stood by the sound system. I squinted my eyes at him as I twirled the glue gun in one hand. I noticed the big bag in his hand.

"What did you get?" A smirk suppressed his lips as he handed me the bag. I looked inside and saw a pair of Victoria's Secret underwear.

"We got Kendall her fave. She can show you tonight." He winked.

"For the tenth time today, it's Kelly." I turned my head. Our eyes locked for a second, then she looked away. "Hi," Lana whispered. I turned to my brother, who had a goofy grin.

"Your parents know that you're here?" I asked her. She stood in the corner of the living room, behind the sofa, as if not sure if she should come any closer. Her hair curled as a strand fell down her face onto her glasses.

"Yeah, and somehow they're fine with me hanging out with a twenty-two year old."

"Okay, now that we've all caught up, how's the vase?" Axel asked.

"Getting there."

"Thanks for buying this. It's…err…very kind of you," I said in an ominous tone.

"Only the best for your girlfriend," Axel sang as

I set the bag on the ground. Lana scoffed and turned away. I turned back to my brother and smirked as he returned the gesture. She faced us with an innocent look.

"What?" she snapped. Axel let out a dry laugh as I shook my head in amusement. He walked to the kitchen, which left me with Lana.

"How are you?" My voice sounded quieter than I expected.

"I'm all right."

"All right, you reckless teenagers, I'm heading out," Axel announced as he entered the room in a different shirt, jingling keys. I squinted my eyes at him as he smiled at Lana.

"No, no, no—you're helping me with this shit!" I pointed to the vase.

"No can do, brother. I have places to go and people to see," he said, then rested his hands on my shoulders. "Lana can help you. I've heard she's quite handy at fixing things." Axel released his grip from my shoulders then spun around. "See you later, pumpkin." He winked at her. I scoffed at my brother's pet name for Lana as she gave him a kind smile. As he passed the sound system, he turned it on. Nirvana blared through the speakers. Lana twitched. I was used to the loud music. I walked to the sound system and reduced its volume. The familiar engine roared as I let out a frustrated groan. Axel took my motorcycle on purpose, so I had to take the car to drop off Lana. The only sound to be heard was the music as I looked over my shoulder. Lana remained in her spot as I raised a brow.

"Make yourself comfortable," I mumbled. My

jaw clenched as I approached the coffee table. Lana took a seat on the sofa. I joined the pieces back together and couldn't help but divert my eyes to the Victoria's Secret bag. I licked my lips at the thought of Axel and Lana shopping together. "Let me guess, it was my brother's bright idea to get Kelly some lingerie?"

"Yeah, he was determined to get her something." Her voice was soft as she laughed.

"How was the game last night?"

"Jefferson High always wins. Ethan played well. Liam was his goofy self, while Nick and Benny were focused." I squatted to the opposite side of the coffee table so that I faced her. I felt her eyes on me as I tinkered with the super glue. I'd look at Lana and sometimes watch as she lip-synced to a few songs. Her eyes met mine as she stopped and looked down, clearly embarrassed by the fact that I caught her. My lips twitched up into a smile as she blushed. That was the side that everyone knew, the kind and smiley Lana Willson. I thought back to yesterday, her weak frame wrapped in Benny's arms as she cried. I wanted to yank her away from him, but I knew that she'd cause conflict. It seemed like hours as Aidan and I watched her cry in his arms. All he did was lean his head back on the wall, a blank look on his face as he caressed her. It's like he felt sorry for her and understood what she went through. Me, on the other hand, I couldn't comprehend as to why she'd do such a thing. Then again, we all have secrets. For the past few months, I tried to figure out Lana. One thing was for certain: we had a few things in common. Yet there was something else about her that I couldn't crack. I could stare at her for hours, but I knew that I wouldn't get anything out of her.

"Blake!" Her voice snapped me out of my thoughts, and I saw her rush toward me. An alarmed look was on her face as she glanced down. I followed her gaze and saw the glue on my hand.

"Fuck," I exclaimed as I shot up and stared at my right hand. Three fingers dripped in glue. As I took my other hand to pull it apart, Lana smacked my hand away, and I glared at her.

"You idiot, then you'll glue that hand as well!" she said, then gripped my wrist. I followed her into the kitchen and snickered. She placed my hand under the tap as she opened the faucet. The lukewarm water soothed my palm as Lana pushed up my sleeve so that it wouldn't get wet. She crouched down and opened the cupboards under the sink. She came up with two paper towels and olive oil then set them aside. She was really focused. Her hand reached out for mine under the water. She cupped her left hand underneath my right one as she took her other hand and poured a few drops of olive oil on it. I bit my lip as her soft fingers grazed over my hand to gently rub it in. The only sound to be heard was the water running down the sink. Once she finished, she closed the faucet and gently wiped my hand. After she finished, I stretched my fingers, happy that they weren't stuck.

"Thanks." I awkwardly chuckled as we walked back to the living room.

"I'll finish it," she offered. I gave her an unsure look, and she playfully rolled her eyes. Since I wasn't going to get out of it, I grabbed us two sodas.

"I'll order pizza," I exclaimed over the loud music. She gave a short nod as I tossed the can. Since Lana was here, I didn't want to go to Kelly West's party anymore.

***

"Your fault!"

"It's me!"

"Shut up!"

I blinked rapidly and groaned. I got up from the sofa, only to be met by darkness. Lana and I talked for hours, then decided on a movie. I must've fallen asleep. I squinted my eyes as I heard movements on the other side of the house. I glanced at the clock on the wall, and my brows rose since it was 11 p.m.

"No, please!" A familiar voice snapped me out of my thoughts as I frantically searched for Lana.

"Lana?" I called out as I got up.

"Blake!" she screamed as I picked up my pace. I went down the hall, and something told me to go to the second door. I followed my instincts and went to the bathroom. Axel swayed on one side of the bathroom as he held a beer bottle in his hand. His shirt was unbuttoned as he dropped a cigarette to the floor.

"It's your fault, you whore!" he yelled. I followed his gaze to see Lana in the bathtub, a frightened look on her face as she looked at him. It was dark in the bathroom; the only light available was from the moon that glistened through the

426

window.

"Axel, what the fuck?" I yelled.

"It's her fucking fault, Blake!" Axel shouted, then stepped closer. Lana backed away in fear as her back hit the wall.

"I-I don't know what you're talking about!" she belted out.

"Shut up!" he demanded as he threw the beer bottle in her direction. Everything happened so fast. She let out a scream; I raised my fist and punched Axel. I heard the glass hit the wall in one ear and my brother growl in the other. He collapsed to the floor, clearly unconscious. My breaths quickened as I stared at him. He came home drunk and shouted at Lana. He barely knew her. I clenched my fist as I stared at him in the dim light. I saw something move. Lana was trying to get out of the bathtub. I scurried to her side as I held a hand out. She hesitated first as she looked at Axel, but accepted my hand. As I watched her every move, I noticed something red drip.

"You're hurt." My voice was hoarse as I looked at Lana's thigh. She shrugged her shoulders, but I grumbled. I wrapped my arms under her legs then picked her up. I slowly walked out of the bathroom and into the living room. I placed her on the sofa as I examined her cut. One of the pieces of broken glass must've cut her. Blood oozed out of her jeans as I walked to get the first aid kit.

"Take off your jeans," I said and returned with the bag, only to see her blank expression. "You have to," I stated as I placed the bag on the coffee table and took out stuff. I watched as she stepped

427

out of her jeans. Once she was done, I looked at her bare legs, her flannel extending below her waist. She stared at the cut as I crouched down on my knees. She was only in her underwear as I stared at it. Lana's eyes widened as she got up. She raised her brow at me and motioned for me to sit on the sofa. I gave her a confused look as I sat on the couch. She sat on the armrest and placed her legs over mine so that the cut was right on my lap. Thankfully the cut wasn't too deep, so it didn't need stitches. If it did, her dad would've killed me. I glanced at the stuff beside me and grabbed the cotton swab along with the hydrogen peroxide bottle.

"I'm just going to clean it," I murmured as I looked up. Her eyes were bloodshot, which made them bluer. She had an unsettled look on her face as she stared at the injury. Her arm wrapped around my shoulder for support as she gave me a nod. I gently poured the liquid onto the cotton swab, then dabbed it onto the wound. Lana winced from the coldness as her hand gripped my shoulder. I applied the ointment onto the gauze then covered the gash. While I worked, she'd pull down her flannel. I stared at the bandage on the coffee table, then down to the injury.

"Oh," she mumbled, then slowly got up. Once she was on her feet, she staggered forward, and my arm wrapped around her waist as the other held her injured thigh. "I'm all right," she whispered as our eyes met. She looked to the side as I followed her gaze and saw the bandage. I gently placed her leg on the ground, and my hand grazed up her back as she stabilized. I grabbed the bandage and crouched down to my knees. She pulled down her flannel again as she looked at me.

"Err…you need to spread your legs so I can wrap the bandage around your thigh," I mumbled up at her. A blank look appeared on her face as she gave a nod. I sucked in a breath as she shifted her legs so that they were broad. Shit. I swiftly wrapped the bandage around her thigh and brought my face closer to tie it.

Once I finished, I stood and cleaned up. Lana sat on the sofa as I strolled down the hall. I grabbed a pair of sweatpants from my drawer and walked back. I saw a figure on the ground. I rolled my eyes as I dropped the sweatpants and walked into the bathroom. I grabbed Axel by the ankles and pulled him out of the bathroom. As I dragged him through the hall, I wondered why he yelled at Lana. Then again, he always said absolute shit when he was drunk. This time, though, he went too far—he injured someone. I pulled him into his bedroom and debated on whether to leave him on the ground or put him in bed. I shrugged as I left him on the ground and shut the door. He wouldn't even remember any of it by morning. I picked up the sweatpants and walked into the living room. Lana was in the same position as when I left, which made me suspicious.

"I'm sorry for what my brother did. He gets really violent when he's drunk," I lied as I helped her into the sweatpants. She gave a minor smile as she stood up. The bags under her eyes became worse by the second as I observed her. Her face

429

drained of color as I put a lock of hair behind her ear.

"Lana, are you oka—" She cut me off when she grabbed my hand and removed it from her face.

"Blake, just take me home, please."

Chapter Twenty-Seven

Lana

Today I gave everyone a lift. Since Carter lived five minutes away from me, I got him first, then Aidan, Liam, and Benny.

"How was your weekend?" Benny asked as he leaned forward. I bit my lip as I placed my hand on my thigh. When Blake dropped me off Saturday night, I expected Mom and Dad to question me. However, as soon as they heard Axel's name, they were utterly okay with it. It confused me that Dad was protective when the guys were around, but when Axel came into my house, he was suddenly treated like a long-lost son.

"*Lana!*" I blinked quickly as Liam yelled out my name. The car swerved as I dodged a guy offloading things from his truck. I kept in a laugh as everyone took sharp breaths and glared at me in the rearview mirror.

"Note to self—never catch a ride with Lana ever again," Aidan sighed.

431

"Sorry, I was just distracted."

"You never answer my question," Benny piped up. Everyone was silent as they waited for a reply.

"Dull, like any other weekend. How was the party?"

"It was sick! You should've been there, Lana," Liam said as I rolled my eyes.

"Yeah, where were you? We came to get you, but your parents said you were out," Carter inquired as he turned to me. Flashbacks of when Axel threw the bottle against the wall and one of the pieces slashed into my thigh entered my mind. It happened so fast that I didn't even feel the glass open my skin. Then when Blake wrapped the bandage around me, that was awkward. I put on a fake smile then glanced back at the road and spoke.

"I just had a few errands."

"The party was huge! It was killing two birds with one stone. Kelly's birthday party and celebration of another win for Jefferson High's football team." Liam smiled.

"Glad that you enjoyed it." I glanced down at my thigh again and sighed. I wore sweatpants today because the jeans would be too tight and a skirt was too cold. Blake's sweatpants were still at my house. I haven't heard from him at all since he dropped me at home. I wondered if he went to the party? Axel, on the other hand, called me. He said he was terribly sorry and he'd take me out to dinner to make up for acting recklessly. He also said we'd catch up, whatever that meant. I didn't want to go to dinner with Blake's brother. "Was Blake there?"

"Err…yeah, he was," Aidan mumbled. The car

fell into an uncomfortable silence after that. We arrived at school five minutes later and decided to hang around the front since the bell hadn't rung yet. Miranda, Melissa, Nick, and Ethan joined us as we talked.

"Remember when you rolled down the stairs and pulled the dude's pants down?" Miranda chuckled as she looked at Liam.

"Not my fault that he was in the way," Liam said.

"Where's Marcus?" Melissa asked as she leaned her head onto Nick's shoulder.

"He left the party early, saying he felt sick. I wanted to give him a ride, but he said someone was already taking him," Aidan explained.

"Is he sick?"

"Uh huh! Yesterday he sounded so weird on the phone, and I wanted to take him some soup, but he said everyone in his house is sick," Miranda responded with a frown. Liam swung his arm around her shoulder, and she immediately looked up at him.

"Don't worry, he'll get better soon," Liam assured her.

"I hope so. I miss my baby."

"But I can keep you company," Liam added, wiggling his brows.

"Ready for Physics tomorrow?" Benny asked as he placed one hand on the wall, then leaned. Our faces were inches apart as he eyed me up and down. Every second I took to answer, Benny leaned in as he licked his lips.

"I just need to rev—"

"Come on, we can work this out!" a familiar voice cut me off. Everyone who stood outside seemed engrossed by the voice. I looked and saw Blake heading toward the school doors. Kelly trailed behind him with makeup smeared on her face. "Blakey, plea—"

"No, fuck you! You self-centered bitch!" Blake yelled. Everyone's eyes widened as they looked at the couple.

"I thought it was you." Her voice trembled as she tried to catch up to Blake. He was a few feet away from the doors as he spun around. There was a troubled look on his face as he fixed his leather jacket. Kelly sniffed as a smile broke onto her face.

"That asshole had no tattoos, no piercings, weird curly hair, and he was fucking shorter," Blake hissed. "Don't talk to me ever again; I don't waste my time on stuck-up bitches like you." He spun around and ripped the doors open. They banged against the walls as he walked in. Everyone was quiet for a minute as they tried to absorb what they'd witnessed. I was confused by it all and wondered who he was.

"What happened?" I asked. Benny's jaw tightened as he looked away. I looked at Melissa and noticed the smirk plastered on her face.

"Kelly cheated on Blake."

The rest of the day was spent in silence as we studied. I hadn't seen Blake anywhere, yet Aidan told me he ditched. I was in a cubicle when I heard girls gossip outside.

"Blake's hot, but he scares the shit out of people."

434

"It was obvious they wouldn't last. But Kelly sleeping with someone else?"

"What I've heard is Blake showed up at the party late, and she was already drunk. When he finally showed up, he looked for her, only to find her upstairs with someone."

"Well, I heard she only dated him to get closer to one of his friends."

***

"Arabella" by *Arctic Monkeys* echoed through the store as I bobbed my head to the beat. With my books spread out on the table, I reviewed the work in preparation for tomorrow's test. Rodney didn't care if I smoked in his store; he said people did it all the time. He even gave me a new pack. People around my age and older lurked the store, but most of them were on the second floor for the merchandise. I was at the store for almost two hours when Rodney approached me with a warm smile. I glanced around and noticed that most of the people were gone and the music was off.

"Store is going to close soon."

"Wow, time flew. Thanks," I said as I gathered my things. Once I had everything, I lit a cigarette then turned to Rodney. "Thanks, have a good night."

The clouds looked faded as I strolled to my mother's car. I watched as the ash hit the ground when I hit the cigarette. I dropped it to the ground and crushed it with my shoe.

"Becoming my bad girl again?" I whipped

around to see Blake, his motorcycle behind him as he approached me. I swallowed the lump in my throat as I backed away; my legs hit the edge of the car as he reached me.

"N-no." My voice came out as a whisper as I leaned back. He trapped me, resting each arm on either side as he placed it on the hood. Our faces were inches apart as he smirked. I bit the inside of my cheek as he neared me. I felt his mouth on my skin as his lips soared up my jawline until he stopped by my ear. I heard his slow breaths that sent shivers up my spine. Again, he leaned closer, which resulted in me almost falling onto the hood, but I placed my hands behind me for support.

"Who am I kidding? You've always been my bad girl." Blake's husky voice sent chills through my entire body as I pushed myself up, so I sat on the hood. A playful smirk appeared on his lips as he backed away and leaned on the hood beside me.

"Are you high?" I blurted out as he sat next to me. Blake ignored the question as he looked at me with a grave expression. He lowered his gaze to my thigh and gently rested his hand on it.

"How's your thigh?"

"It's okay," I mumbled as he rubbed it. "How are you?" His hand moved from my thigh to his neck as he awkwardly scratched it.

"I'm good," he replied with a dry laugh. "I think this is the time where you tell me 'I told you so' and laugh?"

I badly wanted to say that, but something told me not to. Instead, I asked something I wanted to express to him from the day I saw him with Kelly.

"Just…why?" I asked. Blake let out a sigh as he glanced around before he spoke.

"Do you remember when we got arrested and your dad interrogated us?" he began, and I nodded. "Your dad told us to leave you alone, to not get too attached to you otherwise you'll just end up being unhappy. That James guy is a huge criminal and is known for getting what he wants. The less that you were involved, the better. So we did what we could, and what better way to start than to go to Homecoming with Kelly West?" Blake sighed.

"So you guys went through all that to protect me?"

"Yeah, I didn't mean for things to go this far," he replied, then let out an awkward laugh. "But every time something happened, Kelly would be there. It was hard to, believe me. I wanted to break up with her before winter break, but she beat me to it."

"By cheating on you."

"Yep, and I'm kinda glad that I forgot her gift," he added with a smirk. My jaw dropped as we laughed.

"Do you know who she slept with?" I asked after we composed ourselves. Blake's delighted expression blanked, which meant he wasn't going to answer. His lips were sealed as he glanced down at my sweatpants. I followed his gaze to my cigarettes. I quickly slipped my hand into my pocket and took them out.

"Want one?" I asked as I opened the pack. "Looks like you need it."

He held a blank expression as he looked at the box, then me. I watched as he squinted his eyes and got off the car.

"How many do you have?" he asked as he stared at the pack. I let out an awkward chuckle as I looked at the box in my hands.

"Well, Axel bought me one on Saturday, then Rodney gave me a pack today, so I guess," I hummed as I took out a cigarette and lit it, "two packs left."

I left out the part where I had his one pack at home; I kept that for emergencies. He observed me as I inhaled the tobacco smoke and blew out rings. I watched as his jaw clenched, then looked down.

"So, what, is this your new addiction? We get rid of the pills then you're smoking like there's no tomorrow?" Blake yelled as he raised his arms in frustration.

"Yet who's the one who can smoke a pack in a day?" I tilted my head. That seemed to hit a nerve as he banged his fists against the car. We were in the same position as earlier, but his smirk was gone as it filled with anger.

"The bad girl with glasses thing is kinda hot, but smoking isn't for you, Willson," Blake grunted. He pulled the cigarette out of my mouth, threw it to the ground, and crushed it. I gaped at him as I pushed myself off the car and shoved him.

"*Who the hell are you to tell me what I can and cannot do?*" I yelled in his face. His features hardened as he stepped closer and pressed me against the car. A smirk tugged at his lips as he stared at me.

"Your little sheriff daddy told me to protect you, and you're not doing a good job of cooperating here," Blake hissed at me. I used all my energy to push him off me as I sighed in relief.

"Bullshit! You owe me a fucking cigarette!" I yelled. He stared at me, then laughed. Yet it wasn't a funny laugh; it was filled with irony and strain. He reached into his leather jacket and pulled out his pack. He did the same with his back pockct and pulled out another.

"Since our lives are already so fucked up," he shoved the packs in my chest, "what difference will this make?"

***

"We are test-free, people!" Liam cheered as we plopped down at our regular lunch table. Physics was a challenge, but with all those nights I pulled, I ought to pass. When we came out of the classroom, everyone seemed relieved, but Benny was nervous. Every time I glanced up at the clock, Benny would run his hand through his hair.

"How was Biology?" Ethan asked Miranda, who sat down next to me.

"Ugh, I swear I failed," she mumbled.

"You say that every time, yet you get a good grade." Carter laughed.

"I didn't even study!" she exclaimed.

"I bet that you'll pass!" Liam chimed in as he threw a grape at her.

"Whatever, I'm just glad mid-terms are over, and there's only one more week of school until winter break," Miranda sighed in relief.

"We don't have to come to school on Friday," I

said.

"Cool, what's the plan then?" Aidan asked as he rubbed his hands together. I squinted my eyes because there was no plan. Since mid-terms were finally over and I didn't have the pills anymore, I wanted one night of peace. I struggled to get things done and eventually gave up as I felt a sudden exhaustion lap over me. A screeching noise snapped me out of my thoughts as the person pulled the chair out and sat down. We stared at each other as everyone else conversed. His black coat seemed to make his face broader since the collar was up. His nose piercing gleamed as his nostrils flared. Blake's lips were drawn into a thin line but immediately pulled up into a smirk. I watched as he took a glimpse at everyone.

"Anyone got smokes?"

Ethan had a puzzled look on his face. Blake Gunner always had cigarettes. He slowly reached into his pocket, but I beat him to it as I pulled out a pack and slid it across the table. Blake caught it in time as he stared at me with a blank expression.

"Returning them so soon?" He tossed it back.

"Just being generous." I faked a smile as I flung it across the table.

"I wasn't asking you," Blake hissed as he threw it back.

"Well, I'm offering," I declared, hurling it toward him.

"I don't want yours," he argued, then threw it.

"In actual fact, it's yours!" I added, then flung it back to him. Nick leaped forward and slammed his hands onto the box before Blake caught it. The whole table went silent as we watched Nick glare at the two of us. He let out a huff as he slowly sat down and left the pack in the center of the table.

"Now I don't know what the hell is going on between the two of you, but you guys better make up. Fucking hell." Nick muttered the last part. "This is getting really fucking annoying. Evcry week you two are fighting."

Melissa calmed her boyfriend down as Blake and I stared at each other. Every week since the bet, we'd fought and it'd be over the smallest of things. Yet every time we forgave each other, it'd be out of trust, care, desperation, or the thought of not having to speak to one another. Plus every week we got to know each other a little bit more. Whether it was about our goals in life or our pasts, we'd have something to say to each other. Yet right now I had nothing to say to him. He asked for smokes, and I offered.

"Apologize," Carter said. I scrunched my nose up as I glared at the blond boy.

"For what?"

"For taking my cigarettes," Blake pointed out. I snapped my head in his direction and huffed. He gave me his cigarettes yesterday, but he knew that I wouldn't tell.

"Sorry," I mumbled. Everyone turned his or her heads to look at Blake as we waited for his apology. He gave us a blank look, then turned to me.

"Apology accepted," he said with a broad grin. I let out a scoff as everyone started talking again. Aidan slowly stood up while everyone conversed. He leaned across the table as his eyes met mine, an innocent look on his face as he took the cigarettes.

"Don't worry, I'll get rid of them," he said as he put them in his jacket.

***

A groan escaped from my lips as I sighed. I sat on the sofa and watched *Titanic* as I rubbed my tummy. I received my period this morning, and it only pained hours later. I called Miranda and Melissa, but they were on a double date. Dad was at the station as usual, yet Mom was keen and made me a cup of tea when she came home from work. Miranda suggested that I call the guys since some of them were at Ethan's house, but I didn't want to ruin their night. We finished mid-terms, so everyone wanted to chill. Yet I was at home on the sofa as I watched a beautiful young Leonardo DiCaprio.

Chapter Twenty-Eight

Miranda

I wanted to be with my best friend on her period. Yet Melissa and I had made plans before she got it, so I had no choice but to go. We were in the restrooms, and I got off the phone with Lana. Melissa suggested that we call one of the guys to go over and keep her company. So I decided to call Benny while she tried Blake, but I preferred Benny, because Blake was a bad influence, like Levi, and he'd made her smoke.

"House of Beauty, you're speaking with a cutie!" Liam sang on the phone.

"Are you with the guys?"

"Yeah, where else would I be on a Wednesday night?"

"Is Blake there?" I whispered as I turned to Melissa, who typed on her phone.

"Nope just Aidan, Ethan, Benny, and of course mwah."

"Put me on speaker."

"Why?"

"Just do it, Sanchez."

"Okay, calm down, Stevens." I heard shuffles through the phone as I waited. Whispers and background music filled the phone as I sighed.

"Whatcha' need, Stevens?" Aidan's voice echoed through the phone. I bit my lip anxiously as I thought of a way to tell them. Obviously, they'd know what time of the month meant.

"Lana's T.O.M."

"What?" Ethan asked. I was about to say that she's on her period and that she needed someone who loved *Titanic* to go to her now, but an old woman came out of a cubicle.

"Lana's under the radar," I muttered as the woman strolled to the basin.

"Huh?" Benny asked. A few whispers sounded through the phone as a realization hit them.

"*Oh!*" they said in unison.

"So how does this affect us?" Liam asked.

"Well, since I'm on a date and can't be there for my best friend, get your asses over there!" I exclaimed. The elderly woman turned to me with a disapproving look. I pulled my tongue at her as she walked out.

"No, no, no, as much as I love Lana, I heard you women can get brutal when it's the red flag," Aidan complained as I scrunched my nose up at his choice of words.

"Oh well, then you certainly haven't met my army!" I hissed as I made eye contact with Melissa. Her phone was pressed to her ear, which made me bite my nails.

"What's in it for us?" Ethan asked.

"Just think about all the things she's done for you," I began. "While you guys are jerking off, she's suffering all alone watching a goddamn ship sink!"

There was silence at the other end of the line as I waited. I glanced over at Melissa, who spoke in a hushed tone.

"She's watching *Titanic*?" Liam asked.

"*Go there now, or I will rip your tongues out, strangle you all until your heads are off, then dump your bodies in a barrel of bleach!*" I yelled into the phone. Again, there was silence, followed by movements, then whispers.

"Goddamn, Miranda, no one wants to know when you're on your peri—"

"I get mine exactly four days after Lana's, so I suggest you guys start preparing for war already," I warned.

"Okay, okay…geez, Miranda, we're on our way," Benny said. "But wait, what do we get her?"

A smile formed on my lips as I looked at Melissa, who frowned.

"Google it," I said, then ended the call. I placed my phone in my back pocket as I walked toward Melissa with a grin. She hopelessly sighed as she put her phone in her purse.

"Can you hear that, Melissa?" I asked as I leaned forward and cupped my ear while looking around. "It's the sound of Blake slowly dying and Benny fucking rising!"

"Shut it, Stevens," she grumbled. I did a happy dance as Melissa stared in amusement. I watched as her relaxed face turned into a worried expression.

"What's wrong?" I asked.

"Are we forgetting something?" she asked. "We have boyfriends who've been waiting for us!"

"Oh, shit!" I yelled. We bolted through the doors and casually walked back to our table. Thankfully Marcus and Nick laughed as we calmly slipped into our seats. I sat next to Melissa with our dates opposite us, and it took a while for them to notice us.

"No way, did he really?" Marcus asked between laughs. Nick turned his head toward us as his expression changed.

"Everything okay?"

"Yep."

"What's so funny?" I asked my boyfriend, who snickered as his curly brown hair fell to his face.

"Liam's hilarious when he's drunk." Nick chuckled.

"Man, I had to leave when the fun started," Marcus mumbled.

"Who picked you up?" Melissa asked as the waiter served our desserts.

"Austin," Marcus said in an ominous tone. We turned to him with curious looks. Marcus was friends with everyone, but he knew that we weren't very fond of Austin.

"Why?" I asked as I sipped on my drink.

"Well, I didn't want to spoil your guys' fun, and I was feeling sick, so I went outside and threw up," Marcus mumbled. "Austin popped up out of nowhere and offered me a ride home since I had a few drinks."

"What time was that?" Melissa asked as she sipped her drink.

"I don't know." Marcus shrugged. "After midnight, I guess."

My jaw clenched at the memory of Blake when he arrived after midnight and then went up the stairs to find Kelly in bed with someone else, a curly-haired someone.

"Heard there was a fight too," Marcus added.

"Yeah." I breathed out as I clenched my fists.

"Wow, I missed out on a lot." He let out a chuckle but immediately turned it into a cough.

"Uh-huh," I said through gritted teeth as I leaned forward to slap him but was held down by Melissa.

"We don't know if it's him," she whispered as Marcus gave me a weary look. Melissa was right; I refused to believe that Marcus cheated on me with Kelly West. There were plenty of guys with curly hair, and it's a coincidence that he left before the fight. Nick saw the discomfort on my face and changed the subject.

After we had our desserts, we decided to check up on Lana since it wasn't too late. I tried to push aside the thought of Marcus and think about Lana. We stood on the Willsons' porch as Marcus held my hand. I turned to the brunette boy with a small smile.

"You okay?" he whispered as he pressed his forehead against mine.

"Peachy."

"I'd kiss you right now, but I don't want to make you sick." He sniffed.

"That doesn't stop me from doing this," I said,

447

then kissed him on the cheek.

"*Life sucks!*" a familiar voice boomed through the house as I turned my head to the door. It wasn't even locked as Nick pushed it open. Marcus gripped my hand as we entered the house. We entered the living room as I took in the scene. I tried so hard not to squeal. My plan had worked! Yet I didn't imagine it to look like Lana was on the sofa with her feet propped up on the coffee table. On her left sat Benny, and on her right was Ethan. Pizza boxes lay around the room as well as many pillows. *Titanic* played on the TV as Benny tried to watch and massage Lana's shoulders at the same time. Ethan sat with a massive bowl of popcorn on his lap, eating with one hand while the other scrolled through his phone.

"Where are the two morons?" Nick asked as he sat on the La-Z-Boy. Lana let out a loud groan as she rubbed her tummy. Her hand immediately went to Ethan's thigh as she gripped it to release the pain. He jumped up, and the popcorn flew as he let out a girly scream. We laughed as Lana cursed under her breath.

"Quit doing that!" Ethan complained as he picked up his phone.

"Then why are you still sitting here?" Lana scolded. Ethan shrugged as he got up and picked up the popcorn. Marcus let out a terrible cough as he held his hands to his face. I comforted him as I rubbed my palm against his back.

"Who's coughing?" I looked over my shoulder to see Lana's mom. She was still in her doctor's uniform, which meant that she just got home.

"Sorry, Mrs. Willson, I just have the flu," Marcus sighed as he straightened his posture.

"And a terrible cough! Follow me, boy. I don't want your germs in my house! I have guests coming soon!"

He gave me a startled look, and I ushered him to follow her. They disappeared down the hall, and I stood while Melissa sat with Nick.

"Ugh, she's such a witch," Melissa complained. I followed her gaze to see Rose's mom on the television.

"Damn, Jack is looking good with that hair." Lana grinned at the part where Jack got ready to have dinner with the rich people.

"You know it's kinda creepy that you can go from moody to smiley in less than ten seconds."

"It's called being a woman, Ethan Baxter."

"Okay, you're creeping me out now," Benny said as he looked down at Lana. I couldn't help but squeal as their eyes met and they smiled. Benny had his arm around her shoulder as her head rested against his chest. A blanket draped around them, which made it cute and cuddly. Everyone turned to me with questioning looks. I shook my head as Melissa let out a huff.

"*It's hot, you idiot!*"

I raised a brow as I glanced at the kitchen door, then at Ethan, who sat on the loveseat.

"They're attempting to make Lana soup," Ethan said.

"I hate soup," Lana said. "I'm on my period, not sick."

"I'm gonna go check up on the soup," I

announced, then walked into the kitchen. I instantly regretted that decision as I entered the kitchen. Ingredients were laid on the table as dishes piled the sink. Aidan stood in front of the stove, humming a tune as Liam chugged down a big glass of water. "What the hell is going on here?"

"'Sup, Stevens? Just making our lovely friend some soup," Aidan replied as his focus was back on the pot. I noticed the apron he wore over his clothes, with **_Kiss the Chef_** in big bold letters. I watched as Liam finished his glass of water. Once he was done, he set the glass on the table and poked his tongue.

"What happened to you?"

Liam stared at me with a grave look on his face, then shifted his gaze to Aidan.

"He burned my tongue!" Liam shouted as he placed a block of ice on his tongue.

"Dude, it's your fault for not waiting for the soup to cool down," Aidan began. "Miranda, he was literally like, 'Oh, can I taste?' then he took a big-ass spoon and slurped it."

I shook my head in disappointment as Liam gaped at me. I heard footsteps behind me and spun around to see Angie and Marcus.

"And you're wearing such a thin sweater!" she complained. "Just be glad I caught you. Otherwise you'll be waking up with a fever."

"Mrs. Willson, don't worry, I'm fine," Marcus assured her as she walked around the kitchen and took out random things. She filled a bowl with hot water and set it on the table, then she cut up an onion and placed it inside. We groaned from the smell as she motioned for Marcus to bend.

"I just steam my face in that?" He pointed to the onion water.

"Yes, so everything can open up! The scent will hit your nose and hopefully loosen up what's inside," she assured him as she placed a cloth over his head.

"Well, it's already hitting my eyes," Marcus grumbled as he put his arms on either side of the bowl and lowered his head. He let out a groan as Angie smiled, satisfied with her work. I saw Ethan come in, but he had Lana in his arms.

"What happened?" her mother asked with a worried look. Ethan shrugged as he let Lana down and placed her opposite Marcus.

"Nothing. Whenever my sister gets hers, she can't walk because it hurts. Lana told me it hurts too, so I just carried her," Ethan said as if it was nothing, then went back into the living room. I squinted my eyes at her because I knew very well that it didn't hurt.

"You lazy." I laughed as I sat opposite her.

"He offered, and plus who wouldn't want Jefferson High's team captain to carry you around bridal-style?"

I shook my head in amusement as I watched Aidan and Liam prepare her soup. Liam placed a bowl of hot soup in front of Lana with a grin.

"Made by yours truly!" Aidan said as he posed in his apron.

"Thanks."

"See, that's common sense," Aidan said as Lana took a spoonful and blew on it.

"Whatever," Liam muttered. Another pair of

footsteps were heard as Melissa entered the room with a horrified look.

"Note to self—never ever be in the same room with a bunch of guys while watching *Titanic*," she mumbled.

"Why?" Lana asked.

"It's getting to the part where Jack sketches Rose right before they hit the iceberg," she said.

"Whoa, my favorite part!" Liam cheered as he and Aidan walked out of the kitchen. I rolled my eyes at their wicked ways and looked at Marcus. His head was still covered by the cloth. I gave him a slight poke, causing him to raise his hand.

"I'm alive."

"What's wrong?" Melissa asked Lana, who poked the macaroni in her soup. I glanced up and watched Lana as her eyes met mine. Her grip on the spoon tightened as she held a poker face.

"How could you send them here?" she hissed.

"Well, I didn't want you to be here all alone."

"You could've sent Mr. Bronx or even Jennifer! But why them?" Lana whined.

"What's the problem? It's kinda cute seeing them act like this," Melissa said.

"Yet awkward! I literally stared at them when they were at my front door. Holding freaking tampons!" Lana complained. I laughed at the thought of them going to the grocery store and buying pads and tampons. "Then being the annoying little weirdo that Liam is, he waited outside of the bathroom while I did my thing!" Melissa and I glanced at each other, then laughed. "It's not funny! I feel like a baby when Ethan's carrying me or when Aidan tries to cheer me up." She huffed then turned to Angie Willson. "And Mother! If that is even the appropriate name to call you! How could you let them stay?"

"Lana, dear, I am your mother, and I only let them stay because I know what a pain in the butt you are when you're on the rag," Angie exclaimed.

"And what about Benny?" I asked.

"He was okay," she mumbled. I pursed my lips. Lana rolled her eyes as her cheeks reddened. "Okay, he kept giving me blankets and checking if I was comfortable. I said my tummy hurts and then—"

"And then he said, 'It helps if someone else rubs it,' and he did!" Angie cut off her daughter, then let out a girly squeal.

"Aww," Melissa and I cooed. From the corner of my eye, Marcus lifted his head and looked at us. "What are we talking about?"

***

Thursday went by in an absolute blur since I slept in class. Exams were finished, so none of the seniors cared about work, but rather the three-day weekend we had, so I was with my best friend in the park on a Thursday afternoon. After last night's fiasco, everyone went home when Lana's dad showed up. Looked like something serious since he came home grumpy. Marcus came to school today since he felt better after Mrs. Willson's homemade remedy. Even though our relationship was okay, I couldn't help but think of the party. Lana turned to me with a question. I squinted my eyes.

"What?" I asked.

"You've been spacing out all day, and that's not normal for Miranda Stevens."

I let out a sigh as I looked down at the grass. We sat under a tree that had bare branches since the cold weather had struck.

"Do you think it's a coincidence that Marcus went home at the same time when Blake found Kelly in bed with someone else?" I rushed out. Lana's eyes widened as she licked her lips.

"I-I don't know…Marcus does have curly hair, but he's not so short."

"He also said that Austin took him home."

"Austin? That's unusual," she commented as she took out a cigarette. I watched as she slowly lit it and inhaled the smoke.

"But he wouldn't cheat on me, right?" I croaked out. Lana stayed quiet as she exhaled. My left eye suddenly twitched as the whiff spread through the air. I snatched the cigarette from her fingers and threw it to the ground in frustration.

"Hey!" she exclaimed as I crushed it with a rock.

"Answer me!" I yelled.

"I don't know," she mumbled. I looked at her with weary eyes, then at the crushed cigarette.

"Those fucking cancer sticks are ruining you, Lana!"

"Please don't you start too."

"I will!" I said, then rose to my feet. "I thought the last time you 'tried' that, it'd be the last, but no," I stated. "One guy comes into your life and ruins it all and gets you back on those!"

"Don't blame him!"

"I will. He's a narcissistic bastard who has too many tattoos, and he's using you!"

"Don't talk shit, Miranda!" Lana yelled. "Just because Marcus might've cheated on you doesn't mean you can turn the tables and start another argument!"

"He did?" I snapped my head to see Parker in his regular attire as he watched us in amusement.

"How long have you been standing there?" Lana asked.

"Long enough." He smirked.

"Well, what do you want? Can't you see we're having an argument?"

"Oh, I know," he said. "You may continue."

I turned back to Lana to tell her off again, and she wanted to do the same, but Parker snickered beside us.

"What are you laughing at?" Lana demanded.

"It's actually kinda funny that you assume Marcus slept with Kelly," he said. "Don't you trust your boyfriend?" I remained silent as he bit his lip. Before I could reply, he cut me off. "But you're right, Miranda. There's more curly-haired dudes in the school." He sighed, then took off his beanie to reveal his curly blond hair. Lana let out a gasp as my eyes widened. Blake did mention curly hair, but he didn't say the color. Parker was shorter than Blake, but he was still tall with no piercings or tattoos. Then I remembered that Marcus had his ears pierced. "Now you're probably wondering why did Austin take Marcus home?" Parker stated. "Well, you must've heard that Kelly used Blake just to get closer to one of his friends. It's dumb to sleep with Marcus, because then she would've dated Blake for nothing."

"So he didn't sleep with her?" Lana asked.

"Yep, Kelly may be stupid, but she's not an idiot," Parker said as I snorted. "So we had to make it seem like it was Marcus, and the only way was to get him drunk so that Austin could take him home."

"So you slept with her so that she and Blake could break up and get closer to one of his friends?" I asked with a confused look.

"I don't know, it's her plan? Don't know how she's gonna get him." Parker shrugged, then shoved his hands in his jacket pockets.

"Who is it?" Lana asked as Parker backed away.

"You'll find out soon," he said with a wink, then walked away. We stood there speechless as I tried to absorb the information. I knew Marcus wouldn't cheat on me; we liked each other a lot. At first, I thought he faked his illness, but the coughs were terrible, and I visited him before I came here. His whole family was genuinely ill!

"Well, that answers that question!" Lana beamed as I turned to her. I didn't even notice the cigarette between her lips up until now. I balled my fists as I stood right in front of her.

"Please, Lana, I know it won't be easy to get over these, but please," I begged. "Don't depend on them."

As soon as those words left my mouth, I stormed off and walked to my car. I whipped my phone out and scrolled through my contacts. I pressed Carter's name and got in the car while I waited. It rang as I started the car and decided to leave it on speaker as

456

I drove. After three rings, he finally answered.

"Parker's porno palace…what's your pleasure?"

"Not in the mood, Halls," I said as I drove. "Where are you guys?"

"Crashing at Benny's place, why?" he asked, and I heard laughter in the background.

"No reason," I said, then ended the call. I spcd down the streets on the way to Benny's house in the hope that they're all there. It's Blake's fault that Lana was back on cigarettes, yet it's Levi's fault she's like that. My car came to a shaken halt as I approached the Nielson's home. All the guys' cars were parked in the driveway. I got out of my car and trudged toward the front door. As I passed the vehicles, I resisted the urge to push Blake's motorcycle to ground. The door wasn't even locked as I pushed it open. His parents were still at work, so it wasn't like I intruded. I heard music along with laughter from the basement. I followed the noise and walked downstairs.

"Hey, Stevens!" Liam greeted as my loud footsteps interrupted everyone. I searched the room for a specific bad boy. He sprawled out on the sofa with a cigarette in his mouth. Just like Lana, I thought. I darted toward Blake with my fists clenched. He slowly stood up and raised a brow.

"*You!*" I yelled as I shoved my index finger in his chest.

"Miranda, are you okay? Don't tell me Mother Nature has struck yo—"

"You broke her!" I cut off Aidan. Blake stared at me in confusion as I let out a laugh. The whole room was quiet as everyone watched me. I laughed so hard that tears formed in my eyes. "At first, I thought that he ruined her, but then she just carried on with life as if it were nothing, but then you came along and fucked everything up!"

"What the hell are you talking about?" Blake demanded.

"You broke my best friend," I whispered. "Guess where she is now? Out in the park probably having her fifth cigarette while sitting on a swing. Adults with their children walk by with looks of concern seeing an intoxicated girl smoking her problems away," I said in one breath. The only sound to be heard was my heavy breaths as everyone sat. Guilt filled their faces because they knew that they were part of ruining her life. "But have no fear, for he shall appear."

"Who?" Ethan asked as I laughed to cover up my fearfulness of Levi's friend, Keene.

"The one and only Levi Radcliff!" I exclaimed.

"That name sounds so familiar," Benny mumbled.

"Since you're all friends with Lana, you must know that he visits once a year, and every year they do something crazy," I muttered, and the reminiscence of summer 2015 entered my mind.

"Who the fuck is this guy? Is he famous or something? What did he do?" Blake asked as his jaw tightened.

I spun and walked toward the stairs. "You'll find out soon, so I suggest you do something so that she slows down on the cigarettes, because once he's here, we're all going on a fucking ride."

Chapter Twenty-Nine

Lana

I was on my fourth cigarette as I stopped to look at my surroundings. Most people my age and younger were in the park since it was a Thursday afternoon. Old people sat on benches and fed the birds while kids played on the playground. My eye caught the familiar boy who hid his blond curls under his beanie. I shook my head in disappointment because Miranda went through all that for nothing. It was a coincidence that Marcus left the same time Blake came to the party. Well, not an accident, since Kelly planned it all. I watched as Parker handed the guy a bag in return for cash. Once the guy was gone, he spun around with a smug look.

"If nobody's gonna come after me, you can still be my customer." He winked.

"Nope, I'm done with those," I said, then inhaled as I put the cigarette to my lips. "Why did you tell us all of that?"

459

"It's a warning," Parker said as his jaw tightened. "Kelly won't stop until she gets what she wants."

As soon as those words flew from his lips, he spun around and walked off. I scanned the park and saw an empty swing set not too far. I walked toward it and plopped myself down onto the tire swing in the center. As I inhaled the sweet scent between my lips, I thought of what Miranda said twenty minutes ago. I hadn't gotten addicted to them, and I didn't depend on them. I only smoked to take the pain away. I didn't know when I last got a full night of sleep, and with everything that happened, I had to have something to take it all away. From the corner of my eye, I saw Carter, Ethan, Aidan, and Blake. They watched me with blank looks as I blew out smoke rings.

"Hey, Lana," Aidan said as he sat on my right. Carter followed in sync as he sat on the swing that was on my left, and Ethan sat on the end by Aidan.

"You reek of tobacco," Carter pointed out as he swung back and forth on the rusty swing.

"You reek of sex, but you don't see me complaining," I muttered, then threw my cigarette on the ground and watched it crumble. Blake chuckled as he walked around us. There were only four swings, so heaven knew where he'd sit. I felt the weight behind me as the front of the tire went up. My eyes widened as Blake tried to balance on the back of the tire swing but failed as I fell backward. I felt the tire go up as my body hit the ground. "Ugh." I groaned as I squeezed my eyes shut from the soreness. I heard laughter and opened my eyes to see Blake Gunner from above. "Jerk," I muttered as Ethan's face came into view. He instantly helped me and gently set me back on the tire swing. I gripped the chains on either side of me as I smiled at him. "Thanks." Ethan bent over as he put his hand on either side of the tire and glanced up. I followed his gaze and saw Blake climb back onto the tire swing. This time I made sure to keep my balance as he wrapped his hands around the chains. He towered over and gave me a cheeky grin. I looked down to see Ethan release his grip. Once he was sure that none of us would fall again, he sat back down. I cautiously clung to the chains as Blake and I slowly moved.

"Don't worry, I got you," Blake mumbled as I felt his knees on my back to keep us steady. After that, silence took over, and the only sound was the rusty noise of the swings. Ethan took out a pack and handed each of us one, but I declined and gave my cigarette to Blake.

"Miranda's quite pissed," Aidan spoke up.

"She'll get over it." I rolled my eyes. "I'm not addicted to these. It just takes the pain away."

"What pain?" Carter asked.

"You know when you first light it then inhale the tobacco for the first time?" I asked, to which they nodded. "Well, for me, when I inhale, everything just seems to drift away. The hurt, the remorse, the feeling of life just goes away. I'm in my own world, and once you're done with the cigarette and throw it out, that's when everything comes back. That's when you're snapped back into reality."

It was quiet for a moment as they smoked. They

didn't know how to answer that or what to say, so I looked at Carter and decided to respond to his question.

"I'm having nightmares."

His slick blue eyes stared into my wounded blue ones. I watched as he took his last drag, then threw the cigarette to the ground and crushed it with his foot.

"We know," Blake said from above. I squinted up at the six-foot giant and raised a brow.

"Benny told us before we came here," Ethan said.

"You don't have to talk about it, but when last did you get some actual sleep?" Aidan asked, and when I turned to him, I noticed the gleam in his brown eyes.

"A few weeks ago," I mumbled. No one said anything, but I watched as Aidan took out his phone and typed. I tried to pry over his shoulder, but Ethan turned to me as he blew smoke toward us.

"Do you guys ever feel like we're being watched?" he asked. I raised my eyebrow as I looked around the park, yet everyone seemed to be doing their own thing. Parker was still here but with another guy, chatting.

"No, why?" Carter asked.

"I don't know, but these past few weeks I just feel like someone is watching me," Ethan pointed out as he continued to look around.

"Dude, there are a lot of girls here eyeing you," Aidan began as he put his hand on Ethan's shoulder. "If you need to get laid and can't decide who to bang, just ask Carter. He must've done them all."

"Hey!" Carter argued as he glared at Aidan and Ethan, who laughed.

"Did you know that Parker slept with Kelly at the party?" I looked up at Blake. He didn't seem fazed by that and shrugged.

"I knew that it was some weird curly asshole."

I then watched as he took his final drag and dropped the cigarette to the ground. I watched as the cigarette burned as the ashes descended. It seemed like we'd jumped from one topic to another. When it got awkward, or nobody talked, we tried to come up with a new topic.

"Dad is gone," I stated after a while. They turned to me with curious looks, and I felt Blake's stare from atop. "James Cornelius was spotted in Detroit last, and he hasn't made a move since. Police became suspicious, so they called in back up. My dad left this morning."

"Do you think they'll get him?" Ethan asked.

"I hope so," I mumbled.

"You'd actually think that he'd be in jail by now," Carter said. "Not just for drugs, but for killing people."

"Who?" I asked.

"He told us that he killed that guy who shoved the bag of parcels into us that day," Aidan replied.

"He told you that? James Cornelius?" I asked as Aidan let out a snort from his last name.

"Yeah, he said if we don't follow the rules, then we'll end up like that guy…dead," Ethan rambled on as I raised my eyebrow.

"Did you guys follow the rules?" I asked.

"Yes, and it would've gone well if Parker didn't

steal those two parcels," Carter muttered, yet it still would've gone well if I didn't show up.

"Let's just be glad that he isn't here," Blake pointed out as I felt him come down slowly. I felt two hands on either side of my waist as I gripped the chains. I felt his breath on my neck as his lips brushed against my skin. "You're safe with me," he whispered as he left a gentle kiss on my neck that made my stomach flutter with butterflies.

"Y-Yeah, he's in another state w-where he should be arrested s-soon," I stuttered as I felt him pull away from me and climb off the tire. Aidan immediately jumped out of his seat with a broad grin spread across his face. We gave him a weird look as we slowly stood up and watched him.

"Liam and I have an idea," he said, then spun around.

"What have the two most idiotic people come up with now?" Ethan sarcastically asked as he shoved his hands in his pockets.

"You'll just have to wait and see," Aidan exclaimed as he skipped toward the car.

***

You'd think that Mr. Bronx being the cool teacher he was, he wouldn't give us homework, but Liam and his jock friends had to annoy the class, which resulted in four pages of textbook homework. Thus I had my homework sprawled out on the coffee table while I rested on the sofa. Benny decided to come over so we'd do it together. We'd been like that for the past hour, snacking on things as my record player echoed through the living room.

"Here you go," my mother said as she entered the room with a fresh batch of cookies. I raised a brow as she placed them on the coffee table.

"Thanks, Mrs. Willson," Benny said as she walked off with a goofy grin. She'd been acting weird all day. I asked if she's going to work yet and she said she was going later. She'd been in the kitchen all day, and that was our third plate of cookies. "How's your…?" Benny snapped me out of my thoughts. He rubbed his tummy, and I couldn't help but smile.

"Yeah, I'm good, and thanks for keeping up with my stubbornness the other night." I chuckled.

"No problem. It was fun." He laughed as he set his books aside. I watched as he got up and looked around the room. I quietly got back to work as I heard movement in the room. From the corner of my eye, I felt his stare on me. "Do you remember our first dance together back in middle school?"

I looked up into his brown eyes to see the smile on his face. Benny held his hand out, and I gradually accepted. He helped me to my feet and entwined our hands together as we stood in the middle of the room.

"Yes, you were horrible. You kept stepping on my feet." I giggled as he took my other hand. Even though that was the start of when he bullied me, I threw those horrible memories away and finally made new ones.

"I was frustrated because I couldn't dance," he groaned. "But you kept telling me not to give up."

"We were not that bad."

"True, but over the years I've learned a thing or two," he said, then twirled me around to "Single" by *The Neighbourhood*. I laughed as we came face to face, our hands still intertwined as the music echoed through the room.

"Care to show me what else you've learned?" I teased. Benny's smile twitched up into a smirk as his hands went to my hips and he pulled me closer. I took my hands and placed them around his neck as we swayed to the beat of the music.

"I never gave up," he whispered in my ear. I lowered my head to see his hands firmly placed on my waist as his head rested on my shoulder. I closed my eyes as the alternative music played.

The song ended, but we didn't stop as Benny's arm went around me and up my back, caressing it. I opened my eyes and saw my mother over Benny's shoulder. She had an amused look as she leaned on the doorframe with her arms folded. Her mouth opened, but it cut off as we heard a loud honk from outside. A coldness swept through me as Benny and I pulled away from each other. I raised my brow as I strolled to the front door and opened it. I stepped outside with Benny right beside me. We stood on the porch as I overlooked the garden. Miranda, Ethan, and Aidan's cars stood in the driveway as everyone piled out. I was puzzled. They were busy taking bags out of their cars.

"What are you guys doing here?" I asked as Marcus took out sleeping bags from Miranda's trunk. Liam and Aidan rushed out of the car and stood in front of me with big toothy grins.

466

"Sleepover!"

My eyes widened as realization hit me. It was part of Aidan and Liam's idea. I watched as they set out their overnight bags on the porch. Benny went to his car and took out his bag and smirked at me.

"There must be a huge mistake," I said as they formed a circle around me. "You can't sleep here! Do you know how my dad will fre—"

"Lana, sweetie, he isn't here," my mother piped up. I snapped my head to her as she held another plate of cookies. Liam and Aidan stood next to her as they devoured them.

"Mom, you knew?" I gasped.

"She was part of it!" Liam cheered.

"It will get your mind off things. Plus they'll witness what you face at night," my mother stated as she handed Aidan the plate. I watched as she walked up to me with a genuine look.

"Yeah, we wanna know about these nightmares…" Ethan trailed off.

"So you're gonna help me by sleeping here?" I asked with a blank look.

"We'll take it in turns," Carter stated. "When we go to sleep, two will be up to watch for forty-five minutes. Then when that's up, another two will be up."

"And this will benefit us how?"

"Maybe if you have different people around you, it might make you sleep better," Melissa said as her eyes shifted toward Blake. I rolled my eyes as I looked at my friends. Each of them had an overnight bag.

"Besides, it's rare that the sheriff isn't in town.

We should use it to our advantage," Nick said with a smirk plastered on his face.

"No parties!" Mom blurted out as she took the empty plate from Aidan. "I have guests coming on Sunday, and it took me a very long time to get this house into shape."

"Don't worry, it'll just be us." Liam grinned.

"And I'm leaving Miranda in charge!" Mom added as she walked back into the house.

"Oh, shit, there goes our fun," Aidan commented, which resulted in Miranda flicking him. My mother came back outside with her doctor's coat and bag. I watched as she approached me and left a gentle kiss on my forehead.

"Behave," she warned everyone but managed to smile. "And I hope everything goes well."

***

Blake

It was weird to spend my Friday night at Lana's house, especially since her mother invited eight teenage boys. Although I was curious about her nightmares. We loaded in the living room and watched movies for the first few hours. After the films, the girls decided to get changed into their sleepwear. Us guys decided to get changed down here. Once they were upstairs, I spun around to look at Ethan.

"I call dibs on the sofa," I announced as I watched him eye it with interest.

"Dude, you never bring a sleeping bag." Nick

468

groaned.

"Yeah, because I don't want the only thing separating me from the ground be a piece of material," I scoffed as I took off my shirt and slipped on a hoodie.

"Do you even have a sleeping bag?" Marcus asked.

"Nope," I said as I collapsed onto the big sofa.

"These are my favorite winter pajamas!" When I glanced up, I saw Liam in a pair of baby blue pajamas with small trains on it, while my cousin wore his stupid nightgown.

"You look stupid." Aidan eyed Liam.

"Look who's talking." Liam scoffed as he motioned to Aidan's nightgown. The rest of us wore hoodies, shirts, sweatpants, or pajama pants. Not like the two idiots who thought it was a real sleepover.

"I look ridiculous." We turned our heads to see the girls. Melissa wore white sweatpants and a black tee while Miranda wore black sweatpants and a white tee. I bit my lip as I looked at Lana. She wore similar pajamas as Liam, but hers were purple with teddy bears. Liam ran toward her. He embraced her and literally picked her up.

"Twins!" he cheered as Lana tried to pull away. "I knew you'd back me up, Lana."

"You guys look fucking adorable," I said, and Lana glared.

"Isn't she cute?" Miranda cooed. "I got her those for Christmas last year."

Lana managed to pull away from Liam's tight grasp and walked toward me. To be honest, she looked cuddly; the pajama top was big, which made the sleeves overlap. I watched as she sat next to me with a smile displayed on her face.

"Mom said you guys can sleep in the guest room, but you have to keep it clean," Lana said to Melissa and Miranda. They nodded then sat down next to their boyfriends. After that, everyone seemed to get into his or her own conversations. Yet I felt Benny stare in my direction. I looked at Lana, who made eye contact with him. I raised a brow as I watched the two communicate with their eyes. It was creepy the way everyone talked, and they'd look at each other. I remembered that Benny was here before all of us. Please don't tell me we interrupted their little study session—yet if we did, I was glad. I turned to Lana and knocked my knee against hers. She blinked then looked at me.

"Do you know the time?" I asked and mentally slapped myself.

"Err…it's almost midnight," Lana answered as she pointed at the clock displayed across the room.

"You should probably get some sleep," I said, then rested my palm on her thigh and caressed it. "I have a feeling you'll get a nice rest."

"Yeah, you're right," she whispered, then stood up. "Err…I'm gonna call it a night, guys. You can chill or whatever."

"Goodnight." She strolled to the stairs. The TV played in the background as I watched her walk upstairs. Once she was out of sight, I saw Melissa's grin. I sent a questioning look to which she shook her head.

"Who's taking the first forty-five minutes?"

470

Miranda asked. It was quiet as everyone looked at each other. Nick let out a sigh as he raised his hand. I shrugged and raised my hand too. Melissa smiled. Weirdo. "Okay, cool, then Melissa and I will go to the guest room while you two stay up," Miranda said as she grabbed a blanket that Mrs. Willson left for us.

"Wait—then who will take the second shift?" Aidan asked as the guys started to set out their sleeping bags.

"Marcus and me," Liam volunteered as he raised his hand and held up Marcus's with the other. I decided to get up and fulfill my duties, as I didn't want to be in the same room as Marcus and Liam, who quarreled. Nick said he'd be around the house and would call me once we're done. I was kind of surprised when Benny didn't volunteer to go first. I knew he liked Lana, heck everyone knew that, but I couldn't wrap my head around as to why. He bullied her, and now suddenly, he's her knight in shining armor. I mean, what did he do that made her forgive him for all the brutal years he put her through? I shook the thought away as I reached Lana's room. I entered it and took in the familiar surroundings. Her room was still in top shape as everything was neatly placed on her desk, books in the shelves, and posters in line as they stuck to the wall.

"You my first babysitter?" Her voice sounded soft as we made eye contact. Lana was in bed as she fluffed her heart-shaped pillow. My lips turned into a grin as I shut the door and strolled toward her. The bags under her eyes showed as she stared at me. I gave her a blank look as I raised a brow.

"Sleep," I demanded as I shoved my hands in my pockets. Lana seemed taken aback by my tone but eventually turned to her side and brought the blankets up to her chin. I watched as she slowly closed her eyes as silence filled the room. I got curious as to what kind of nightmares she had. Benny told us that they're kind of sad since her parents were worried. They even insisted on a psychologist, but Lana refused.

"I can't sleep." Her voice snapped me out of my thoughts. I looked down to see her gaze on me. I let out a huff as I pulled the blankets open and climbed in. Lana moved a bit and gave me space as I laid next to her. I took my phone out and glanced at the time. Thirty-five minutes to go. I didn't know why I got in, but it's way better than standing next to her bed and watching her like a creep. "Can you put music on?" she asked. I playfully rolled my eyes as I went to my music and scrolled through the artists.

"*Aerosmith*?"

"Nah."

"*Calvin Harris*?"

"No."

"*The Killers*?" I asked with a grin.

"Nope," she murmured, to which I scoffed. I felt her head on my chest as I scrolled further. I was taken back by her actions but gladly wrapped my arm around her as I went through the music.

"*Coldplay*?" I asked. Thankfully, she nodded, and I hit shuffle. "Spies" came on, and I raised a brow at the first song. I turned the volume up as I set my phone on the table. I felt Lana's breath on my chest as we listened to the beat. I ran my hand through her hair as *Coldplay* echoed through the room.

After a few *Coldplay* songs, I decided to turn the music off. I picked up my phone and realized there were ten minutes left. I heard Lana's light snores on top of me as she slept. I tried my best to slip out of her hold, trying not to wake her. Once I was out of her bed, I pulled the blankets over her. She looked so peaceful. Her brunette locks fell to her face as she breathed in and out. I looked around her room, since I had plenty of time. I walked to her desk and sat on the chair as I gazed around. From the corner of my eye, I saw a plain box peek out of a drawer. I squinted my eyes as I reached out for the carton of cigarettes. Yet they weren't any box of cigarettes…those were mine. However, it was an old pack that could be from two months ago. I slowly opened the pack and noticed a few were missing. It confused me.

"Mm." I snapped my head up to see Lana stir in her sleep. I put the cigarettes back in the drawer and got up to stand next to her bed as I observed her. She moved and mumbled out, "no, stop" and "please," yet I watched. The sweat ran down her forehead as she grabbed imaginary things. I realized she tried to get her pillow. My hand suddenly jerked forward as she gripped onto it.

"Please, no," she cried as her grip on my hand tightened. I crouched down on my knees so I was eye level.

"Lana."

"*No!*"

"Lana!" I yelled as she gasped and sat up. I swallowed the lump in my throat as I watched her. Our hands were still entwined as she breathed rapidly. She had a horrified look as we made eye contact. "A-are you okay?" I blurted out as I stood up. She looked away, then let go of my hand. I watched as she tied her hair up and lay on the pillow.

"No."

Not knowing how to answer that, I crouched down and hovered over her, our faces inches apart as she watched me. I placed a gentle kiss on her cheek, then her forehead. I replaced my lips with my own forehead as I pressed mine against hers.

"Please...don't ever let me witness that again," I whispered as I shut my eyes.

"Then just go, Blake," she whispered. I pulled away from her as I stood up tall and gazed at her. Her eyes were bloodshot as the dry sweat made her glow. The moonlight shone through the window, which suddenly made her stand out.

"Get some sleep," I said, then stormed out of the room because I didn't want to be there anymore. I got downstairs to see Nick on his phone while everyone slept. It was almost one in the morning, and I felt the tiredness kick in.

"Is everything okay? I heard voices," Nick whispered. I gave a curt nod as I walked to the sofa and saw Miranda and Marcus. I raised an eyebrow because she was supposed to be upstairs in the guest room with Melissa. I woke Marcus up and told him that it was his turn, as well as Liam. Miranda woke up, and I asked her why they're not sleeping in the guest room, yet I had the sudden urge to roll my eyes at her response.

"There's a spider in there."

I collapsed on the sofa and placed the blanket on me as I watched Liam go upstairs to check on Lana. Marcus followed, and I relaxed because everything would be okay.

As time went by, my eyelids got heavier as I watched Marcus come back down and cuddle next to Miranda. That was the last thing that came into view before my eyes shut.

***

"*No—please!*"

My eyes shot open as I jolted up. I glanced around the room to see everyone asleep, yet something didn't feel right.

"*I'm sorry!*" The familiar voice echoed through the house as my eyes widened.

"What's going on?" Benny murmured from his position on the floor. Everyone got up as we heard a commotion from upstairs.

"What the hell is going on?" Aidan asked as he rubbed his eyes. A loud bang erupted through the house as I jumped up and searched the room.

"Who's supposed to be on watch?" Carter asked as he turned on the lights. I glanced at the clock and paled since it was three in the morning.

"Where's Liam?" Miranda asked as she looked around the room.

"*Stop!*" someone yelled, and we froze for a second.

475

"*Lana!*" Miranda shouted as she bolted upstairs. We followed behind her as Lana's screams drove my anxiety through the roof. It wasn't a scream from a nightmare; it was a cry for help.

"*It was an accident!*"

We ran down the hallway to see Lana's door closed. Benny grasped the handle as he rattled it to open. He suddenly stopped and turned to us with a frightened look on his face.

"It's locked."

"*What?*" I yelled as I began to bang on the door. Aidan tried to pick the lock. Everyone else stood there hopeless of the situation as Benny and I banged on the door.

"Lana, it's just a dream," Aidan shouted out as he pressed his ear against the door.

"Where's the spare key?" Benny asked Miranda.

"We-we'll go look for one," Miranda said as she, Marcus, Melissa, and Carter ran down the hall.

"*N-no please!*" Lana cried as I heard shuffles on the other side of the door.

"I just wanna break the fucking door down!" I yelled as I fell to my knees. While everyone twisted the doorknob, banged on the door, and assured Lana that it was a dream, I looked through the hole below the doorknob. I didn't know what made me more nervous—Lana's screams for help or the figure I saw in her room.

Chapter Thirty

Blake

It was like a shadow, yet it seemed so real. I couldn't tell from the small hole. The way the figure moved around the room made me jolt up intently. Everyone ran around the house, either in search of a key or something to knock the door down.

"W-wait, where's Liam?" Nick asked, and we froze. I glanced around, and there was no sign of the tall brunette. Benny let out a huff as he banged on the door.

"Liam, if it's you in there, open the fucking door. It's not funny!" he shouted as he rattled the doorknob.

"Huh?" a familiar voice asked as we turned our heads. There he was, Liam Sanchez, in his "choo choo" pajamas with a bag of chips in one hand and a fruit cup in the other. Nick walked to him and flicked him on the head, which made all his food fall.

"Lana is locked in her room, and here you are

477

demolishing her kitchen!" Nick yelled.

"My shift ended two hours ago," Liam said with an innocent look. "I was hungry."

Nick threw his hands up in exasperation as Liam held a look of confusion. Behind him, Miranda ran toward us with a keychain in her hand.

"I got these from her dad's study."

"Okay, which one is it?" Benny rushed out as we made way for her.

"I-I don't kn-know," she stuttered as she began to try various keys.

"Don't worry, Lana. We're coming!" Aidan yelled beside me with a frying pan in his hand.

"Do you guys hear that?" Melissa asked as we halted.

"Hear what?" Ethan asked.

"Exactly," she whispered as the only sound to be heard were the attempts of multiple keys. It was quiet as Benny leaned his head against the door. Not a sound to be heard, which made me anxious.

"Fucking hurry up!" I scolded Miranda. After a few more keys, one finally went through. She turned the key and pushed the door open. We stood there ready to take on the figure in her room as Carter held up his shoe, Aidan held a frying pan, and Liam held his bag of chips in one hand and a chip as a weapon in the other. The first thing that we saw was Lana with her back toward us. I saw movement by her window. Aidan, Carter, and bolted toward it as we saw a guy climb down. A frightened look crossed my face as I nudged Carter. He gave me a short nod as he, Aidan, and Ethan dashed out of the room to capture the guy. I looked over my shoulder to see Miranda's arms wrapped around Lana. I noticed something dangling between Lana's fingers as she froze. Melissa took the pair of shoes and raised a brow. They couldn't be Lana's because they were a pair of black high tops. They looked dirty as well as big for her small feet. I looked at everyone else and noticed a panicked look on Benny's, Liam's, and Nick's faces. Their attention was on the shoes as mine was on Lana and the way she hugged her best friend like there was no tomorrow. Her hair in all directions was sweat soaked, and tears streamed down her face. She finally released from Miranda's hug, and her eyes immediately locked with Benny. Like earlier, they stared at each other and communicated. I raised a brow at their strange actions as I stepped forward and gently placed my hand on Lana's shoulder. I caught her by surprise, because she jumped, then turned to me.

"Are you okay?" I asked. She gave a short nod as she nervously bit her lip. I was taken back as she slowly wrapped her arms around me. I went stiff but soon relaxed as she tilted her head up and whispered in my ear.

"I'm scared."

I swallowed the lump in my throat as I absorbed those words. Whoever or whatever was in her room suddenly made her afraid, and I couldn't do anything about it. I felt useless.

"I'll make you some tea," Miranda mumbled as we pulled apart. Lana gave her a nod as Marcus followed her. Melissa placed the dirty shoes on the ground and exited the room. I turned back to see

Benny's jaw clenched as he stared at the floor. Liam's jaw was still open as he stared at the shoes, while Nick held a blank expression. From the corner of my eye, I noticed Lana's glare at them, but I was confused by it. The dim light by Lana's bed didn't make the situation better as it gave off a depressed mood. I felt everyone's eyes on me as I glanced around.

"I'll be going then." I awkwardly coughed. Even though I didn't want to leave Lana again, especially with her past tormentors, something told me to go. As soon as I was out of the room, I heard the door shut behind me, followed by whispers. I let out a huff as I walked downstairs. I was about to go into the kitchen until I saw the front door open. Carter sat on the stairs of the porch with his head in his hands. Then I remembered that I sent them to catch the guy who was in Lana's room. We could've called the police, but no one was hurt…besides, I didn't think the police would've been keen to find eight guys and three girls in a house on a Friday night. I heard the kettle boil as I looked over my shoulder and into the kitchen. Miranda leaned against the counter as Marcus kissed her. I scrunched my nose up and shuddered as I looked away. I walked outside onto the porch and saw Aidan in the middle of the road in his nightgown. The frying pan was abandoned on the ground. I raised my eyebrow as I looked down at the blond boy. "What the fuck is going on?" I demanded as Ethan stood next to me. Carter shook his head as he pointed to Aidan. I walked down the stairs and slowly approached Aidan, who had his back toward me. "Aidan, dude? What the hell?" He slowly spun around with a horrified look. "Did you get him?" I asked as Carter and Ethan stood next to me. We stood in a circle, everyone silent. Ethan stared at the ground with a look of guilt, while Aidan had no expression. Carter ran his hand through his blond locks and shook his head. "Well, do we know who it is?" I asked. Aidan picked up the frying pan and studied it. He turned to me with a blank look.

"It was one of James's men," he stated. My eyes widened. Why was one of his men here? What did he want with Lana? How does he know that we're all here? Then again, we're talking about the most wanted man in the USA.

"What happened? What did he say?" I blurted out as I frantically looked at my friends. Ethan looked at me with his dull brown eyes. They had bags under them as he sighed.

"He's not done with us."

***

Lana

"*You had one job!*" I yelled as soon as I heard Blake's footsteps descend.

"We kinda sorta lied," Liam mumbled as he let out a chuckle.

"Well, you know what?" I rhetorically asked as he picked up his black Converse shoes. "We are kinda, sorta fucked!"

Benny paced up and down the room as Nick placed his hands on either side of my shoulders. I stared into his round blue eyes as he told me to remain calm. Once he was sure I was calm, he slowly let go of my shoulders and stopped Benny from pacing. I turned to look at Benny and noticed his eyes were bloodshot from the lack of sleep. His hair was messy, and his clothes were wrinkled.

"We dumped the stuff, but we couldn't stay," Benny said as he approached me. "If we stayed, it'd only make things suspicious as to why a bunch of teenagers are lurking around a junkyard!"

"Well, you didn't have to lie to me!" I cried as I shoved him away from me.

"Lana, you were going through so much already we didn't want to you stress even more," Liam whispered as Benny and I glared at each other.

"Well, now I'm going to stress twice as much because the shoes that you wore that day are here!" I pointed to Liam's high tops.

"How did they get here? Who was that guy?" Nick asked.

"I don't know," I lied. I couldn't tell them that it was one of James's men. They didn't even know who he was. It still gave me goosebumps when he entered my room. I wasn't asleep; I stared at the wall. One minute I was alone, then the next he was there, dressed in black. It didn't make sense as to how they knew. He didn't even talk loudly, just whispered as he told me what a murderer I was. I got too paranoid and yelled out that it was self-defense. Then when Blake rushed through the door, he was gone like a speck of dust. His last words still echoed through my mind. *We're watching you.* I snapped out of my thoughts as Benny laughed. It was a psychotic laugh that scared me.

"Now someone else knows what we've done," he said after a while.

"Maybe he doesn't know that I ki—" My optimism cut off when Benny scurried toward me. He pressed me up against the wall as he glared at me.

"*That you killed someone,*" he finished, then banged his arms against the wall so I couldn't escape. "*Bullshit. Not only does he know about you, but it concerns us too!*"

"Benny, dude," Nick mumbled as my bottom lip trembled. I looked at Benny, his chest pressed against mine. His eyes filled with rage and anger that seemed oddly familiar. The position that we were in felt familiar as the thought of him bullying me came to mind. Benny's facial features softened as the realization hit him. His shoulders slumped as his arms dropped to his side. He licked his lips as he backed away and spun around. Liam tried to comfort Benny, but he shoved Liam away as he walked toward the door. Only then I noticed Blake, Miranda, Aidan, Ethan, and Carter by the door. Blake glared at Benny as the three walked out and the other five walked in. I was still against the wall as everyone else stood on the other side of the room. Miranda slowly approached me and placed the hot cup of tea on my bedside table. She looked at me with those sad eyes as she brought me in for another embrace. I wrapped my arms around her as I let out a sigh. The worst part of it all was that I couldn't tell her. I didn't want to involve her too. Drugs were one thing, but a dead body was a whole lot different. I'm only doing this to protect her; if I went down, I didn't want her to come with me. She had Melissa and a boyfriend who cared about her.

"He wouldn't hurt you; he's just worried," Miranda whispered. Once she pulled away, I gave her a sad smile. Miranda walked out of the room, which left the five of us. I sat down on my bed and looked at the ground.

"He almost hurt you," Blake mumbled.

"Almost…and he wasn't going to," I said as I looked up at Blake.

"Bullshit, Lana, we all saw that back there," Blake demanded. "The dude's got a short temper."

"He's scared!" I shouted as I rose to my feet. "I'm scared; we're all fucking scared!"

My heavy breaths were the only thing to be heard in the stuffy room. Blake stared at me with no emotion as Aidan rubbed his eyes.

"What do we do?" Aidan asked after a while.

"Go to the cops," Ethan stated, causing Blake and me to grab him.

"*No!*" we exclaimed as he sent us a questioning look.

"And tell them what?" Carter tilted his head at Ethan. "Hey, we'd like to report a guy who's working for James Cornelius. He broke into the sheriff's home and left us a warning, along with a goddam pair of shoes!"

"Cornelius." Aidan snorted as we glared at him.

"Where do the shoes fit in?" Blake asked with a puzzled look. I searched the floor for the familiar black Converse, but they were nowhere to be found. Liam must've taken them.

484

"Did he tell you anything?" Ethan asked as he placed his hands on my arms.

"You're right, they're watching us," I mumbled up into his dull eyes. He let out a deep sigh as he brought me in for a hug. I slowly wrapped my arms around him as he placed his chin on my head. Ethan let go, and I ran my hand through my hair. I sat down on my bed as the four discussed the situation. I drank the tea Miranda made me and thought of what she said earlier. Surely Benny wouldn't hurt me—he changed, and I knew it. He was just afraid of what would happen to us.

"Okay," Aidan said. "It's been a long night; we'll figure this out in the morning."

I nodded as Carter, Ethan, and Aidan walked over to me. Each of them said goodnight and kissed my forehead. I felt my cheeks warm up, but thankfully the room was dim. I watched Blake as he strolled toward me. He sat down next to me and looked straight ahead as if it were too daring to look at me.

"We failed," he mumbled as I raised a brow. "Your dad said, 'If you care about my daughter, you'll stay away, that's the only way that she'll be safe.' I failed."

"Blake, it's not your fault," I said as I rested my palm over his. He flinched as he pulled away and shook his head.

"No, Lana, we fucking failed. I failed to protect you, and now you have to go through all this shit," Blake said as he put his head in his hands.

"Blake, it's not your fault. James is just a terrible person." I mentally slapped myself as those words came out.

"We should've never met," he said after a while. "Your life wouldn't be so fucked up if I didn't enter it."

"Blake, please don't say that."

"It's my fault. My life wouldn't be so exciting if I hadn't met you," I said as we let out a chuckle. "I wouldn't have amazing friends caring for me. I wouldn't have you," I whispered as he finally turned to me. His dark brown eyes seemed to glow from the moonlight. His nose piercing shone as he licked his lips. I couldn't help but stare at it as he moved closer. I felt his breath on my face as he leaned in and placed his forehead on mine. He closed his eyes as our lips touched, and I did the same. I heard a sigh as Blake's forehead left mine. My eyes shot open as I saw him on the bed while he avoided eye contact. A strange feeling whirled through my stomach as I thought of what we were about to do. Then a stinging pain of rejection swept through me as Blake pulled away. Heck, we didn't even kiss. The only kiss we ever shared was at the cottage, and that was short. I felt embarrassed as I bit the inside of my cheek.

"Come on." He snapped me out of my thoughts. I noticed he stood in front of me and rolled his eyes. His back was turned to me as he walked toward the door. "You're not sleeping here tonight. No way in hell are we letting you out of our sight after that; you can sleep on the sofa."

And just like that, Blake Gunner could take something special and act as if nothing happened.

***

"What in the world?" My eyes fluttered. I finally opened them to see my mother's stare at the teenagers sprawled out in her living room. I was on the sofa, while Marcus and Miranda shared another couch, and Blake slumped across the La-Z-Boy. Nick and Melissa took my room while everyone else was on the floor.

"Morning, Mrs. Willson," Aidan greeted from his position on the floor. His nightgown creased as he stretched.

"Morning?" my mother repeated as she raised a brow. "Kids, it's already the afternoon."

My eyes widened as I shot up from the sofa along with everyone else. The clock on the wall stated three o'clock as the winter sky beamed through the window.

"Holy crap, what a night," Carter muttered as he ran his hand through his blond locks. I turned to see Marcus on the sofa with Miranda on his lap. He tried to wake her up as she groaned and snuggled into his neck. Everyone else got up as my mom walked into the kitchen. My eyes landed on Blake, who scrolled through his phone. I bit my lip as the thought of him pulling away from the kiss entered my mind. With everything that happened, a gut feeling of myself preferred him with Kelly West.

"Earth to Lana." Liam waved his hand in front of my face. I squinted my eyes at him as I swatted his hand away and got up. For once, I was glad that we had three bathrooms because the guys already argued about who's going to shower first. I strolled upstairs and opened the door to my room. Melissa sat on my bed, already showered and dressed. Off to the side, I saw a shirtless Nick with a towel wrapped around his waist. He looked like heaven with his six-pack and tanned skin. His blond hair was soaked, which made me nervous.

"Oh crap!" I said, then turned away. "Sorry."

Melissa let out a laugh as Nick walked back into the bathroom and shut the door. I turned to her with flushed cheeks as she smirked at me.

"Should've knocked," I mumbled as I sat down next to her.

"It's your room," she stated. Silence took over as I planned the rest of the afternoon. It seemed like we'd chill since it's so cold. "So what happened last night with you and Blake?" Melissa asked with a grin. I let out a sigh as I looked down at my hands.

"We almost kissed," I began as her eyes lit up, "but then he pulled away and acted as if nothing happened."

Melissa frowned as she placed her hand on my shoulder and rubbed it.

"Do you like him?"

"I-I don't know…" I trailed off.

"Lana, he likes you a lot." I scrunched my nose up as she spoke. "Maybe he's holding back because he doesn't want to end up hurting you."

"Can't he see he's already hurting me?" I demanded. "You don't hurt the people that you care about!"

Melissa stayed quiet as I took sharp breaths. I felt like a crazy person as I let out a laugh.

"Who am I kidding? He doesn't even care."

"Lana, don't say th—"

"Well, it's the truth!" I snapped. I heard my bathroom door open, and Nick walked out entirely clothed. He raised his brows, and Melissa nodded. She stood up and faced me.

"Just remember that you can't always choose the people who're there for you."

I rolled my eyes and watched them walk out. Once they were finally gone, I got up and walked to my closet. I didn't feel bright today, so I decided on a big black sweater and ripped blue jeans. I gathered my things, then walked into the bathroom.

I entered the kitchen and saw Benny dish up lasagna. He wore a faded tee and a jacket on top of it. His hair was damp from the shower, and it covered his eyes as he glanced up with a remorseful look. I leaned against the island as I took a plate and dished my potato wedges. Mom was behind me. I heard footsteps approach, and I turned to see Blake enter. He wore a gray hoodie and a leather jacket over it, with black jeans and Doc Martens. The dog tag that Blake wore around his neck swayed against his rock-hard chest. I locked eyes with Blake as he gave me a blank look, but soon looked down. We stood in silence as we dished our food. As I was about to reach for the garlic bread, Benny got the same idea and beat me to it. Our hands touched as I looked up at him and sheepishly pulled away.

"Sorry, you were first," Benny mumbled as he pulled away from the food.

"No, you go," I said with a smug look.

"I insist, ladies first," he sang as he pushed the plate toward me. I was about to push it back to him until I heard a groan. Benny and I turned to look at Blake, who stared at us.

"I'll go," he said with a fake smile as he took a piece of garlic bread. Benny and I stared at each other as Blake picked up his plate and walked toward the living room. He mumbled something along the way, but I couldn't hear what he said. I quickly took a piece of garlic bread and added it to my plate. Benny finished and left the kitchen. I soon followed, and eventually, everyone gathered to watch a movie. I noticed the tense atmosphere that surrounded us as we ate in silence. Liam tried to lighten the mood, but nobody was interested; even Aidan was in his own world.

I was back in the kitchen as everyone else collected his or her things. I placed the leftovers in the fridge and shut the door. When I spun around, I saw Benny leaning against the counter.

"How'd you sleep?" he casually asked.

"Err…good, and you?"

"Good." Benny let out a deep sigh as I watched him tug on his hair. He pushed himself off the counter as he approached me. I took a step back as my body hit against the sink. "Lana, I'm sorry," he breathed out. "I don't want you to fear me. I would never hurt you, I'm jus—"

"It's okay," I whispered. "We all had a rough night. I understand."

Benny stared at me, then nodded. I watched as he bit his lip and took a few steps back. We heard laughter followed by footsteps as Liam and Nick entered the kitchen. I watched as Nick leaned against the doorframe while Liam propped himself up on the counter.

"What are we gonna do?" Nick asked, then looked over his shoulder.

"I don't know. First we have to find out who was in Lana's room, the—"

"Or we can visit him," Liam cut Benny off.

"Visit who?" I asked. Liam held a mischievous grin as he looked both ways. Once he knew that it was sure that nobody heard us, he spoke.

"Jack August."

My eyes widened as Benny snapped his head to Liam. Nick didn't seem fazed by it as he looked at his shoes.

"Are you crazy? You want us to go visit the guy we buried?" Benny asked.

"Why would we do that?" I asked.

"Well, think about…how do people get over their fears?" Liam asked.

"By facing them," Nick answered as if he waited for Liam to ask.

"So Lana's nightmares are the same thing. You think Jack August is haunting you and you 'almost' saw him in your room, so now we go there and you'll see that he's in the ground," Liam finished with an innocent smile on his face.

"That's stupid," I muttered.

"It's the only way that you're gonna get sleep," he sang. I turned to look at Benny, who stared at the ground. Nick held a blank expression as I squinted at him.

"What do you guys think?" I asked.

"Not such a bad idea if you think about it." Nick shrugged.

"Besides, we got rid of him on the other side of the city. We won't get caught," Liam insisted as he looked at Benny.

"What do you think, Benny?" I asked as he nervously bit his lip. He looked at his friends, then me. I didn't want to do it, but I'd do whatever it took to stop Jack August from haunting me.

"If it lets you sleep at night, then let's do it," Benny said as he nervously rubbed his hands together.

"Do what?"

My head snapped to the door Nick was supposed to guard as I saw Blake walk in. He had his plate in his one hand and overnight bag in the other as he watched us.

"Go out to the place…" Liam trailed off as he looked at Benny and me.

"What place?" Blake asked.

"The place to get the things…right, Benny?" Liam asked as he glared at him.

"Wha—oh! Yeah, the things. We'll go get the stuff," Benny said as he tugged on Nick's arm.

"See you later, Lana; we're going to get the 'things,' and thanks for letting us stay," Liam said as he followed Benny and a confused Nick. Blake had a puzzled look on his face as he watched them tumble out of the kitchen. Once they were gone, he turned back to me and set the plate on the counter.

"I better get going," he mumbled as he slowly approached me.

"Err…yeah. Thanks for staying," I mumbled.

"No problem," he replied. "And don't worry, things will get better," Blake assured me as he placed his hand on my arm and stroked it. I avoided eye contact as he awkwardly stood there. I think he noticed my discomfort as he pulled away. We walked into the living room as I greeted everyone. Melissa got a ride with Miranda because she said that Liam, Benny, and Nick were gone so fast.

After everyone left, I realized what a mess we made. Mom was going to be annoyed with me, but I couldn't care less, even though we had guests tomorrow. I cleaned up until I heard a knock on the door. I raised a brow but thought it was someone who forgot something. I strolled to the door and opened it to see Liam. Nick and Benny were in the car watching me. I turned back to Liam to see a smug look on his face as he yanked me out of the house.

"Let's go pay someone a happy visit."

***

"Fuck you, Liam!" Nick yelled as he threw the shovel toward Liam. Thankfully, he saw it in time and dodged it. We drove for almost an hour to where we buried Jack's body. Nick got frustrated because it was Liam's idea, and to top it off, it rained. Not to mention the whole ride here Liam annoyed him. I watched the two in amusement as I leaned against Nick's car. Benny took out shovels from the trunk as I turned to him.

"Do you really wanna do this?" I asked as he looked at me.

"I- I don't know," he stuttered. "We can't stop now. Otherwise, we drove here for nothing."

"Fair enough," I stated as he handed me a shovel. We walked as Benny guided us. I didn't remember where he was buried because it was almost two months ago. Thank goodness it drizzled and wasn't hard rain. The sun set, which meant it'd be harder to see. Benny must have noticed it too, as he picked up his pace. After twenty minutes, we finally stopped. Benny looked around at the flat, wet land.

"Come on, let's hurry up," he said as he forced the shovel in the ground and dug. Everyone followed as we dug in silence. Something didn't feel right. I looked up to see Nick's squinted eyes as he dug. Liam didn't seem fazed, as he was too excited to meet his friend again. It became harder to dig as the sun disappeared, which only left us with a little lantern. After what felt like an eternity, I dropped the shovel and ran my hand through my curly hair.

"Go rest, Lana. We'll take it from here," Liam assured me. I glanced at my phone and noticed that it was almost eight p.m. Time flew as we worked so hard. I walked away from where they dug, but not too far, so I could watch them. Nobody spoke, which made me nervous. We're supposed to be typical teenagers who were supposed to go to parties and stuff, not bury bodies and argue. It's funny that at the start of the school year I thought it'd be like any other year with Benny. It's true how things could be fine one moment, and then the next everything crashed down. Three months ago, I'd never imagined myself doing this. I felt a tear run down my cheek as I remembered all the things that happened during the last two months. Homecoming was crap, mid-terms were crap. I didn't want Christmas to be the same.

"Are you okay?" Benny asked as I glanced up. I shook my head as another tear fell, and I opened my arms. Benny immediately came and let me wrap my arms around him as I cried. "Ssh, don't cry, Lana. Everything's gonna be okay."

"I'm a killer," I cried into his chest.

"No, you're not," Benny said as I looked up at him. "You're a smart, beautiful, kind, caring, and brave person. Lana Willson, you're quite mysterious, but you're no killer," he whispered as he buried his head in the crook of my neck. I went stiff as he kissed up the curve of my throat, yet I didn't stop him. My hands went around his neck as he lifted his head and pressed his forehead against mine. He looked at me, then my lips, as I did the same. A sudden déjà vu swept over me as the rain poured down on us. "I just want to feel your lips against mine again," Benny whispered as he leaned closer. He pressed his lips against mine as I shut my eyes. I immediately kissed back as Benny's hand went around my waist. I ran my fingers through his wet hair and gripped it; he responded. A strange feeling went through my stomach as he tugged on my bottom lip to deepen the kiss. I didn't know how long we kissed, but I didn't care. It seemed right in a way because I knew that Benny Nielson had changed.

"Hate to break up your guys' little make-out scene, but we need help here, you know," Nick complained as we pulled apart. I suddenly felt better and more alive after that kiss. Benny's hands glided up my body as he took my hands. A goofy grin spread across his face as we walked back to Liam and Nick. We continued to dig as rain poured down on us.

"What's that?" I pointed to a plain old fabric that stuck out of the ground. Liam reached down and pulled on the material. We thought that it was small, but it turned out to be a big piece of clothing. Nick shone his phone as we observed it. I suddenly paled as the realization hit me. The guys seemed to notice it too as Liam held the jacket up.

"I-If this is his ja-jacket then…" Nick trailed off as he shone his light in the empty hole that we dug. "Where's the body?"

"What do you mean?" I demanded and looked at the jacket, then at the empty hole we dug. No one spoke, but our actions screamed for help. Liam tossed the jacket back in the hole and tried to shine his phone flashlight into the grave, but the rain made it impossible to look. Benny glanced around for who knew what reason, as if he'd know where Jack's body would actually be buried. Nick jabbed his shovel in the ground repeatedly and cussed words that I didn't even know existed.

"Maybe we just dug in the wrong place." Benny shrugged, and a light shone on him. I turned to Liam, who stared at him with squinted brows. Liam's hands trembled as he tried to steady himself because he was nearest to the hole.

"Liam, watch ou—"

"No, we did not. I made sure this was the spot where we left him, and why would his jacket be here? The body was stolen!"

496

"Why wouldn't they take the jacket, though?" I asked, but Liam ignored me as he continued to look around.

"I find it ironic that it was your idea to come out here and the body's suddenly gone!" Nick said as he made his way toward Liam. Nick gave Liam a slight shove, and I gasped because they could've fallen in the hole. The rain made everything worse; our shoes were muddy, our clothes clung to our bodies, and our hair stuck to our foreheads. "*Where's the body, Liam? This is not fucking funny!*"

"*I don't know! Why would I steal it? How?*"

"Hey! Drop it, you two!" Benny stepped in and pulled them back from the hole. I hopelessly stood on the other side as they stared at each other. Benny stood between them, a hand resting on each of their chests as he glanced at them. He looked up at me and announced, "We'll just keep looking, all right? He's gotta be around here somewhere."

We did as Benny Nielson said and dug around the empty hole, which soon filled with rainwater. The night stretched into a dark, eerie silence between the four of us. The rain got to a point where I didn't feel cold anymore. I was covered in a wet blanket that got thicker by the second. My shoes began to fill up with water, but I continued to dig until my hands ached from the repetitive actions. I didn't complain, though, because the only thing I cared about at that moment was finding Jack August.

Acknowledgements

The Wattpad community started it all. The people who read my first few drafts of this book before I had to take it down for it to get published— thank you, because if it weren't for your engagement and helpful feedback, I wouldn't have the honor of writing this.

To my family, who grew curious at the start as to why I'd ask them odd questions and, when I finally told them, fully supported me. My dad, who answered all my questions and gave me the opportunity to start a new life in a new country. My mom, who never bothered me much with everything but knew I liked my space. No one understands me better than she does. My younger sister, who begged me to write more, so I wrote. To my grandparents, who always checked up on me and who I could tell the entire plot to, and they'd find it interesting, that worked for me. Thank you, and I love you all so much. Your response means the world to me because I want to do right.

To Jazmine and Kanita, my dearest friends in Adelaide, South Australia, who encouraged me when things got too hard and I wanted to stop writing. My other friends in Perth, Western Australia, who took me in with open arms, and Tien Doan, who read and gave a different perspective to certain scenes I wrote.

My editor, Toni Rakestraw, who stuck through this complex story and taught me a few things on the way. If it weren't for your guidance, I wouldn't know what page we'd still be stuck on. Thank you for your patience when I didn't know and for helping me bring this all together.

Thank you to Limitless Publishing for accepting my manuscript. That started everything. LP was the first publisher I sent my manuscript to before eight others, and I didn't think the first would be the lucky one. Thank you to all the staff at LP who made me feel welcome, like I was part of them, even if I'm on the other side of the world!

I'd also like to thank the many YA authors as well as TV shows aimed at young adult audiences who inspired me to write something as unusual yet complicated like CBTBB.

If it weren't for all of you amazing people in my life, I wouldn't be where I am today. I doubted myself a lot but stuck through with your words of encouragement.

About the Author

Raathi Chota's writing first began as a hobby and after growing in popularity, her gift for storytelling took off. Since gaining over ten million reads with her first novel on Wattpad, Raathi found her true calling. Being a regular high school student in Australia and a dedicated writer, her imagination knows no bounds. She enjoys random adventures where she knows she will find inspiration. Her stories are general fiction that is packed with young adult, thriller, mystery and romance themes. Raathi's stories are page-turners leaving you yearning for more. She gained over twenty-five thousand followers across Instagram, Twitter, Wattpad, and Inkitt combined. She recently began the second book on Wattpad and additional chapters on Inkitt where it gained its popularity and began trending on their website.

Facebook:
https://www.facebook.com/Raathi-Chota-162715917804333/?modal=admin_todo_tour

Twitter:
https://twitter.com/Raathi07

Goodreads:
https://www.goodreads.com/author/show/164297 04.Raathi_Chota

Wixsite:
https://raathichota.wixsite.com/blog

Instagram:
https://www.instagram.com/raathi07/

Wattpad:
https://www.wattpad.com/user/Raathi07

Inkitt:
https://inkitt.app.link/RA_Raathi_Chota